THE ART OF HALO

CREATING A VIRTUAL WORLD

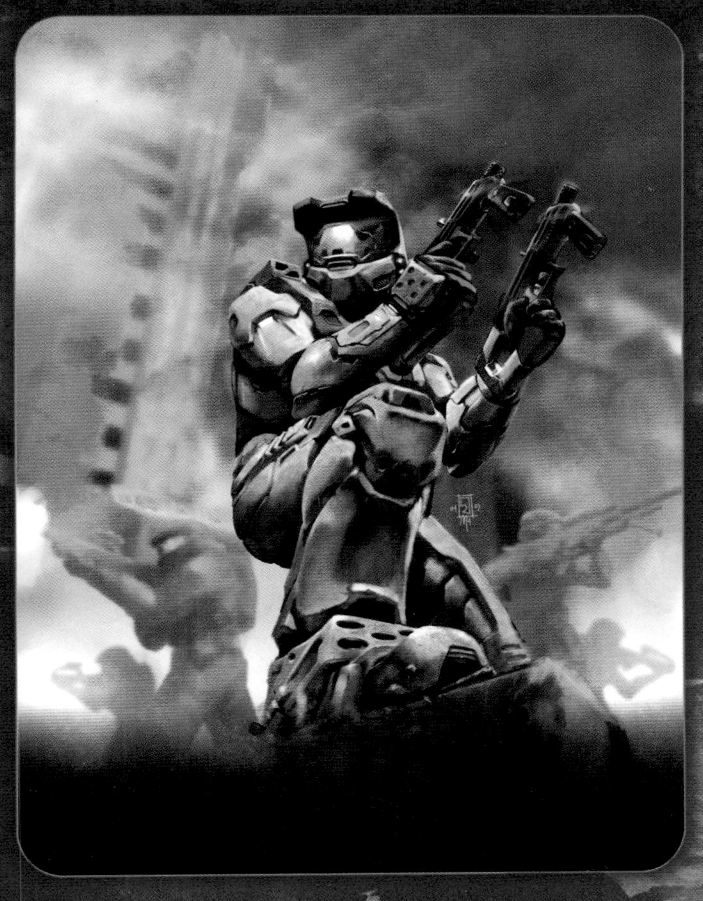

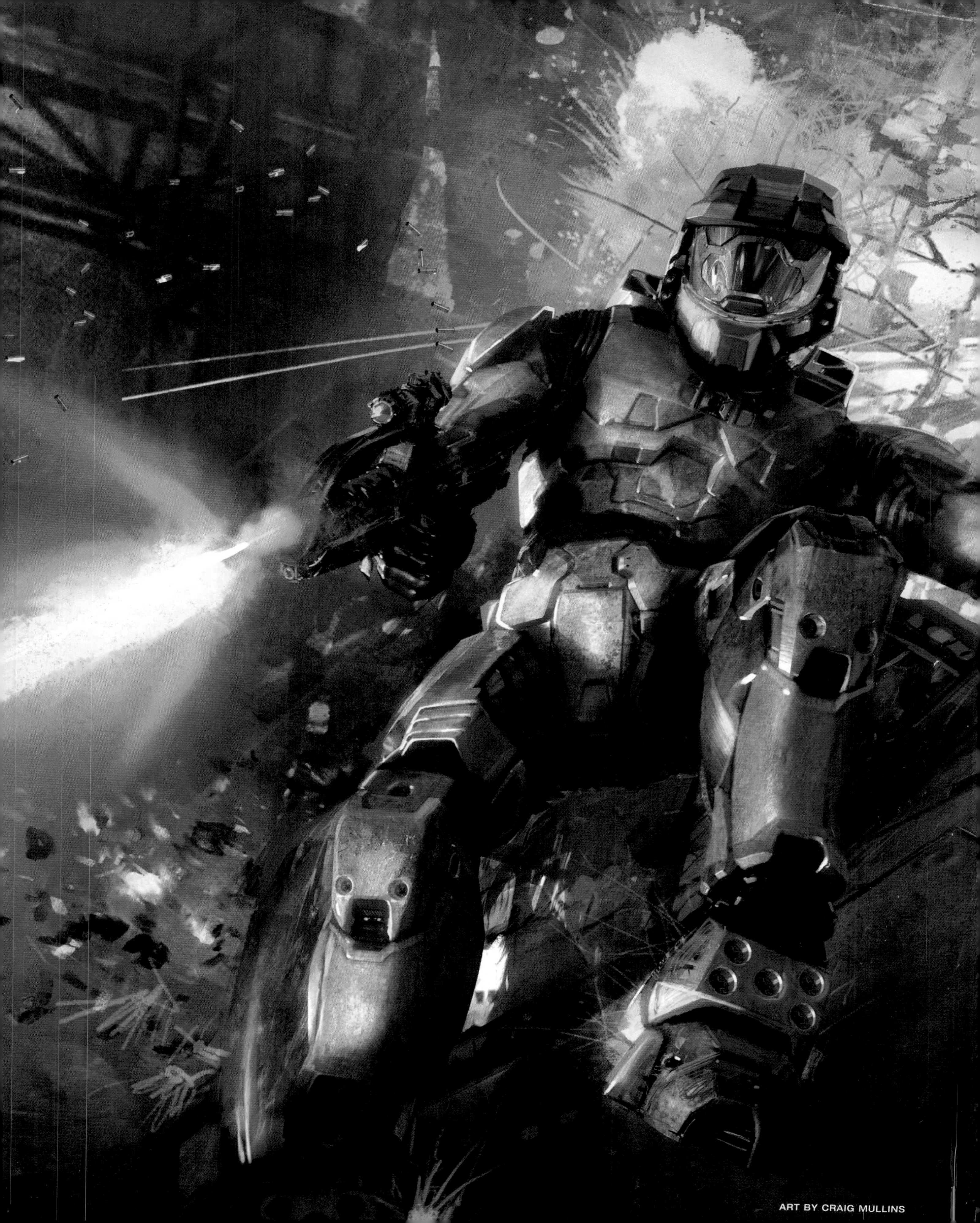

ART BY CRAIG MULLINS

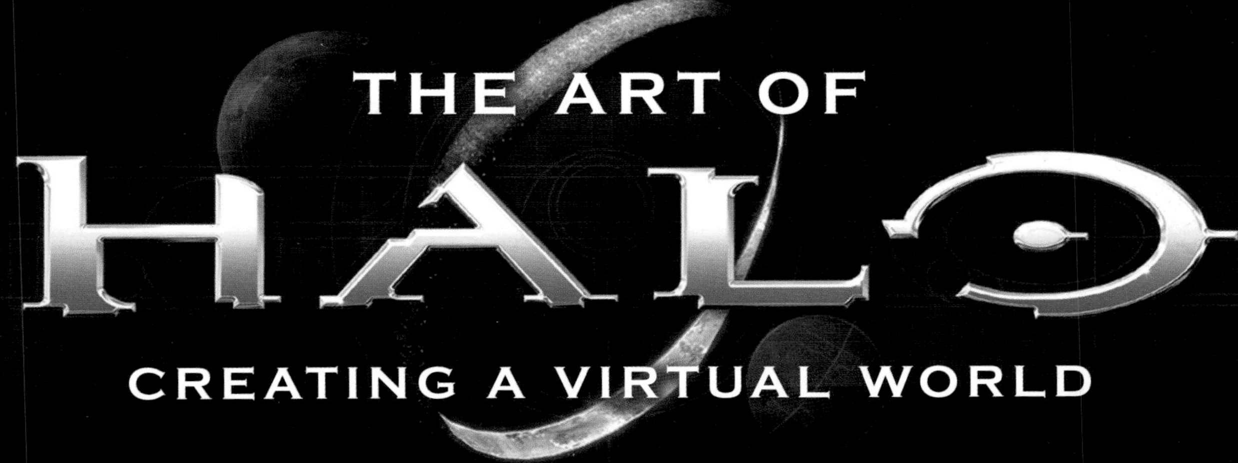

TEXT BY ERIC S. TRAUTMANN

WITH ADDITIONAL MATERIAL BY FRANK O'CONNOR

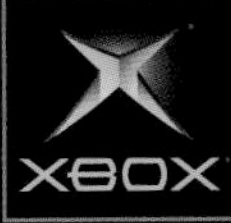

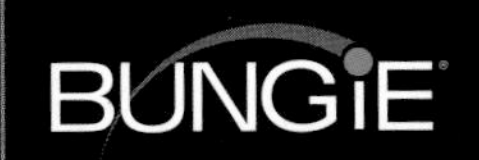

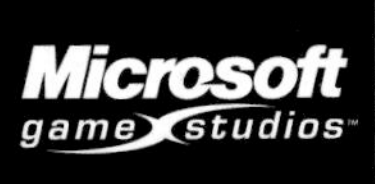

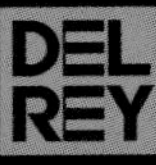

BALLANTINE BOOKS / NEW YORK

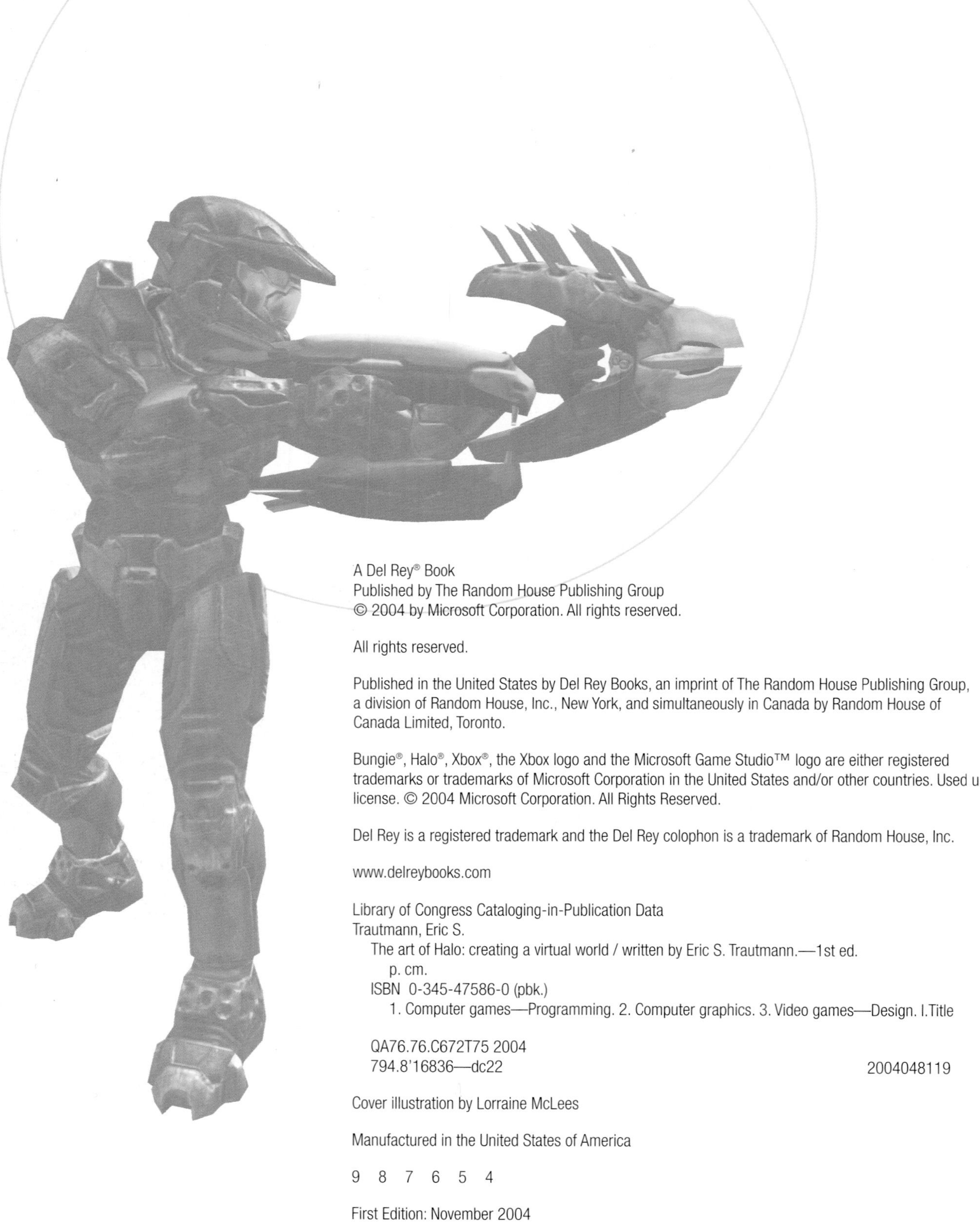

A Del Rey® Book
Published by The Random House Publishing Group

Published in the United States by Del Rey Books, an imprint of The Random House Publishing Group, a division of Random House, Inc., New York, and simultaneously in Canada by Random House of Canada Limited, Toronto.

www.delreybooks.com

Library of Congress Cataloging-in-Publication Data
Trautmann, Eric S.
The art of Halo: creating a virtual world / written by Eric S. Trautmann.—1st ed.
p. cm.
ISBN 0-345-47586-0 (pbk.)
1. Computer games—Programming. 2. Computer graphics. 3. Video games—Design. I.Title

QA76.76.C672T75 2004
794.8'16836—dc22 2004048119

Cover illustration by Lorraine McLees

Manufactured in the United States of America

9 8 7 6 5 4

First Edition: November 2004

Book design by Liney Li assisted by Oliver Martin Ball
Special thanks to Alta Hartmann and Lorraine McLees.
Page i background art by Craig Mullins
Title page, graphic around *Halo* logo: designed by Dave Candland

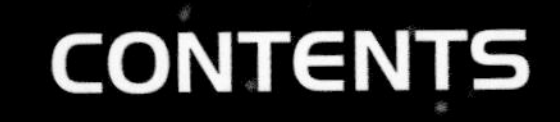

CONTENTS

FOREWORD

I think that an art book is in some ways the perfect tribute to the process and the people that made, built, drew, painted, sculpted, engineered, and imagined *Halo*®. A game, perhaps more than any other medium, is the sum of its parts. In our case, those parts were seemingly disparate elements—concept art, 3D models, network engineering, music, and brutally efficient code. Bring them together in concert, though, and it is, unmistakably, *art*.

But Halo is also a place. We made a living, breathing world and populated it with compelling, interesting beings, buildings, and atmosphere. We did that by utilizing the finest skills of some breathtakingly talented artists. There were animators, environment artists, lighting experts, illustrators, even a few bona fide gun nuts in that mix.

Collecting the assets, the screens, and the renders that comprise this book was both a trip down memory lane and a glimpse into the future. Halo is still growing, organically, exponentially.

Looking at this collection of art—digital and analog—it's overwhelming to think that it all coalesced into such a defined, articulate experience. It's overwhelming to think that this cabal of imaginative, innovative people could also work so beautifully together to make *Halo* and *Halo® 2* happen. And it's overwhelming to think that it's not over yet.

A lot of the things that make up the framework, the essential skeleton of *Halo*, are invisible, but they are as indispensable to the art of *Halo* as a canvas is to a painting. So by all means enjoy the art, enjoy the rich world and vibrant people, creatures, and places we've invented. But remember that underneath it all are mountains of work, lakes of tears, and oceans of sweat. Which is gross, but apt.

—Jason Jones, Bungie development lead
Redmond, Washington

PREFACE

The book you hold in your hands is, at its core, a document of a true labor of love. Certainly, it is a collection of beautiful images and colorful anecdotes. But more than that, I hope it illuminates not just what we did in the creation of *Halo*, but how and why we did it.

There were any number of obstacles to overcome on our way to the completion of the game: tight schedules, deadlines hit and missed, a change from the PC platform to the Xbox®, a move to the West Coast, and many more—too numerous to mention, in fact.

To make all of these eclectic personalities and elements come together into a solid, well-crafted whole requires a team of great pride, honesty, talent, and determination. It has been my good fortune to work in the trenches with these gifted artists; Bungie and its people are truly unique, and I honestly don't believe another group could have succeeded so spectacularly.

As of this writing, work proceeds at breakneck speed on *Halo® 2*, the next step in the evolution of the visual language outlined in these pages—a combined effort by dozens of people, struggling with code, art, animation, and scores of difficult and demanding tasks. New obstacles must be overcome, and a greater anticipation for the game ramps the pressure up even higher.

But beyond the pressure of expectation (which is considerable) is the pressure that Bungie applies to itself. One of the most gratifying aspects of working alongside this team is their unrelenting push to be better, to do more, to make everything as cool as is humanly possible.

A cursory glance at the images on these pages articulates, far better than I ever could, the pursuit of excellence that informs every aspect of Bungie's work.

It is with tremendous gratitude that I salute my fellow artists and team members, without whom none of this would be possible. You have my sincerest thanks and my deepest appreciation.

—Marcus Lehto, Bungie Studios art director
Redmond, Washington

Art by Craig Mullins

The year is 2552 and the human race is on the verge of extinction at the hands of the merciless collective known as the Covenant. A lone starship, the aging cruiser Pillar of Autumn, flees a deadly battle in an attempt to lure Covenant forces away from Earth . . . and in the process discovers an ancient ring-shaped artificial world: Halo.

After a fierce battle with the pursuing Covenant armada, the Pillar of Autumn crashes on Halo's surface, marooning the survivors.

There, this ragtag band of human soldiers, led by a cybernetic superwarrior known as the Master Chief, race against time to harness Halo's unspeakable power, and unlock its most dangerous secrets . . .

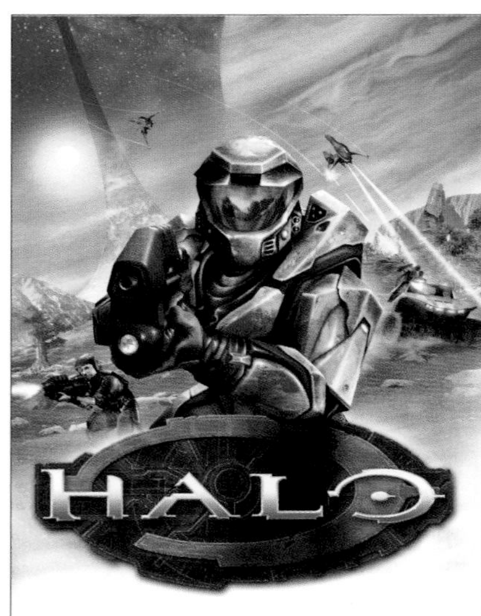

Box art for *Halo* (shown without trade dress).

INTRODUCTION: Halo's Architects

To millions of video game enthusiasts, the word "Halo" is synonymous with pulse-pounding, adrenaline-charged action. *Halo*'s creators—software innovators Bungie Studios—drew inspiration from countless films, books, and other sources to develop the grand, epic scope of the game, and to craft a gripping story that immerses the player in the *Halo* universe.

What follows is a glimpse into the creative processes of Bungie's talented team of artists, from storyboards to level design, from character creation to animation—a look into the world of *Halo*'s architects.

ABOUT BUNGIE

Founded by Alexander Seropian ("in lieu of getting a real job") in May 1991, Bungie Software published a carefully crafted tank combat game, *Operation Desert Storm.*

Bungie Software's next project was *Minotaur: The Labyrinths of Crete,* released in February 1992. *Minotaur* marked Jason Jones's first involvement with the company and built the foundation for Bungie's pattern of creative and technological innovation (despite the fact that the game boxes were originally assembled in Alexander's apartment).

Bungie's first major success was their next game, *Pathways into Darkness,* in August 1993. Again, the software was technologically innovative (the first example of real-time texture mapping on the Macintosh OS, which achieved a realistic, highly detailed 3D effect dur-

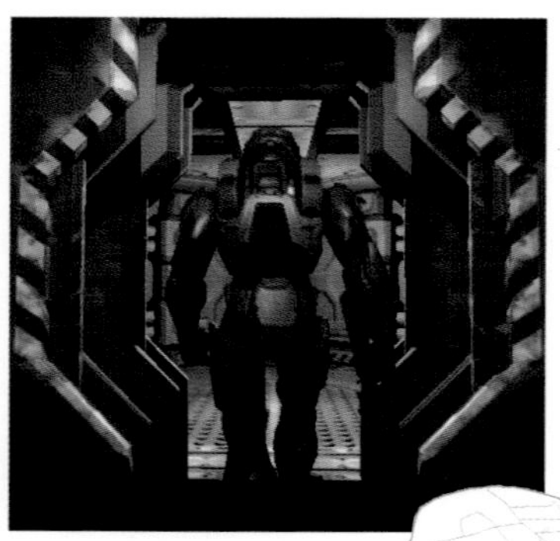

Still from the E3 "announce trailer"—the public's first look at *Halo 2*.

Art by Dave Candland.

ing play). The game won several awards (including being named to *MacWorld's* Game Hall of Fame) and expanded Bungie's burgeoning fan following.

The next title, *Marathon,* was released in December 1994. *Marathon* was tremendously successful, and thanks to a legion of fans and players, the story line (which also featured a cybernetic supersoldier battling a bewildering array of alien foes) became increasingly intriguing.

In November 1995, *Marathon 2: Durandal* was released and topped its predecessor's sales, as well as deepened the story mythos of the *Marathon* universe. Bungie's reputation for intense game play and detailed, rich stories was cemented.

Growing by leaps and bounds, Bungie developed several other titles, including *Marathon Infinity* (the capstone to the *Marathon* story line), *Abuse, Weekend Warrior* (which in 1997 was released in a bundle with the first generation of Mac OS 3-D video cards), *Myth: The Fallen Lords, Myth 2: Soulblighter,* and *Oni.*

In early 1998, Jason Jones and his team began work on *Halo*—though in its early days it was known by a number of working titles. Robt McLees, a Bungie artist, was one of the first people involved with the game: "We always assign working titles to our games, and a lot of times those names just stick. There's always the thought during the development process that we'll come back with a different, better name. But *Minotaur, Myth,* and *Marathon* all shipped with their working titles.

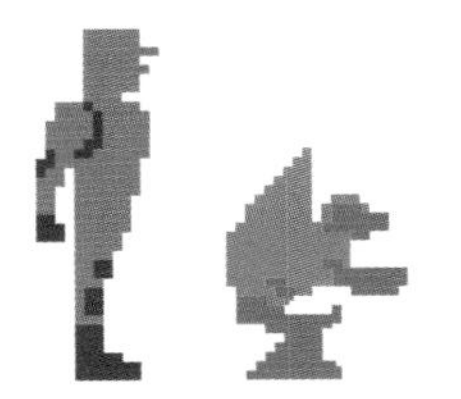

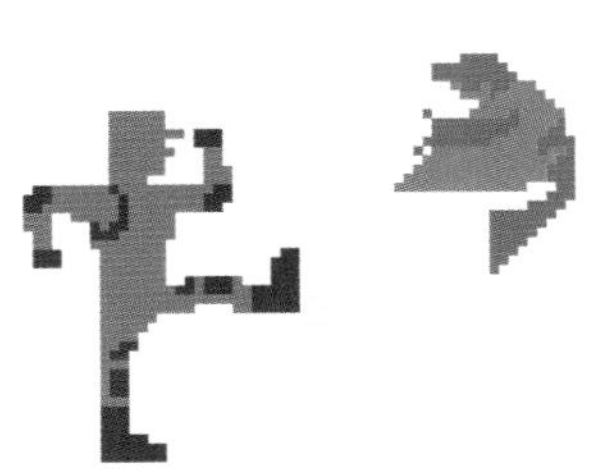

▲ **Two frames of animation used for an amusing prelude to the *Halo 2* demo at the 2003 E3 Expo. Art by Lorraine McLees.**

"So, when we assigned a code name to what would become *Halo,* we originally called it 'Monkey Nuts.' There was no chance that we'd ship a game with that title. Later on, we code-named it 'Blam!' because Jason couldn't bring himself to tell his mother he was working on something called 'Monkey Nuts.'"

(The name "Blam!" stemmed from folks yelling the word in Bungie offices when they were in Chicago. Located near a busy street, the Bungie team could hear numerous near-collisions between cars outside. "You'd hear the screech of tires, and then nothing," explained Robt McLees, "so I'd yell 'Blam!' Just so there was some sense of completion.")

The title *Halo* was announced in 1999 during Steve Jobs's keynote address at the *MacWorld* Expo in New York. A brief display of an early version of the game was enthusiastically received.

In 2000, Bungie joined the ranks of Microsoft's game development studios, and *Halo*—

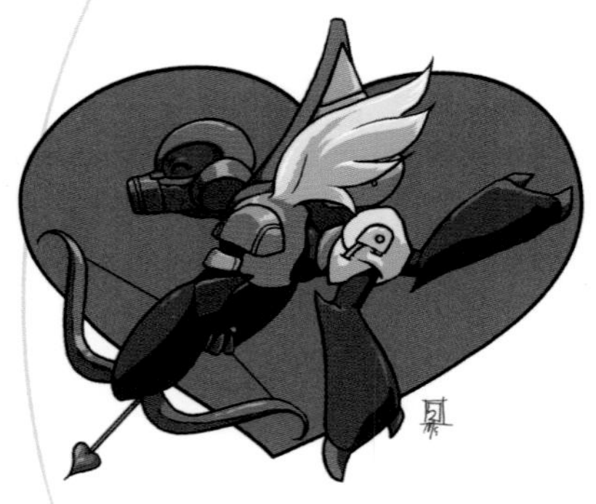

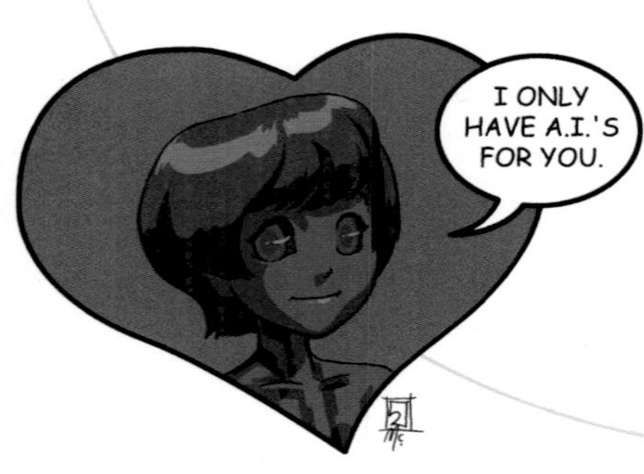

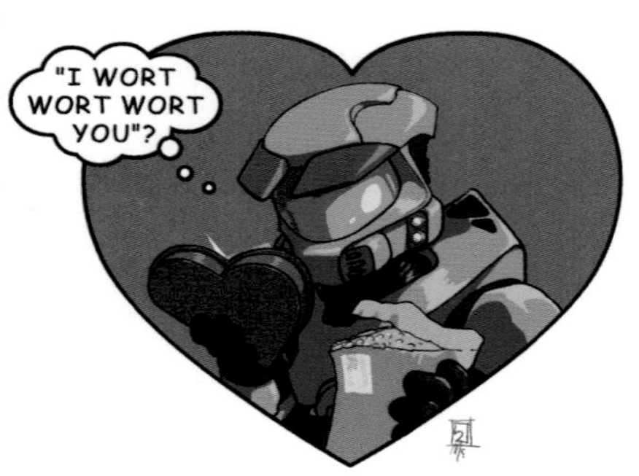

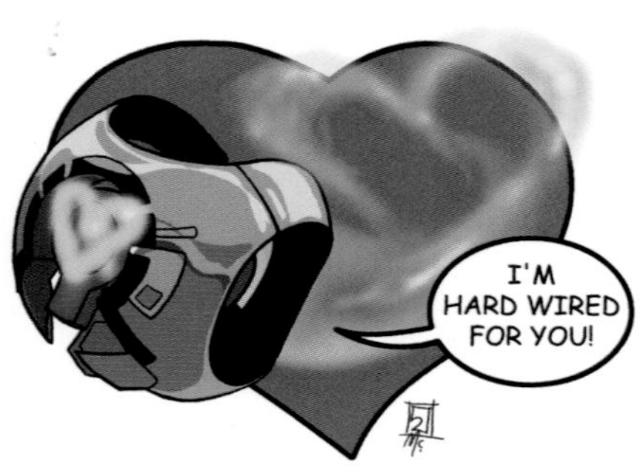

Bungie, for all its emphasis on drama and action, has always had a sense of fun. These *Halo* valentines, by artist Lorraine McLees, proved a firm favorite with romantic Bungie fans.

originally slated for a Macintosh and PC release—became one of the flagship titles for the Xbox® video game console.

Unfortunately, the transition from Mac and PC to the then-unknown Xbox all had to occur under tight production deadlines . . . and while Bungie moved artists, designers, programmers, and community support teams from Chicago to Redmond, Washington. The fact that Bungie produced a game that won many "Game of the Year" accolades—and sold millions of copies—is all the more remarkable.

INSIDE THE STUDIO

The creation of addictive, intelligent, and innovative games is Bungie's primary focus, and every aspect of their creative process reflects this dedication to quality and craft.

Headquartered in Redmond, Washington, Bungie's office is emblematic of their fiercely independent nature. No walls or cubicles separate artists from programmers, level designers from cinematics teams, writers from animators. In this open environment, ideas flow and are investigated or discarded, thanks to Bungie's adherence to a simple philosophy: No idea is out of bounds if it makes the game better.

Even under the best of circumstances, the creation of a hit video game is achieved in an environment of barely controlled chaos. There is a constant pressure to perform, and in the case of *Halo,* there was the added necessity of making sure that the game launched at the same time as the fledgling Xbox game console.

Deadlines came and went, and through the process, Bungie designers, artists, and programmers put in long hours, often staying overnight, and working in grueling shifts. "There were guys who just slept in the office, day and night, during those last few months on the project," said Bungie artist Eric Arroyo.

"One of the things I want to get across here is the state of nearly constant chaos we exist in," added environment artist Paul Russel. "I've never been in any studio situation that is as planned out or scheduled as, say, a Hollywood movie. We're constantly evolving the game designs, the art, the music, everything, so we're always under the gun."

"There were a lot of challenges in completing *Halo,*" said Christopher Barrett, an environment artist on *Halo* and *Halo 2*, "most of them due to the absolute necessity of shipping in time to debut with the Xbox. The deadline crunch and pressure to ship led to some great moments, stuff like: 'Build a level in a month, start to finish.' And I was thinking, this is crazy. But I did it, and that was great."

Virtually all of the artists credit Bungie's open forum as one of the keys to success. With no walls separating team members, ideas are bounced back and forth, debated, and refined.

Marcus Lehto, Bungie's art director, believes that the environment the team works in is vital to success. "There's always a lot of discussion about our production method," says Lehto, "and our 'open forum' setup. All I can say is that when we first moved from Chicago into our offices in Washington, we were all in full-size cubicles. We almost lost all communication—it was just awful.

"Our new facilities are much better. Everything's open, in plain sight, and we can all instantly critique and improve with a minimum of time wasted."

According to environment artist lead David Dunn, "The open forum aspect of Bungie is really unique and a necessary component to what we do. I don't know how other teams function, cooped up in separate offices. How do they mesh? How do they swap ideas?"

"A lot of us jump around from one kind of task to another," adds Bungie artist Robt McLees. "On *Halo*, I did concept art, 3-D modeling . . . including animation and texturing, and some work on the *Halo* story."

The overall vibe of the studio is energetic, even unruly, and reminds one of a college dormitory filled with particularly gifted students. With deadline pressures, long hours, and an environment that fosters communication between all members of the *Halo* team, the atmosphere in the studio offices is as unique as the team members themselves. White boards are covered with sketches—many of them hilariously funny and deeply off-color. Reference sketches, concept art, toys, and models litter tables and shelves. Conversations ebb and flow spontaneously, shifting back and forth from detailed technical concerns about an aspect of the developing game, to scathing critiques of a particular film.

"The challenge to such an open forum is that we're a growing group," said Justin Hayward, an environment artist for *Halo 2*. "It's sometimes tough to sort through all the feedback. But it works. We laugh a lot."

Marcus Lehto sums up the Bungie/*Halo* experience: "*Halo* was the kind of game that *we* wanted to play, but no one had made it yet. It blossomed from being this cool game concept, to this really amazing set of characters, stories, and history, to a final game that blends good storytelling with cutting-edge gameplay and graphics. It was simply amazing to watch it all unfold, to be a part of it."

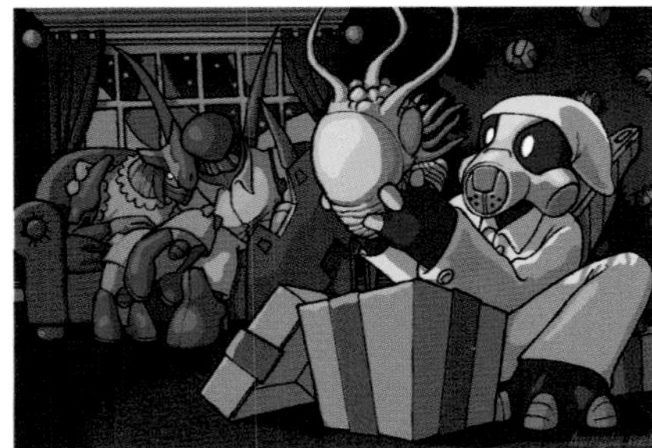

▲ Art by Paul Russel.

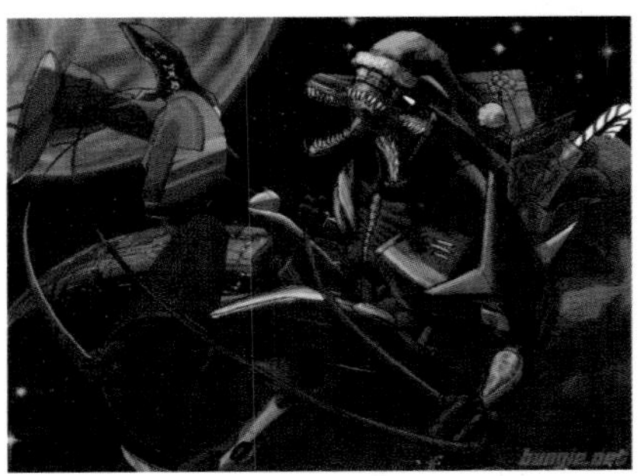

▲ The holiday season is celebrated *Halo* style for Bungie Christmas cards. Art by Ski Kai Wang.

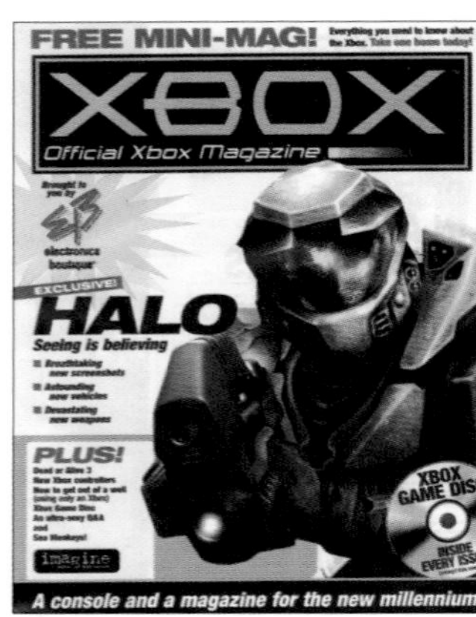

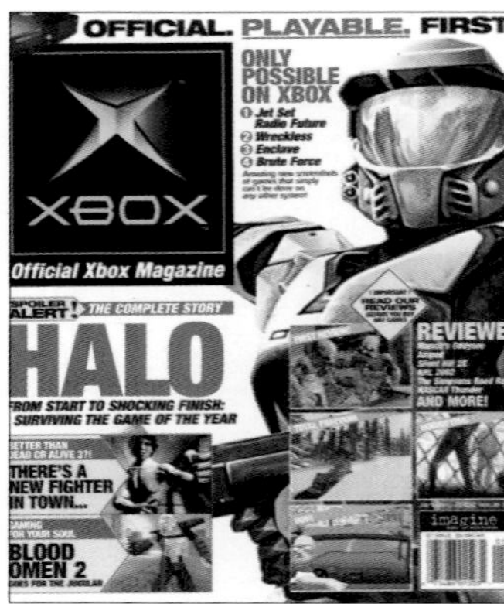

▲ Magazine covers provide a unique challenge for both *Halo* artists and the magazine designers: how to make characters or actions fit within the constraints of coverlines, logos, and more.

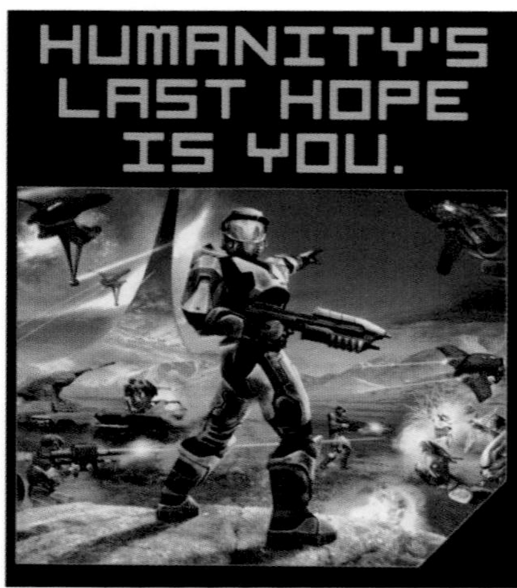

BUNGIE'S HISTORY

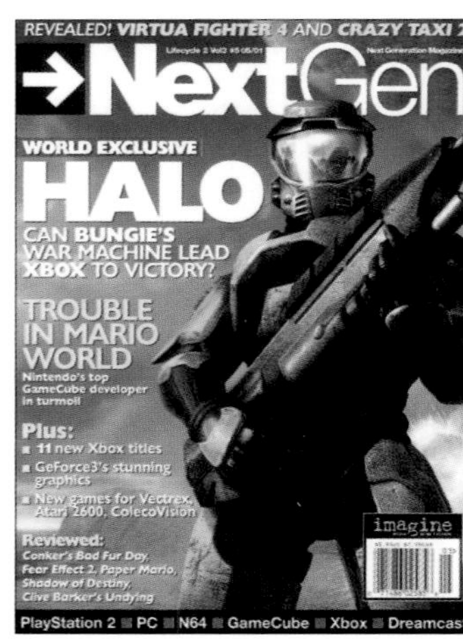

1991

- **May:** Alexander Seropian founds Bungie Software.
- Bungie publishes *Operation Desert Storm.*
- Jason Jones joins Bungie.

1992

- **February:** *Minotaur: The Labyrinths of Crete* published.

1993

- **August:** *Pathways into Darkness* published.
- *Pathways into Darkness* wins several awards, including *MacWorld*'s Game Hall of Fame, the *MacUser* 100, and *Inside Mac Games*'s Adventure Game of the Year.

1994

- **December:** Bungie releases *Marathon.*
- *Marathon* also wins several awards, including *MacWorld* World Class Award, *MacUser* Editor's Choice, and *GAMES Magazine*'s Top 100.

1995

- **November:** *Marathon 2: Durandal* is released on the Mac platform.

1996

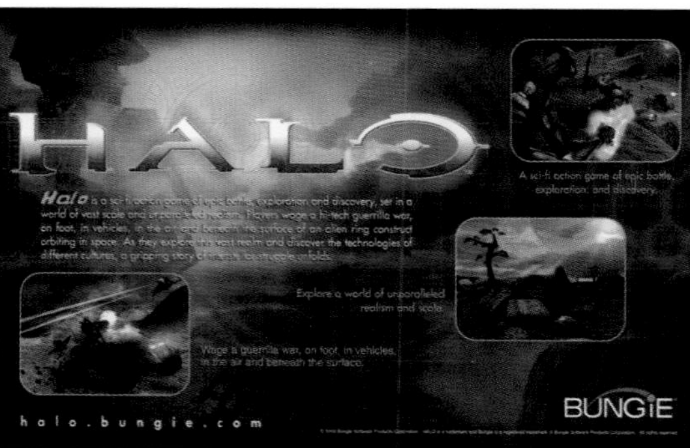

- **September:** *Marathon 2: Durandal* is released for Windows 95.
- **October:** *Marathon Infinity* is released, ending the *Marathon* series.
- *Abuse* (Bungie's first published third-party game) is released, and breathes new life into the side-scrolling platform game genre.

1997

- Bungie.net founded; becomes the central site for the fan community, allowing interaction with each other and Bungie employees.
- **January:** *Weekend Warrior* is released with the first generation of Mac OS 3-D cards.

- **May:** *Marathon Trilogy* boxed set released.
- Bungie Studios West opens in Silicon Valley. Bungie West begins work on *Oni.*
- **November:** *Myth: The Fallen Lords* released simultaneously on Mac and Windows platforms.

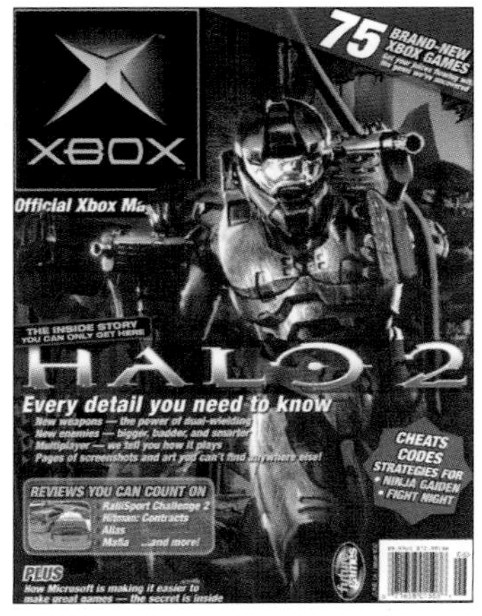

1998

- **Early 1998:** Work begins on "Monkey Nuts"—which eventually evolves into *Halo.*
- *Myth 2: Soulblighter* released. *Myth 2* receives the highest possible review scores from *PC Gamer*, *Game Center*, and *MacAddict*, among others.

1999

- *Halo* debuts for the public as part of Steve Jobs's keynote address at the *MacWorld* Expo.
- Bungie's *Mac Action Sack* released, along with *Myth: The Total Codex.*

2000

- Bungie announces the sale of the company to Microsoft, and that *Halo* is being developed as a launch title for the Xbox.

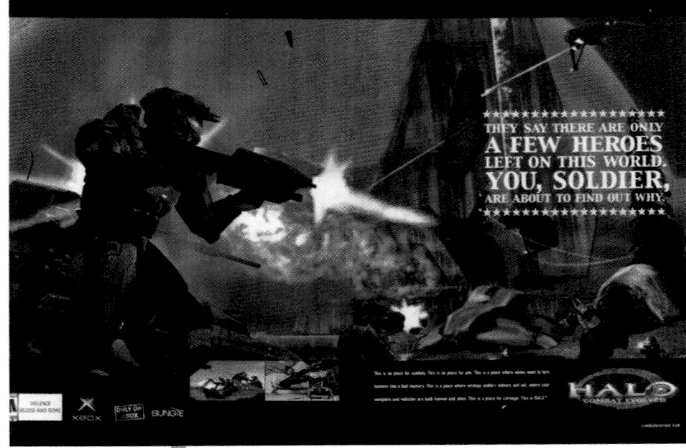

▲ Print ads for *Halo* continued to run in game magazines for months, as the game continued to sell. This one centered on military rather than sci-fi themes.

2001

- **January:** *Oni* is released on the Mac, PC, and Playstation 2.
- **November:** *Halo: Combat Evolved* released for the Xbox platform. *Halo* sells more than two million units and wins several awards, including the Academy of Interactive Arts and Sciences' "Game of the Year" honors.

2002

- Work begins on an Xbox sequel to *Halo.*

2003

- **September:** *Halo: Combat Evolved* released for the PC.
- *Halo: Combat Evolved* released for the Macintosh.

2004

- Bungie.net relaunched. The site is retooled, both in terms of content and graphics. It acts as a nexus for fan-community interaction and as a conduit for "official" information from Bungie.

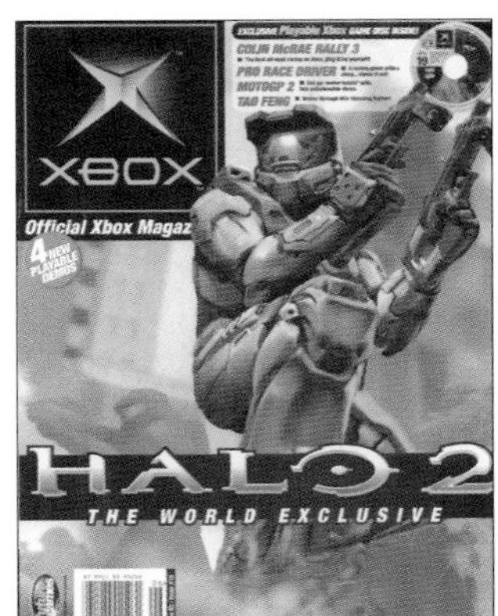

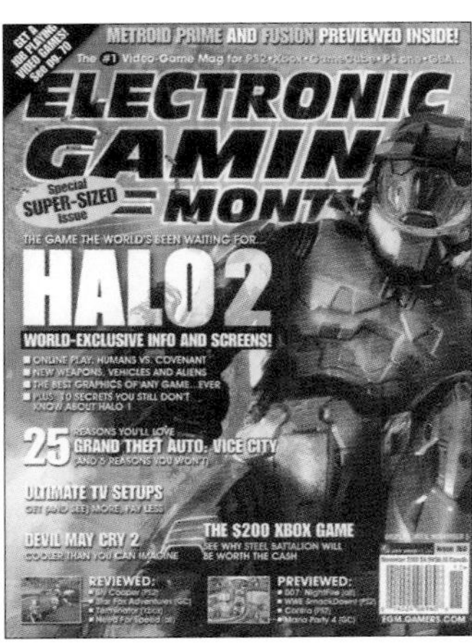

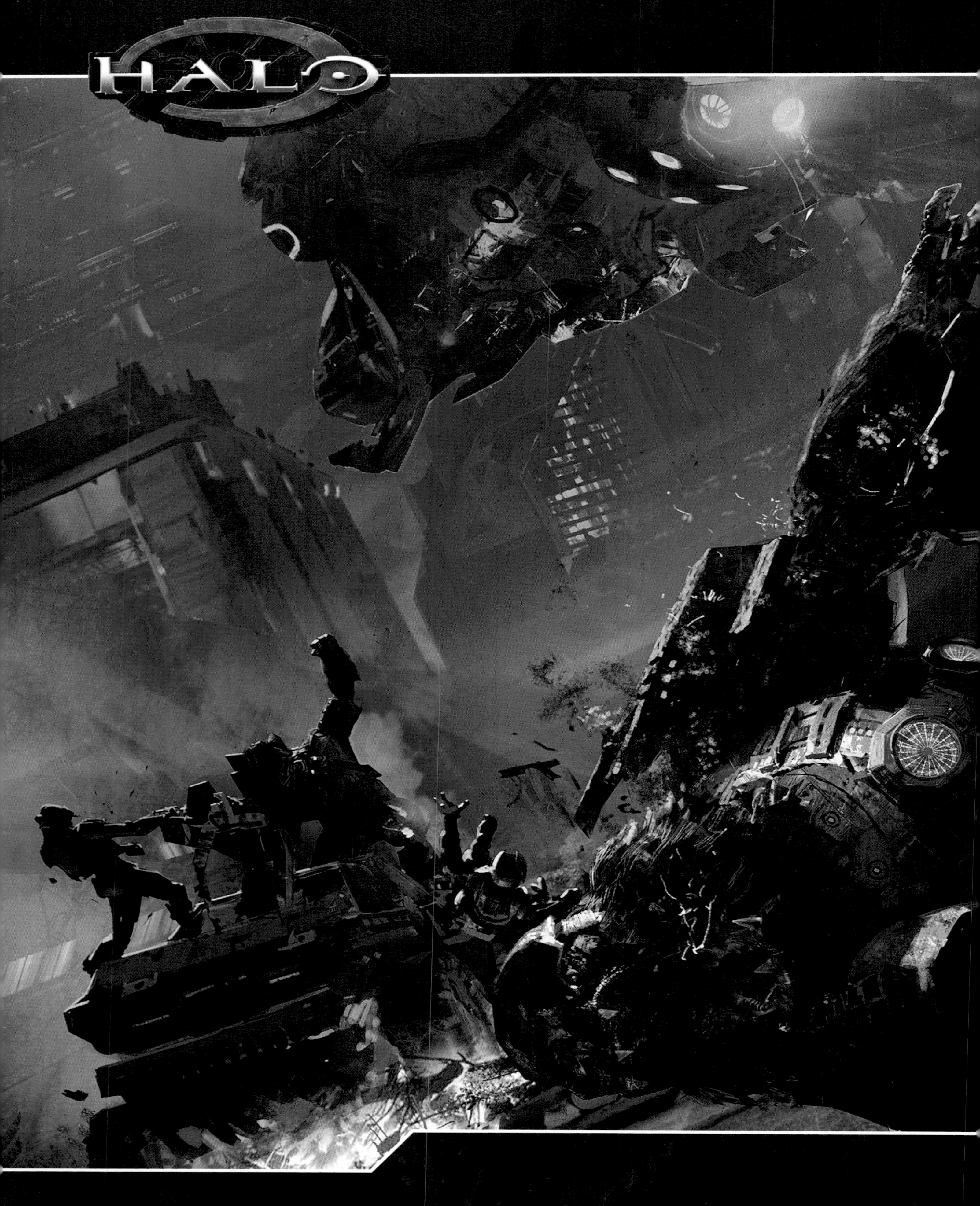
HALO

CHARACTER DESIGN

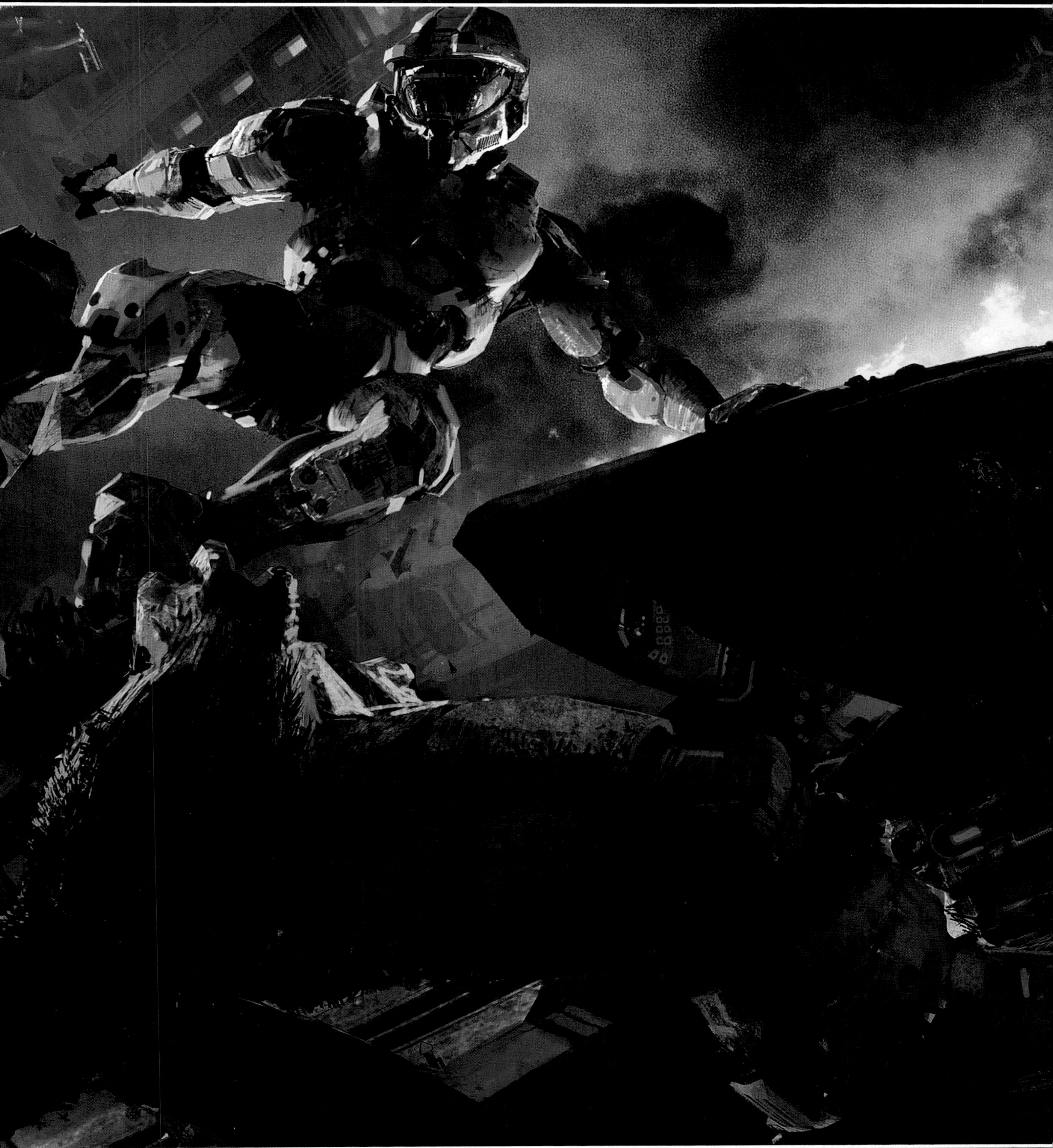

ART BY CRAIG MULLINS

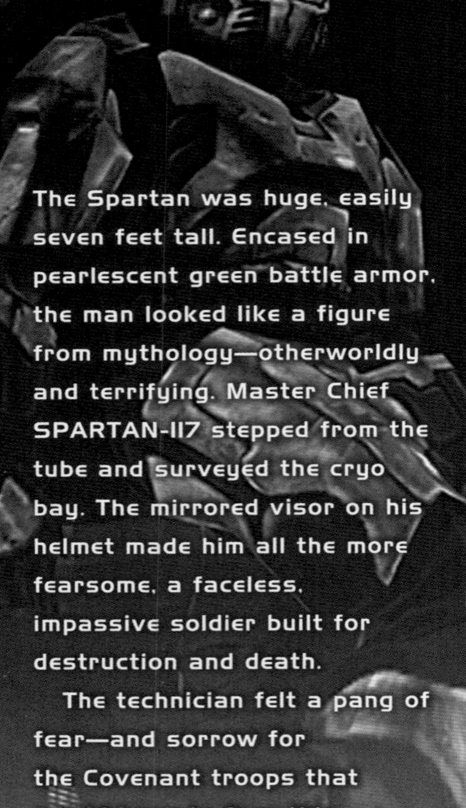

The Spartan was huge, easily seven feet tall. Encased in pearlescent green battle armor, the man looked like a figure from mythology—otherworldly and terrifying. Master Chief SPARTAN-117 stepped from the tube and surveyed the cryo bay. The mirrored visor on his helmet made him all the more fearsome, a faceless, impassive soldier built for destruction and death.

The technician felt a pang of fear—and sorrow for the Covenant troops that would have to face this Spartan in combat.

—Excerpt from
Halo: The Flood
by William C. Dietz.

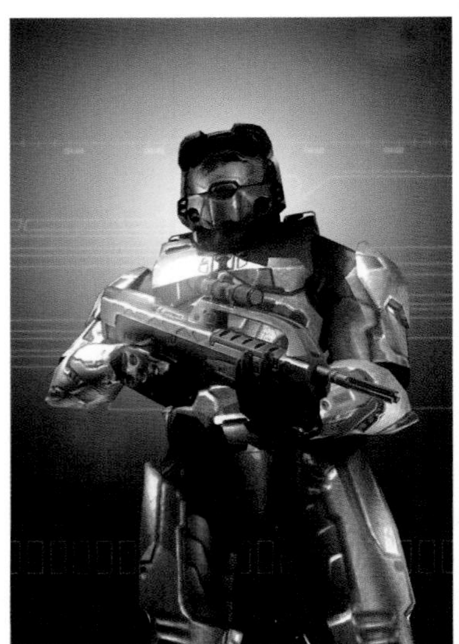

▲ **The Master Chief, ready for war. *Halo 2* 3D render.**

An integral part of creating a good story is the creation of believable and interesting characters. Bungie's 3D modelers craft designs of the various characters that appear in-game, which must then be "textured"—telling the game engine how light and shadow react with the model. From there, the models must be rigged so they can be animated. "Overlap is vital, particularly among modelers and animators," says animator William O'Brien. "We depend on each other for the final product to work—and none of us can settle. We always have to up it a notch."

"Our job is to bring the characters to life in the game," said Nathan Walpole, animation lead for *Halo 2*. "It's what we're best at. We don't use motion capture—most of us are traditional 2D animators, so we prefer to hand-key animation. Motion capture just looks so bad when it's done poorly. We have more control over hand-keyed animation, and can produce results faster than by editing mocap."

Crafting the animations that bring life to the game characters is a painstaking process. "Usually, we start with a thumbnail sketch to build a look or feel," explained Walpole. "Then, you apply it to the 3D model and work out the timing."

"Sometimes the timing's *so* off, it's hilarious," adds animator Mike Budd. "Everyone comes over and has a good laugh. Working together like we do keeps us fresh. There's such a variety of characters—human and alien. And you work on them in a matter of weeks. You're always working on something new and interesting."

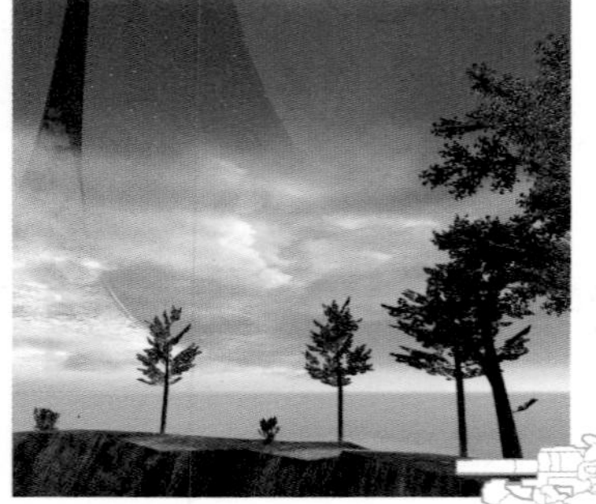

▲ **An image created to showcase the expansive environment on the surface of Halo.**

▲ **Art by Dave Candland.**

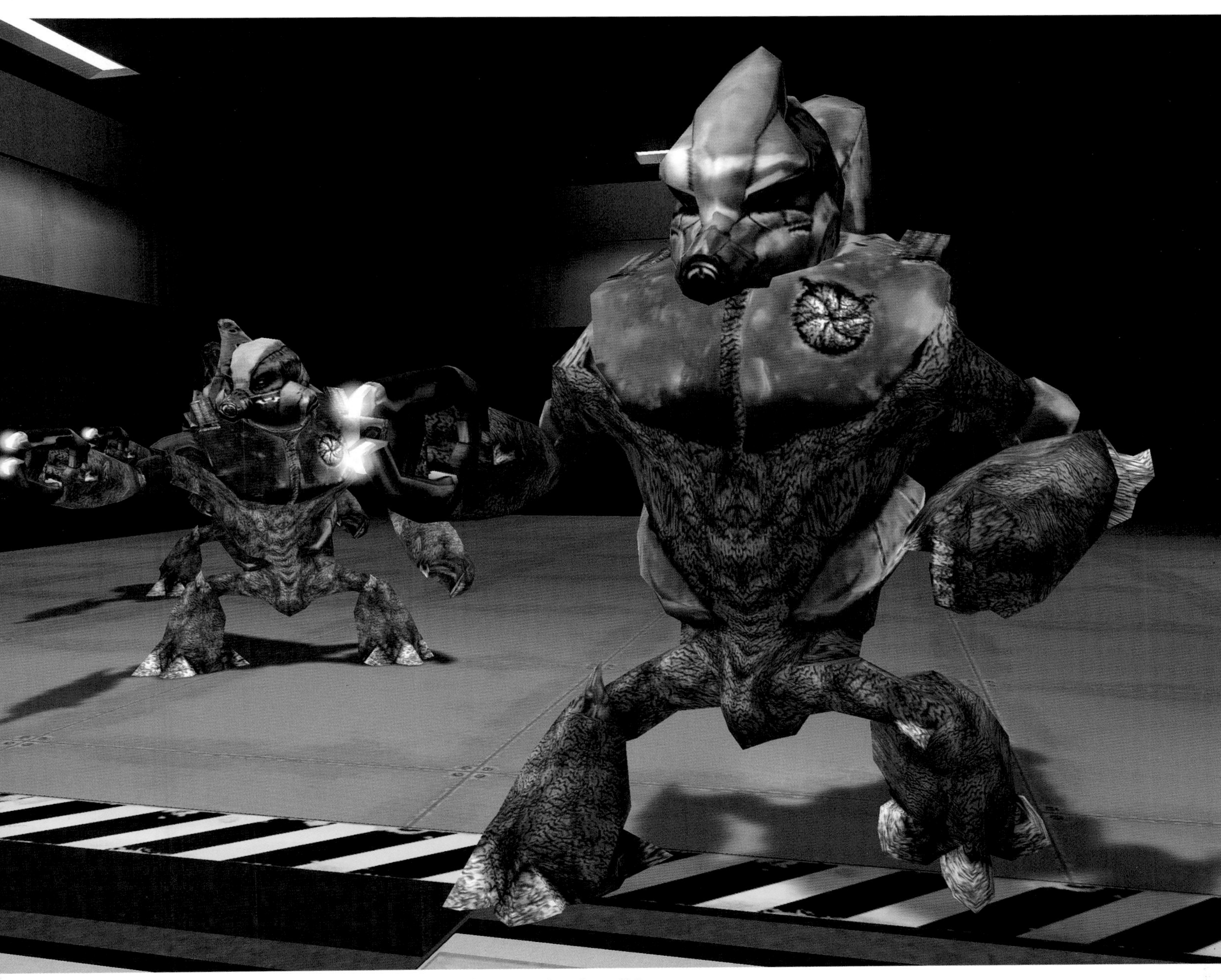

▲ A pair of Grunts prepare to engage the enemy. Screen capture from *Halo.*

To design the characters' motions, the animators study virtually any source of movement for inspiration—though this can create some challenges for animator William O'Brien: "Just being surrounded by people with good senses of humor makes it easier to do your job. The drawback is, I've always had my own office. To animate a character, I often act out motions and movements; this gives you a sense of what muscle and bone actually do. But now, I have an audience. 'Hey, look at the crazy stuff Bill's doing now!' So now, I tend to do that kind of work on video, in private."

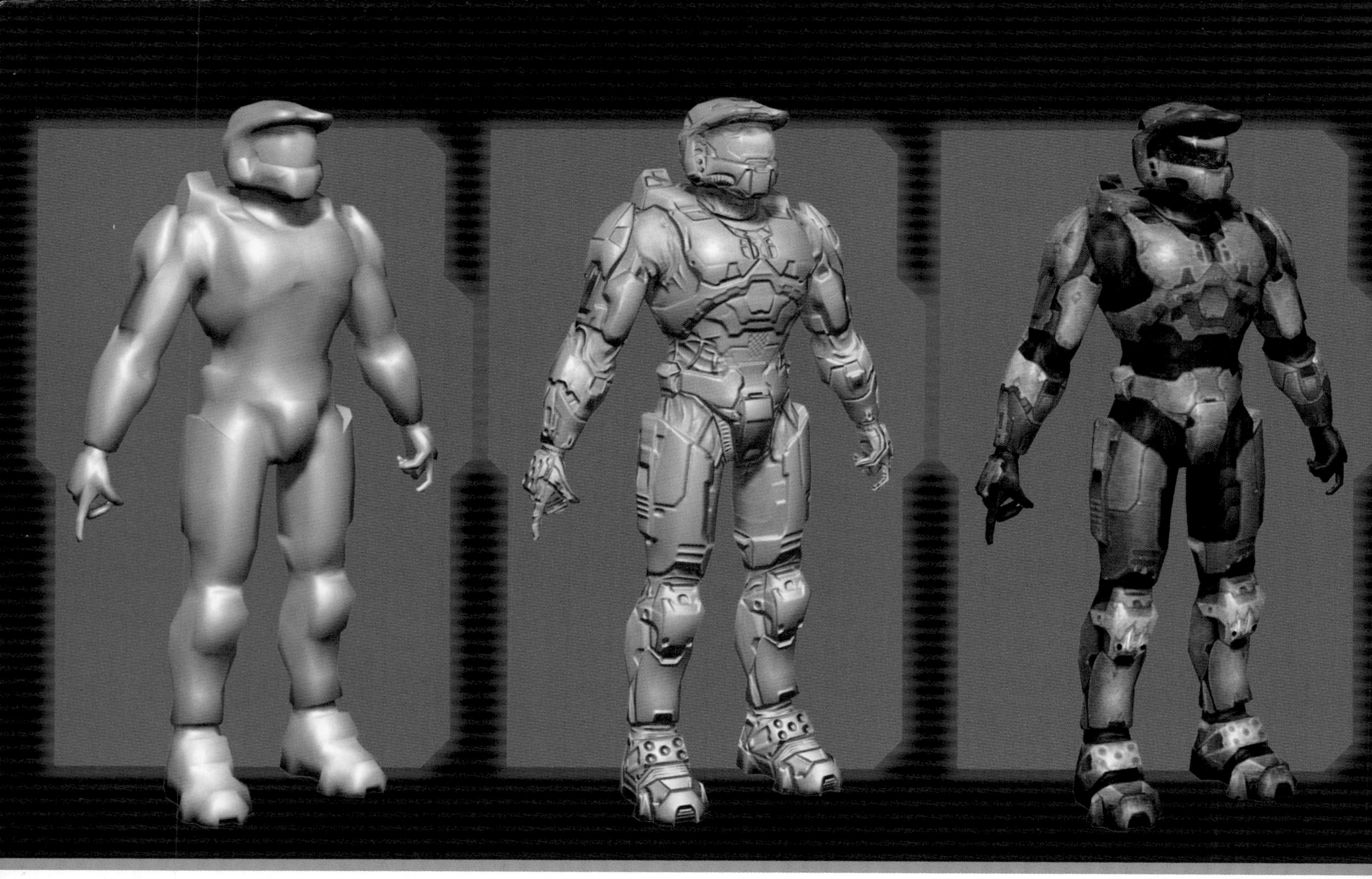

▲ The progression of the Master Chief, from basic geometry, to bump map, to textured, and then final in-game model.

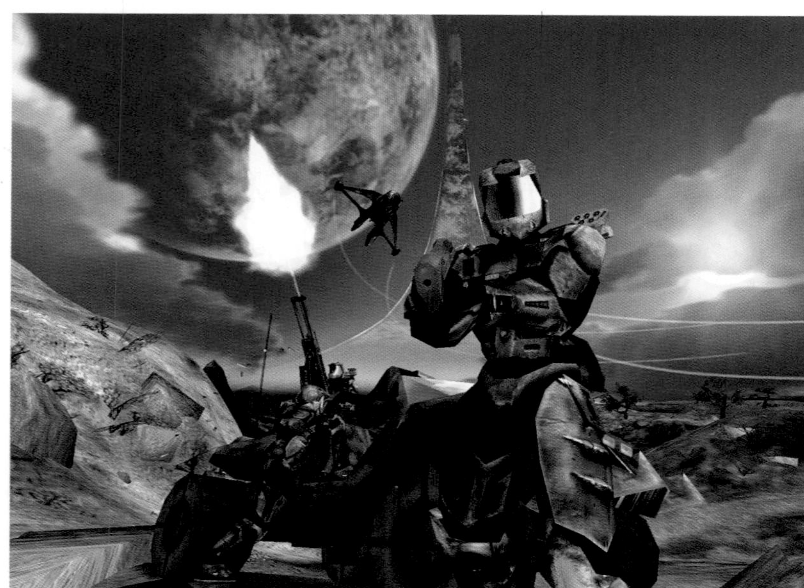

▲ One of the public's first looks at *Halo* came in the November 1999 issue of *Computer Gaming World.*

The collaborative process at Bungie wasn't confined to the *Halo* team. There were several Bungie artists and programmers working on other titles during the various stages of *Halo*'s development. "I didn't do a lot on *Halo*—I was assigned to a team working on a different project," said character artist Juan Ramirez. "But most of us would weigh in on what we saw. I like monsters and animals and creatures—plus I'm a sculptor, so I did some sculpture designs of the early Elite.

"When I came on, I wasn't really a 'computer guy'—I was more into comics, film, that kind of thing. I try and apply that to my work here—to look at our games as more than just games. Better games equals better entertainment. A lot of that is sold through character design."

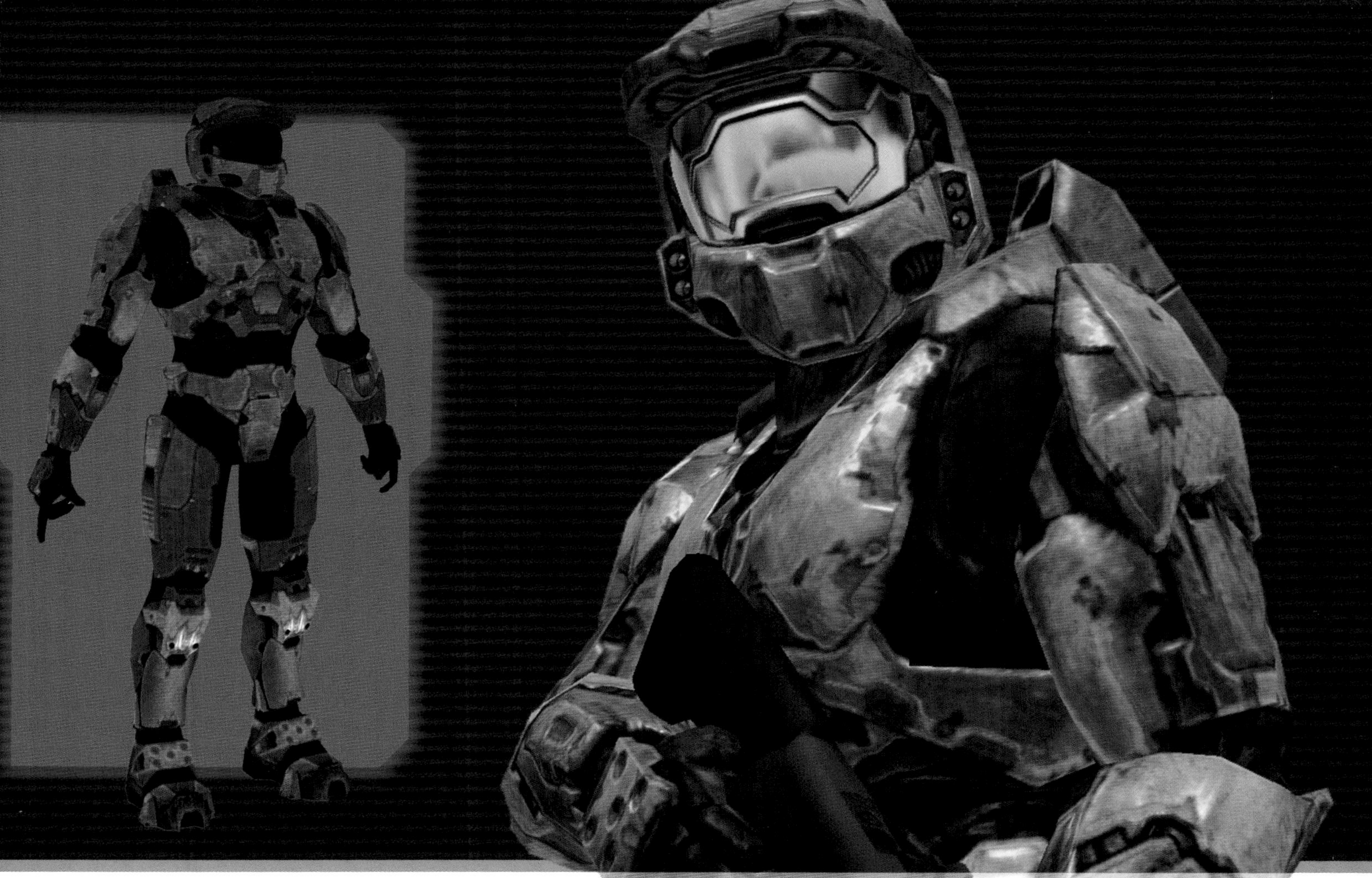

THE MASTER CHIEF

Seven feet tall and clad in fearsome MJOLNIR Mark V battle armor, the warrior known as the Master Chief is a product of the SPARTAN Project. Trained in the art of war since childhood, he may well hold the fate of the human race in his hands.

MARCUS LEHTO, ART DIRECTOR: *"At first, Rob [artist Robt McLees] and I were the only artists working on* Halo*. After that we hired Sheik [artist Shi Kai Wang], who's just great from the conceptual standpoint. I'd do a preliminary version of something, then Sheik would work from that, and really enhance the concept.*

"The Master Chief design sketch that really took hold came after heavy collaboration with Shi Kai. One of his sketches—this kind of manga-influenced piece, with ammo bandoliers across his chest, and a big bladed weapon on his back—really caught our imagination.

"Unfortunately, when we got that version into model form, he looked a little too slender, almost effeminate. So, I took the design and tried to make it look more like a modern tank. That's how we got to the Master Chief that appears in the game."

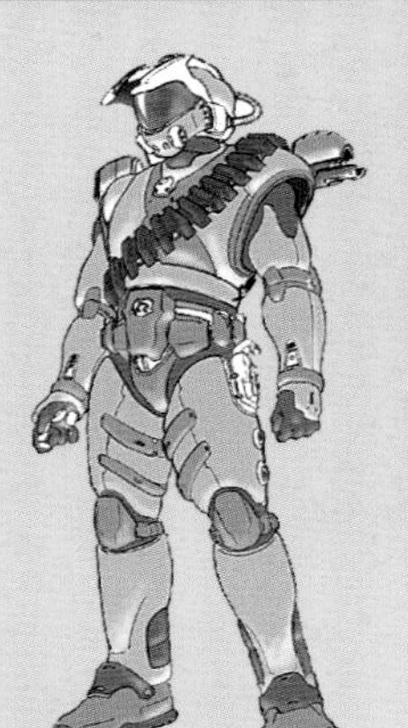

THE MASTER CHIEF

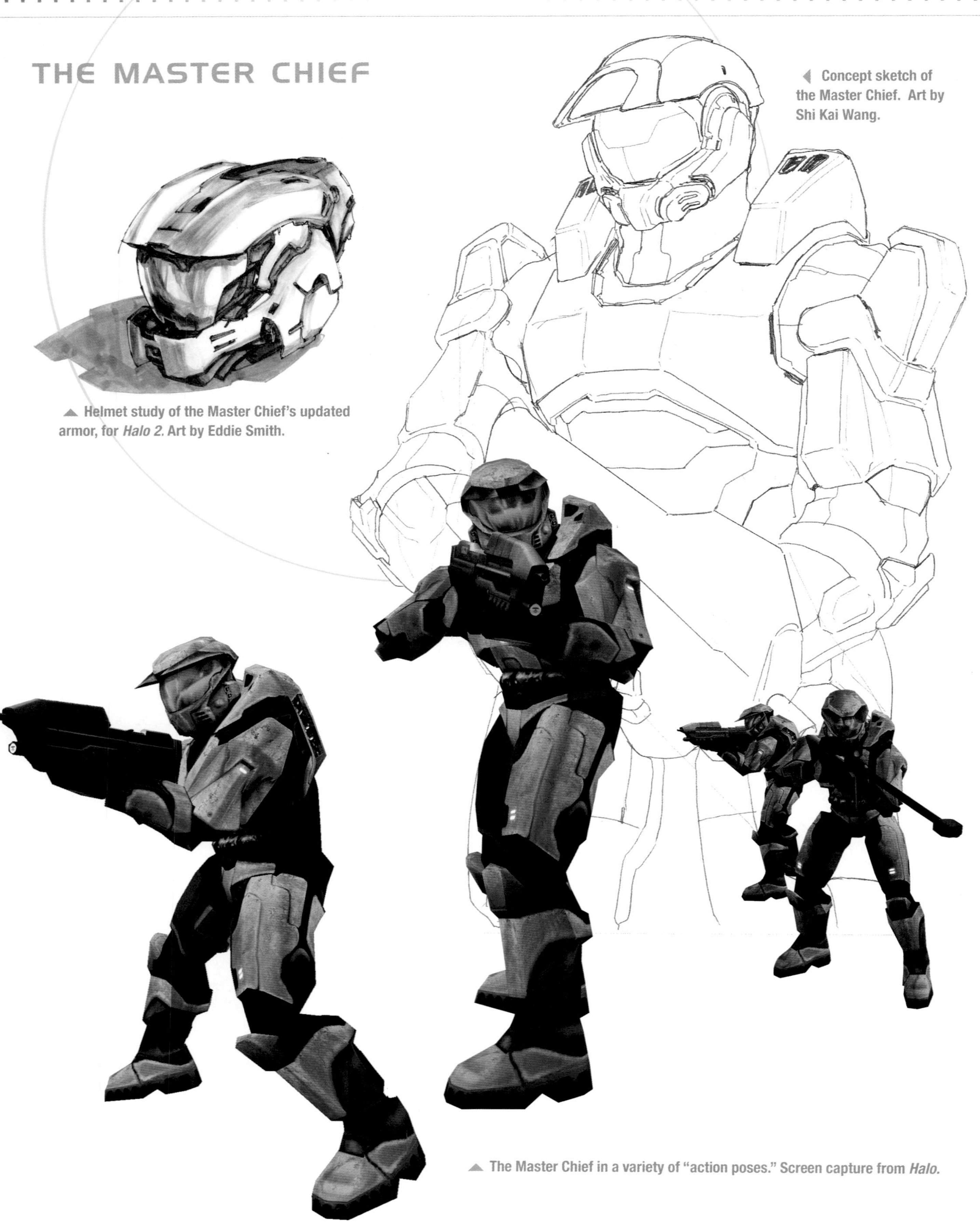

Concept sketch of the Master Chief. Art by Shi Kai Wang.

Helmet study of the Master Chief's updated armor, for *Halo 2*. Art by Eddie Smith.

The Master Chief in a variety of "action poses." Screen capture from *Halo*.

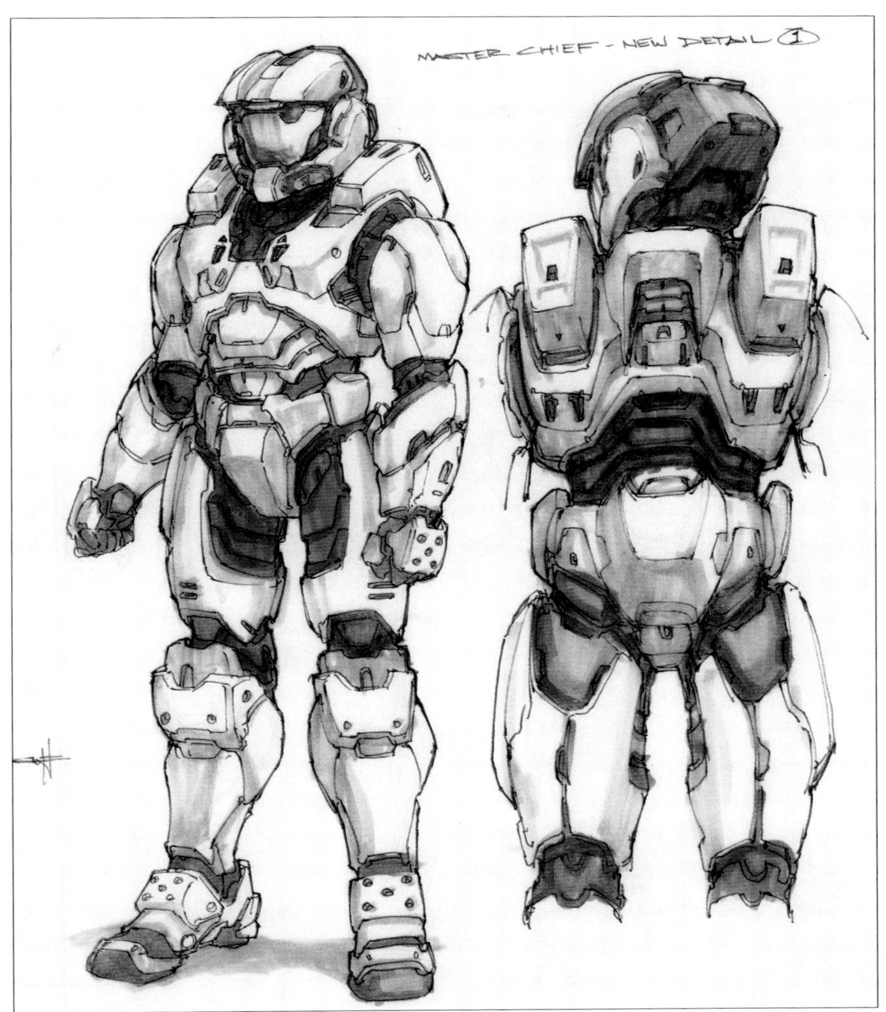

◀ Concept art for the Master Chief's updated MJOLNIR armor. Illustration by Eddie Smith.

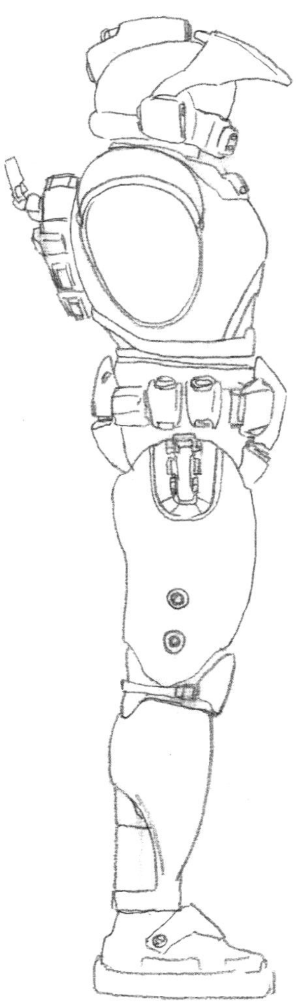

▲ An early profile view of the Master Chief. Illustration by Marcus Lehto.

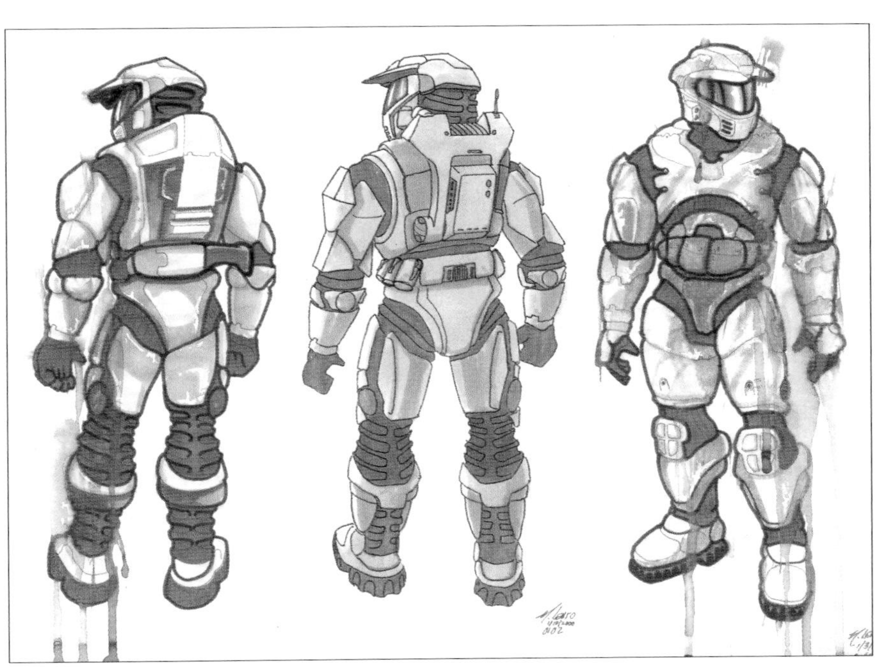

◀ Studies of the Master Chief. The original artwork was damaged when the walls of Bungie's Chicago offices leaked during a rainstorm. Illustration by Marcus Lehto.

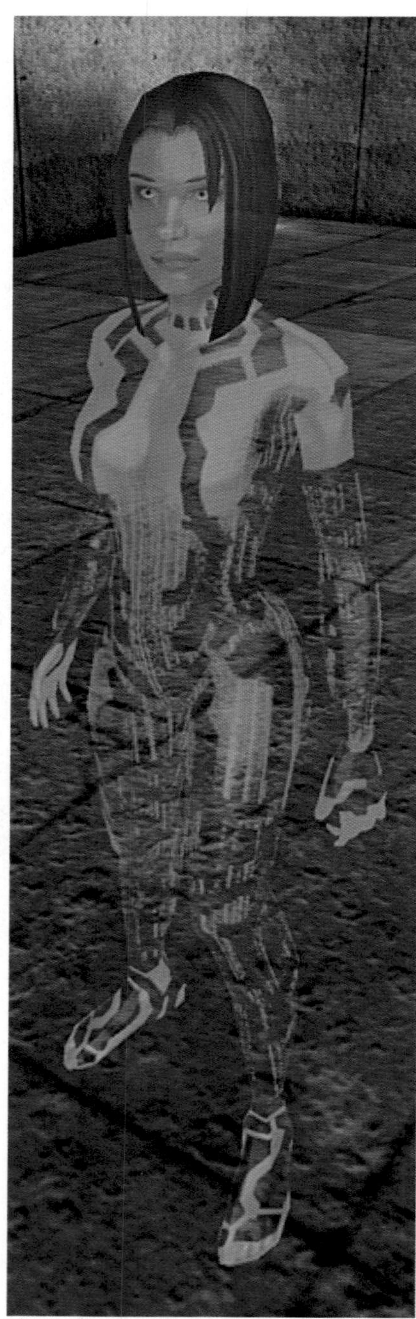

▲ A more realistic take on Cortana; an in-progress shot taken from *Halo 2*.

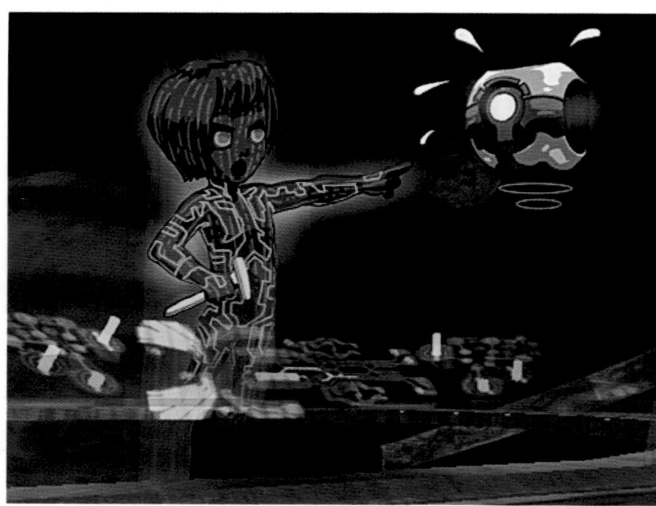

◀ One of a handful of "Halo Babies" art that graced the pages of Bungie.net on April 1, 2001. Art by Lorraine McLees.

CORTANA

Cortana is the *Pillar of Autumn*'s shipboard artificial intelligence. The Master Chief's armor is designed to store and power Cortana, which gives the Chief tremendous tactical advantages. She only appears as a hologram.

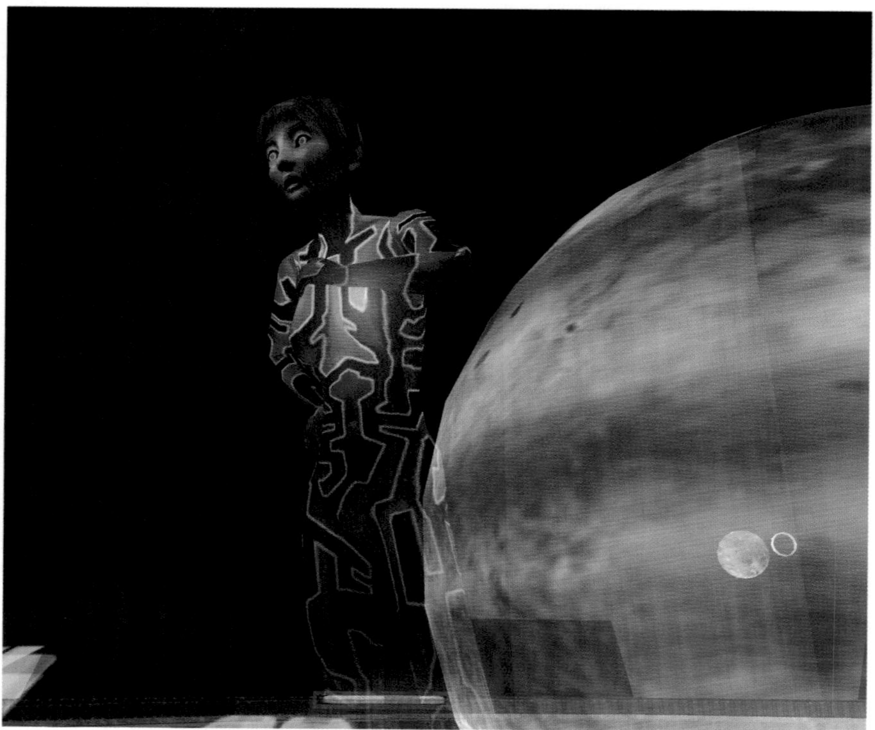

▲ Cortana's holographic form, as projected by Halo's titanic computer infrastructure. Screen capture from *Halo*.

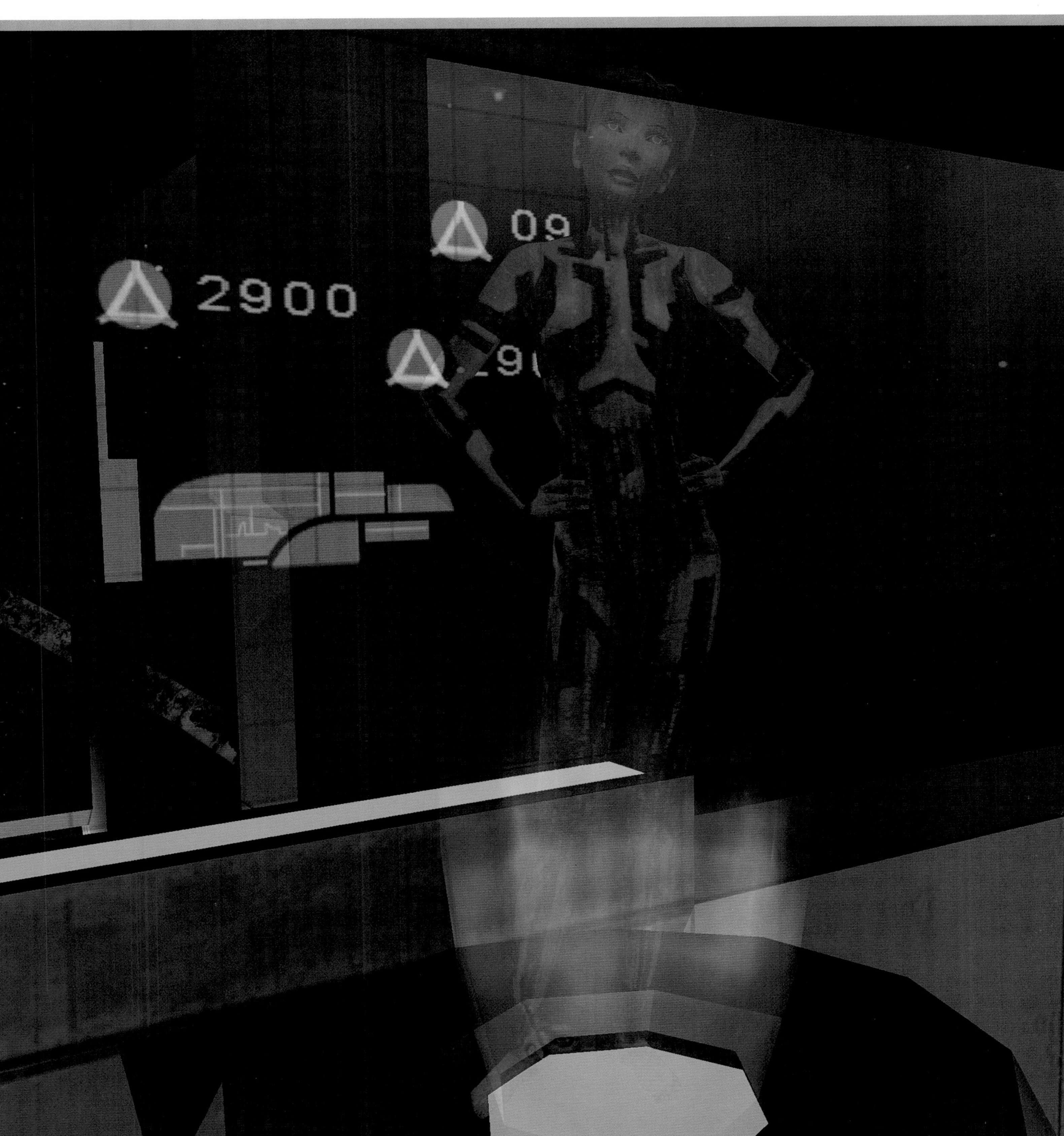

▲ Cortana, the *Pillar of Autumn*'s shipboard AI construct, appears in holographic form on the ship's bridge. Screen capture from *Halo*.

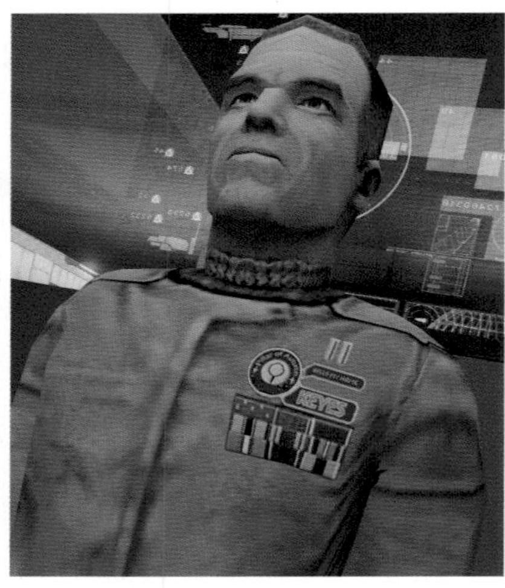

CAPTAIN KEYES

Captain Jacob Keyes is the *Pillar of Autumn*'s tactically brilliant commanding officer. Gruff and occasionally stern, he nonetheless is well respected by his crew. After crash-landing the *Autumn* on Halo, Keyes spent time in Covenant captivity before being rescued by the Master Chief.

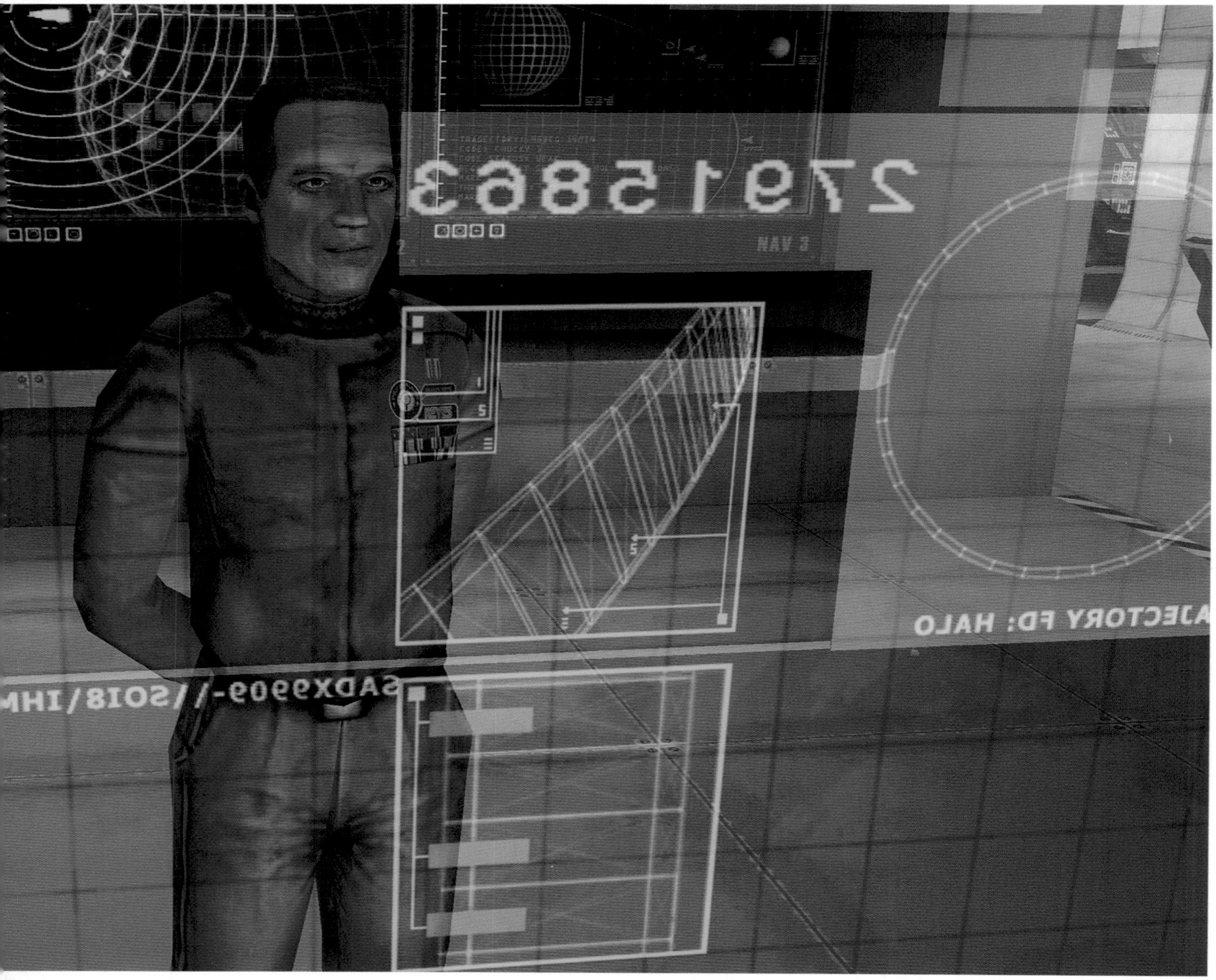

▲ Captain Jacob Keyes, the heroic commanding officer of the *Pillar of Autumn*. Screen shots from *Halo*.

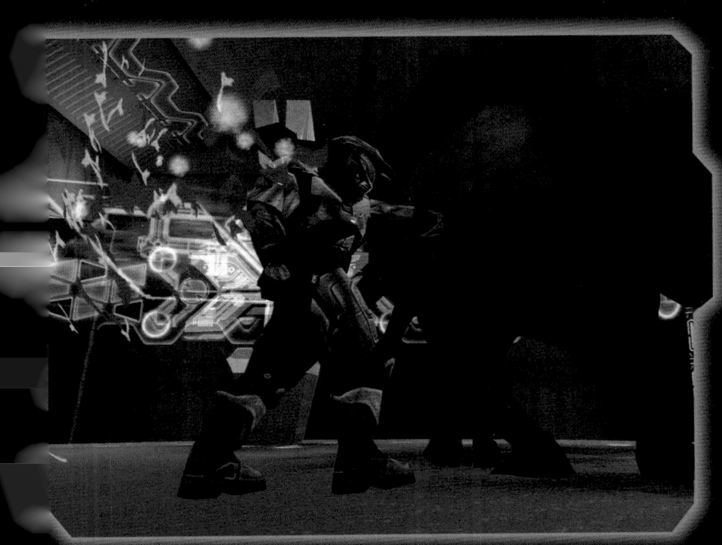

The final fate of Captain Keyes—absorption into the Flood. Screen capture from *Halo.*

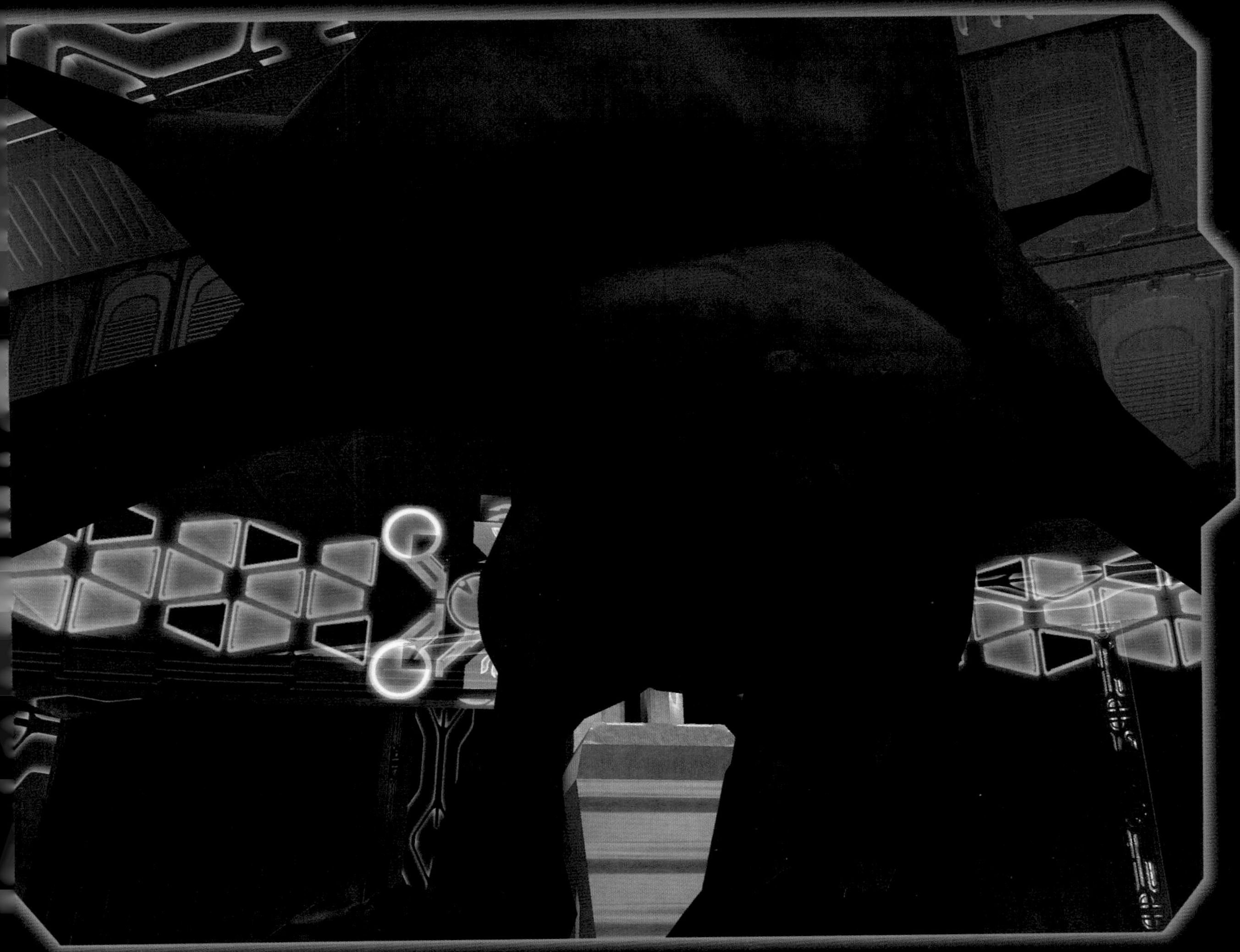

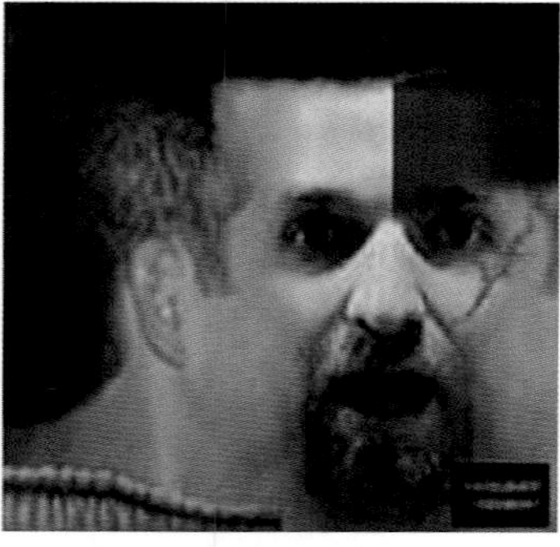

▲ The faces of the Marines are generated by building various portrait images into a form that can be "wrapped" around a 3D model (right).

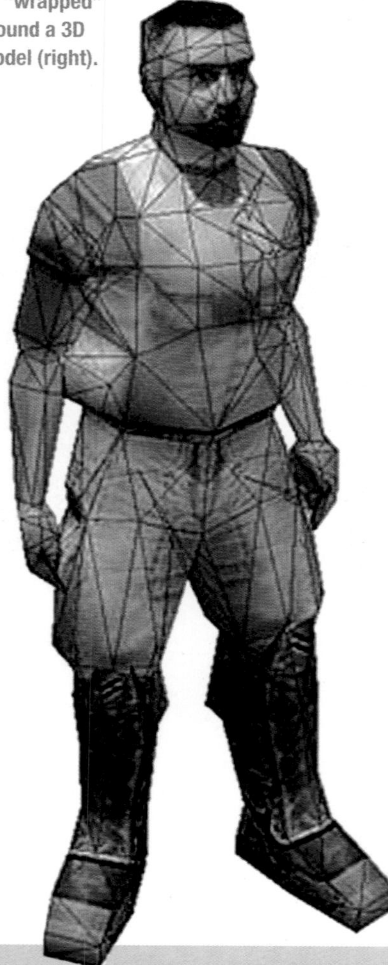

UNSC MARINES

The Marines of the United Nations Space Command are hard-core, aggressive fighters, willing to do the toughest jobs imaginable—from facing down Covenant forces on the ground, to repelling alien boarding parties in space.

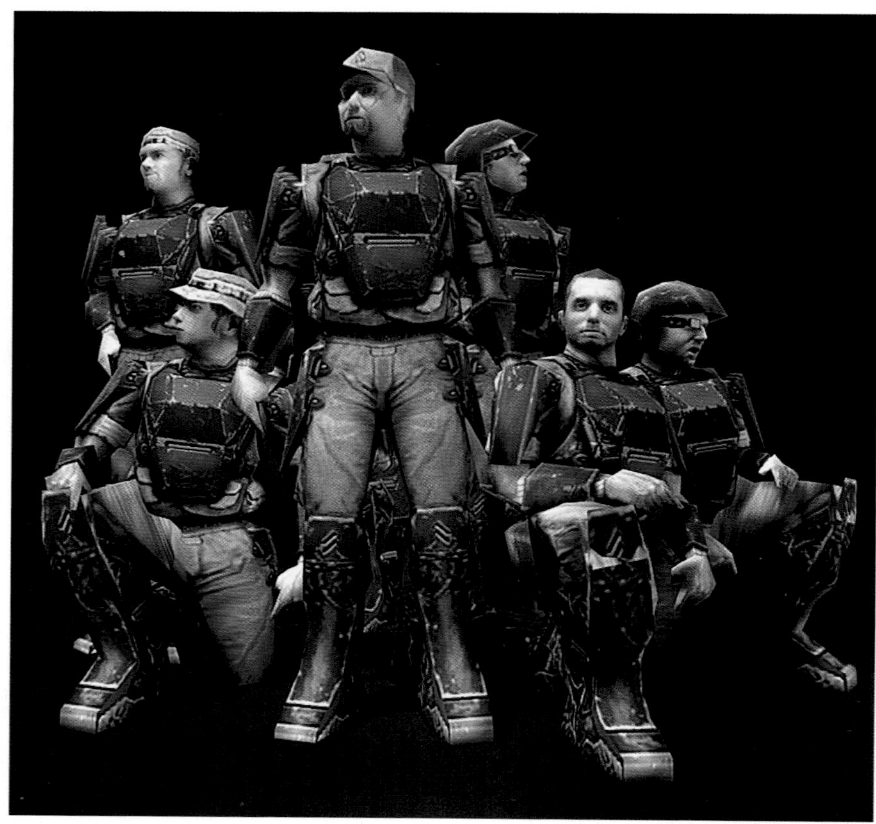

▲ *Halo* Marines, as they appear in the game. Nearly all of them wore the head of a *Halo* development team member. Screen capture from *Halo*.

"I was one of the only animators working on the game in its early days, and I wanted the Marines to look as realistic as possible," says art director Marcus Lehto. "But I could only glean so much watching war movies, so I had to find additional sources of reference to tweak the character animations for the Marines. In the end, my wife videotaped me running around a field with a two-by-four, playing soldier."

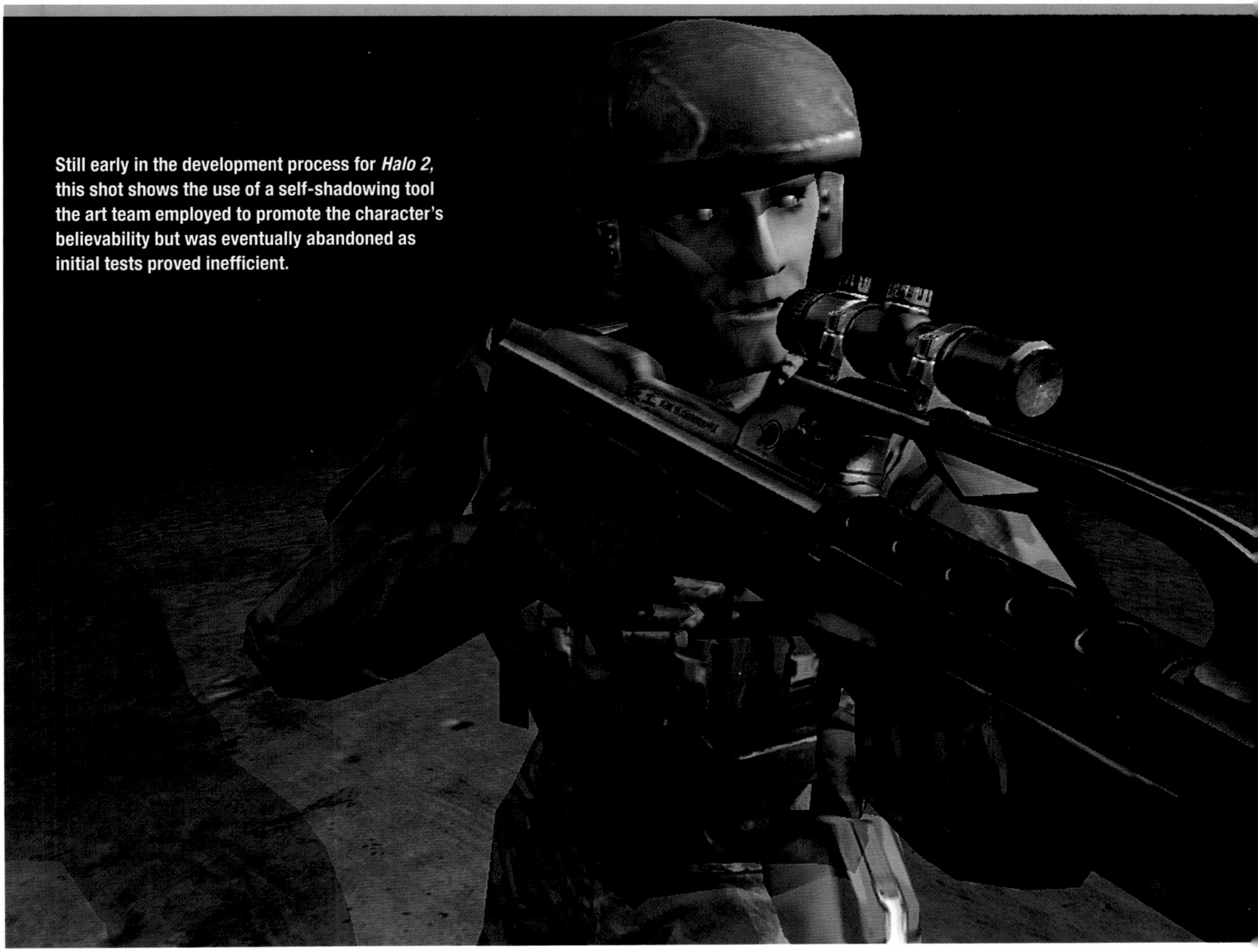

Still early in the development process for *Halo 2,* this shot shows the use of a self-shadowing tool the art team employed to promote the character's believability but was eventually abandoned as initial tests proved inefficient.

"I'm doing a lot of the Marines in Halo 2,*" says animator John Butkus, "so I've been looking at lots of World War II movies, military science fiction films, stuff like that. It's important that these guys move around like real soldiers, that they look as real as we can make it, but with some real energy and excitement, too. I want the player to think he's starring in the coolest movie ever made."*

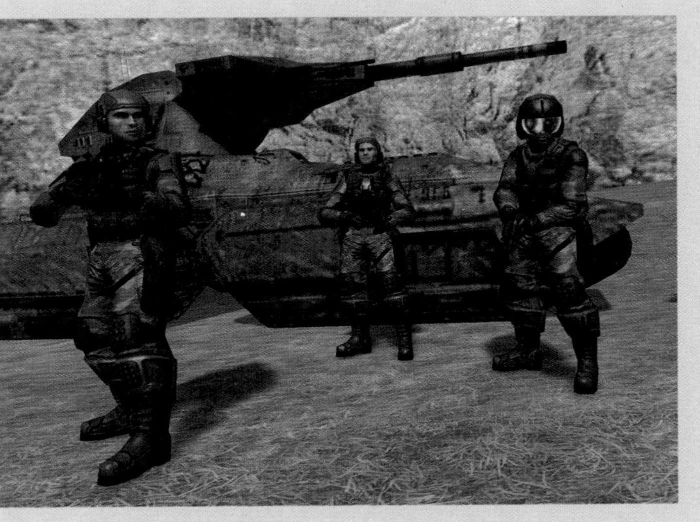

◀ Screen shot from a *Halo 2* test level called "Meat Grinder."

UNSC MARINE STUDY

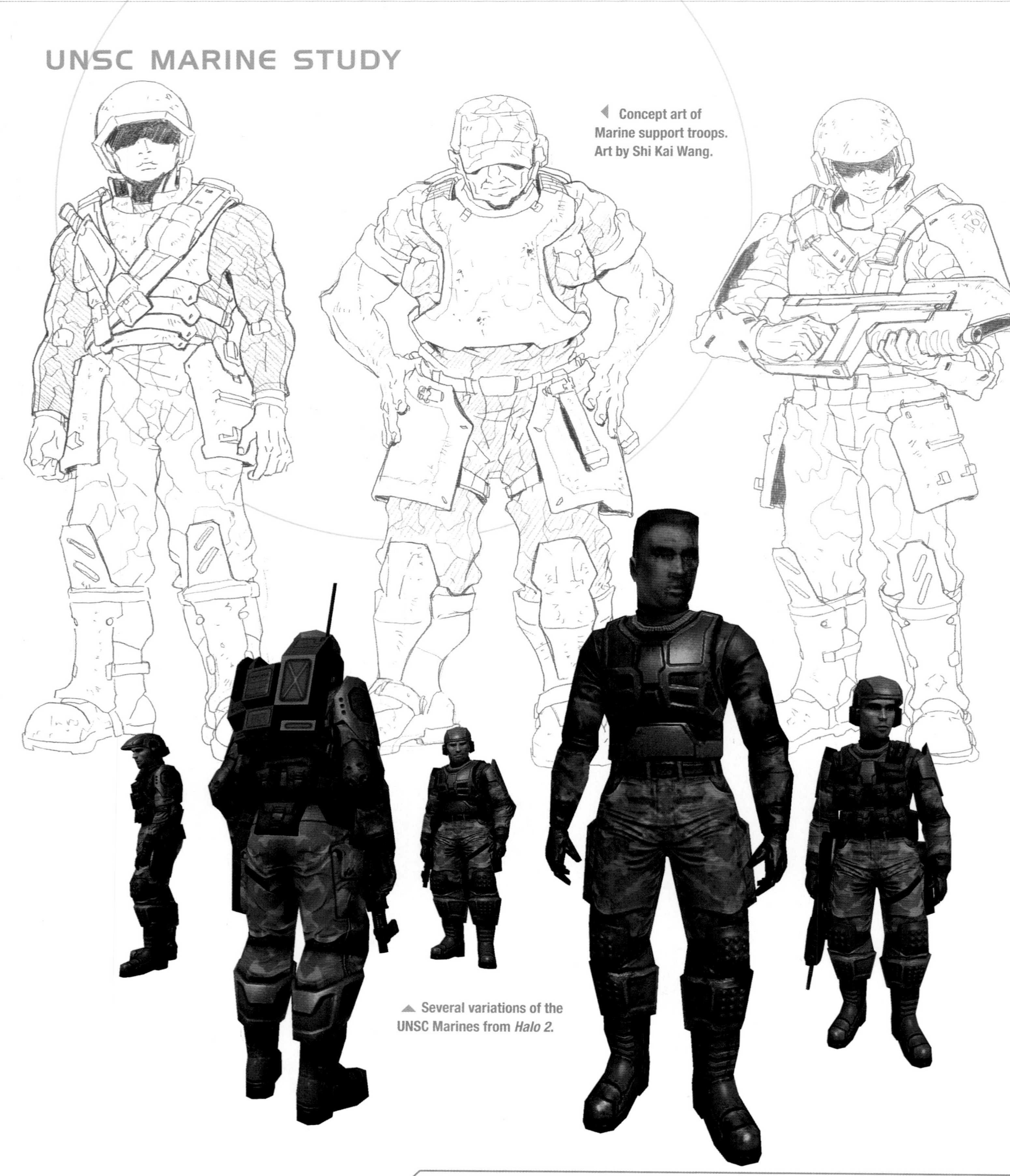

Concept art of Marine support troops. Art by Shi Kai Wang.

Several variations of the UNSC Marines from *Halo 2*.

A Marine infantryman, as seen in *Halo* (left), and an updated pilot Marine from *Halo 2* (right).

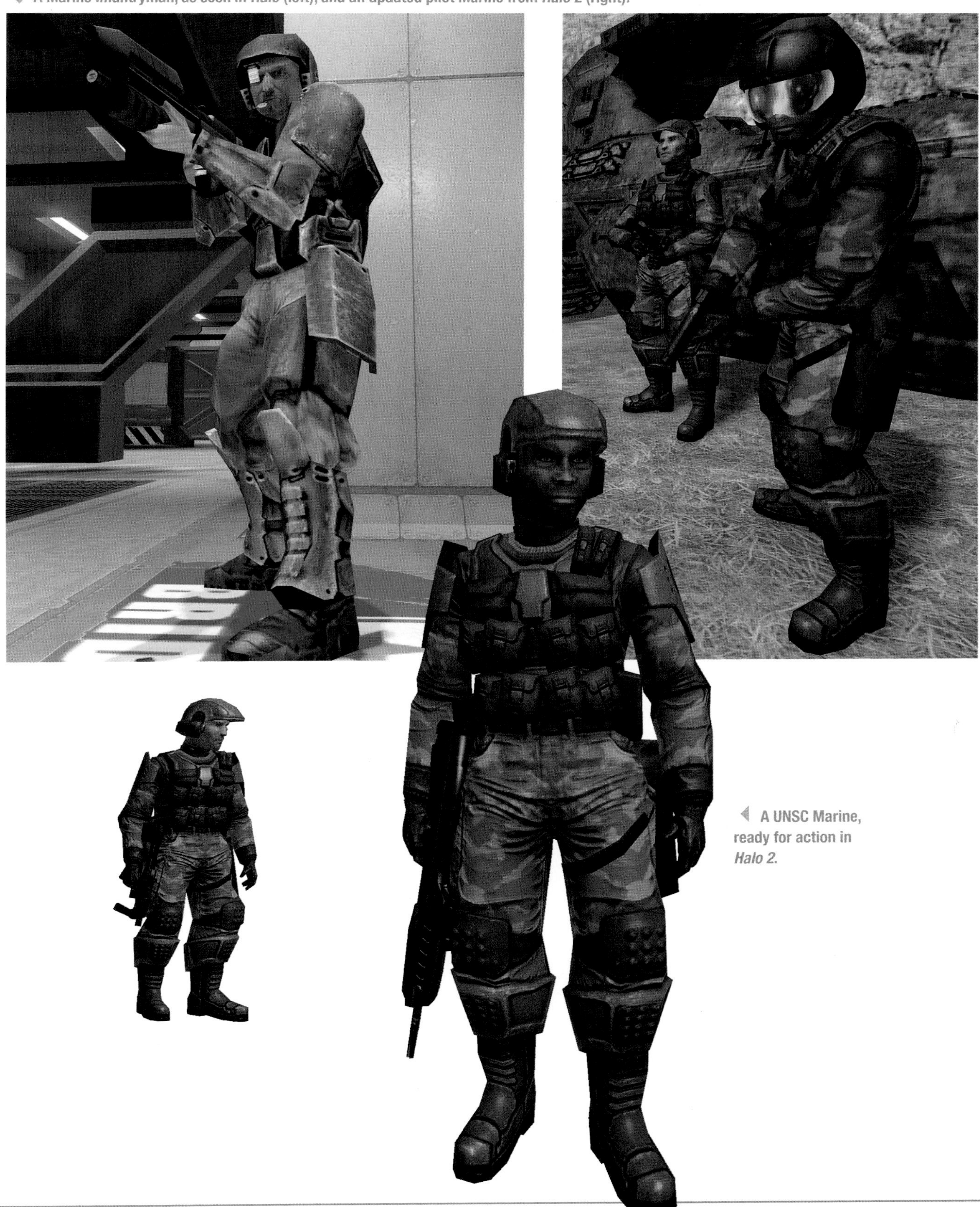

A UNSC Marine, ready for action in *Halo 2*.

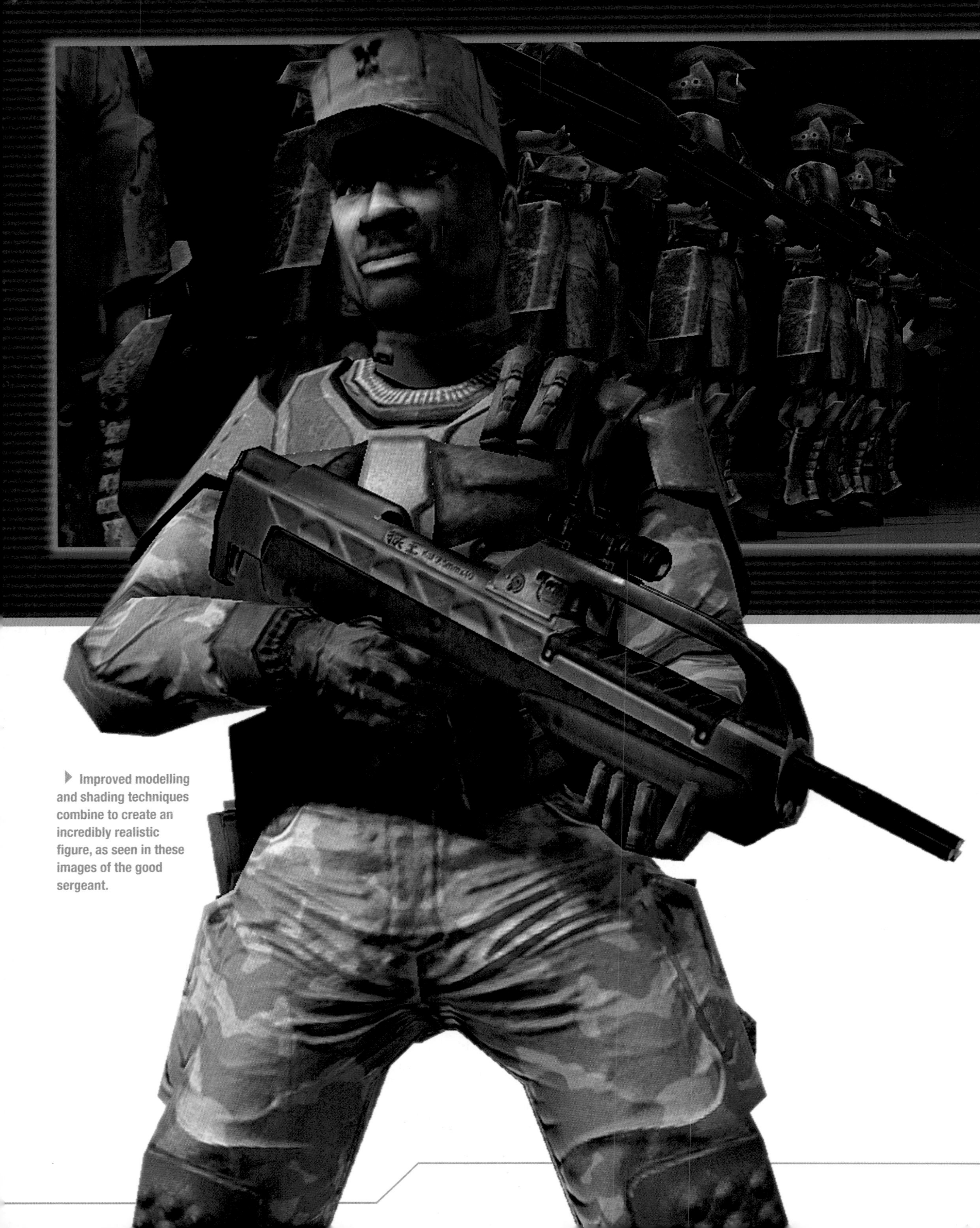

Improved modelling and shading techniques combine to create an incredibly realistic figure, as seen in these images of the good sergeant.

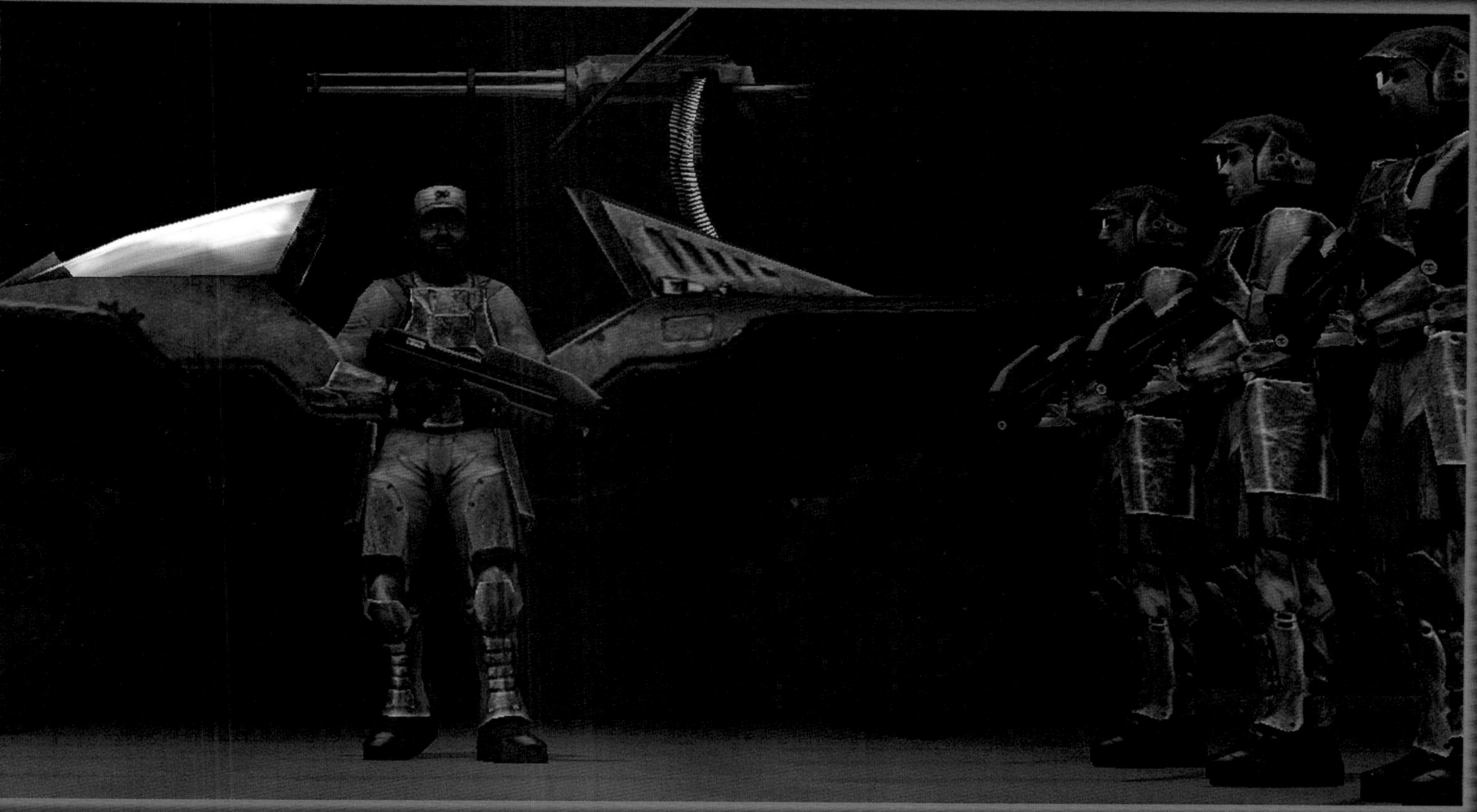

▲ Sgt. Johnson rallies his troops. Screen shot from *Halo*.

SGT. JOHNSON

Sgt. Avery Johnson is a veteran Marine who has fought in countless engagements against the Covenant. Bombastic and gung-ho, he is arguably one of the toughest Marines in the Corps.

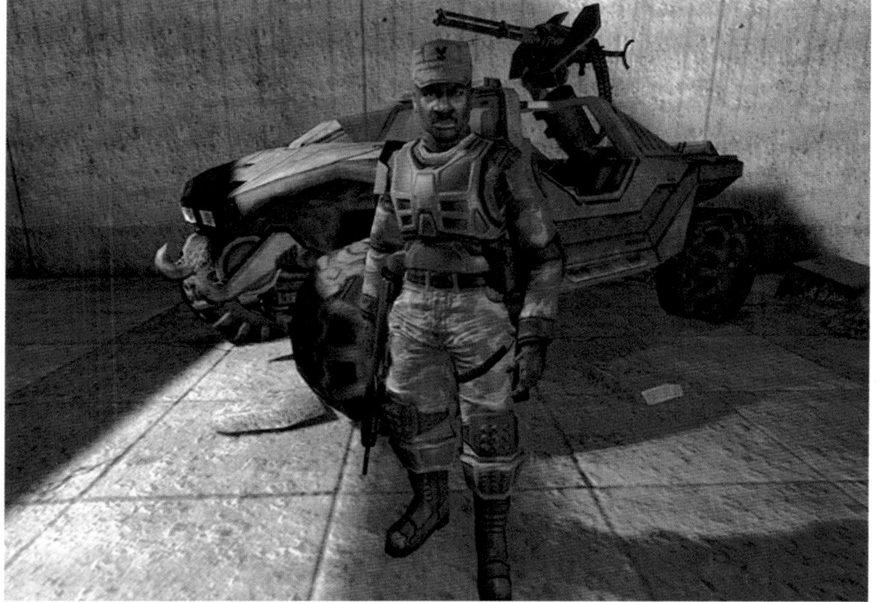

◀ The tough-as-nails Sgt. Johnson survived *Halo*, only to be thrown into an even bigger crisis. Screen shot from *Halo 2*.

UNIFORM STUDY

◀ Uniforms are clearly based on existing military outfits and insignia. Lord Hood's medals and epaulets distinguish him from the rank and file. Art by Lorraine McLees.

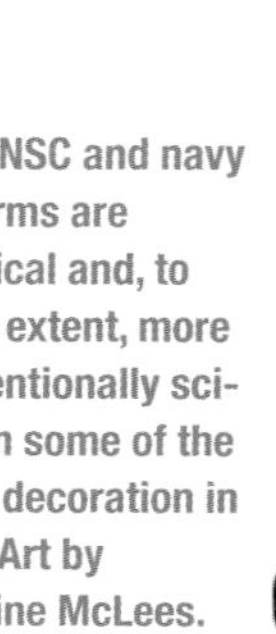

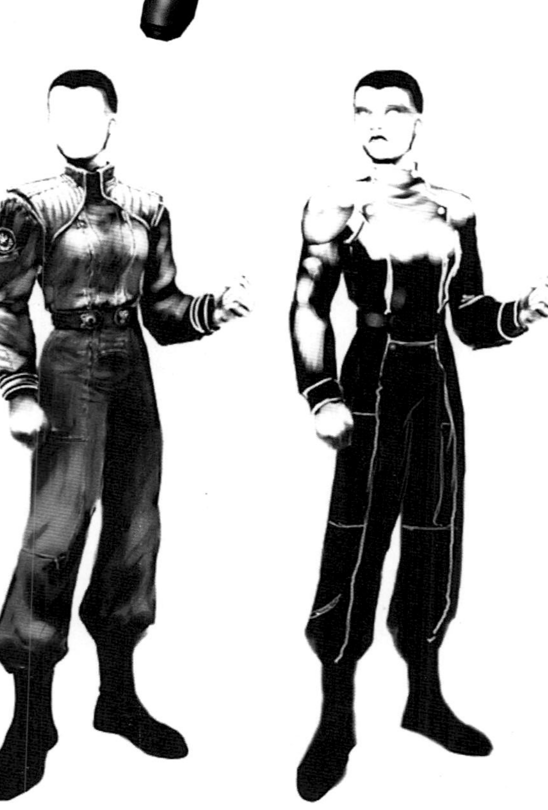

▶ UNSC and navy uniforms are practical and, to some extent, more conventionally sci-fi than some of the other decoration in *Halo*. Art by Lorraine McLees.

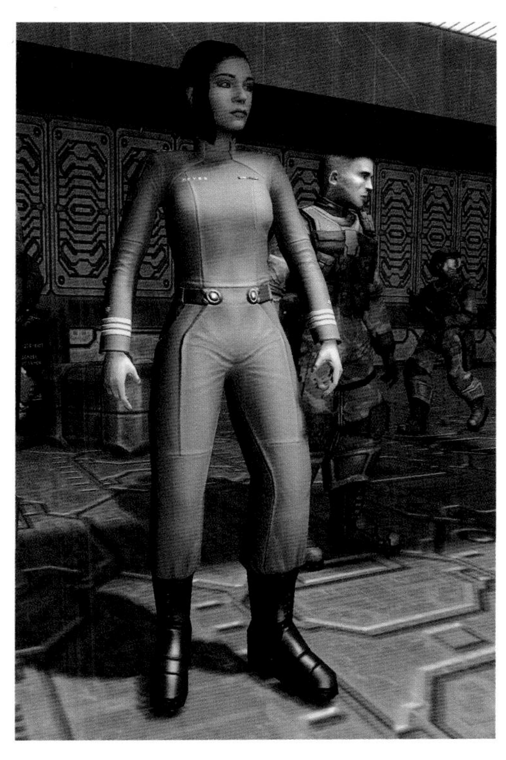

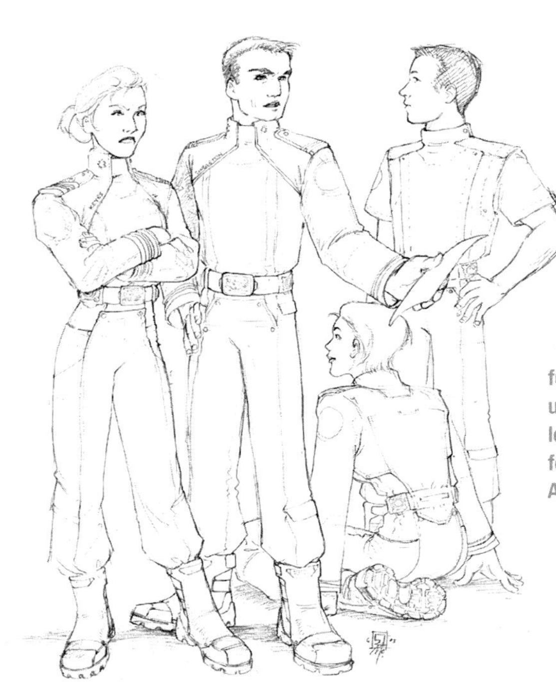

Naturally, real future uniforms will be unisex, so no skintight leotards for enlisted females in 2552. Art by Lorraine McLees.

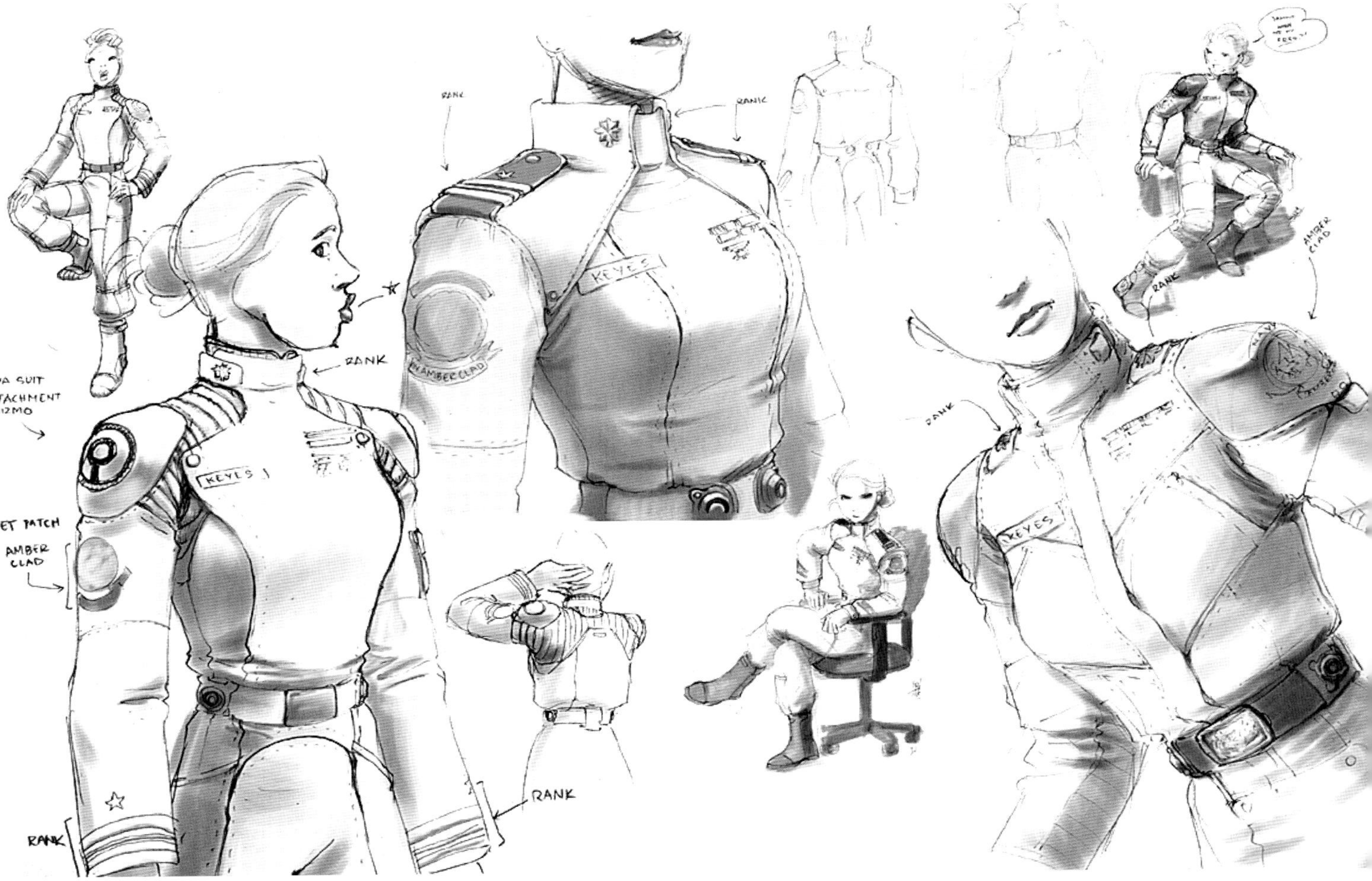

ELITE STUDY

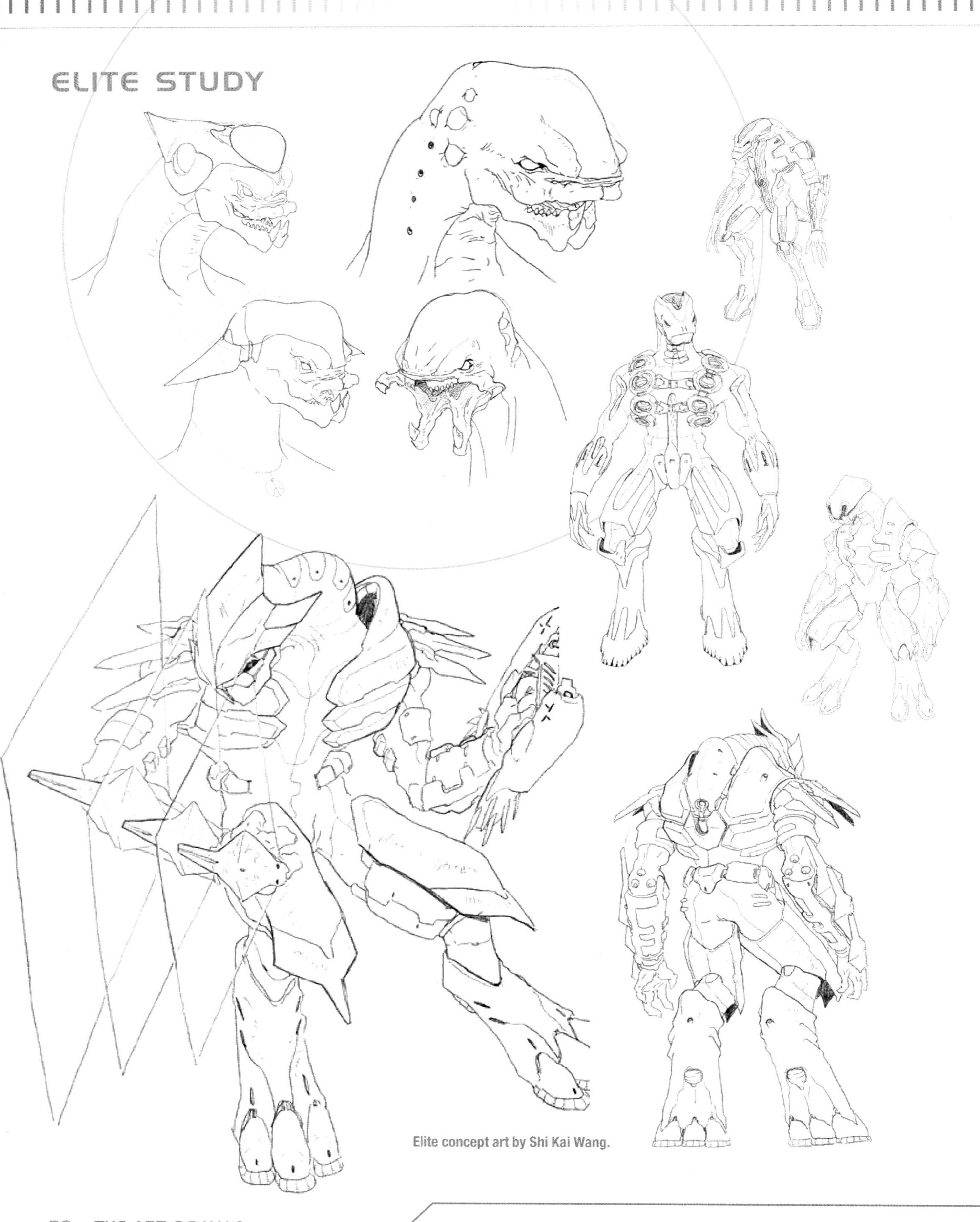

Elite concept art by Shi Kai Wang.

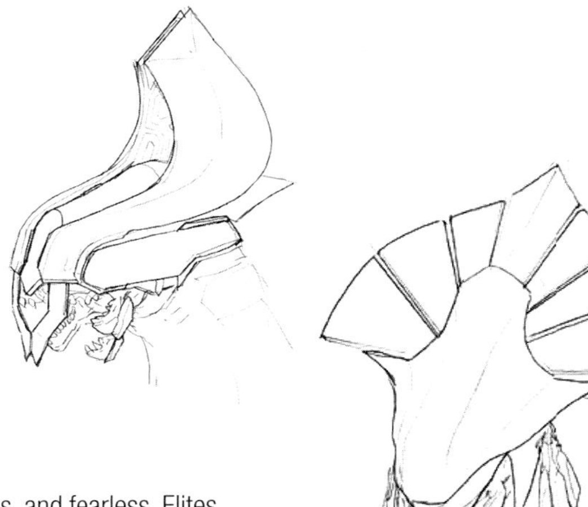

ELITES

Elites are the primary warrior class of the Covenant—relentless, merciless, and fearless. Elites possess energy shields, and fight with a variety of energy and hand-to-hand weapons.

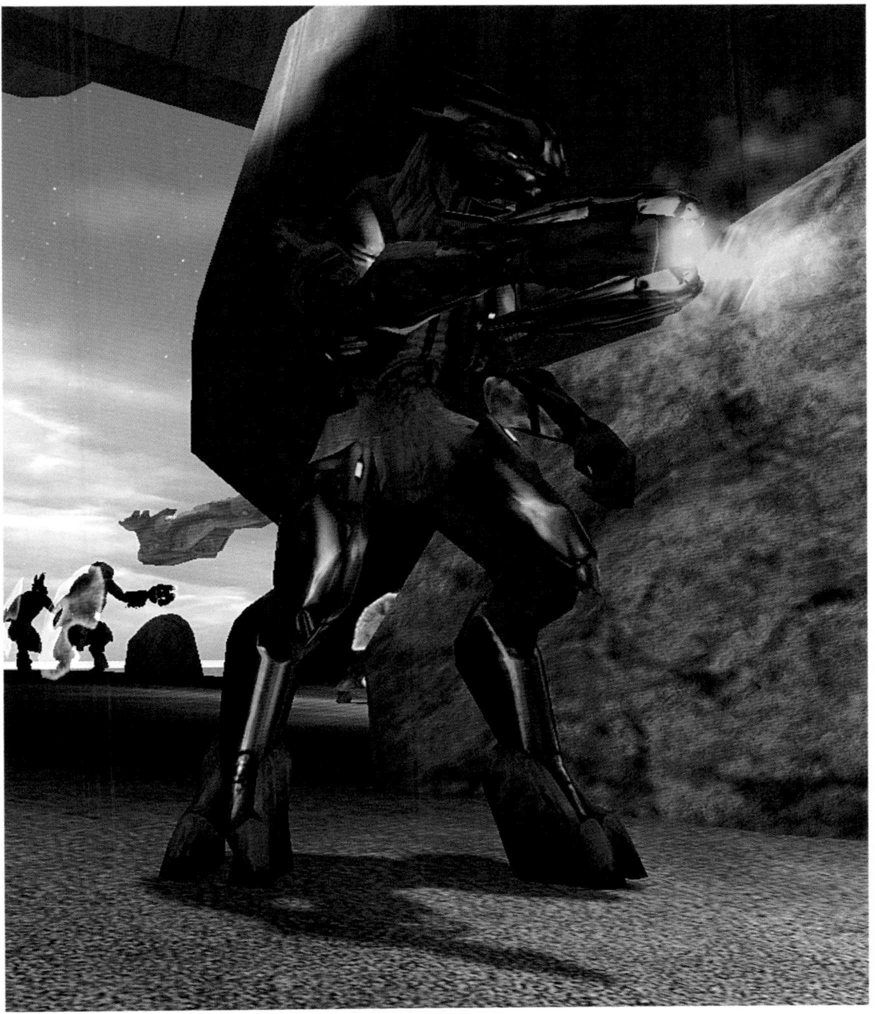

Elites' rank can be determined by the color of their armor. Gold-armored Elites are field commanders; black armor denotes a commando or "special ops" role; red armor indicates a veteran (the equivalent of a sergeant or other noncom); and blue armor indicates a low-ranking "rookie."

Screen shot from *Halo.*

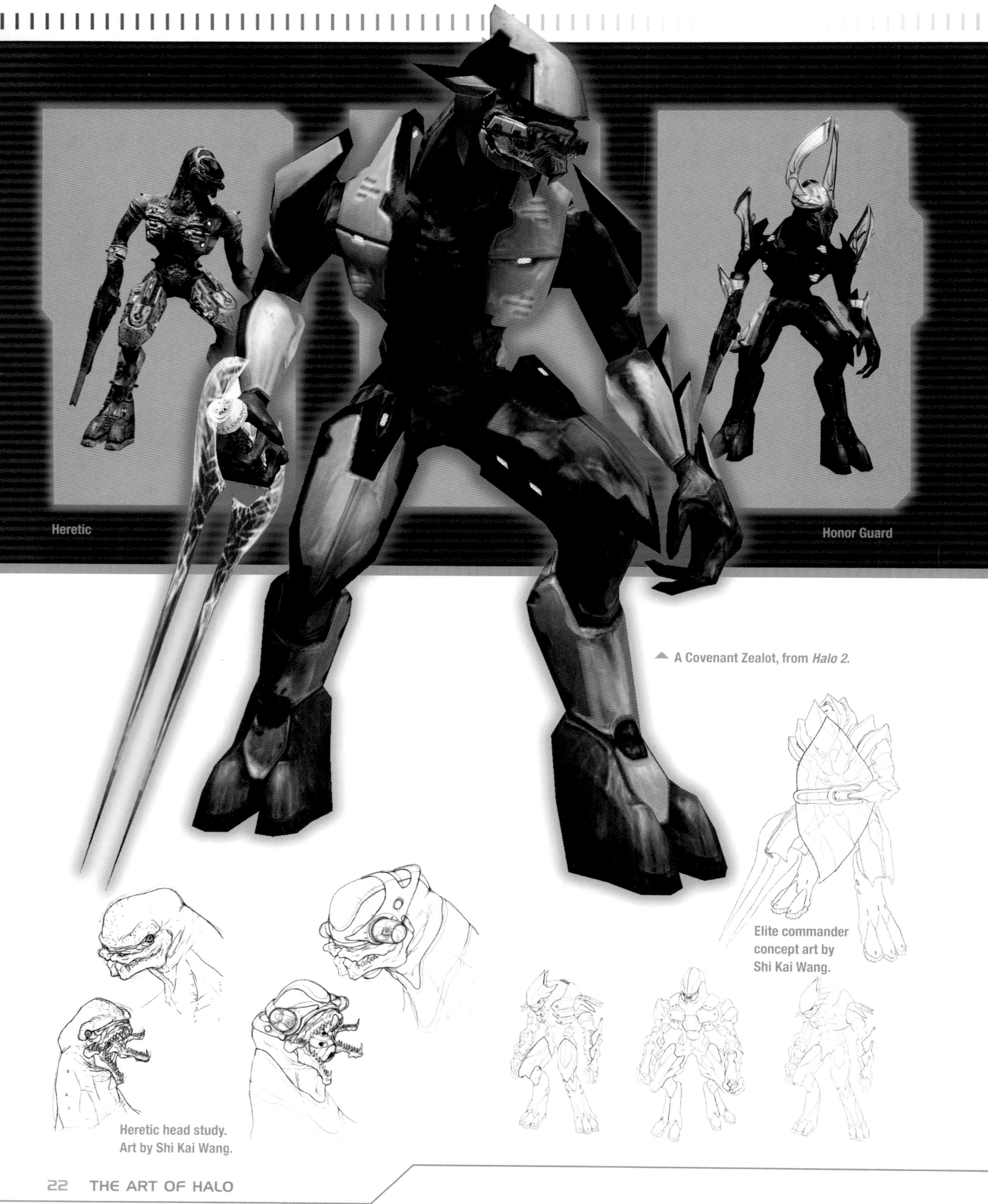

A Covenant Zealot, from *Halo 2*.

Elite commander concept art by Shi Kai Wang.

Heretic head study. Art by Shi Kai Wang.

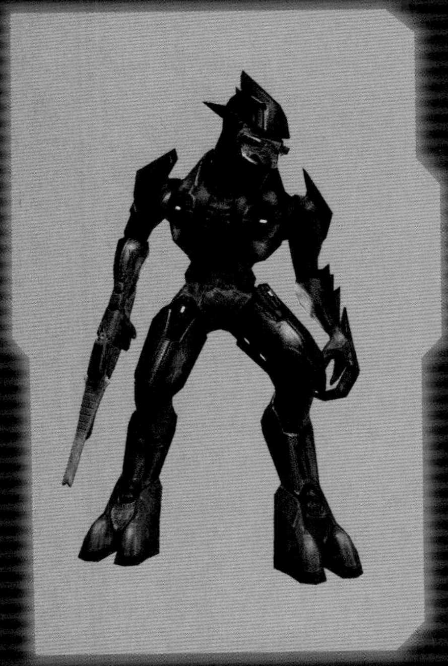

Elite Major

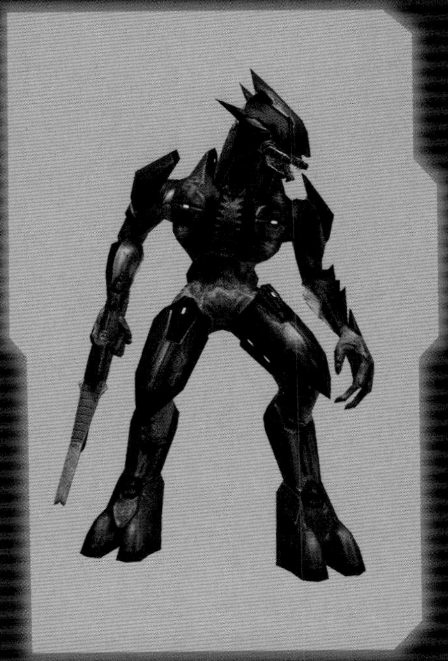

Elite Minor

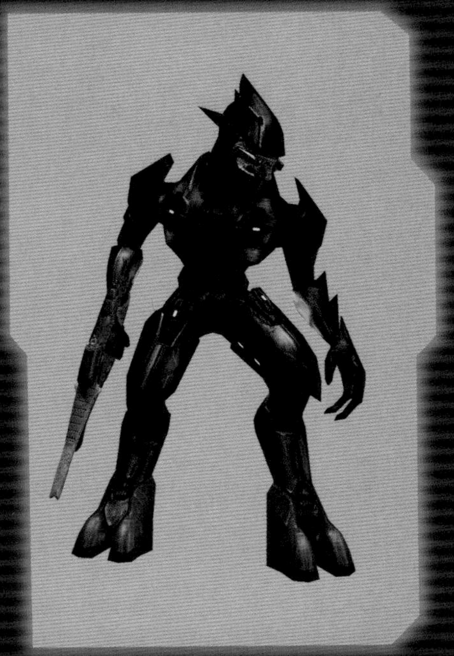

Elite Spec Ops

"Jason Jones always wanted to put a tail on the Elite," explains Shi Kai Wang. "That became the source of a lot of debate. I felt it made the alien look too 'animalistic,' rather than a sentient, technologically enhanced creature. Plus, we would've had to figure out where to put his tail when an Elite sat in a vehicle. At one point, we considered just having the Elites tuck their tails forward, between their legs, but abandoned that . . . for obvious reasons."

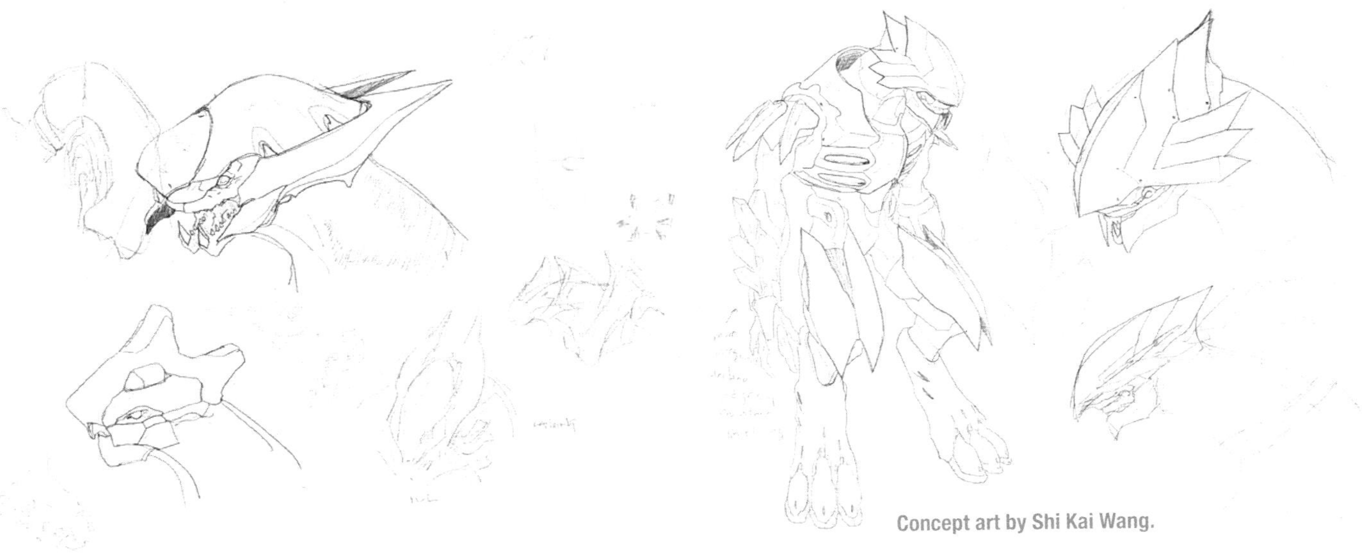

Concept art by Shi Kai Wang.

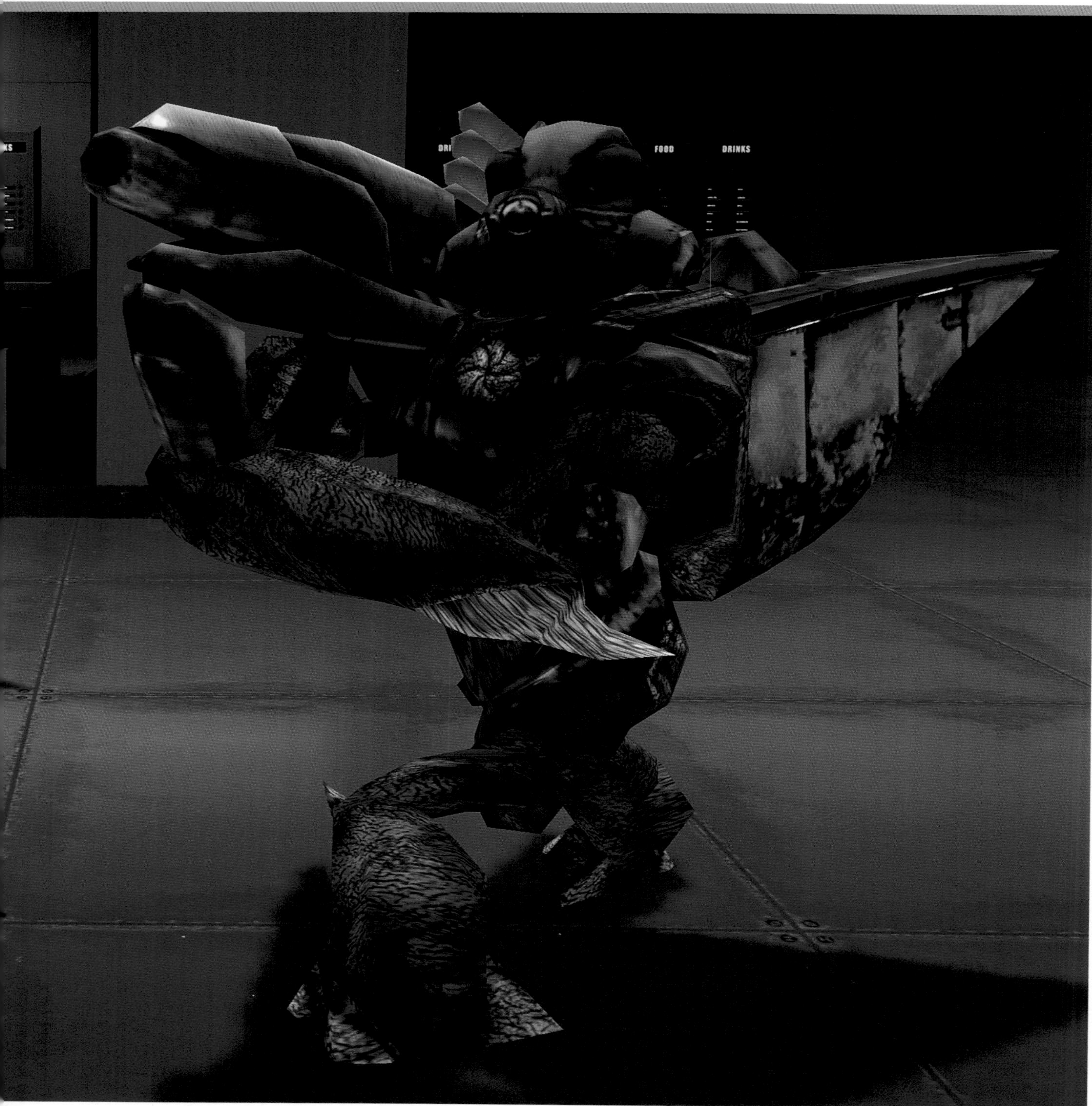

▲ Covenant spec-ops Grunt wielding a fuel rod gun. Screen capture from *Halo*.

GRUNTS

The bulky, low-slung Covenant soldiers known as Grunts typically roam in packs, often accompanied by Elites. Individually, they are not terribly threatening, but in large numbers can be deadly.

They breathe methane and wear sealed environment suits to contain suitable atmosphere.

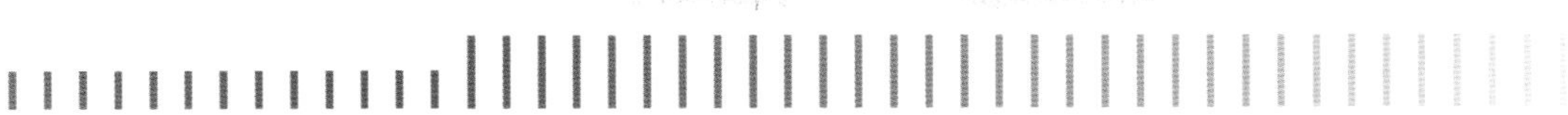

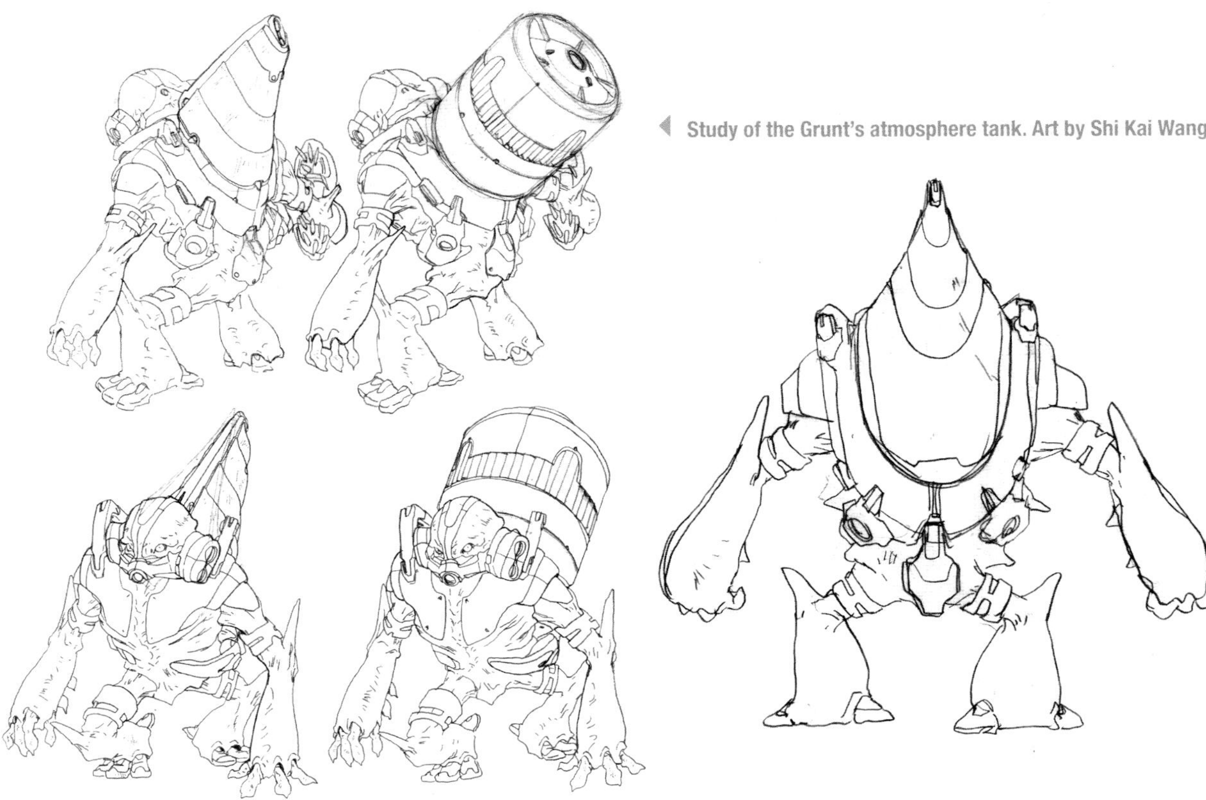

Study of the Grunt's atmosphere tank. Art by Shi Kai Wang.

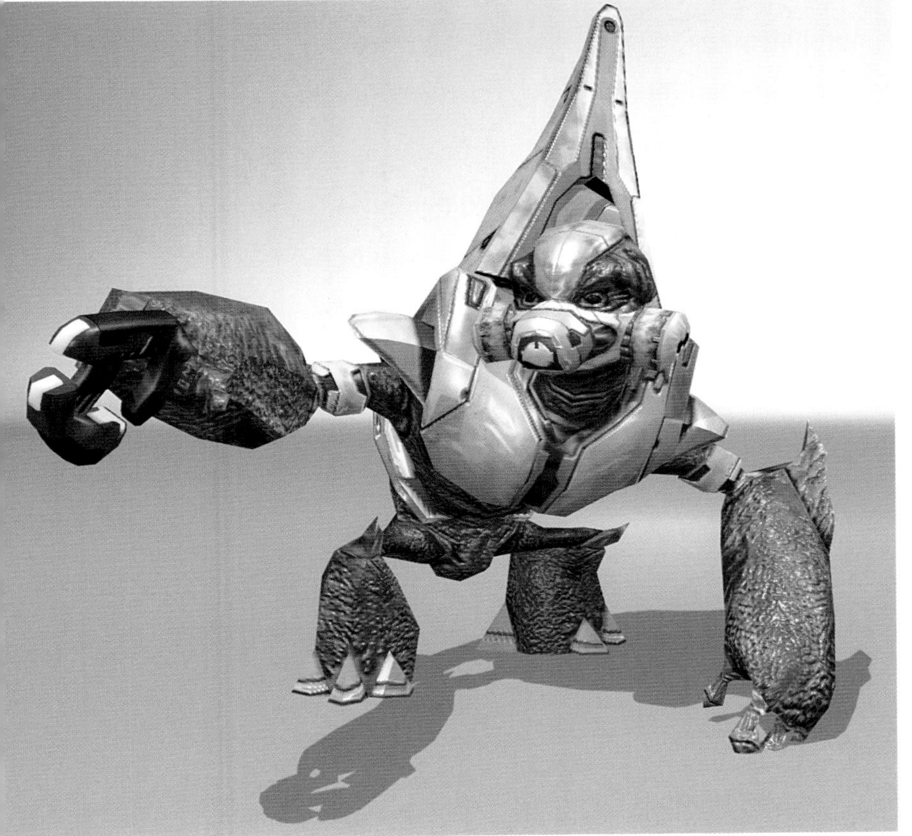

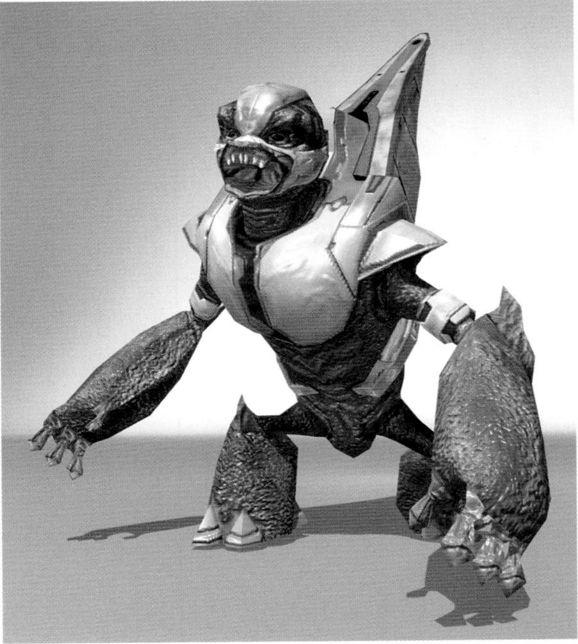

Covenant Grunts rendered with their breathing apparatus and without. Renders from *Halo 2*.

GRUNT STUDY

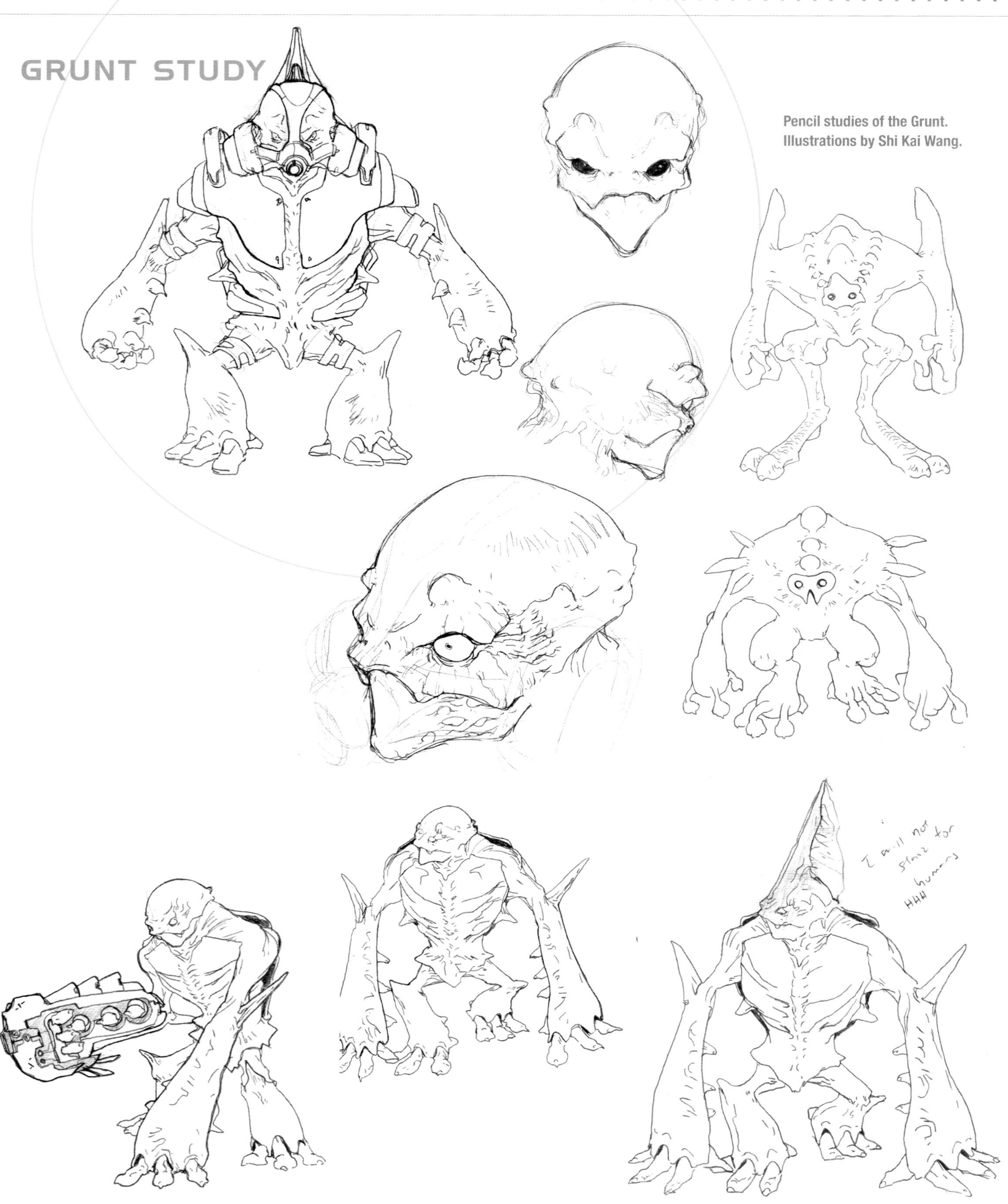

Pencil studies of the Grunt. Illustrations by Shi Kai Wang.

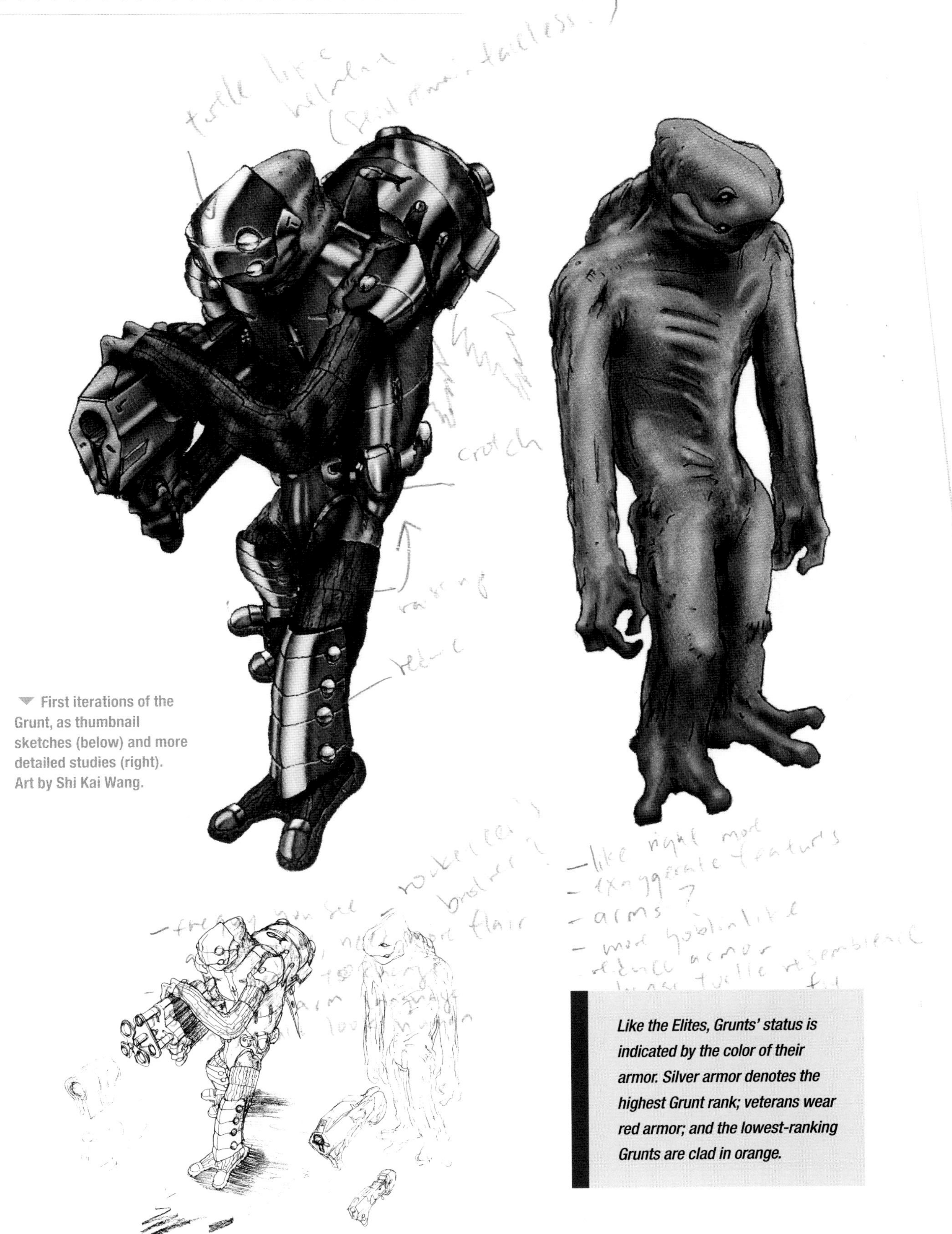

First iterations of the Grunt, as thumbnail sketches (below) and more detailed studies (right). Art by Shi Kai Wang.

Like the Elites, Grunts' status is indicated by the color of their armor. Silver armor denotes the highest Grunt rank; veterans wear red armor; and the lowest-ranking Grunts are clad in orange.

JACKAL STUDY

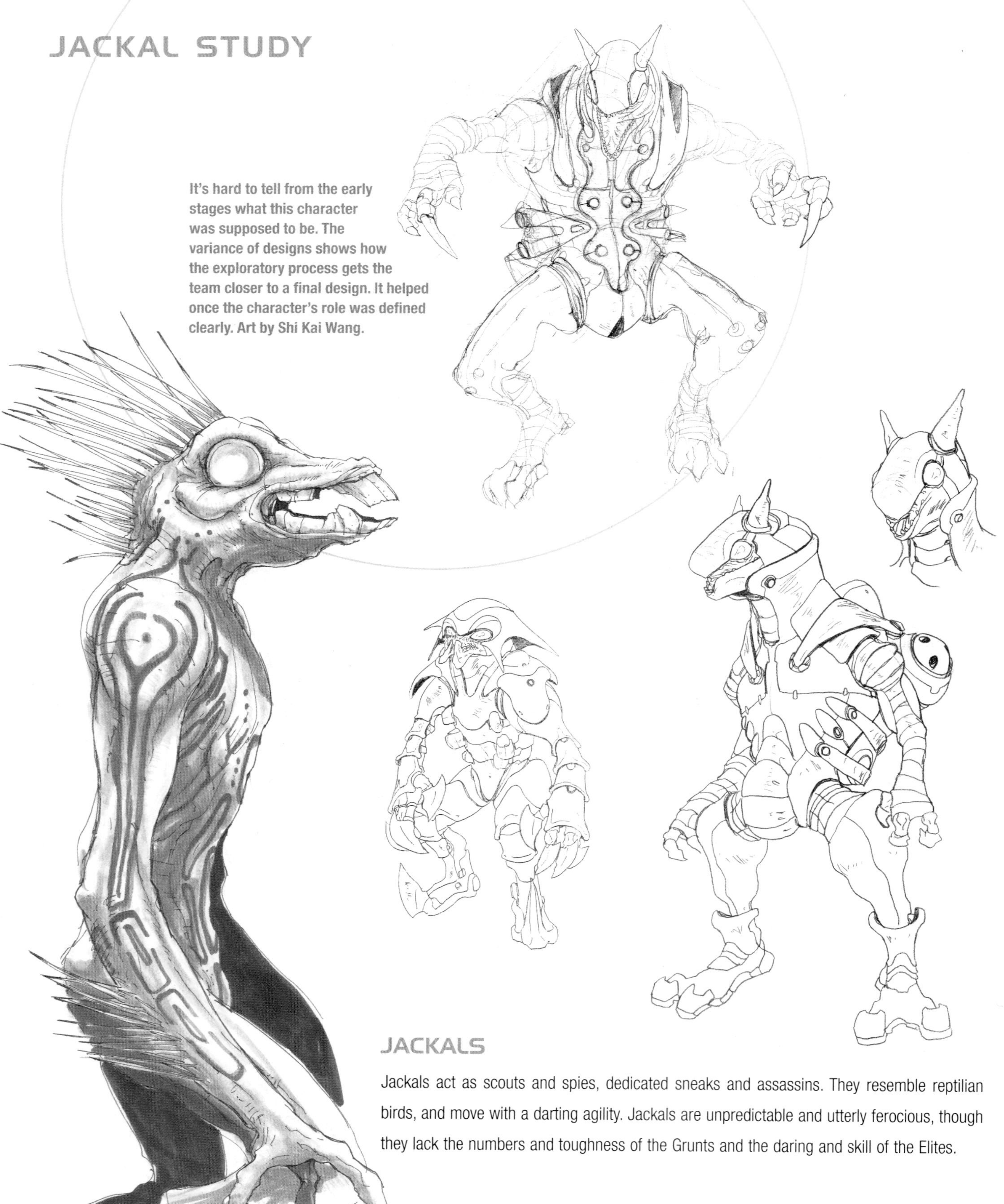

It's hard to tell from the early stages what this character was supposed to be. The variance of designs shows how the exploratory process gets the team closer to a final design. It helped once the character's role was defined clearly. Art by Shi Kai Wang.

JACKALS

Jackals act as scouts and spies, dedicated sneaks and assassins. They resemble reptilian birds, and move with a darting agility. Jackals are unpredictable and utterly ferocious, though they lack the numbers and toughness of the Grunts and the daring and skill of the Elites.

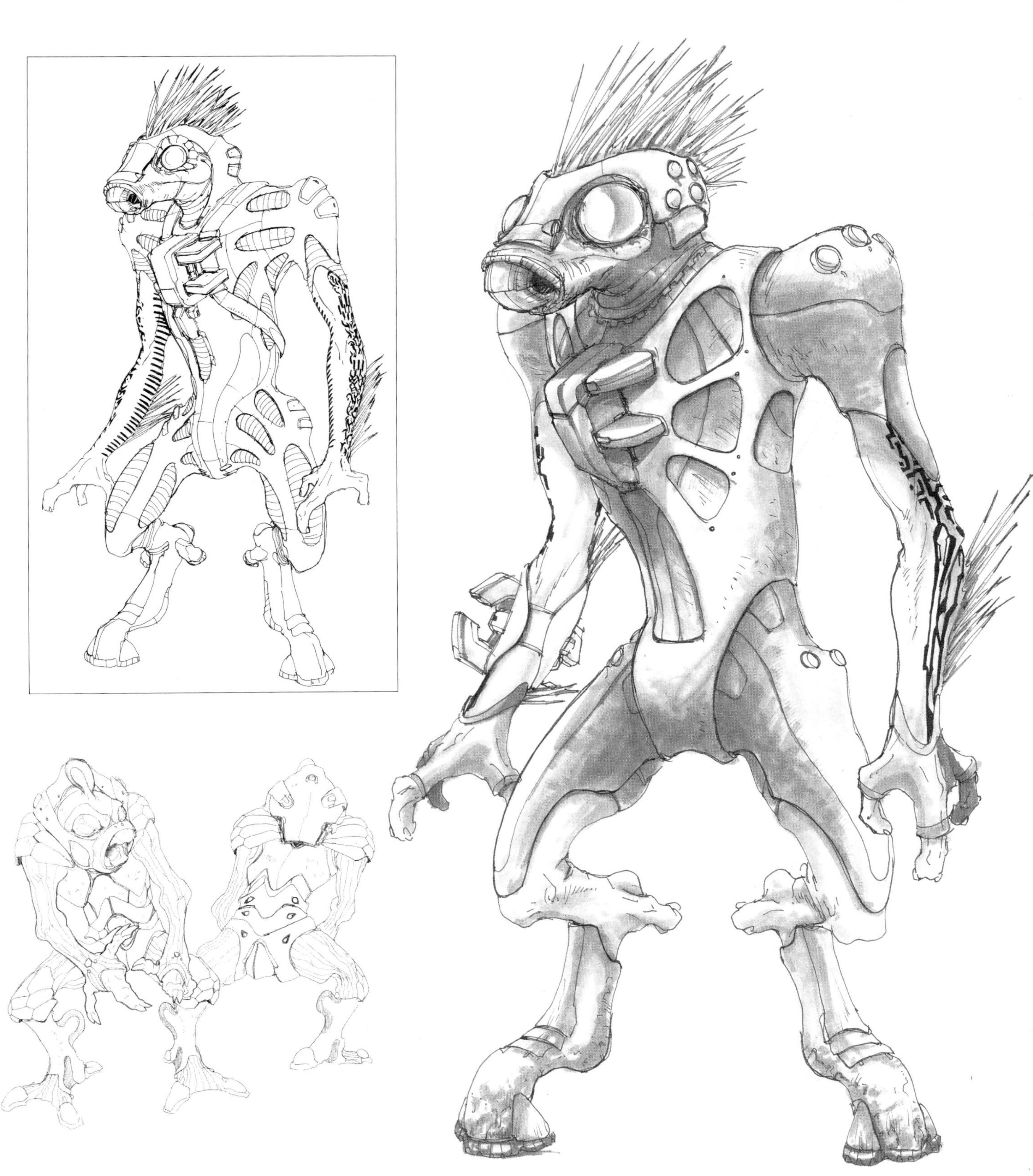

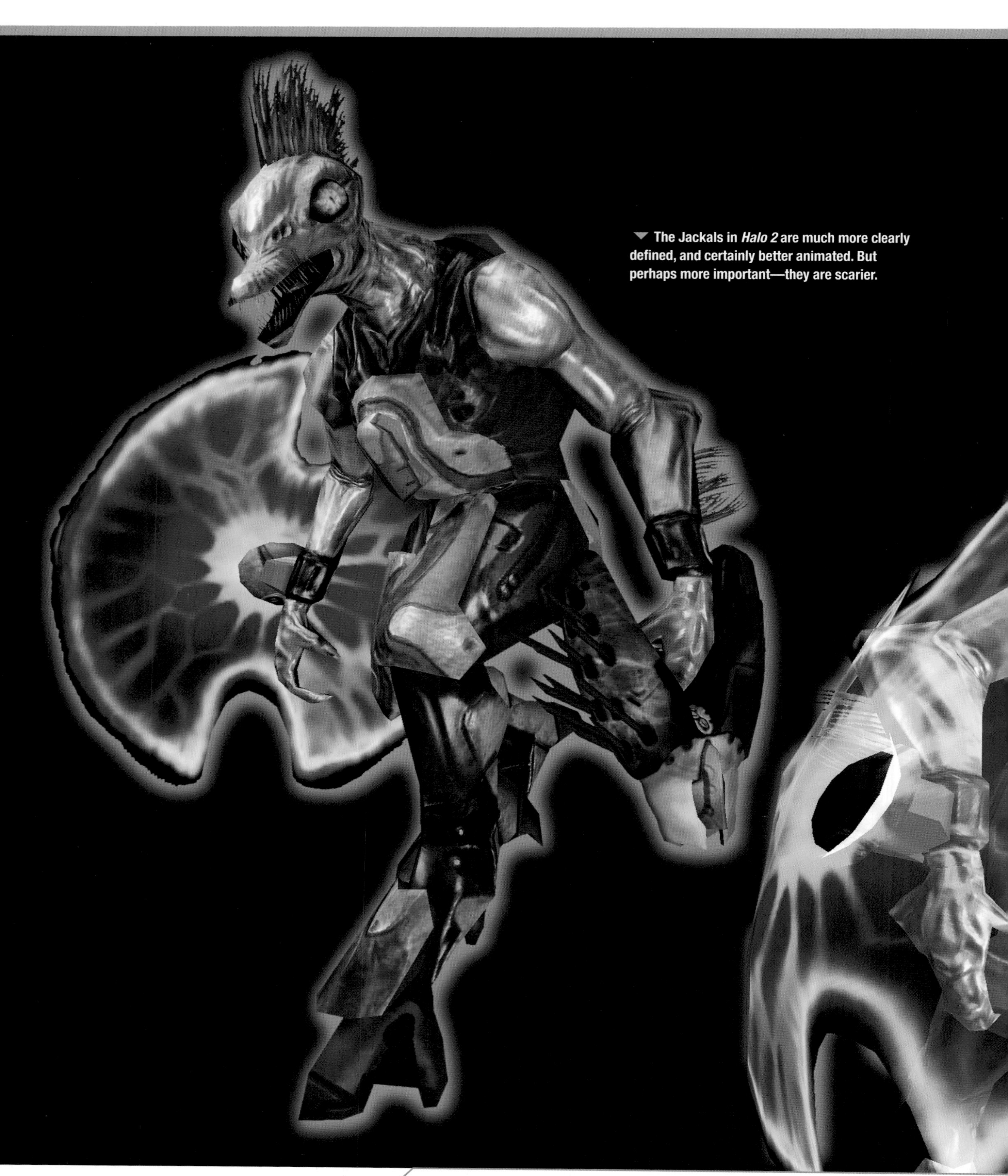

▼ The Jackals in *Halo 2* are much more clearly defined, and certainly better animated. But perhaps more important—they are scarier.

▲ A screen shot from *Halo*

▲ A screen shot taken early in *Halo 2* development; it was shot in a dark alley on an "Earth" level.

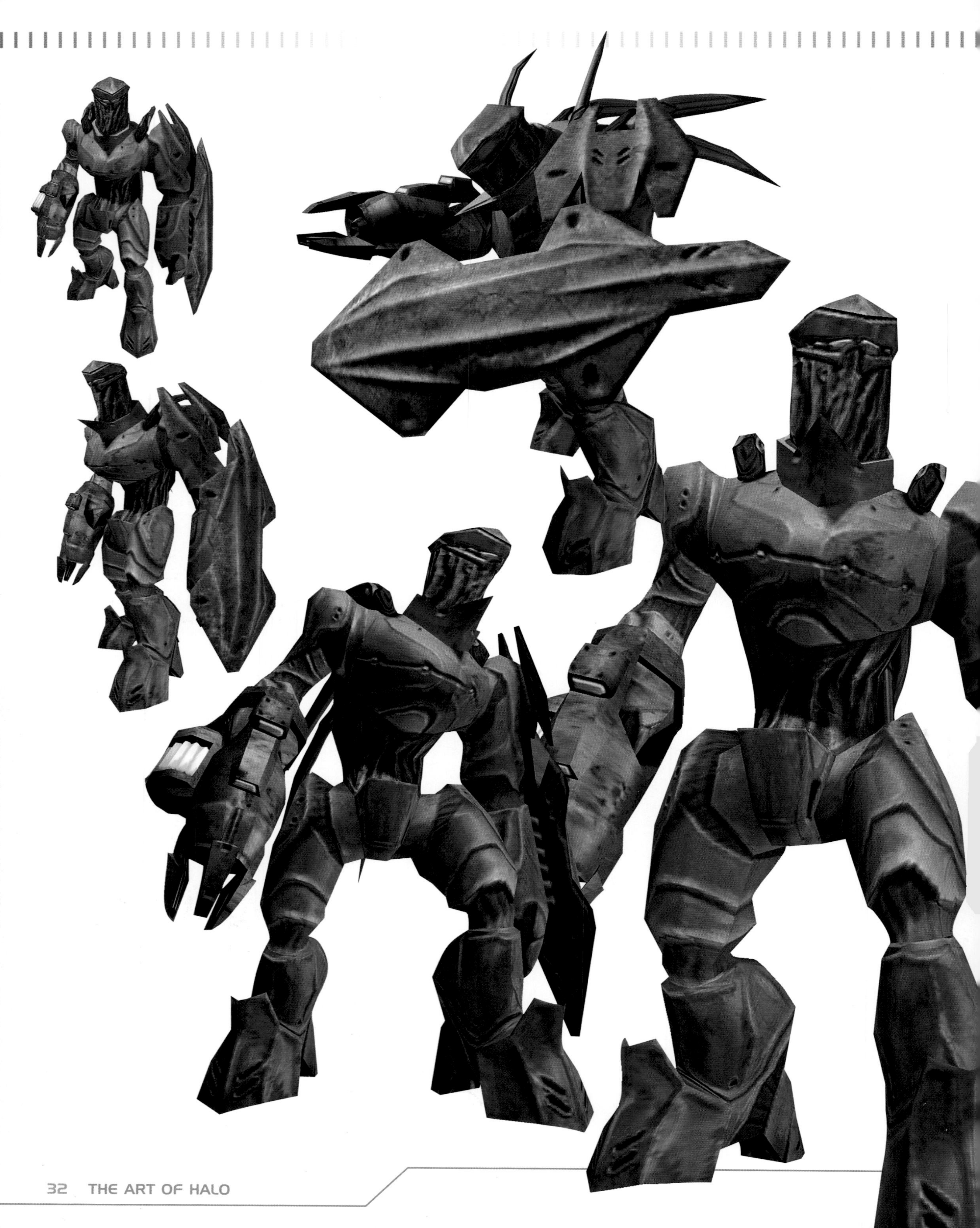

HUNTERS

Titanic armored juggernauts, Hunters are among the most powerful combatants in the Covenant. Hunters operate almost exclusively in pairs, and have a reputation for being nearly invulnerable.

The massive Hunters are actually something of a mystery to human scientists. Consisting of a kind of colony of spineless worms, they assemble into ferocious and massive form.

The Hunter's relative weakness in its consistent "parts" means that it requires generous armor and shielding to maintain the Hunter form.

Hunters are not only found in pairs, they fight in pairs, often performing a kind of pincer movement on unsuspecting foes.

The original concept looked "softer" and slightly less humanoid/bipedal in aspect.

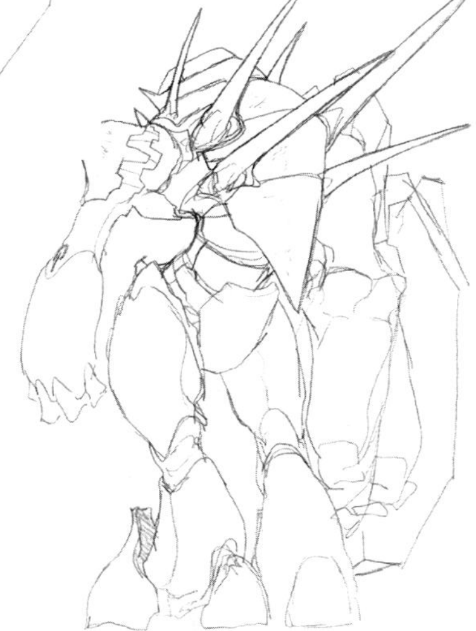

▲ **Concept sketches of the Covenant Hunter. Art by Shi Kai Wang.**

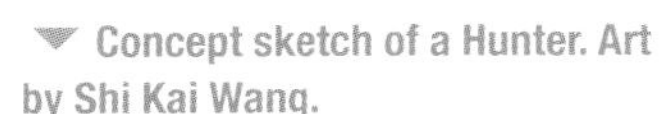

▼ **Concept sketch of a Hunter. Art by Shi Kai Wang.**

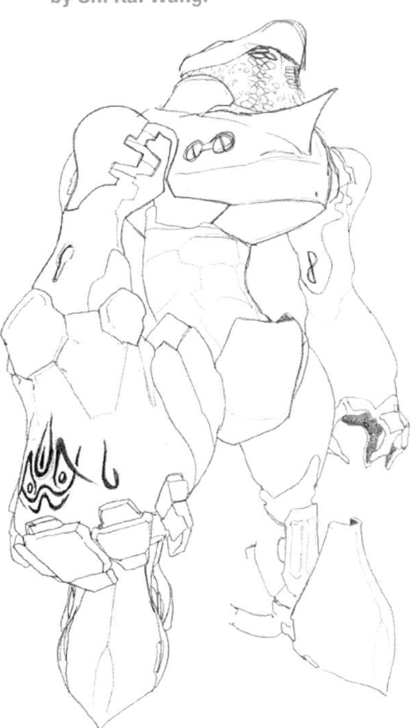

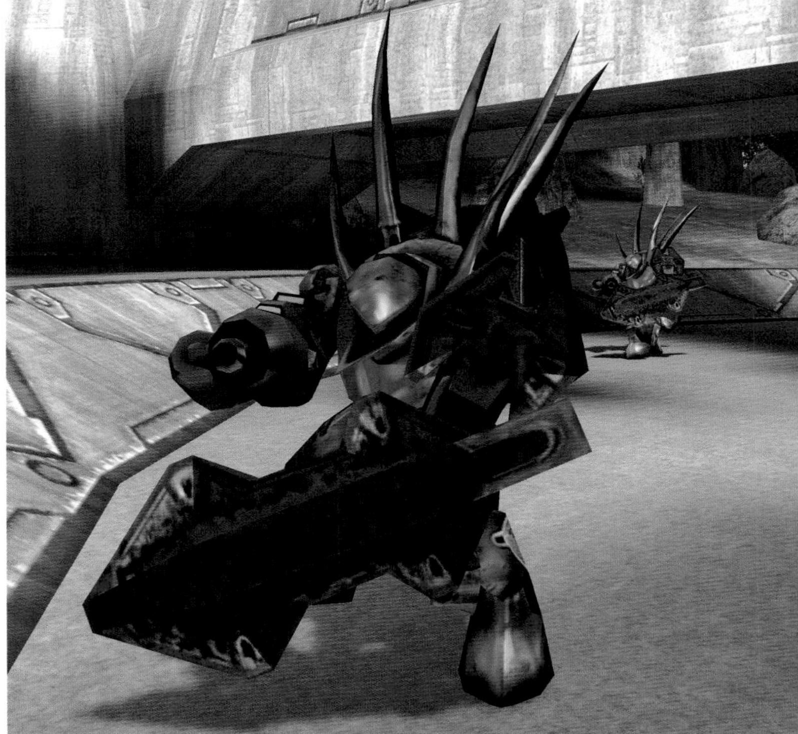

▲ **Screen shot from *Halo*.**

HUNTER STUDY

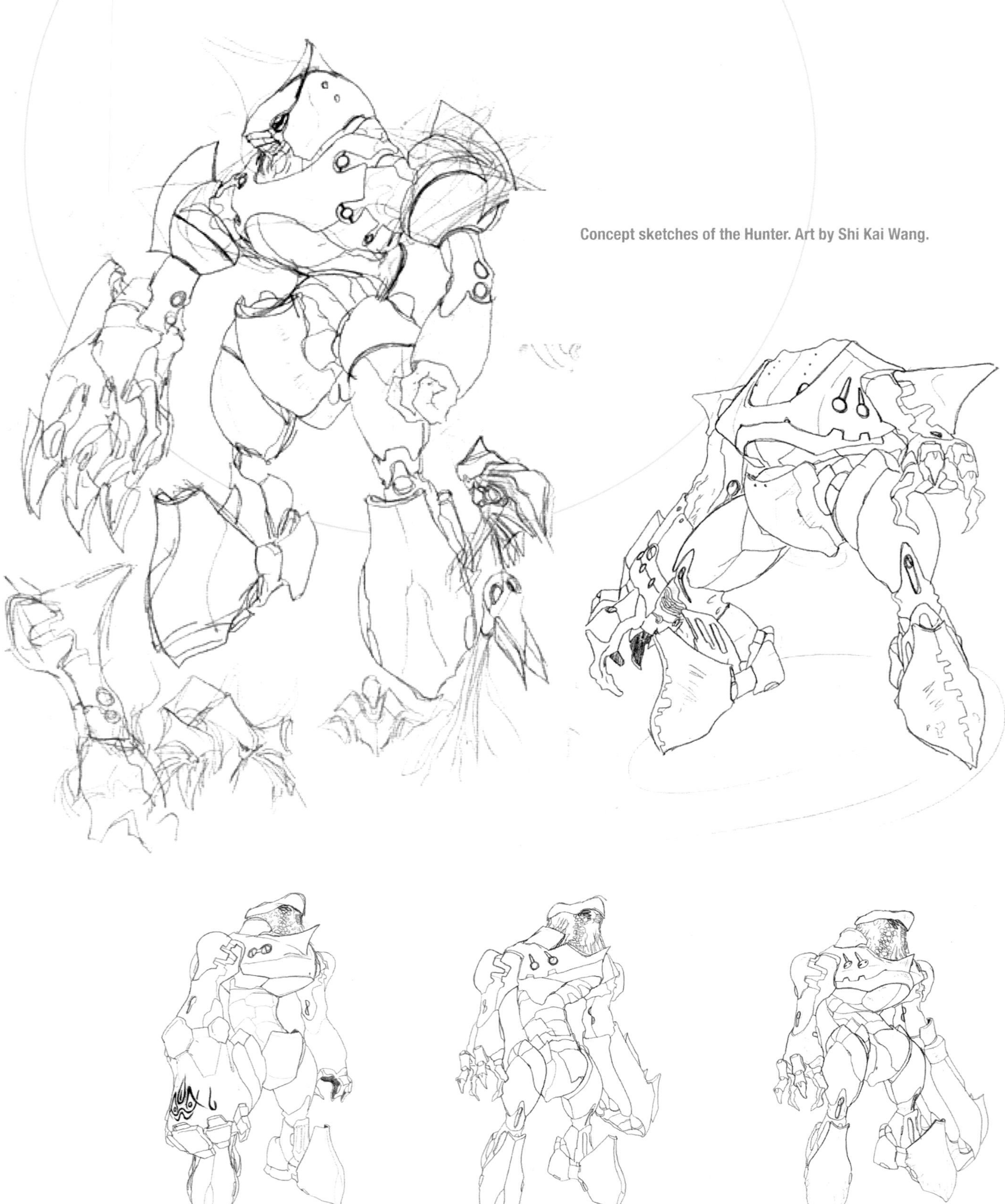

Concept sketches of the Hunter. Art by Shi Kai Wang.

▼ Several designs were considered for the Hunter's massive arm-mounted weaponry, as seen in these early sketches by Shi Kai Wang.

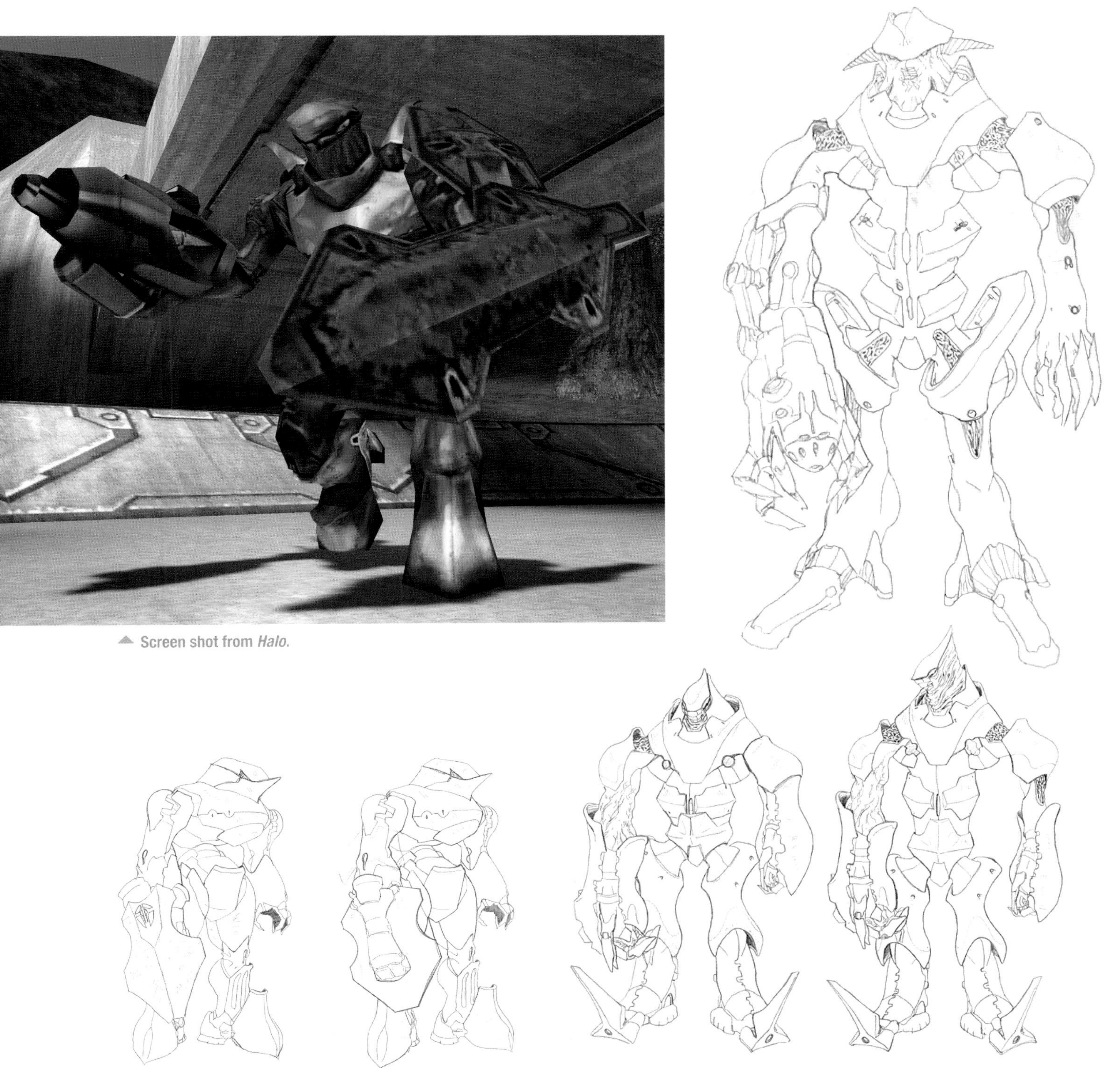

▲ Screen shot from *Halo.*

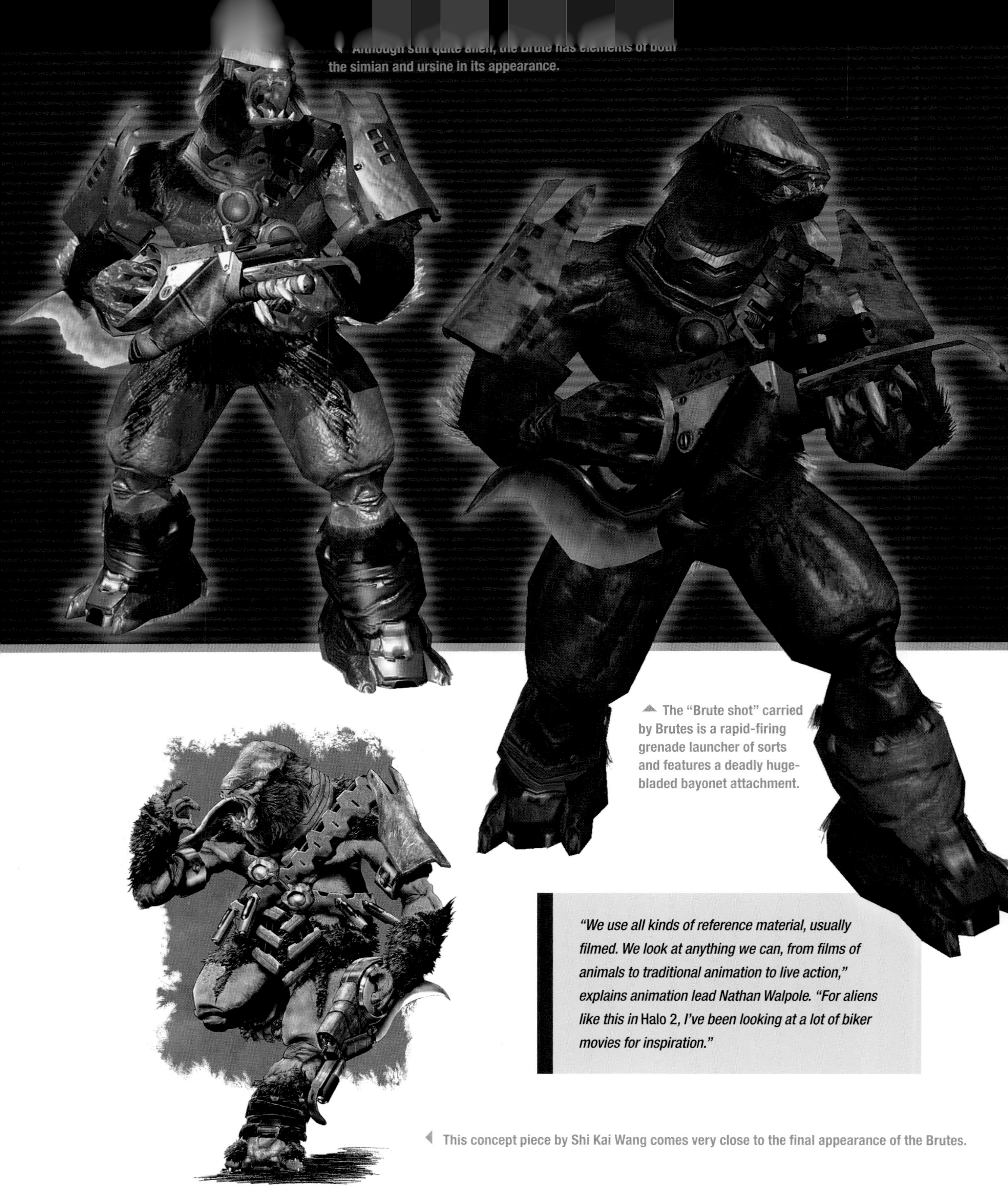

Although still quite alien, the Brute has elements of both the simian and ursine in its appearance.

The "Brute shot" carried by Brutes is a rapid-firing grenade launcher of sorts and features a deadly huge-bladed bayonet attachment.

"We use all kinds of reference material, usually filmed. We look at anything we can, from films of animals to traditional animation to live action," explains animation lead Nathan Walpole. "For aliens like this in Halo 2, *I've been looking at a lot of biker movies for inspiration."*

This concept piece by Shi Kai Wang comes very close to the final appearance of the Brutes.

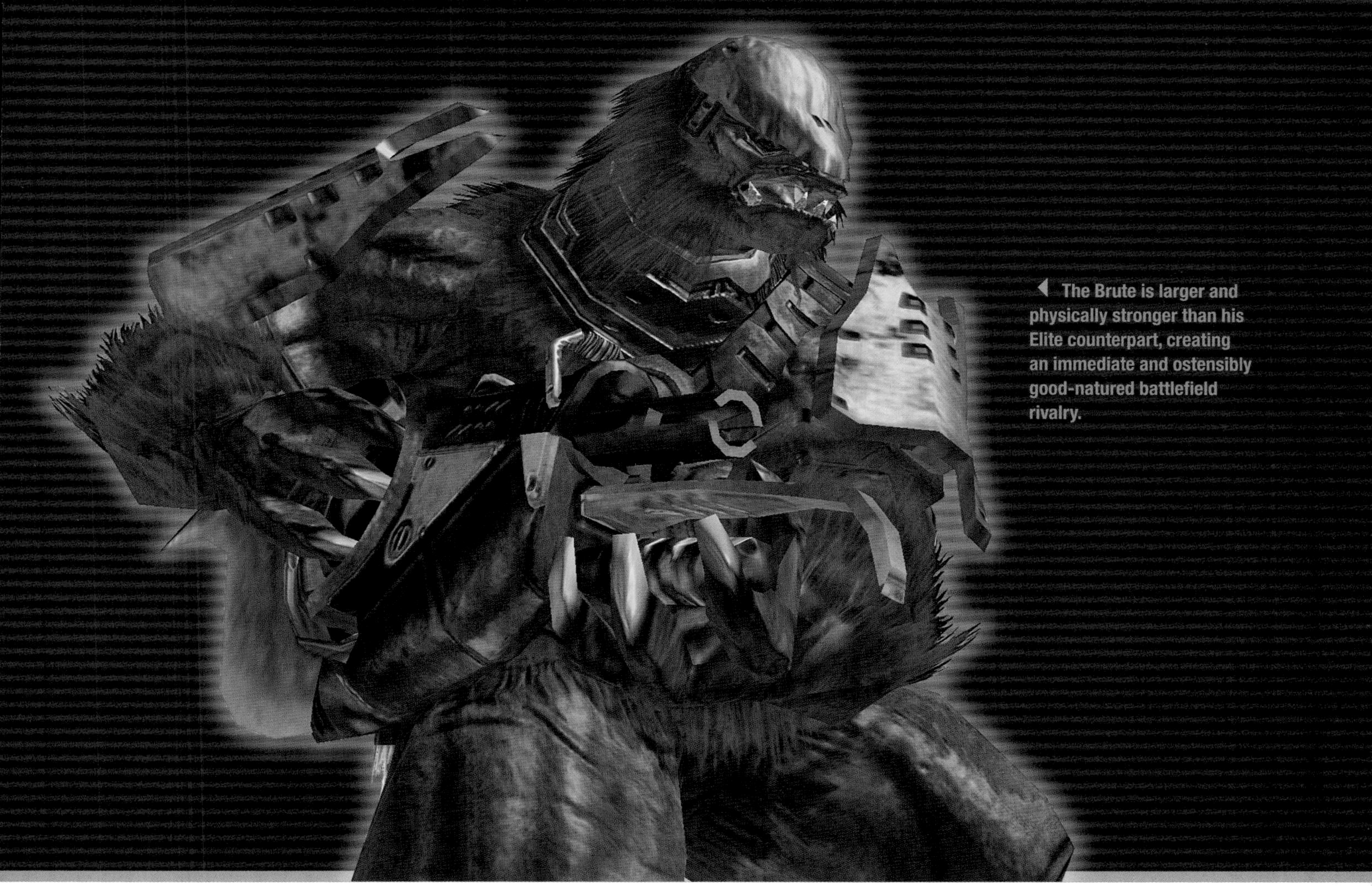

The Brute is larger and physically stronger than his Elite counterpart, creating an immediate and ostensibly good-natured battlefield rivalry.

BRUTES

Tough and relentless alien warriors, Brutes are new aliens featured in *Halo 2*. They are designed to look like particularly fearsome simian monsters.

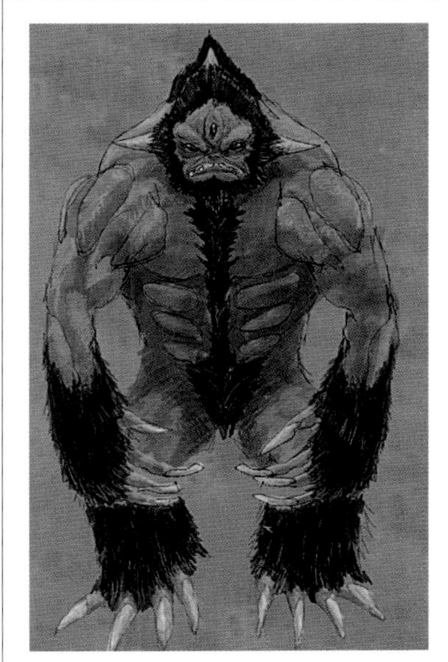

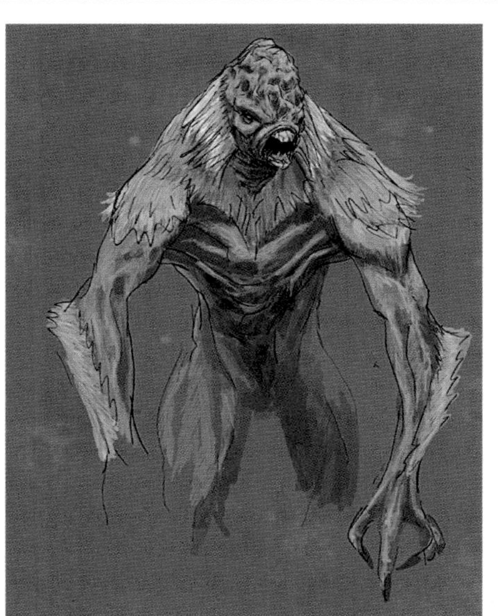

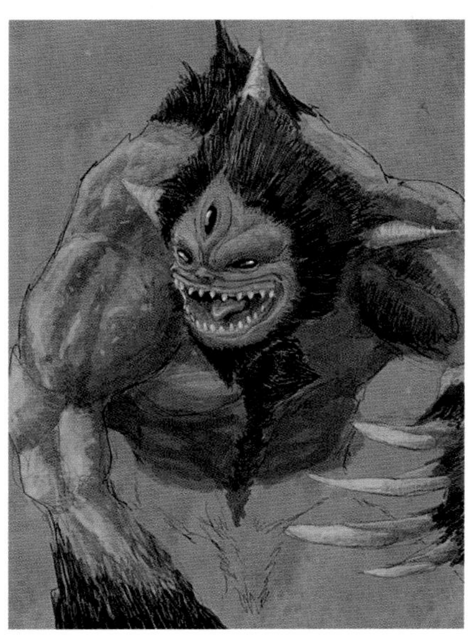

Concept art by Shi Kai Wang.

BRUTES STUDY

▶ The Covenant's breadth of species includes the vaguely simian, vaguely ursine Brutes—physically stronger than Elites and noticeably bulkier. Art by Eddie Smith.

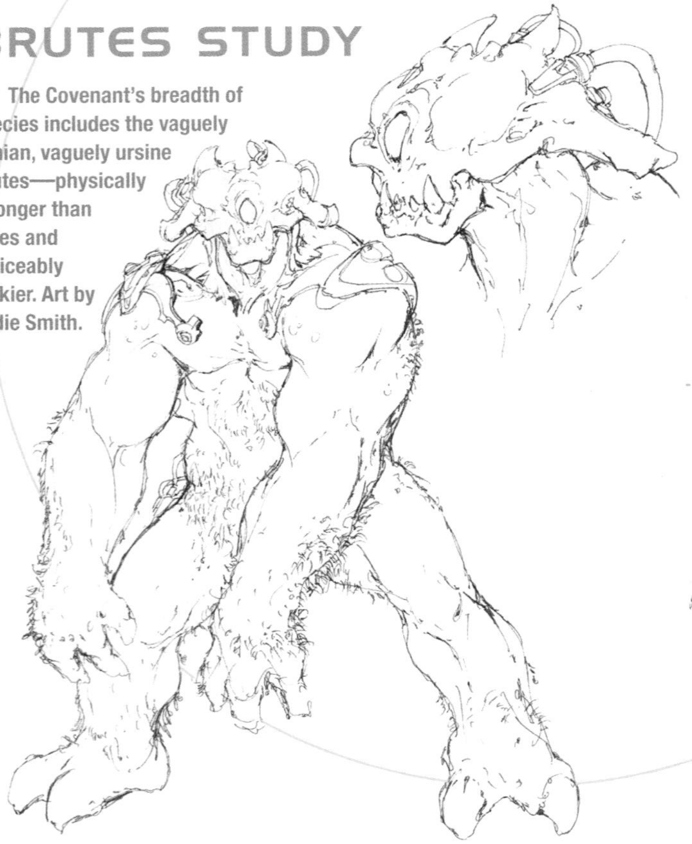

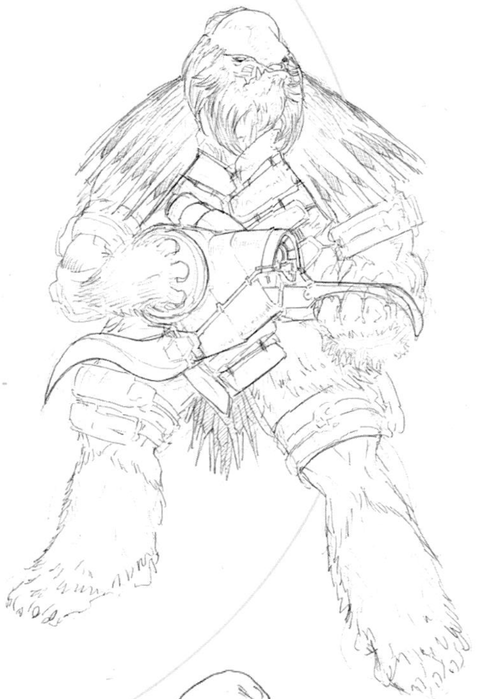

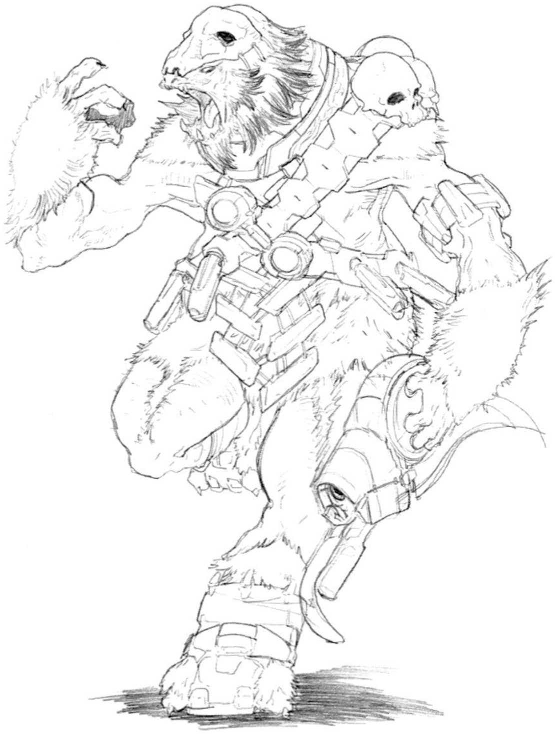

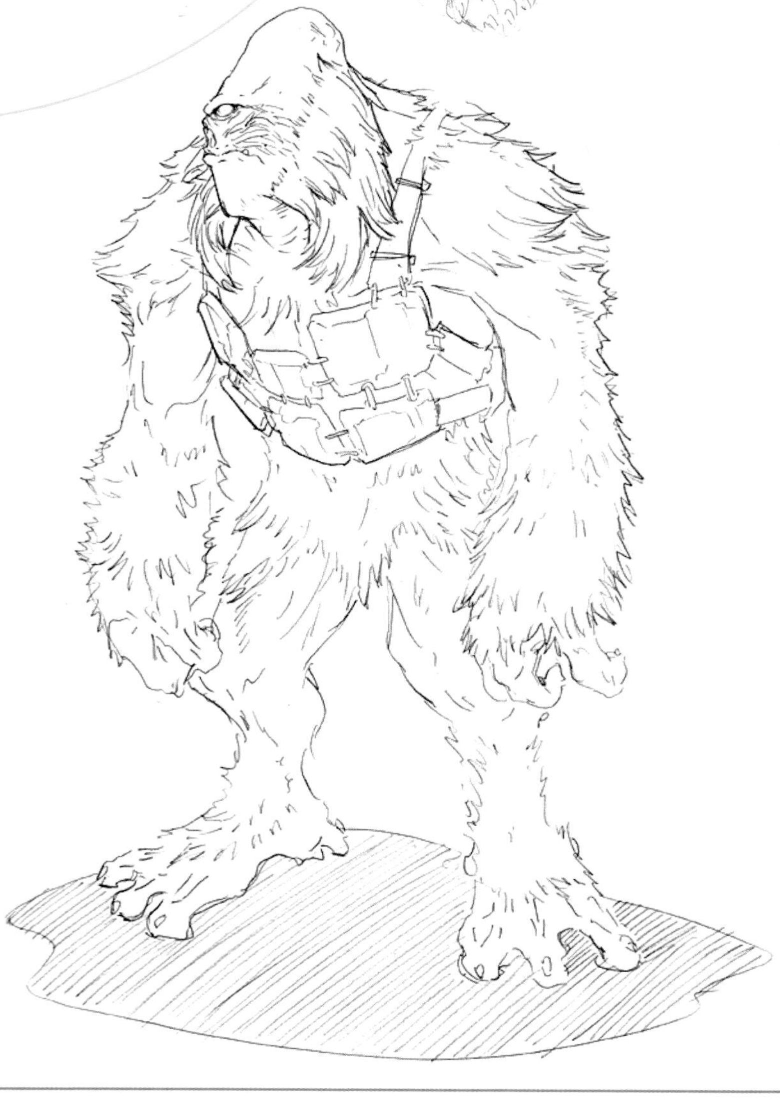

▲ Final Brute concept art by Shi Kai Wang. The final model was later simplified.

These screen shots of the Brute captain, Tartarus, show the small but distinctive changes to his armor and mane that help distinguish him from other Brutes. Early Brute concepts by Shi Kai Wang.

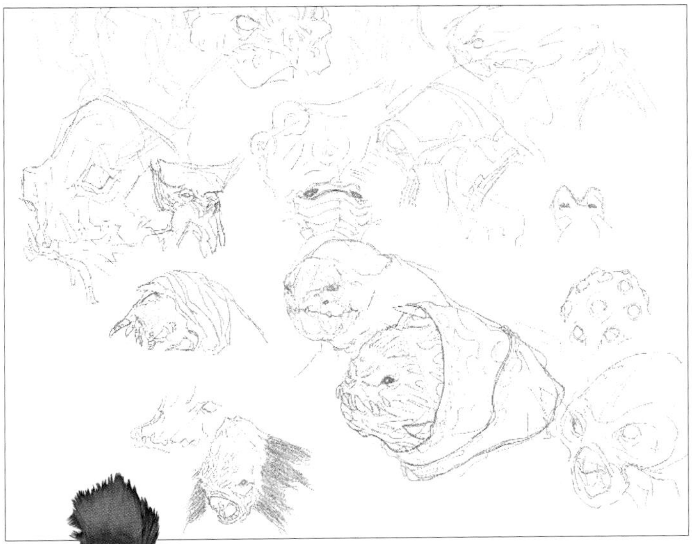

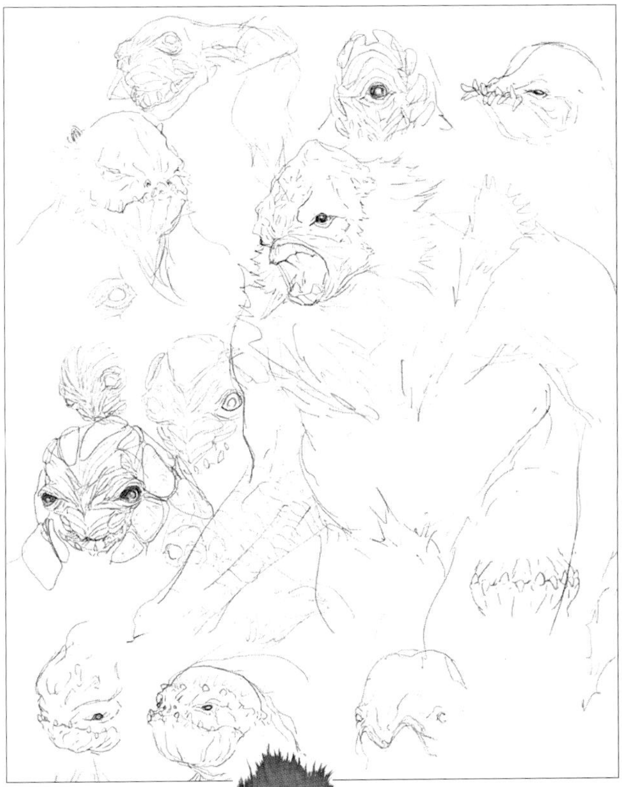

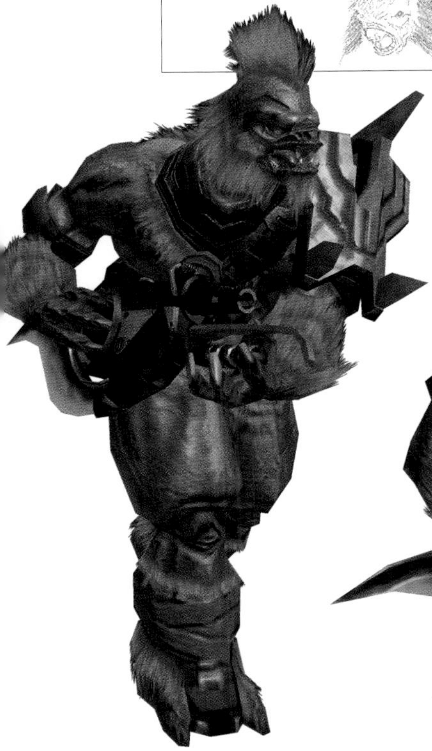

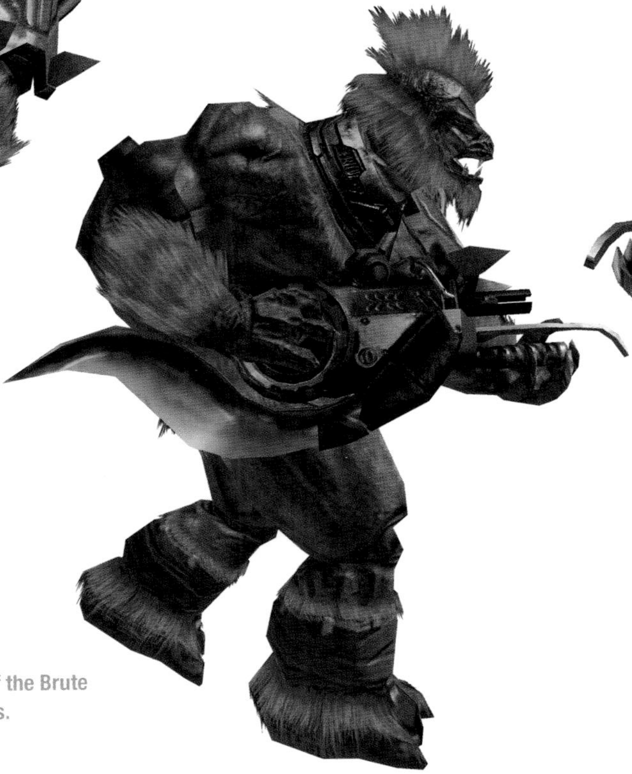

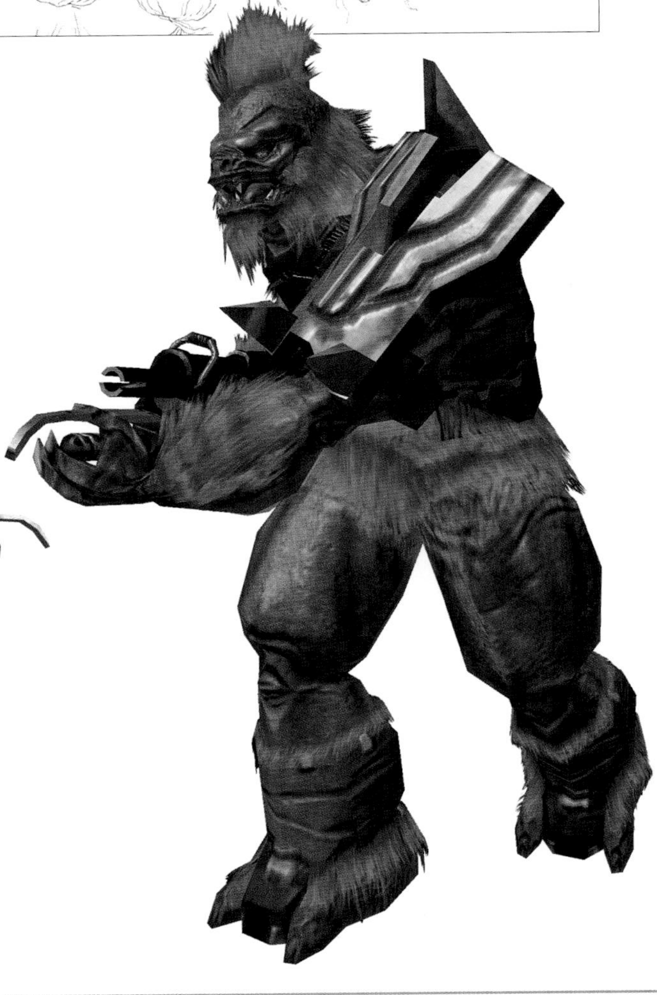

Screen capture of the Brute chieftain, Tartarus.

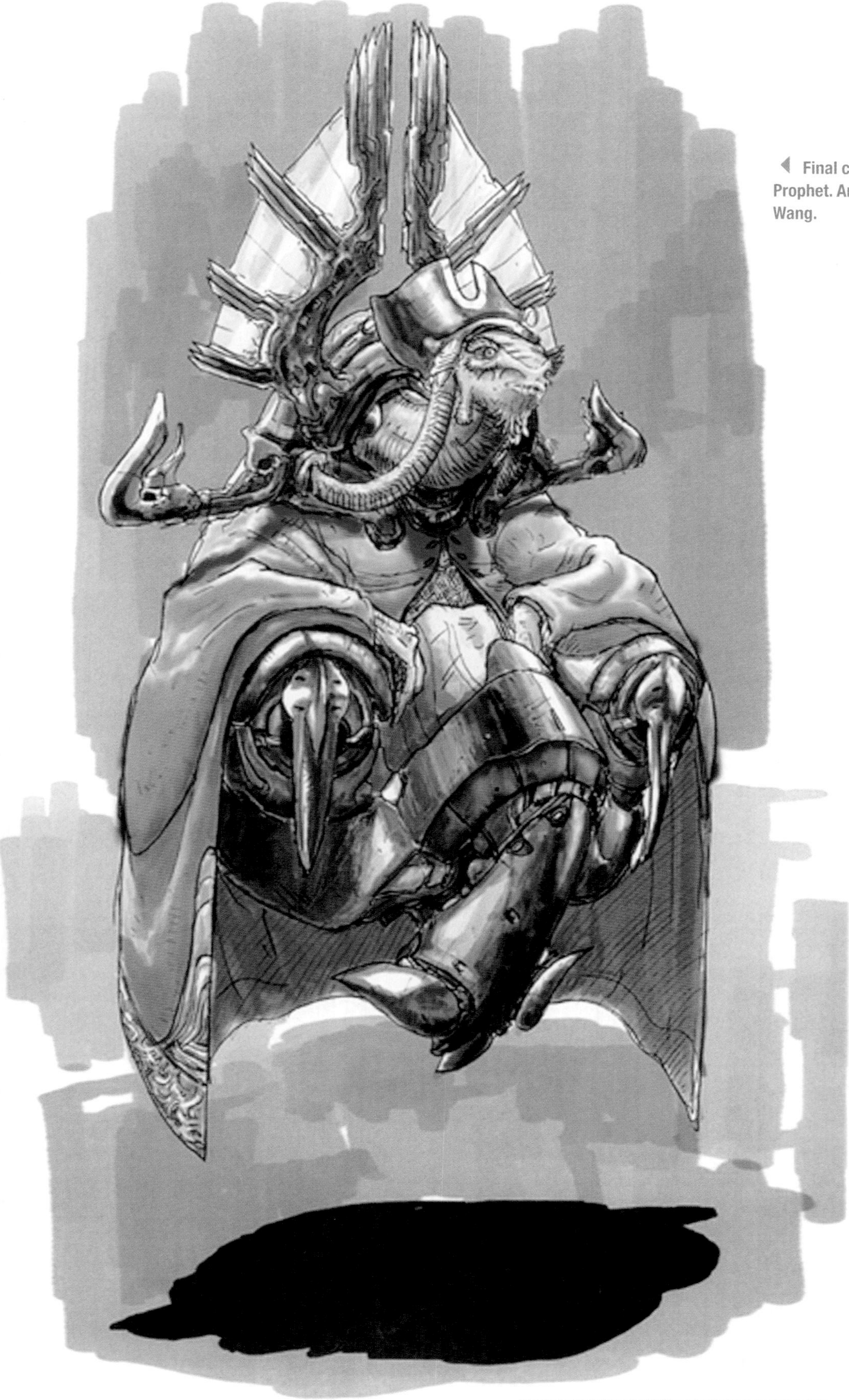

Final concept art of the Prophet. Artwork by Shi Kai Wang.

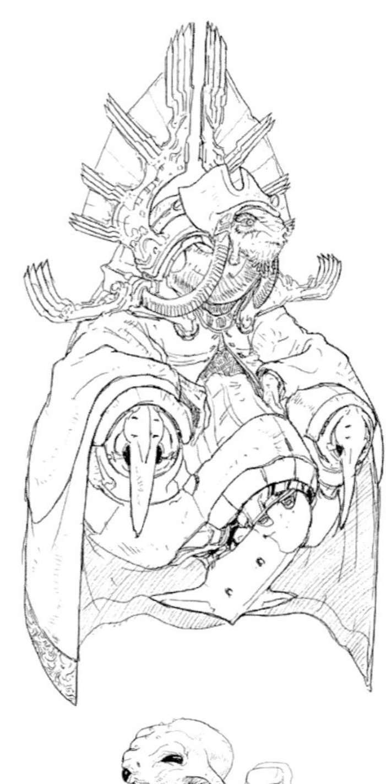

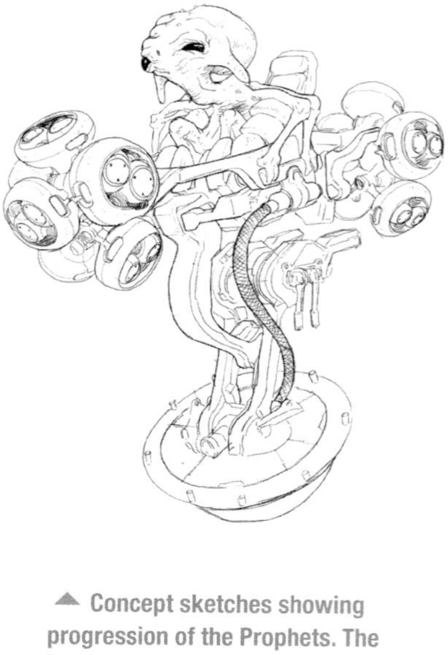

Concept sketches showing progression of the Prophets. The Prophets were always designed to look feeble, yet sinister. These early sketches of the Prophets had a far more integrated feel, with the Gravity Throne more fused with the Prophet's organic structures.

PROPHETS

The Prophets rule the religious arm of the Covenant, and have authority over the military ranks. Mysterious and enigmatic, almost nothing is known about the Prophets.

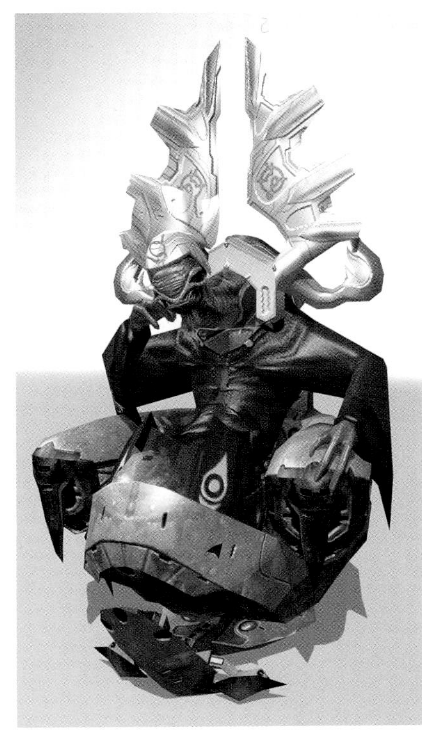

▲ A 3D render of a Covenant Prophet, complete with Gravity Throne.

▼ Concept art of the Prophet. Artwork by Shi Kai Wang.

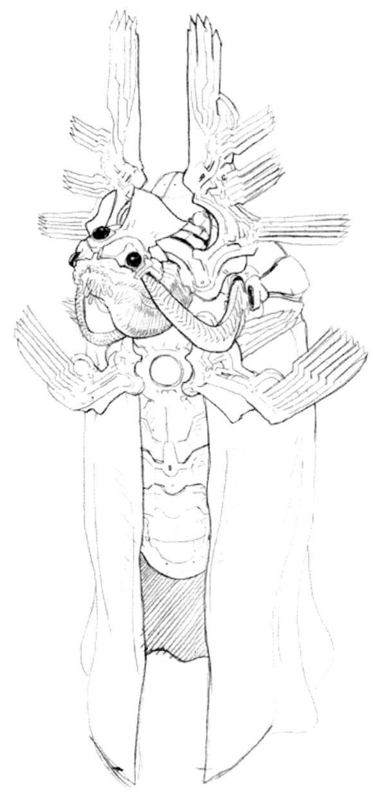

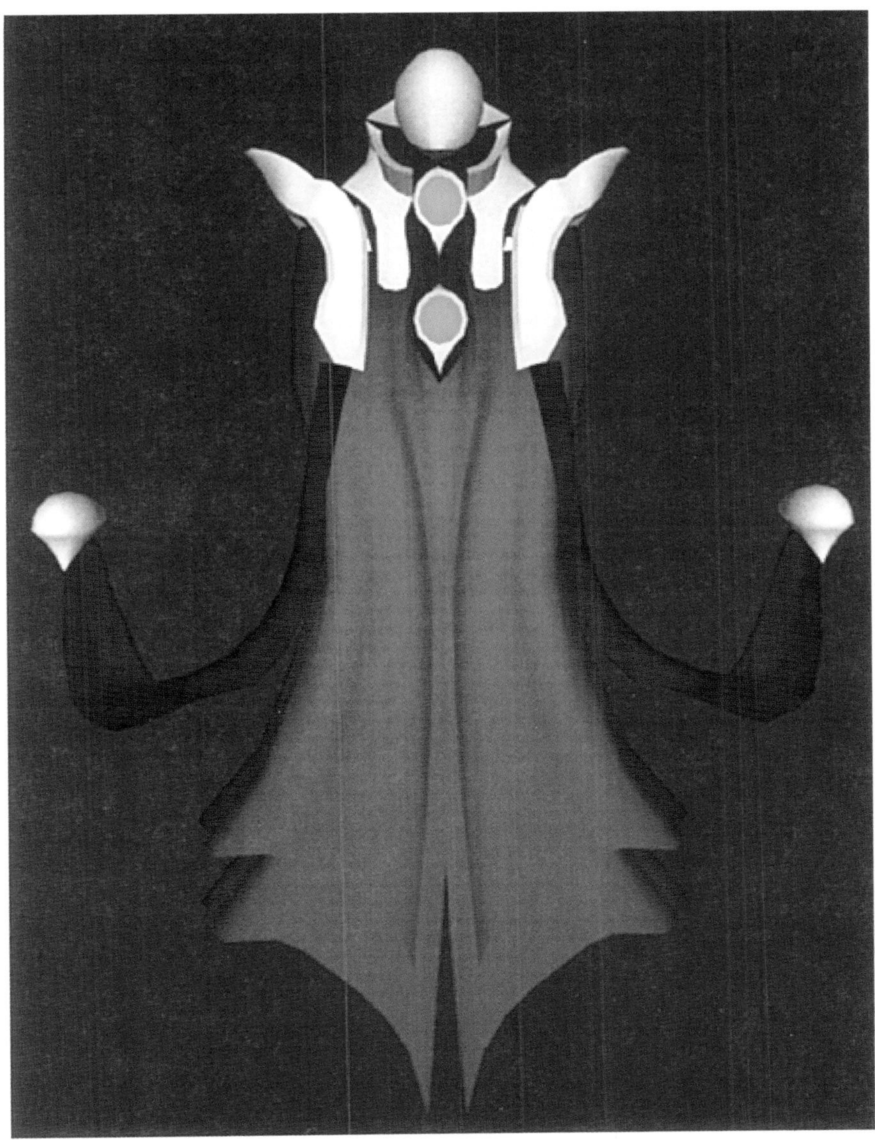

▲ This is the first concept for a Prophet, inspired, in fact, by an earlier Bungie game. It evolved into the character pictured to the right. Art by Shi Kai Wang.

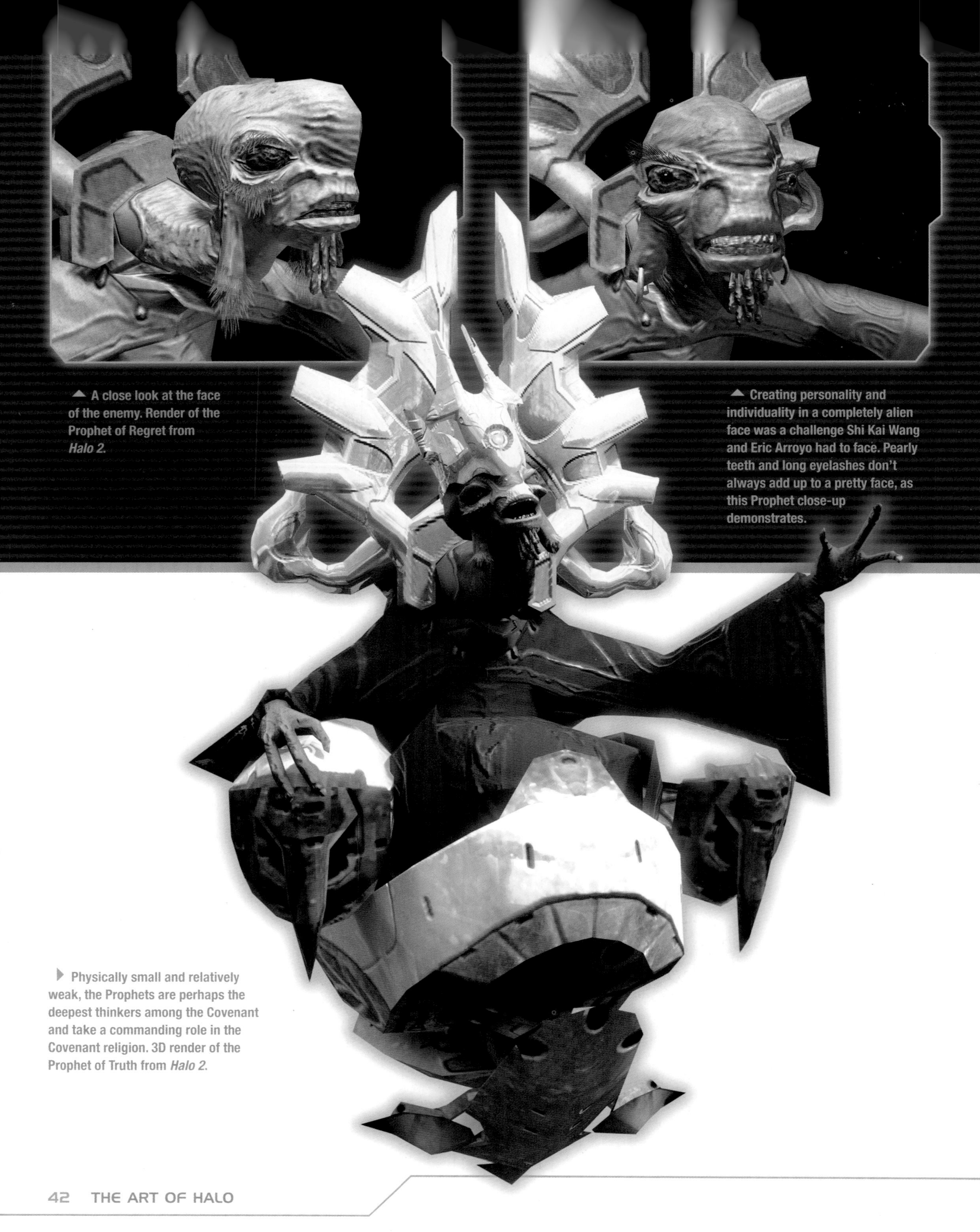

▲ A close look at the face of the enemy. Render of the Prophet of Regret from *Halo 2*.

▲ Creating personality and individuality in a completely alien face was a challenge Shi Kai Wang and Eric Arroyo had to face. Pearly teeth and long eyelashes don't always add up to a pretty face, as this Prophet close-up demonstrates.

▶ Physically small and relatively weak, the Prophets are perhaps the deepest thinkers among the Covenant and take a commanding role in the Covenant religion. 3D render of the Prophet of Truth from *Halo 2*.

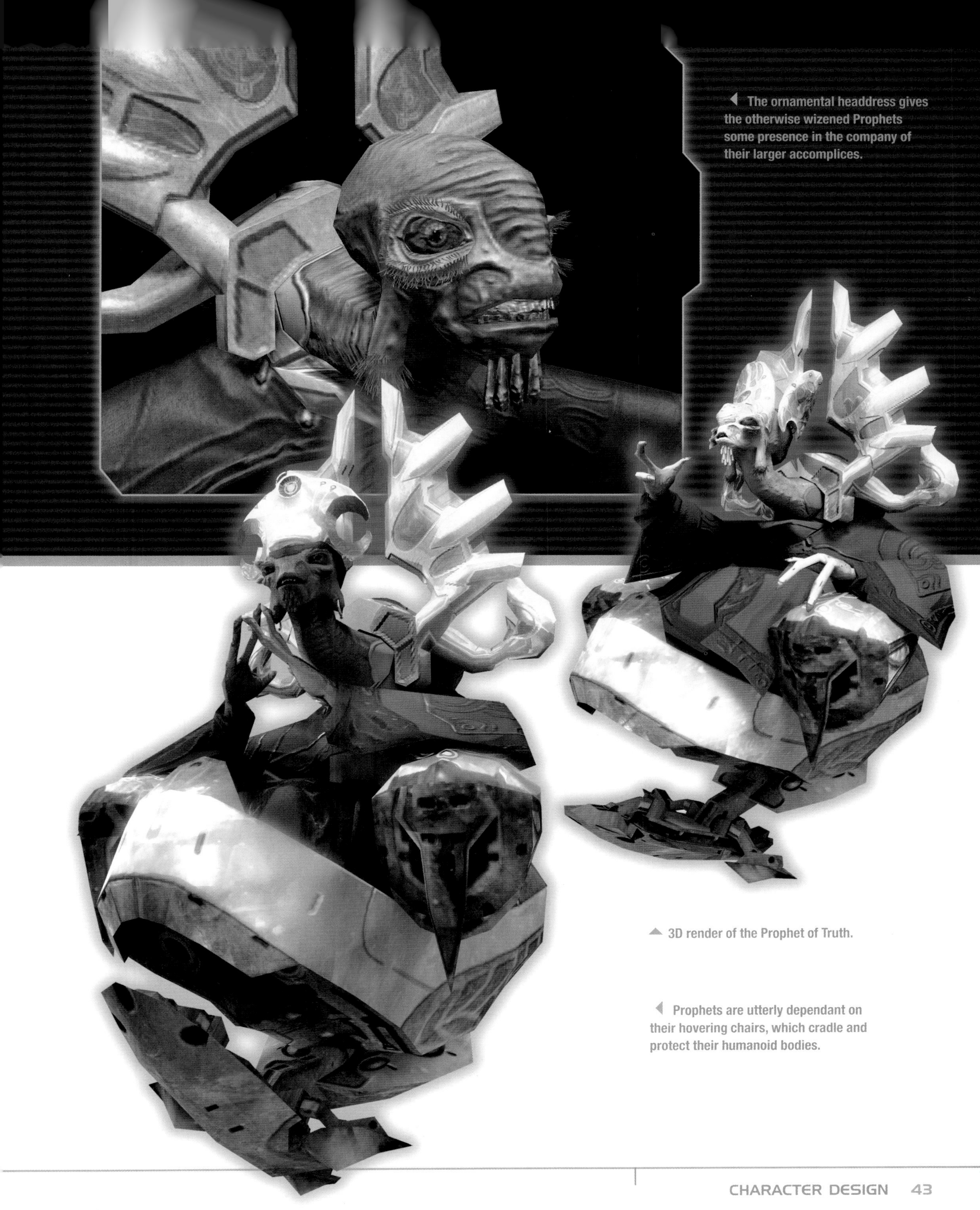

◀ The ornamental headdress gives the otherwise wizened Prophets some presence in the company of their larger accomplices.

▲ 3D render of the Prophet of Truth.

◀ Prophets are utterly dependant on their hovering chairs, which cradle and protect their humanoid bodies.

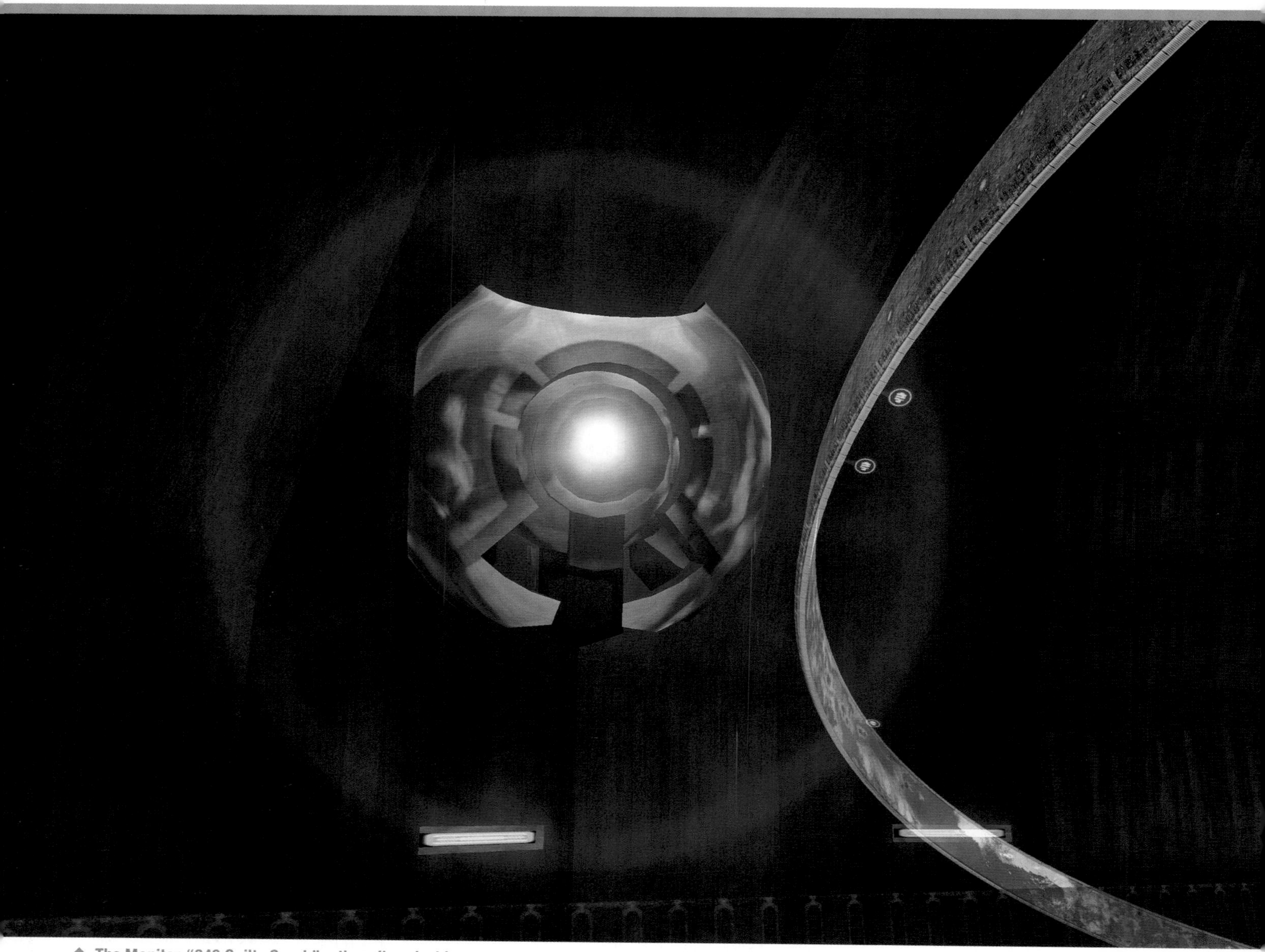

▲ The Monitor, "343 Guilty Spark"—the wily, mischievous caretaker of Halo. Screen capture from *Halo*.

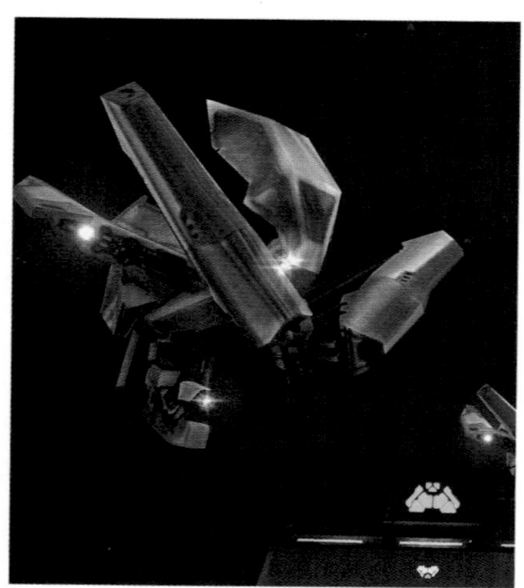

343 GUILTY SPARK AND OTHER HALO INHABITANTS

343 Guilty Spark is the caretaker AI that monitors Halo. A creation of the Forerunner—Halo's mysterious builders—he is erratic and possibly insane.

He controls a number of defensive mechanisms—the Sentinels. These flying, crablike constructs employ destructive energy beams as a form of "pest control."

◀ The final model of the Sentinel was loosely based on the concept art. Chris Hughes created a crablike machine with many animating parts that gave it life and character. Screen shot from *Halo.*

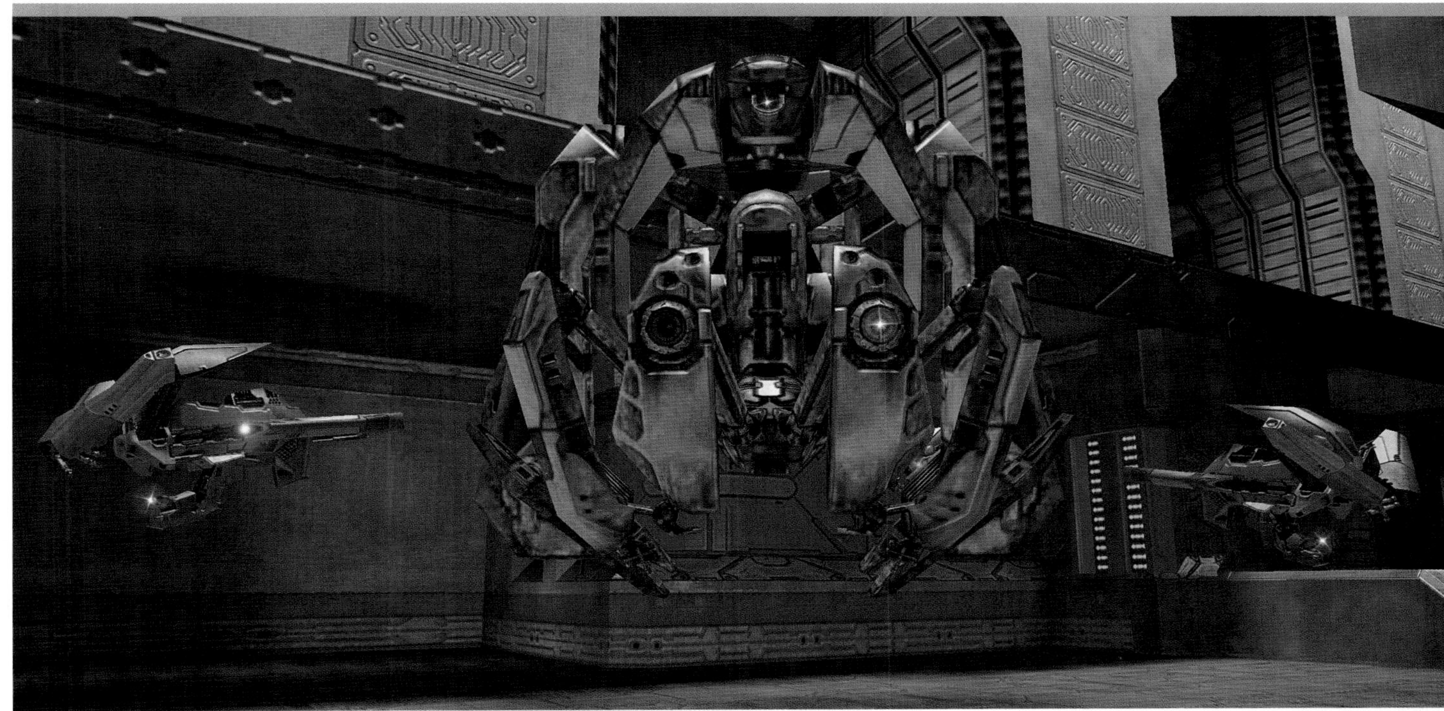

A larger, more advanced Sentinel Enforcer. Screen capture from *Halo 2*.

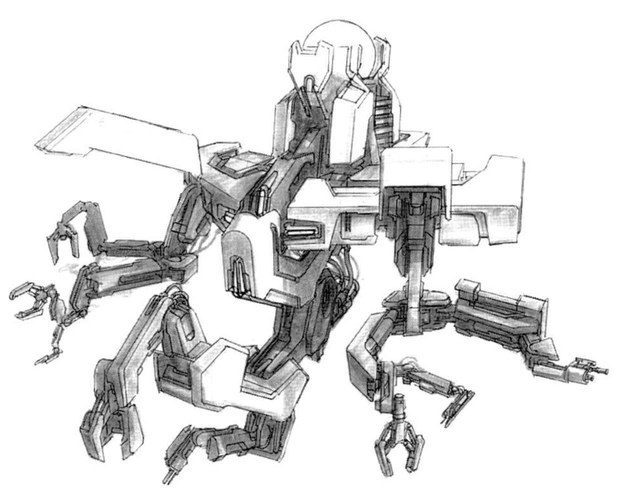

Orginal Sentinel Enforcer. Concept art by Eddie Smith.

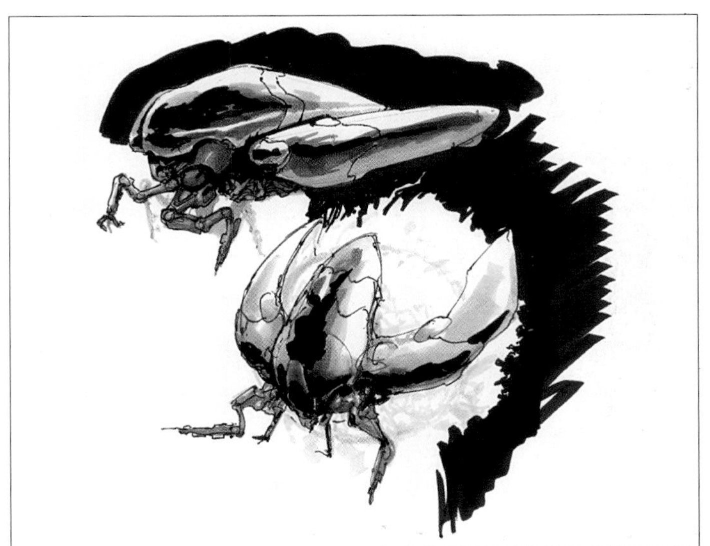

Concept art of a Sentinel. Illustration by Shi Kai Wang.

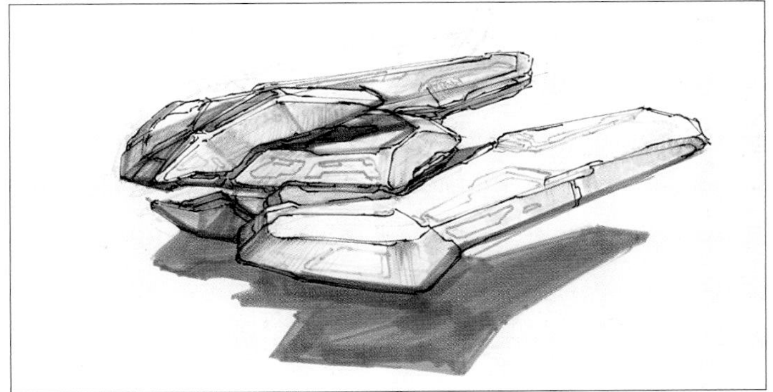

Concept of a Sentinel, by Eddie Smith.

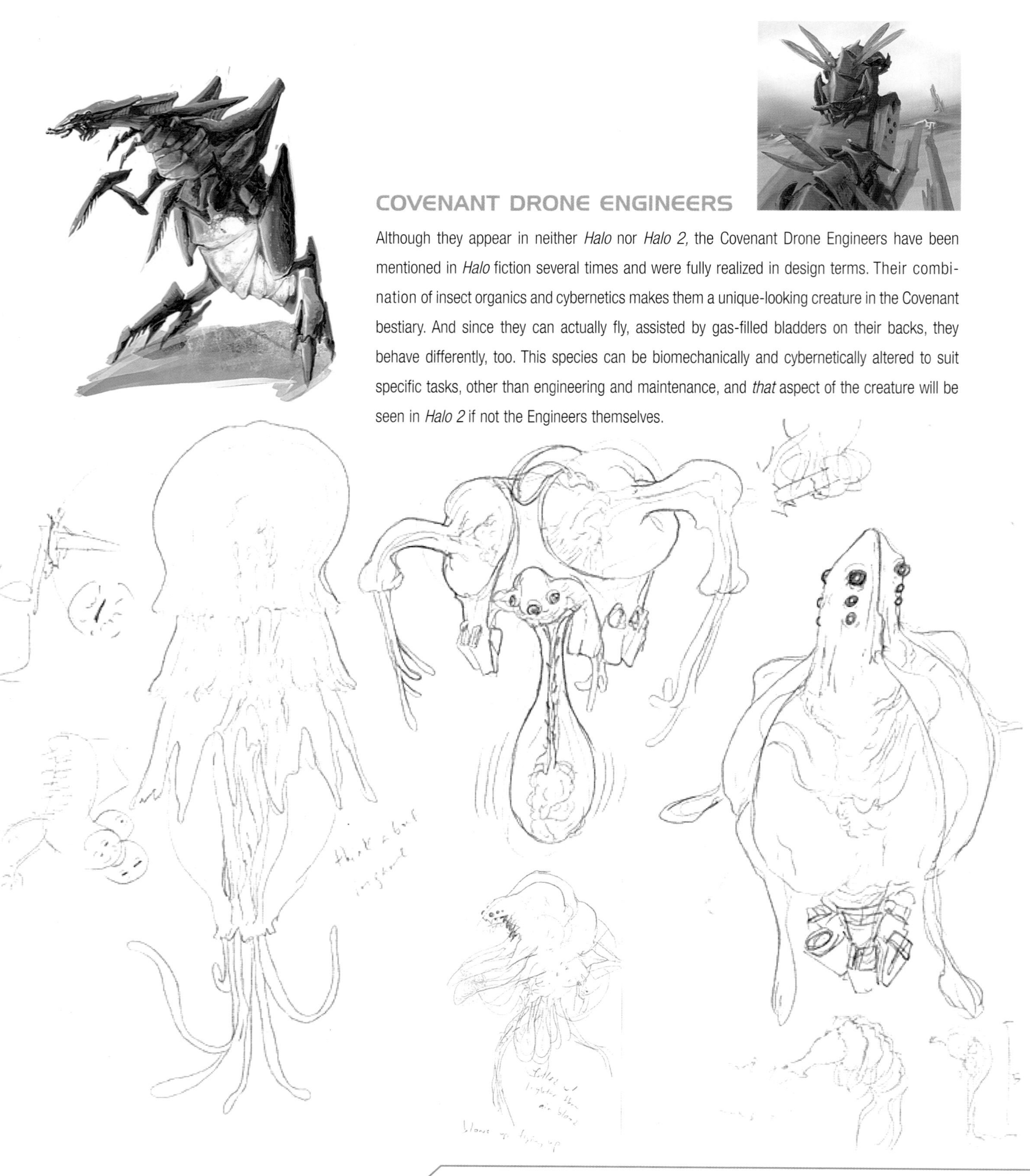

COVENANT DRONE ENGINEERS

Although they appear in neither *Halo* nor *Halo 2,* the Covenant Drone Engineers have been mentioned in *Halo* fiction several times and were fully realized in design terms. Their combination of insect organics and cybernetics makes them a unique-looking creature in the Covenant bestiary. And since they can actually fly, assisted by gas-filled bladders on their backs, they behave differently, too. This species can be biomechanically and cybernetically altered to suit specific tasks, other than engineering and maintenance, and *that* aspect of the creature will be seen in *Halo 2* if not the Engineers themselves.

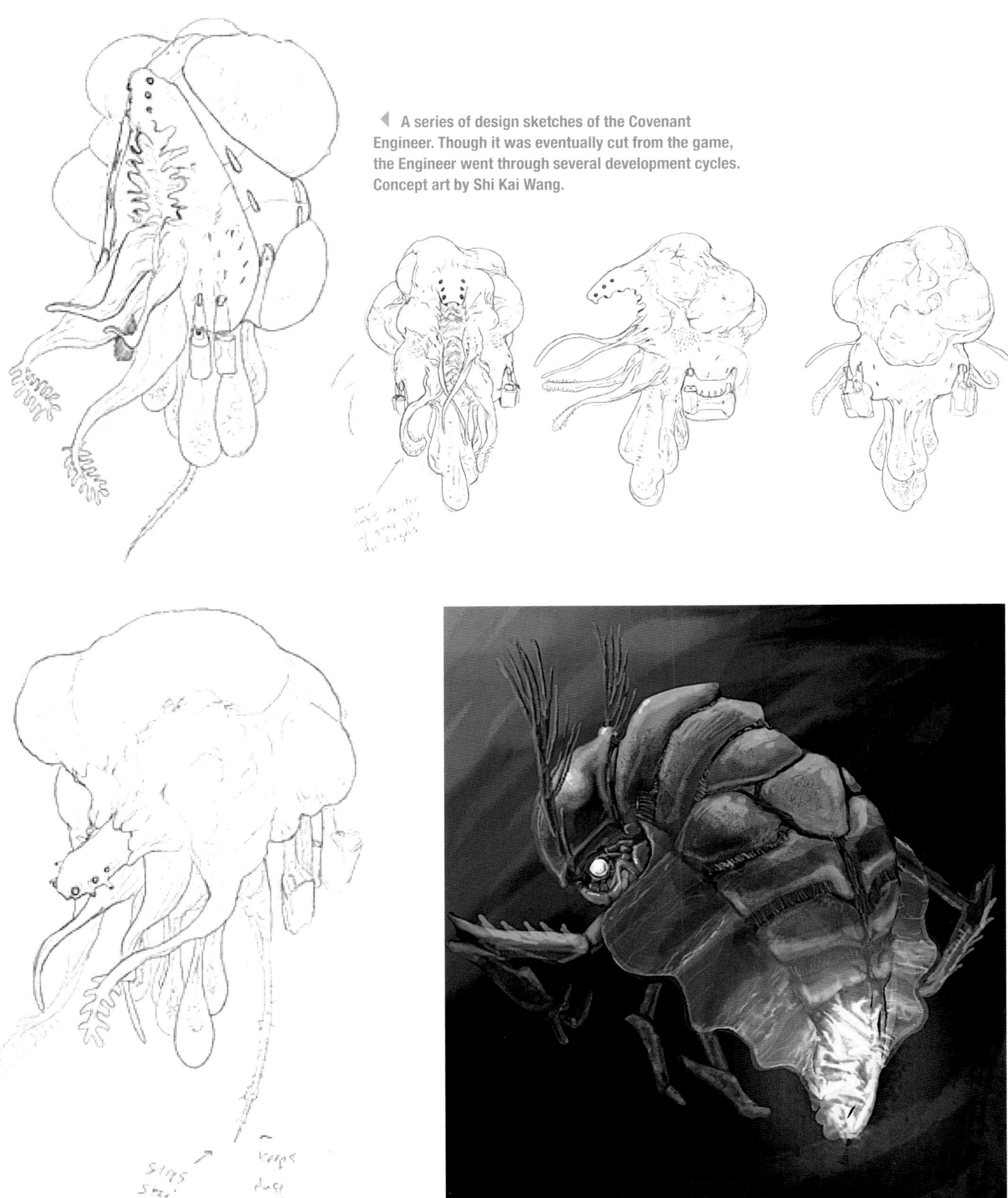

A series of design sketches of the Covenant Engineer. Though it was eventually cut from the game, the Engineer went through several development cycles. Concept art by Shi Kai Wang.

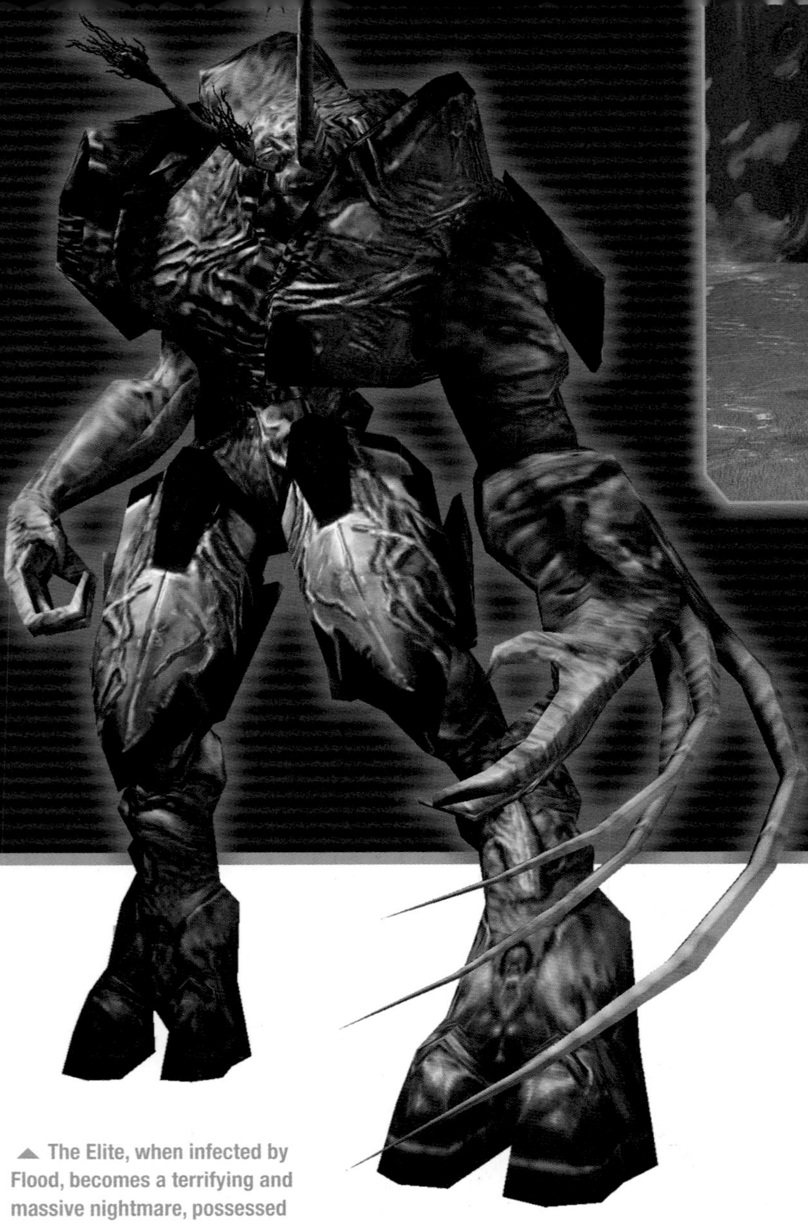

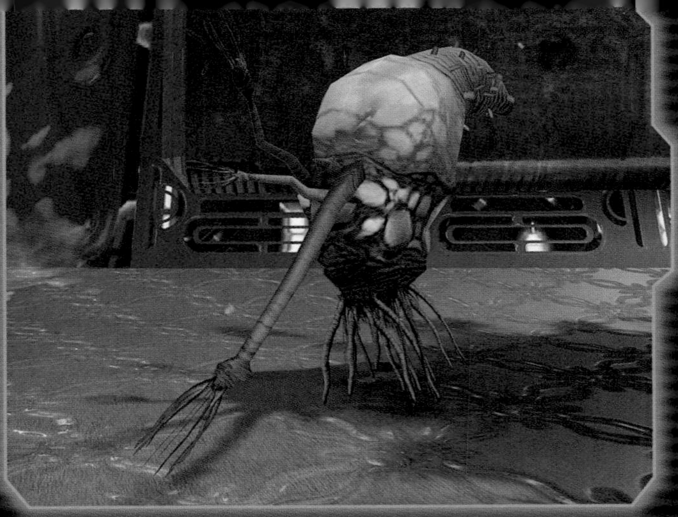

▲ A Flood Infection Form.

▲ The Elite, when infected by Flood, becomes a terrifying and massive nightmare, possessed of lethal speed.

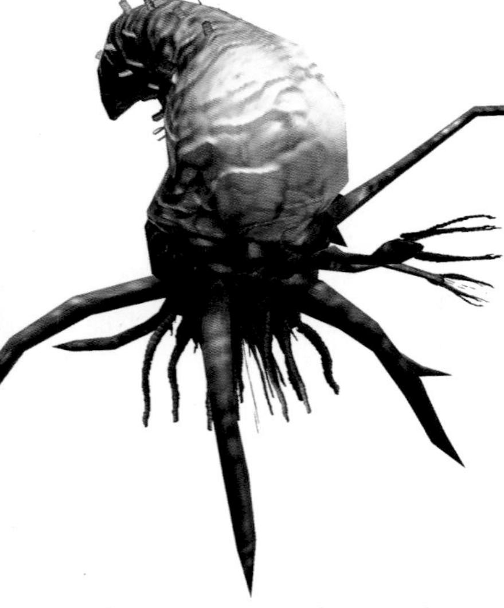

THE FLOOD

Perhaps Halo's deadliest secret is the terrifying parasitic life form known as The Flood. The Flood's origins are shrouded in mystery. Clearly intelligent, Flood can operate vehicles and fire weapons—and are utterly without mercy.

THE FLOOD'S LIFE CYCLE

The Flood appear in three common forms. The Infection Form, which swarms over a victim and consumes its host, replacing the host's biomass with the Flood's super-cell biomass.

The host is rapidly transformed into a Combat Form. The host's brain is chemically blocked from all but autonomic systems—keeping the body alive as it is devoured/converted.

Combat Forms that have been damaged to the point where they are no longer combat-effective are converted into Carrier Forms—mobile incubators for more Infection Forms.

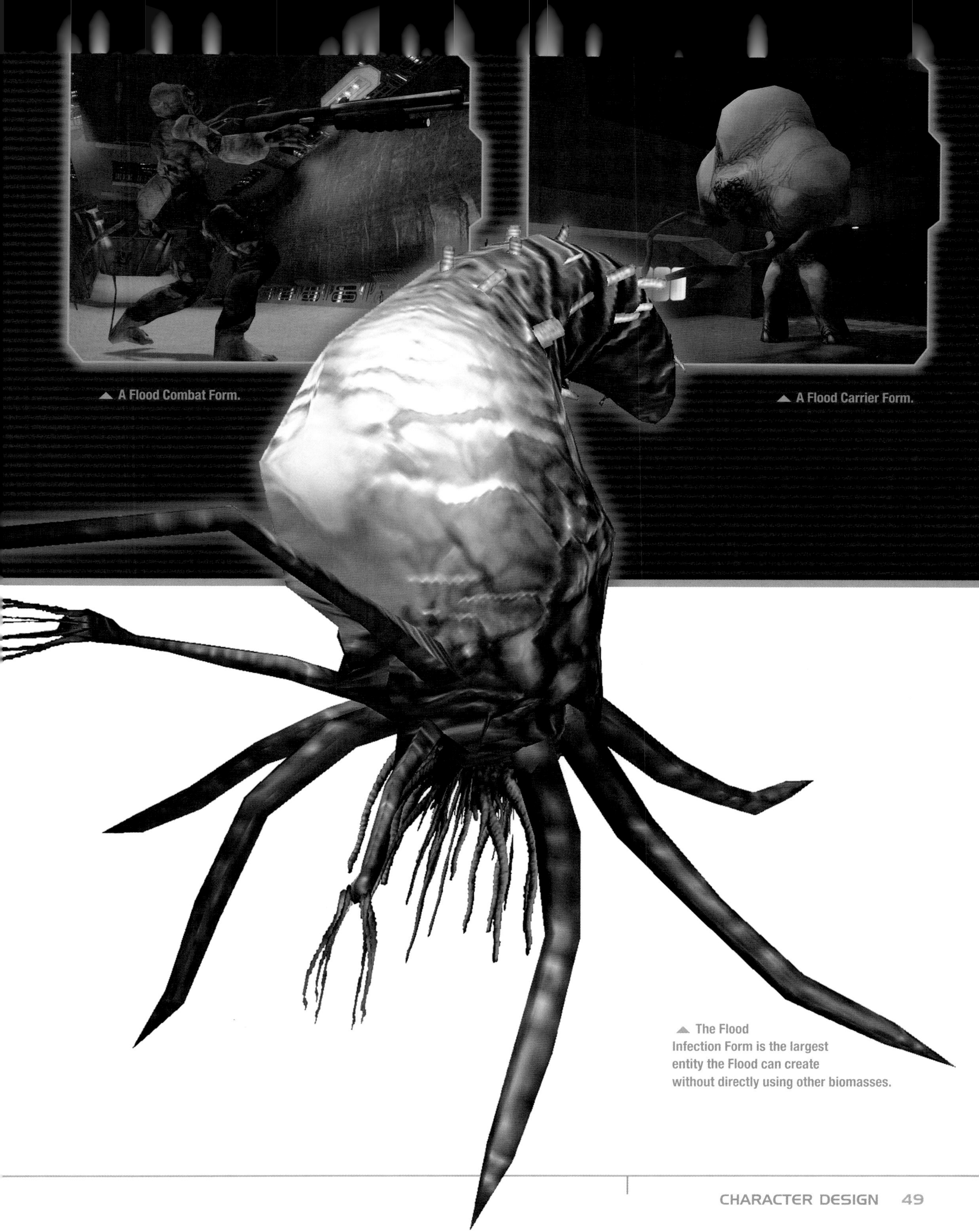

▲ A Flood Combat Form.

▲ A Flood Carrier Form.

▲ The Flood Infection Form is the largest entity the Flood can create without directly using other biomasses.

FLOOD HUMAN TRANSFORMATION

▼ The Flood Infection utilizes its host organism's nervous system and calcium store to create forms it needs to reproduce and fight. Art by Juan Ramirez.

▶ The Flood have full access to the host's skills and memories as long as the host's brain was still intact when it was taken.

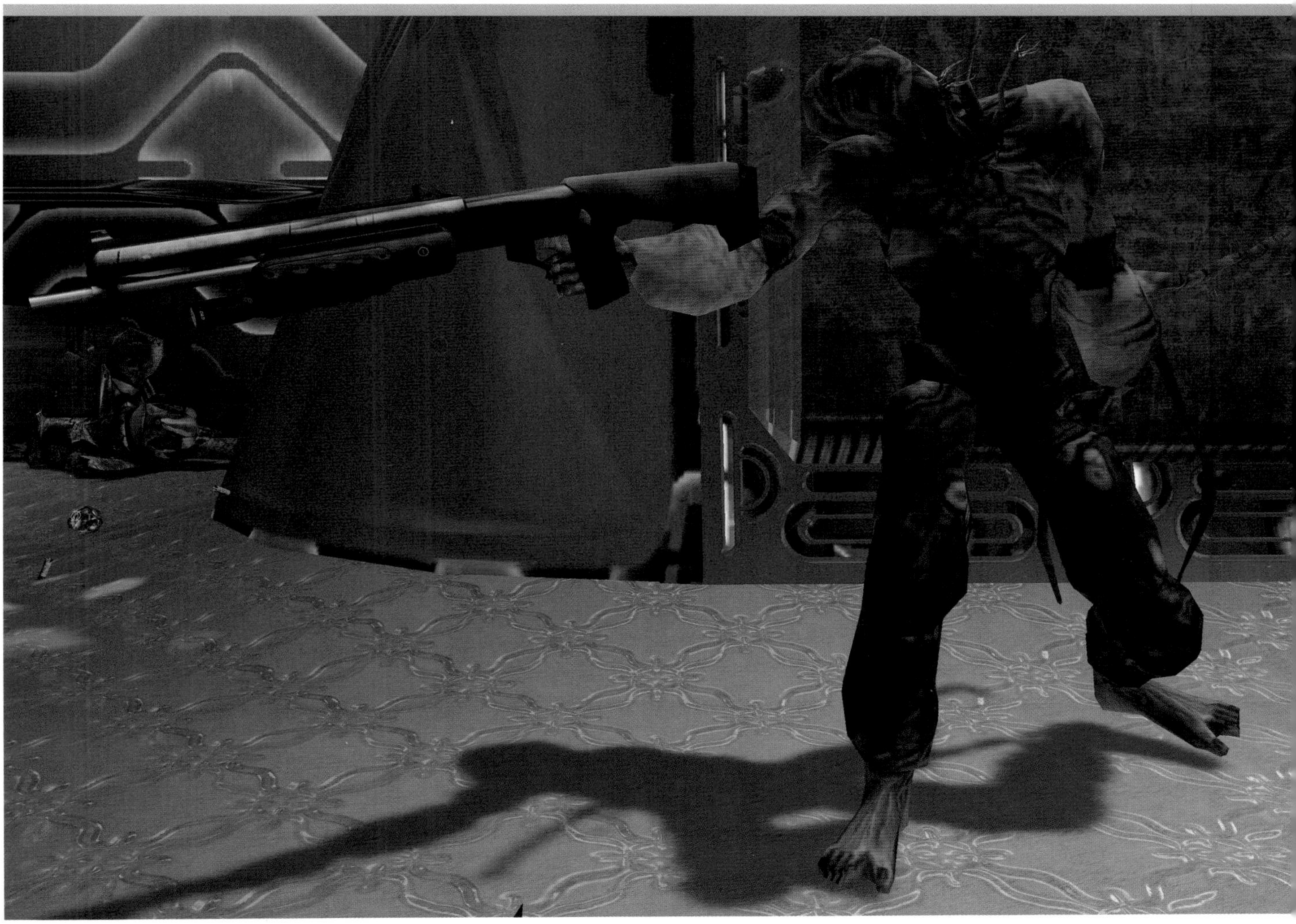

▲ Trying to build a grotesque alien form, while still retaining some of the original subject's humanity, was clearly part of the mission here.

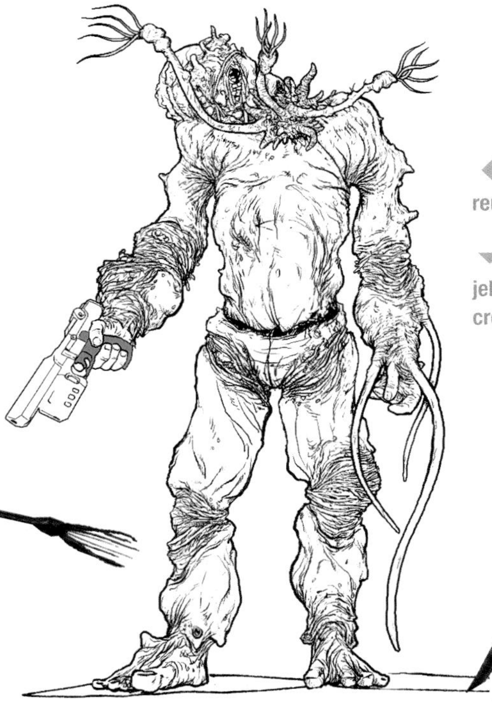

◀ Combat Forms are crippled, deformed, but largely intact reuses of their original hosts.

▼ The gassy, fragile Infection Forms incorporate elements of jellyfish, fungus, and disease to create a uniquely disgusting creature.

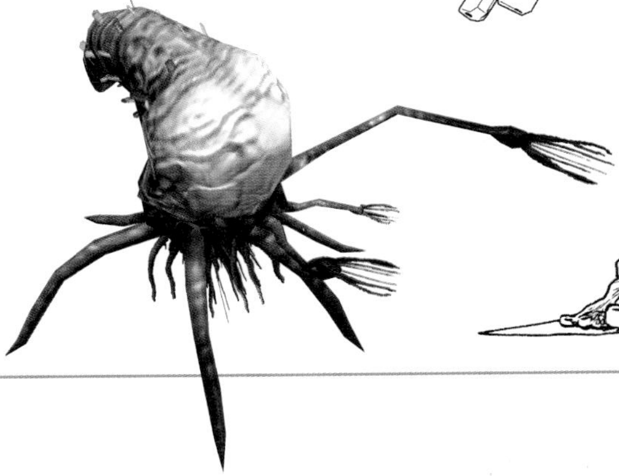

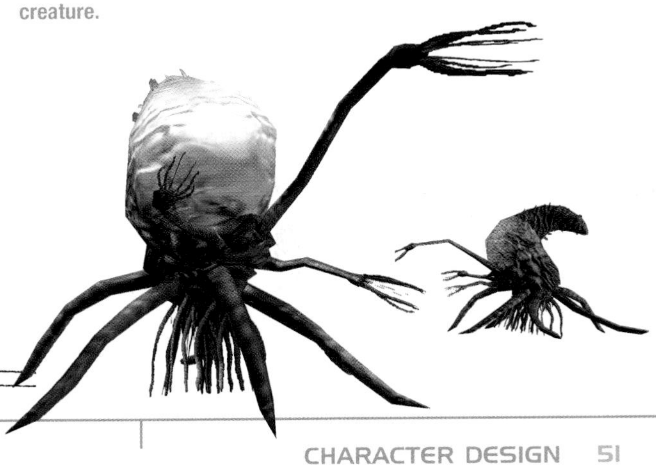

FLOOD STUDY

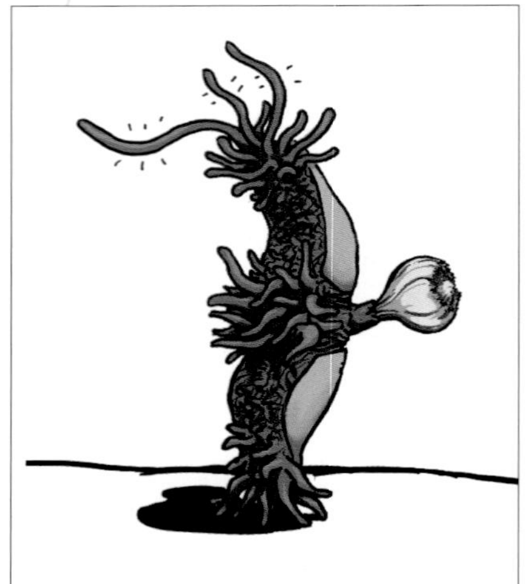

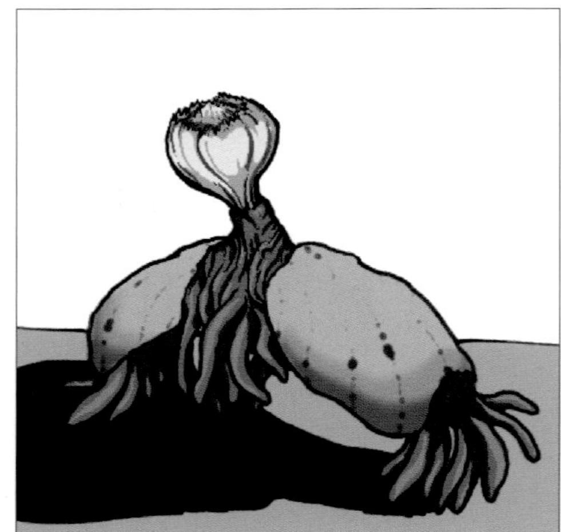

Flood concept art by Robt McLees.

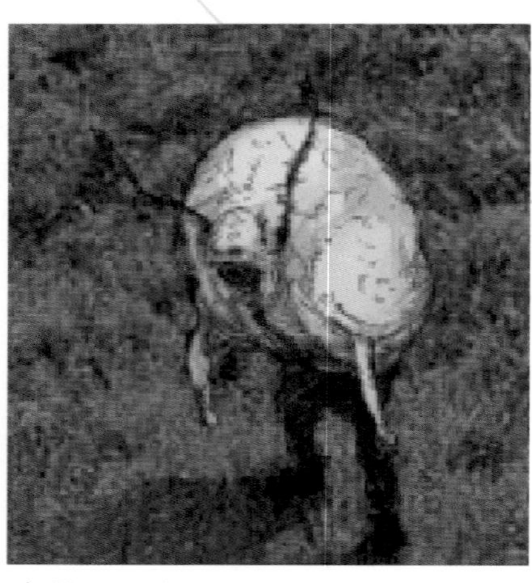

The very first Flood concept art from *Halo*'s early days as a real-time strategy game, circa 1997. Carrier Form concept by Robt McLees.

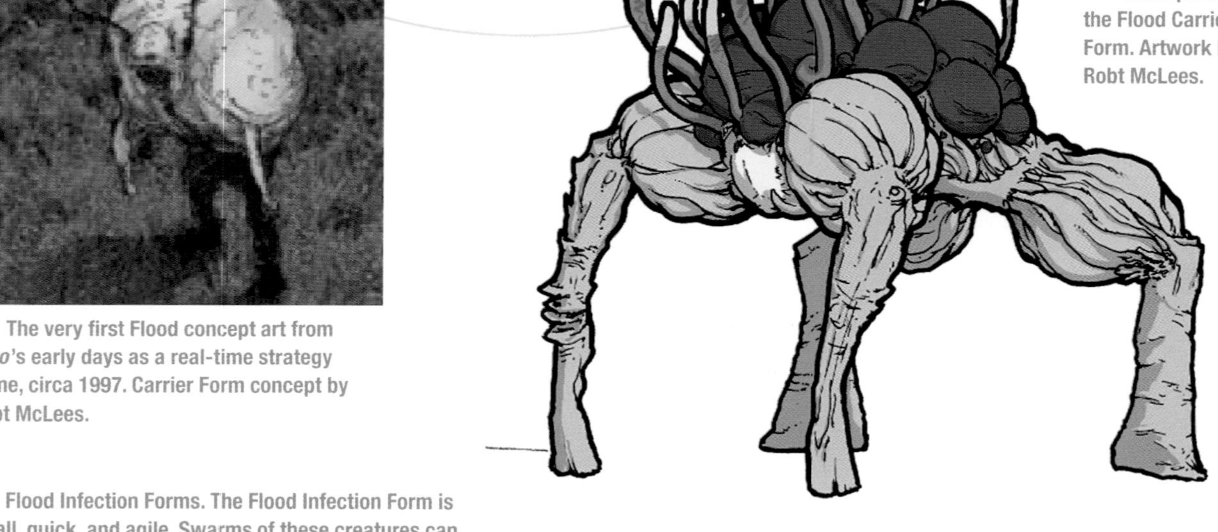

Concept art of the Flood Carrier Form. Artwork by Robt McLees.

Flood Infection Forms. The Flood Infection Form is small, quick, and agile. Swarms of these creatures can overpower a victim and begin his absorption, creating the vicious Combat Forms. Concept art by Robt McLees.

Early concept art of the Flood Combat Forms by Robt McLees.

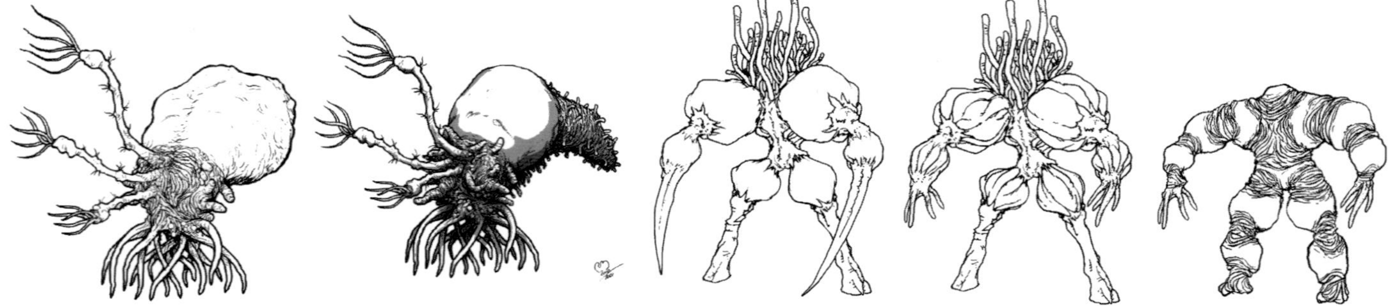

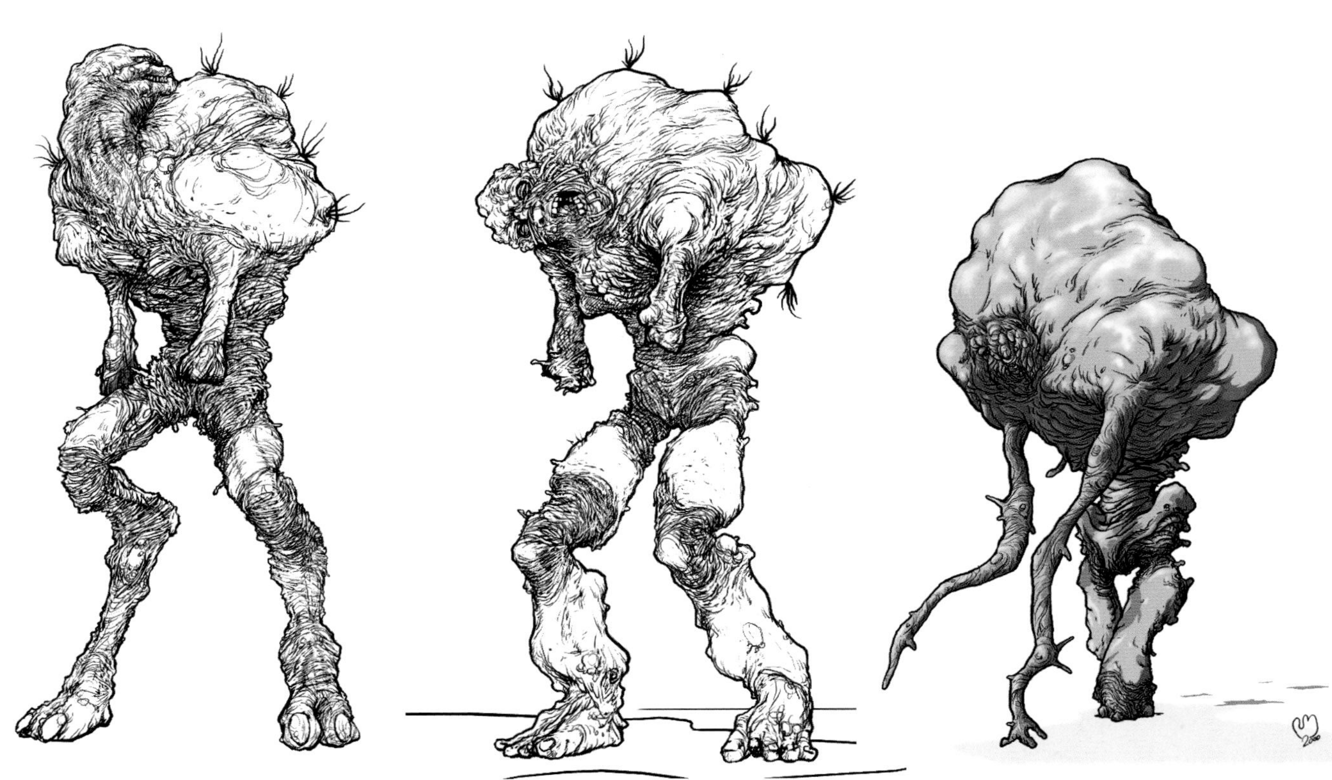

Several iterations of the Flood Carrier Form. Concept art by Robt McLees.

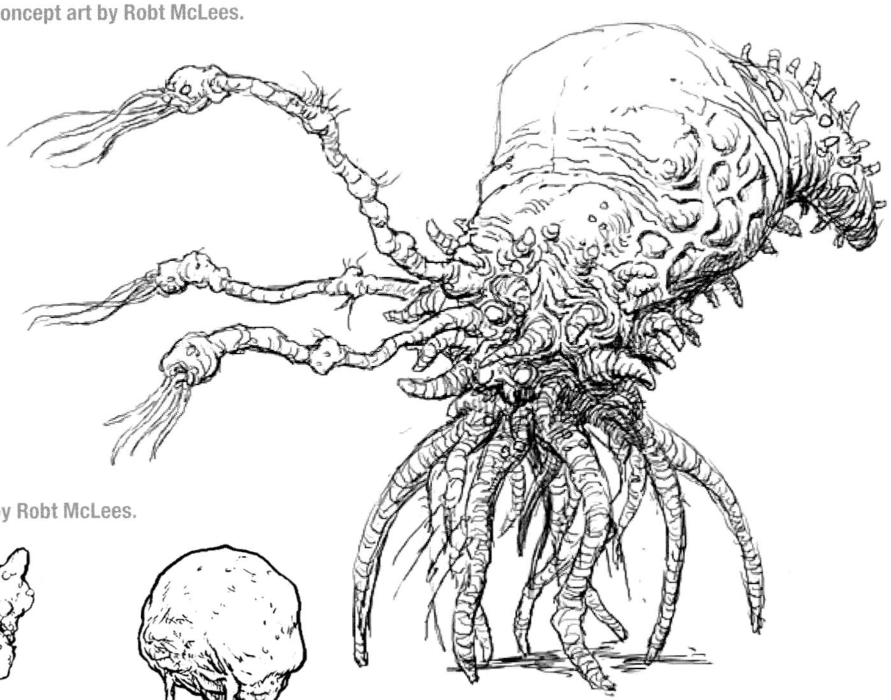

A particularly gruesome look at a Flood Infection Form. Concept art by Juan Ramirez.

Concept art by Robt McLees.

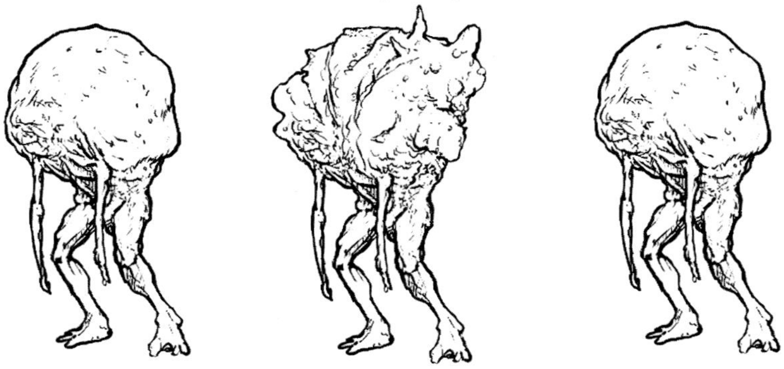

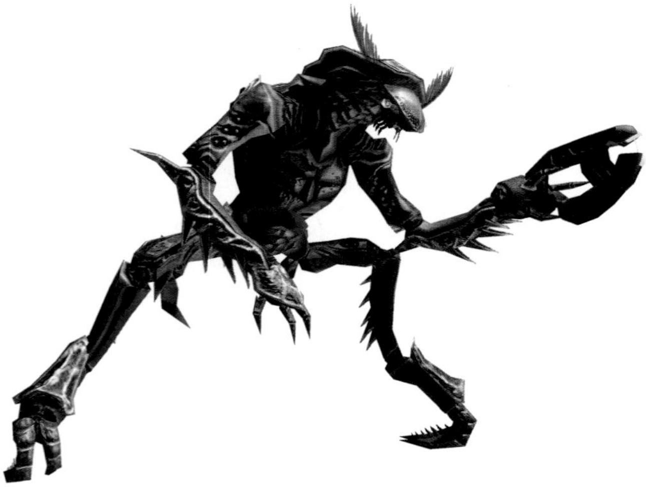

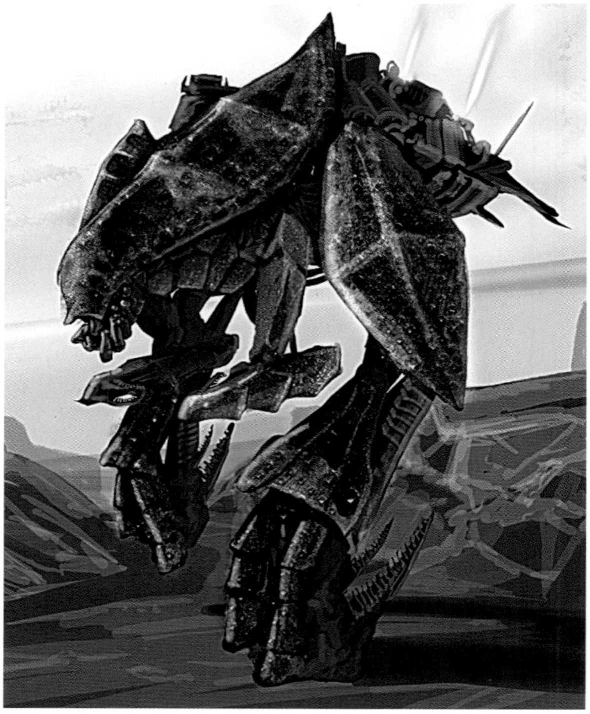

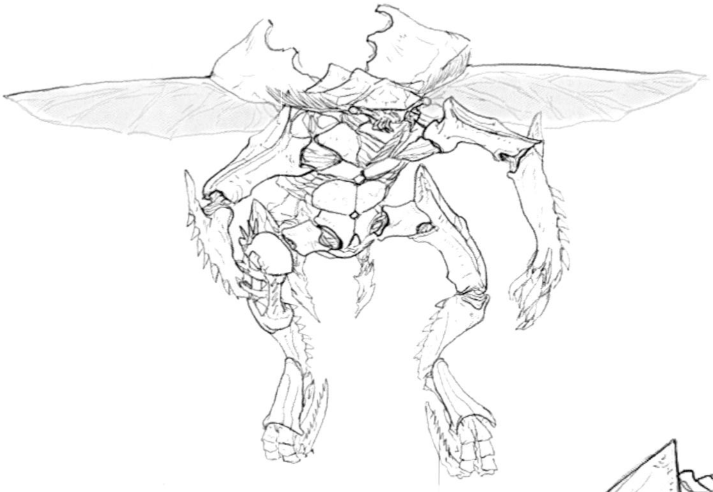

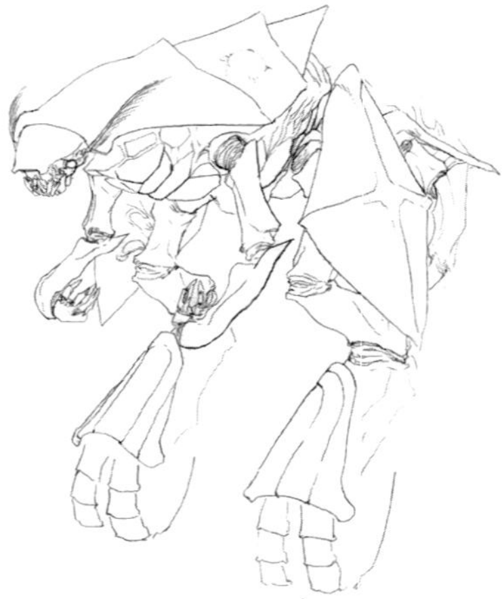

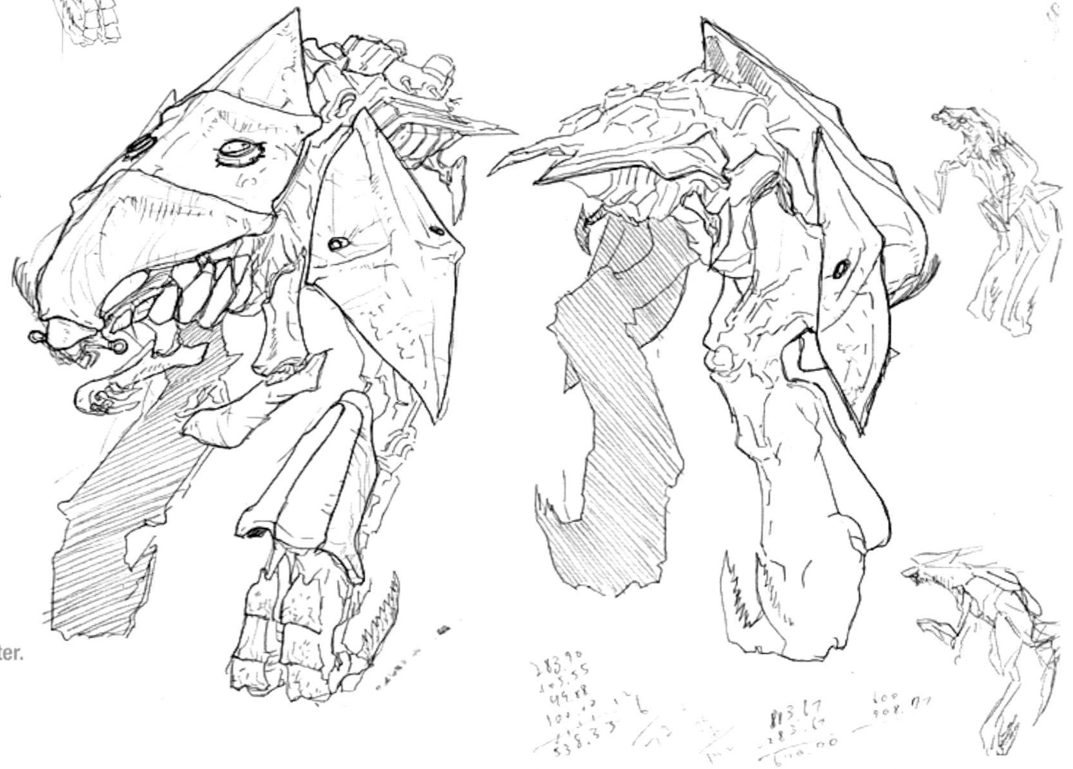

▲ Drones' natural armor plating and insectlike body parts make them an immediately charismatic addition to the *Halo 2* bad-guy roster.

DRONES

The Drones are a new addition to the *Halo* universe. These clearly insectoid creatures have elements of grasshopper, wasp, even cockroach. Quite apart from the simple graphic-design challenge was the problem of animating these creatures as they walk, run, crawl, and fly. Their ability to clamber up sheer walls added an entirely new literal dimension to the animation and design process.

In the game, they take on a number of infantry roles, from simple assault troops to lone snipers. What makes them especially interesting from a design vantage is that their ability to move practically anywhere on a map will make the player look in places he or she might never glance otherwise. Watching a Drone suddenly leap across a gap between two buildings, block out the sun for an instant, and show off a combination of high contrast and bloom lighting is a revelation.

▲ This repurposed piece was originally a concept for the Flood Infection Form.

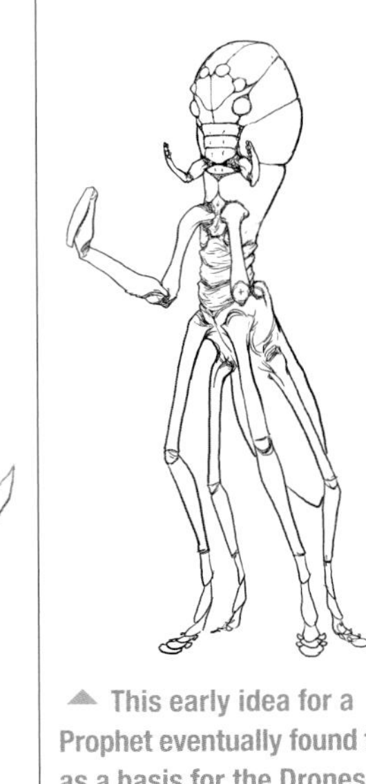

▲ This early idea for a Prophet eventually found form as a basis for the Drones.

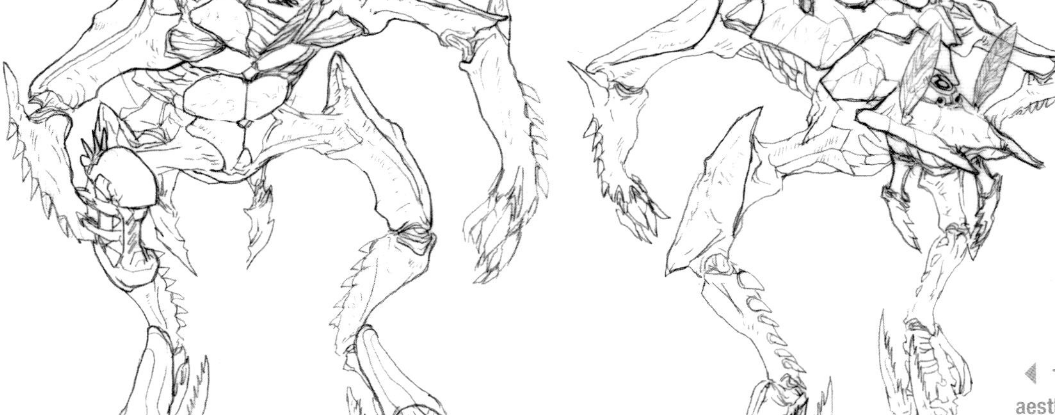

◀ The tiny wings aren't simply an aesthetic choice—the Drones are capable of limited, but not indefinite, flight in Earth's gravity.

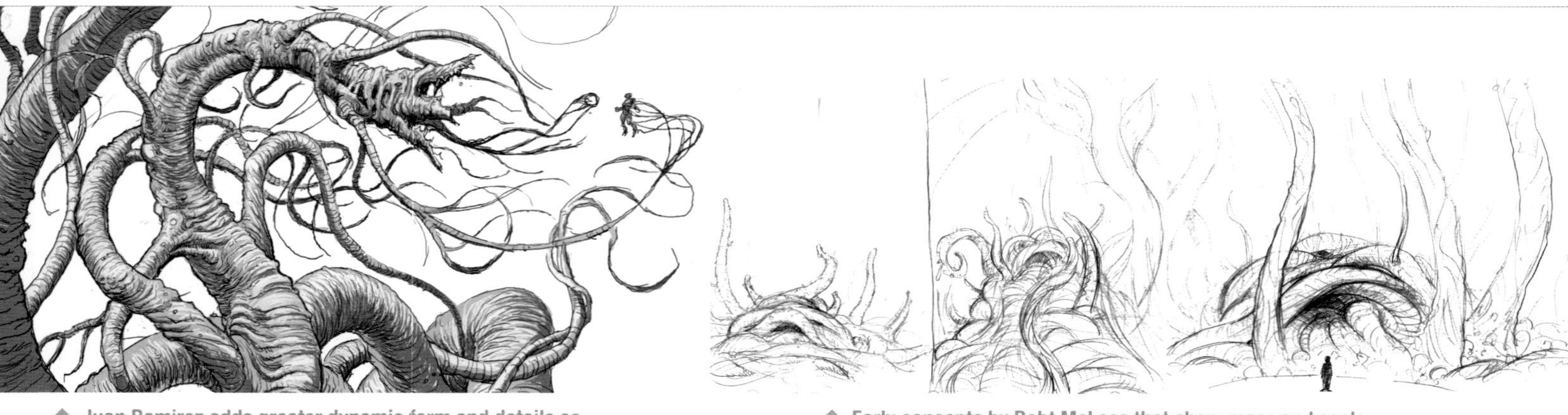

▲ Juan Ramirez adds greater dynamic form and details as the Gravemind becomes even larger.

▲ Early concepts by Robt McLees that show mass and scale.

THE GRAVEMIND

The Gravemind is one of the more shocking moments in *Halo 2*. Discovering that the Flood is not simply a mindless virus comes as quite a surprise. The Gravemind can be thought of as a cross between the Flood's logical evolution and a queen ant. The Gravemind is literally built from the bodies of its enemies and its own fallen warriors reassembled into a massive, tentacled, and intelligent entity, trapped somewhere in this new Halo.

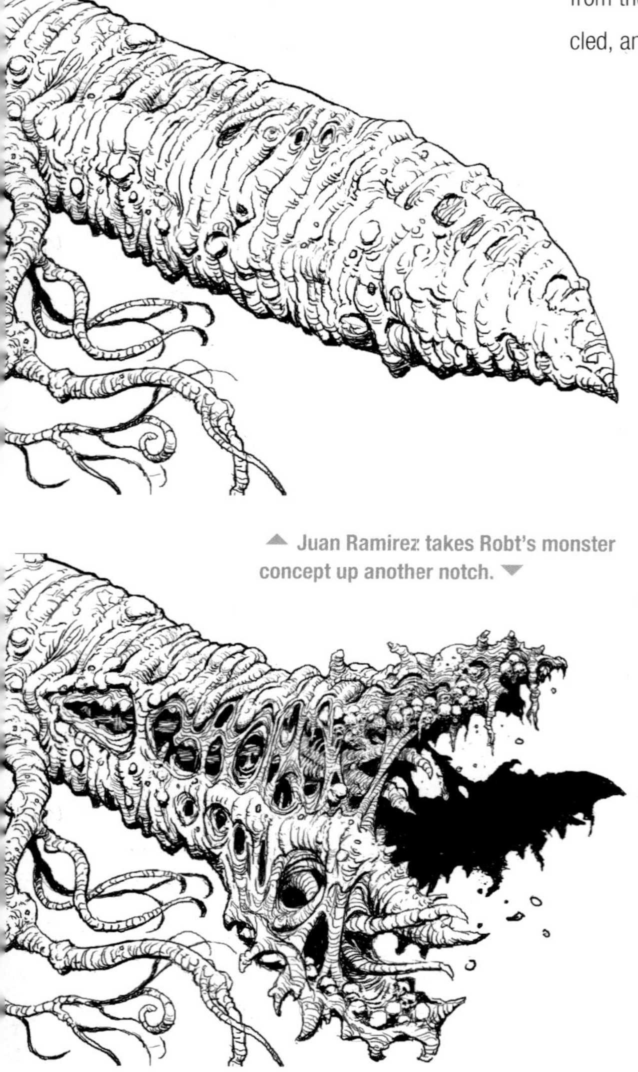

▲ Juan Ramirez takes Robt's monster concept up another notch. ▼

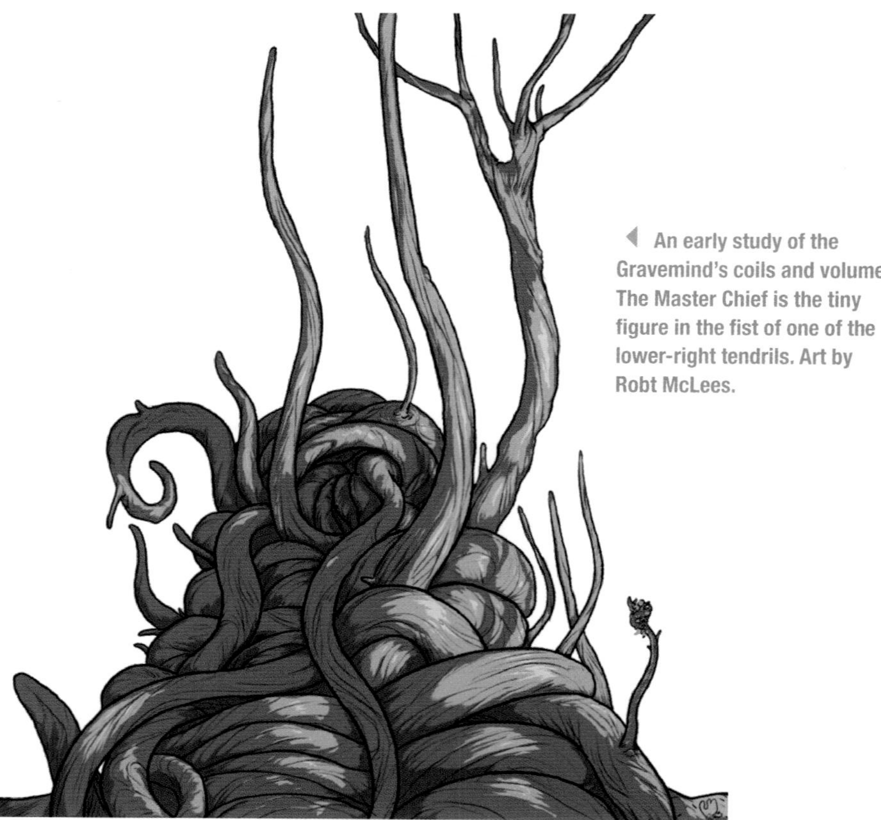

◀ An early study of the Gravemind's coils and volume. The Master Chief is the tiny figure in the fist of one of the lower-right tendrils. Art by Robt McLees.

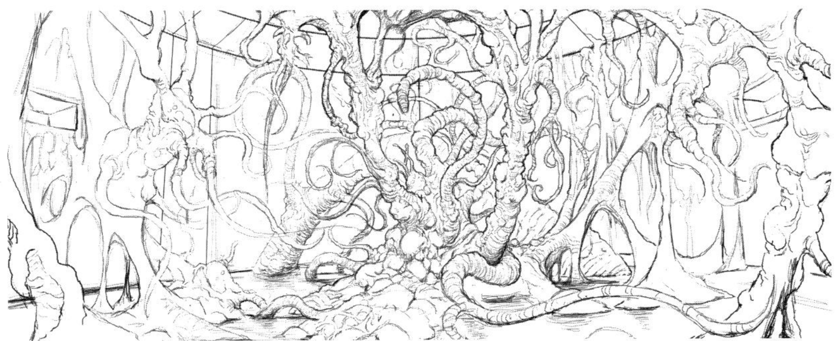

▲ A study of the cinematic space where the Gravemind dwells. Art by Juan Ramirez.

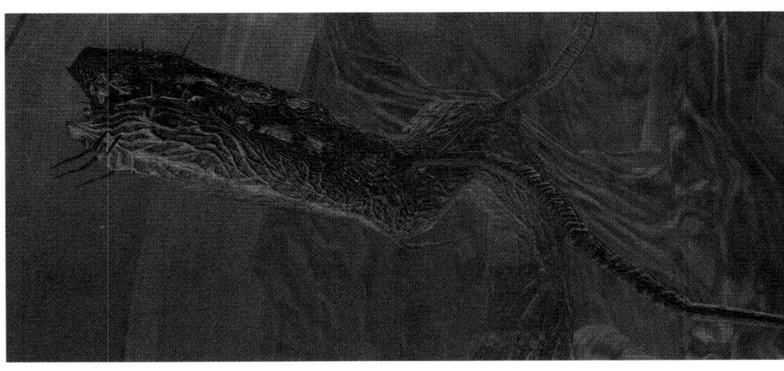

▲ A screen capture early in the game development shows the Gravemind in its massive foggy lair.

Its purpose may be obtuse, but the Gravemind's appearance is always horrifying. Snarls of tentacle, rotting biomass, and reconfigured flesh are naturally a huge challenge for animators as well as artists. But his movement and appearance are unmistakably Flood-like.

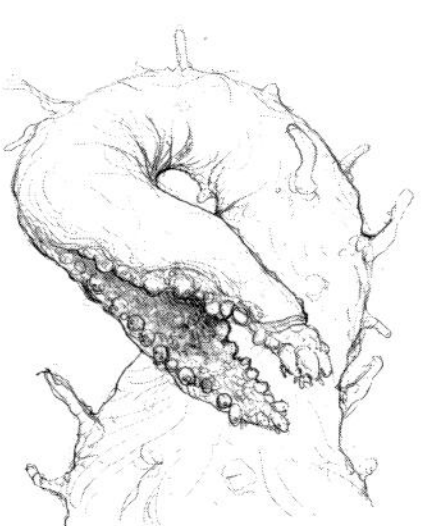

▶ The gaping maw of the Gravemind is more of a tear than a mouth. Skulls from different races serve as teeth. Art by Robt McLees.

▼ One of the first concept images of one of the Gravemind's tendrils shows the horrific nature of the beast. Art by Robt McLees.

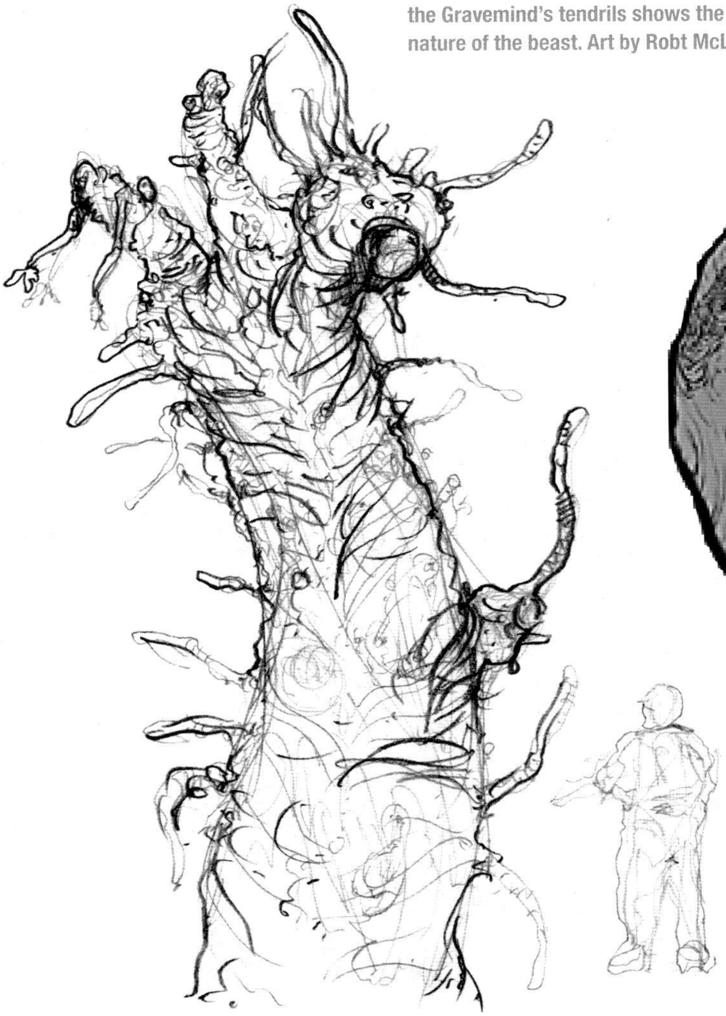

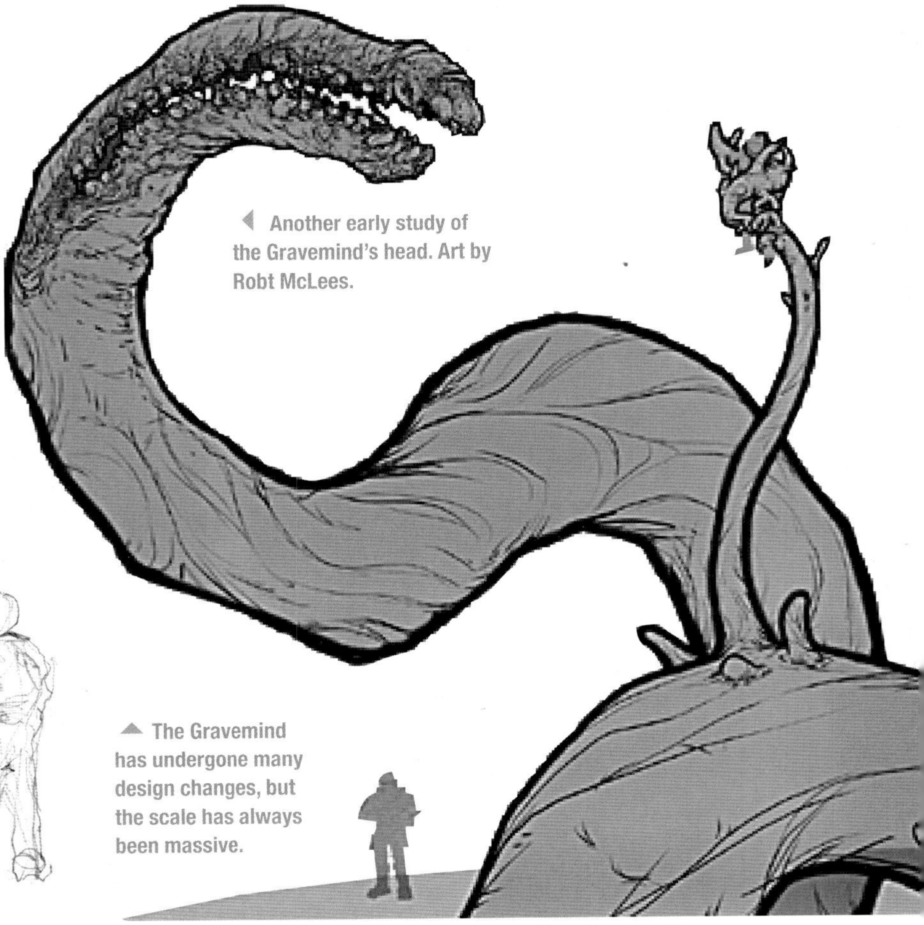

◀ Another early study of the Gravemind's head. Art by Robt McLees.

▲ The Gravemind has undergone many design changes, but the scale has always been massive.

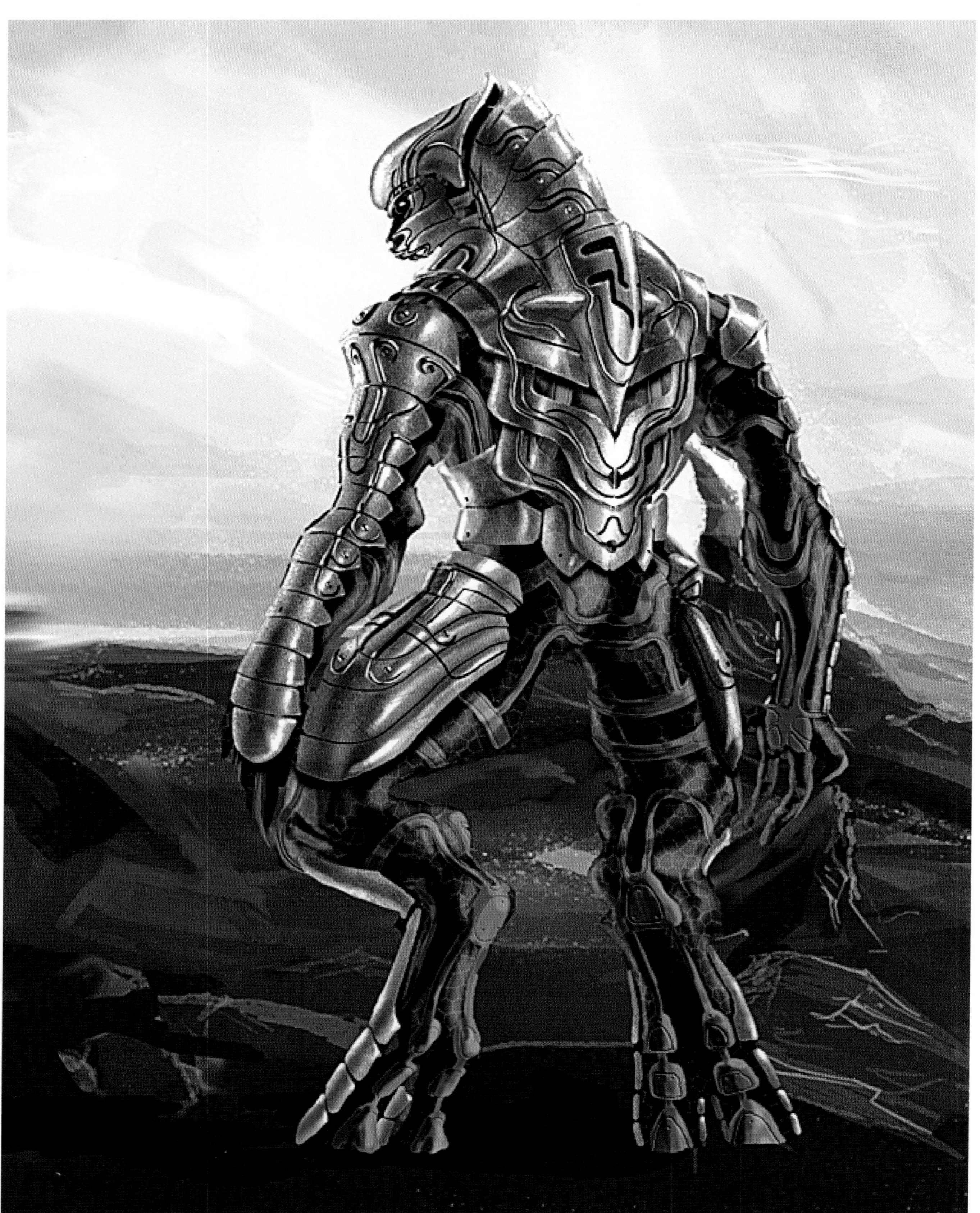

▲ This painting of the Arbiter shows off its ceremonial armor and brooding demeanor.

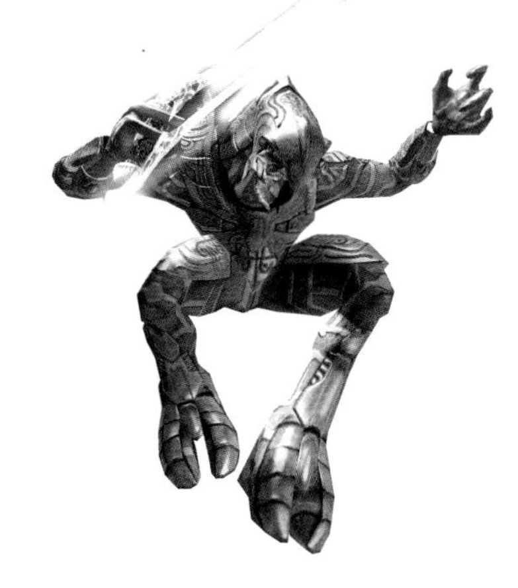

▶ The ornate armor is part shield, part prison—shackling the Arbiter to his task.

ARBITER

One of the most charismatic, complicated, and perhaps shocking characters in the *Halo* universe, the Arbiter redefines what we've come to expect from a video game "bad guy." Rather than playing the part of an aggressive goon or a simply defined hero, the Arbiter has complex political and emotional motives. He is a tortured, dangerous, and ultimately lonely archetype. His story is unveiled carefully in the game and leads to some pivotal dramatic moments.

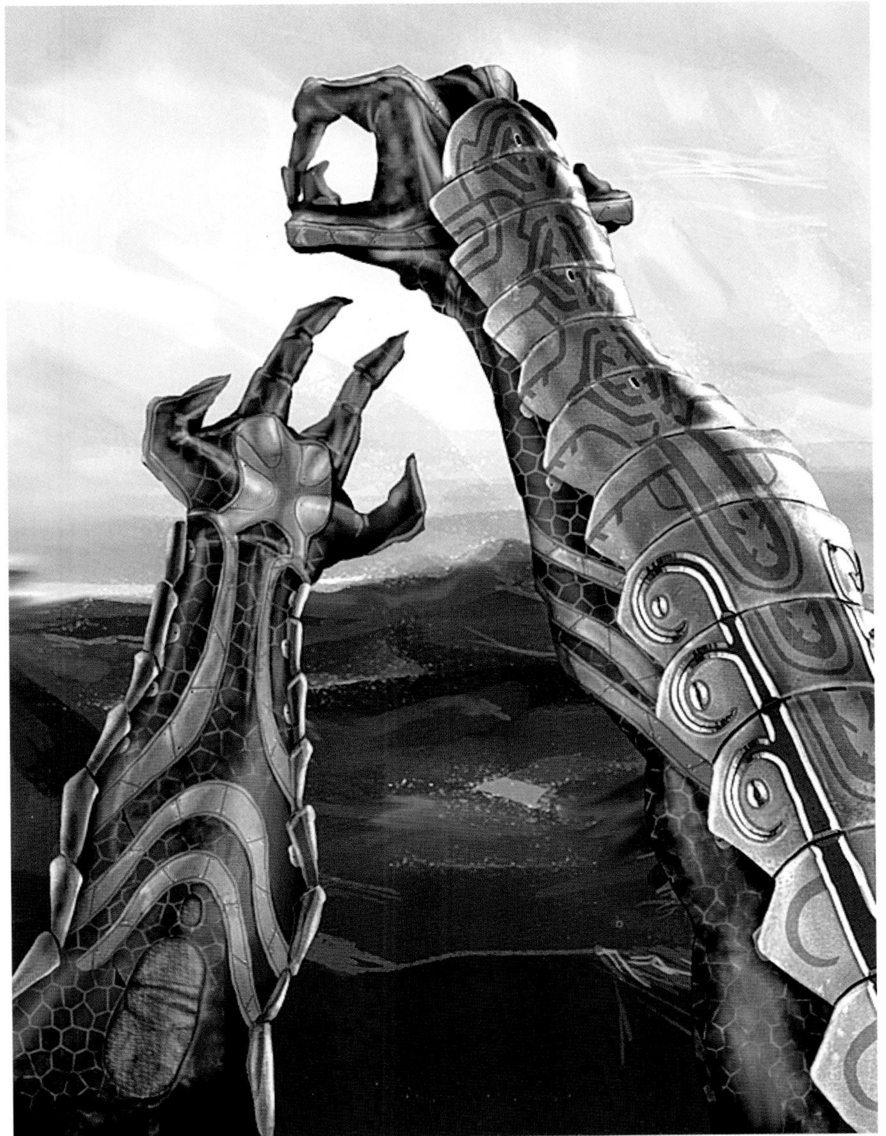

▲ This concept goes some way to demonstrating a first-person perspective of the Arbiter.

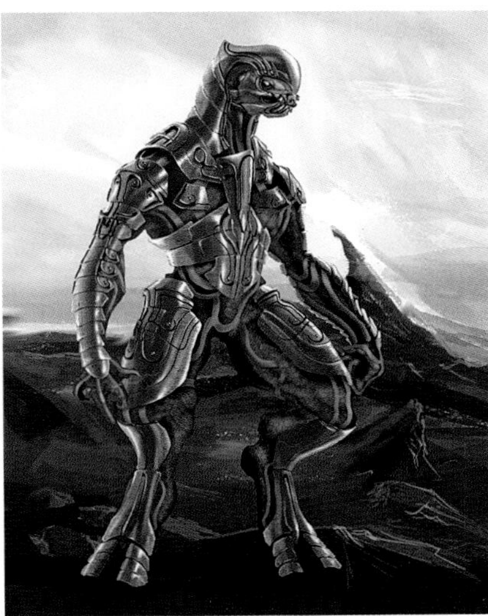

▲ Another concept painting shows a front view of the filigreed metallic shielding.

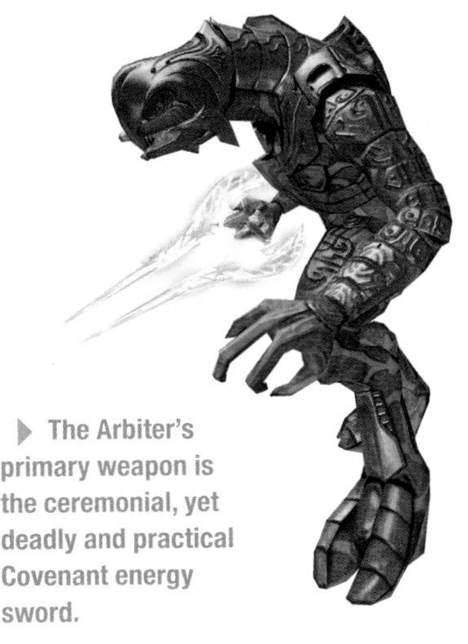

▶ The Arbiter's primary weapon is the ceremonial, yet deadly and practical Covenant energy sword.

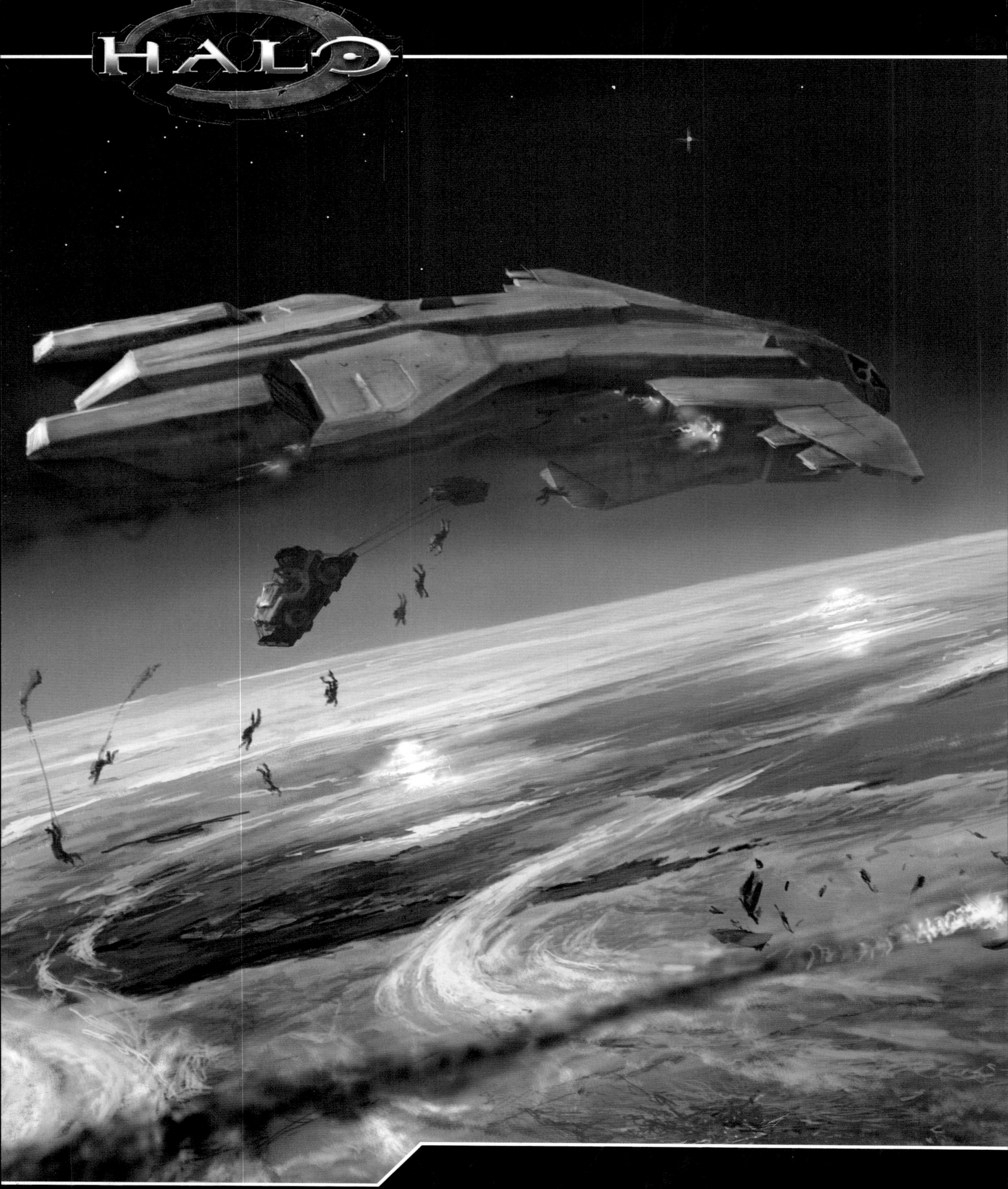
HALO

ENVIRONMENTS

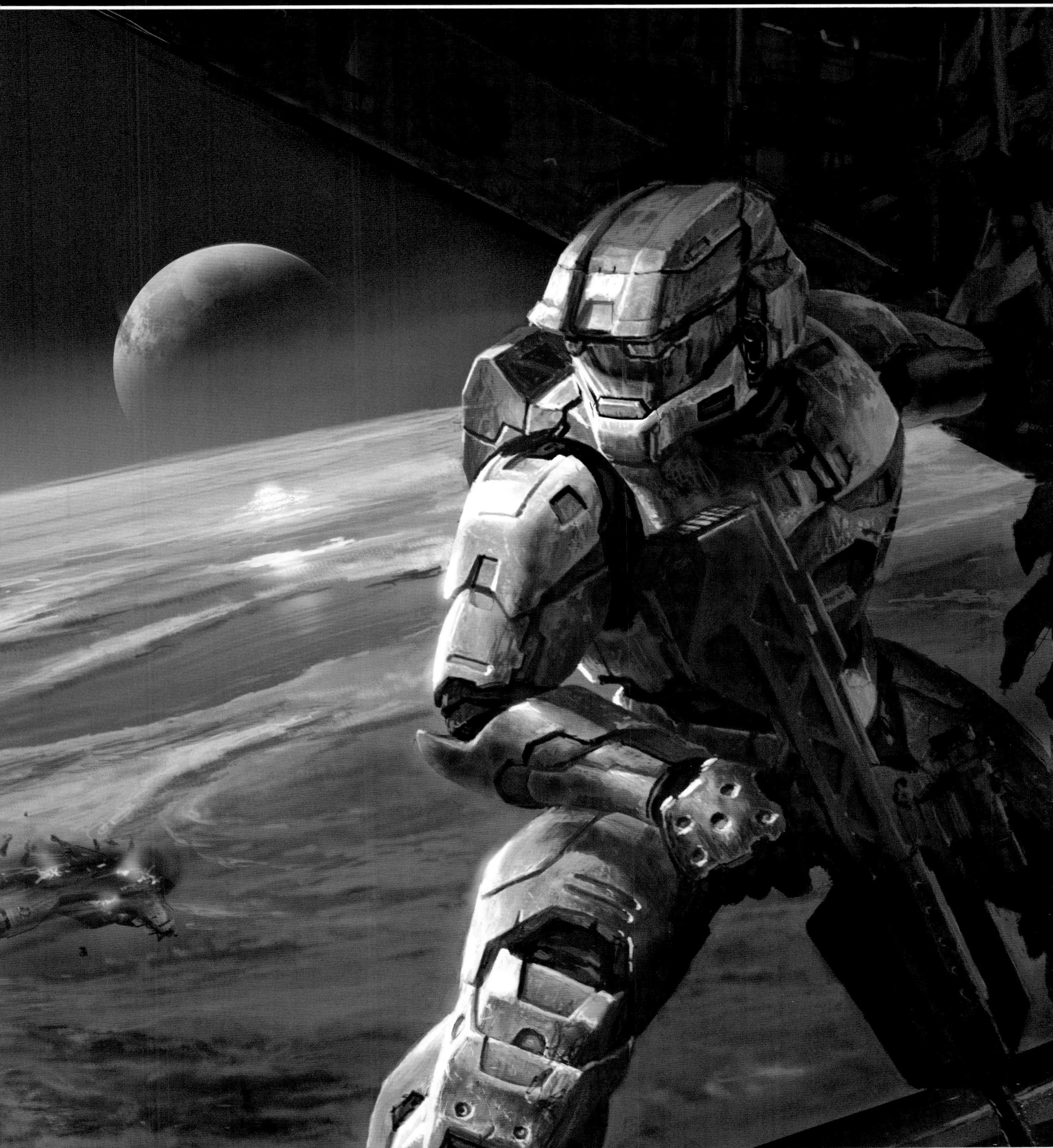

PAINTING BY EDDIE SMITH

As the ship rounded the dark side of the gas giant, the object came into full view. It was a ring-shaped structure . . . gigantic.

The object spun serenely in the heavens. The outer surface was gray metal, reflecting the brilliant starlight. From this distance, the surface of the object seemed to be engraved with deep, ornate geometric patterns.

The inner surface was a mosaic of greens, blues, and browns—trackless desert; jungles; glaciers and vast oceans. Streaks of white clouds cast deep shadows upon the terrain. The ring rotated and brought a new feature into view—a tremendous hurricane forming over an unimaginably wide body of water.

"If it's artificial, who the hell built it, and what in God's name is it?" Captain Keyes asked.

—Excerpt from
Halo: The Fall of Reach
by Eric Nylund.

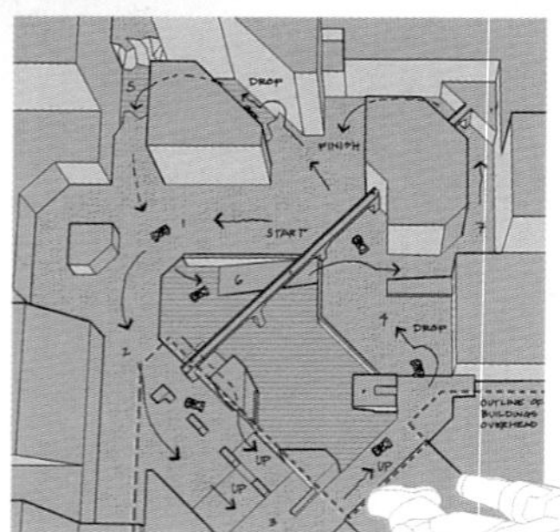

▲ Design for a *Halo 2* multiplayer map, "Headlong." Map by Chris Carney.

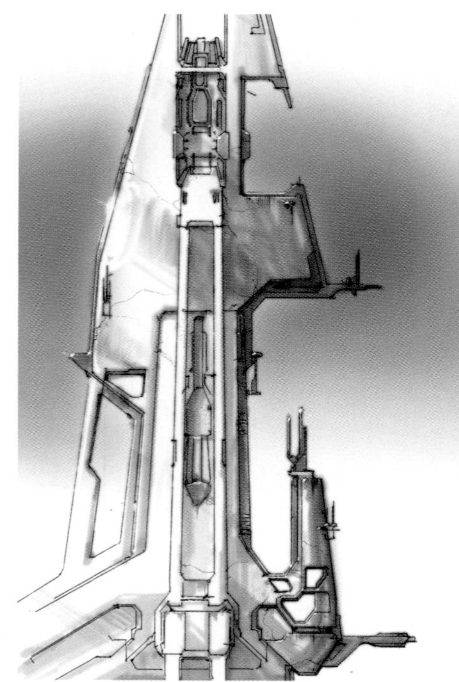

▲ *Halo 2* concept art by Frank Capezzuto.

Halo's success is due in part to the technological innovations of the game; specifically the player's ability to move a character through vast outdoor environments—and then seamlessly enter sprawling interior structures, as well.

Of course, this electronic wizardry is of little value without interesting locations to explore. The task of creating this aspect of the game fell to Bungie's team of environment artists.

Virtually everything a player sees on screen during the game has been developed, polished, and refined by Bungie's environment art team. "Anything that the player can't kill or hold, we do," says Michael Zak, environment artist.

Most of the artists begin with concept art (traditional sketches and drawings) that is either generated by other Bungie artists or, in many cases, by the environment team themselves.

From there, they work with the game and level designers to mock up an environment, be it *Halo*'s sprawling vistas, the sleek, luminous interior of a Covenant ship, or the cramped confines of an escape pod.

Once the basics of an environment are determined, the artists must construct the final shapes and geometry of the area—buildings, swamps, cliff faces, beaches, ancient alien structures, and even trees—using sophisticated 3-D modeling programs like 3D Studio Max.

Once the models are built, they must then be textured, a process by which the artists' creations are "painted"—given color, depth, and shadow. And of course all of this must be done as realistically as possible, without overtaxing the capabilities of the game console.

▼ *Halo 2* concept art by Eddie Smith.

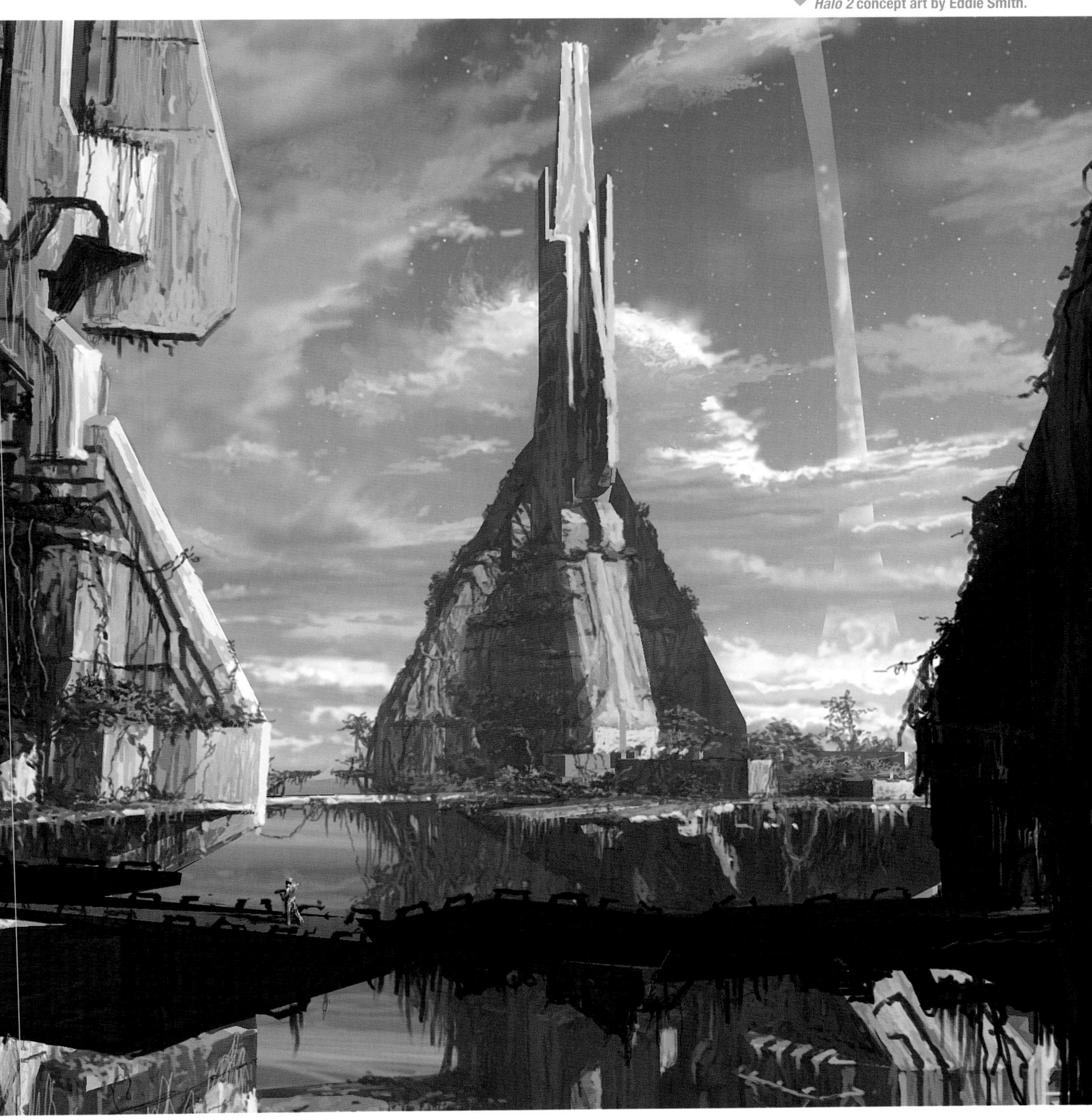

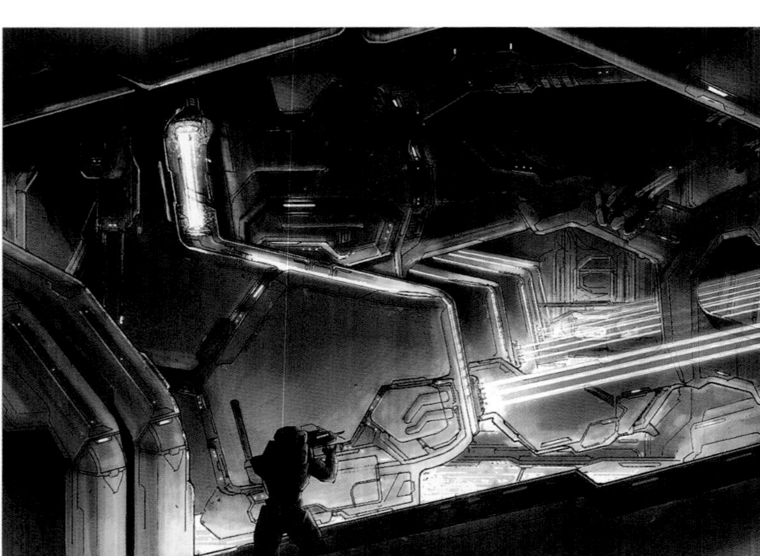

▲ Concept paintings—like this image of a massive Sentinel installation—serve as a style guide, helping define the look and feel of the environment, everything from scale to lighting and color palettes. *Halo 2* concept art by Frank Capezzuto.

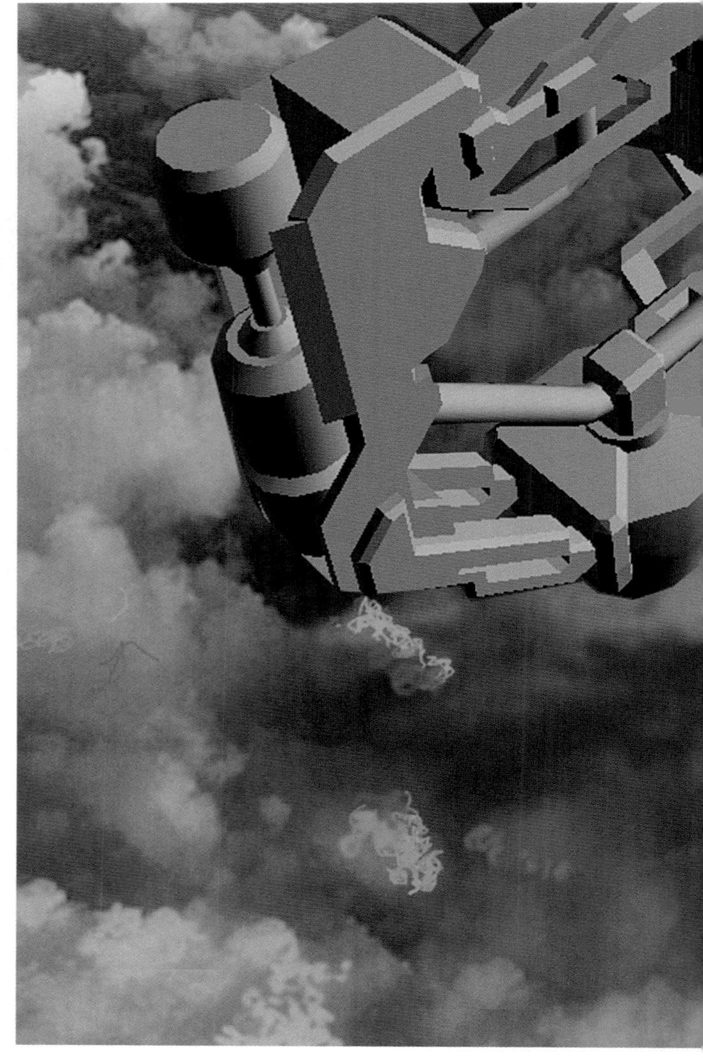

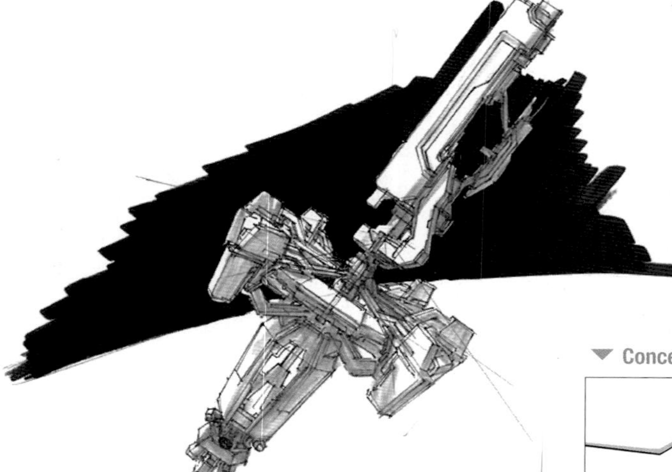

▲ Concept art by Eddie Smith.

▼ Concept art by Frank Capezzuto.

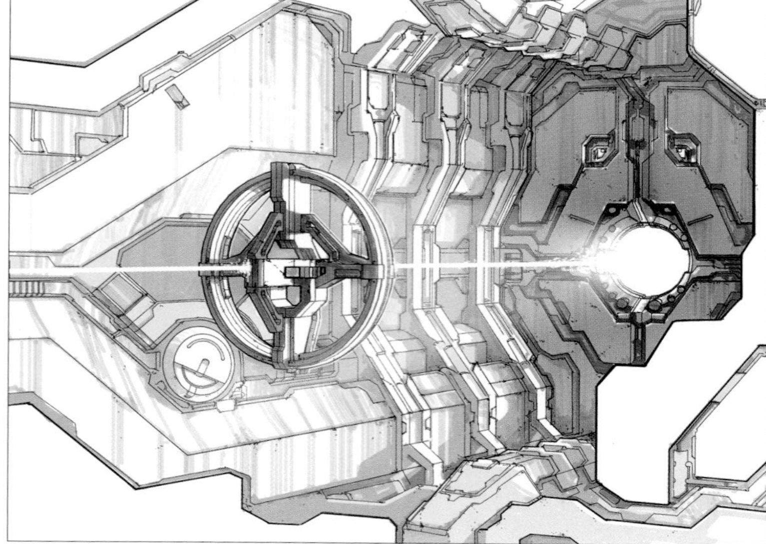

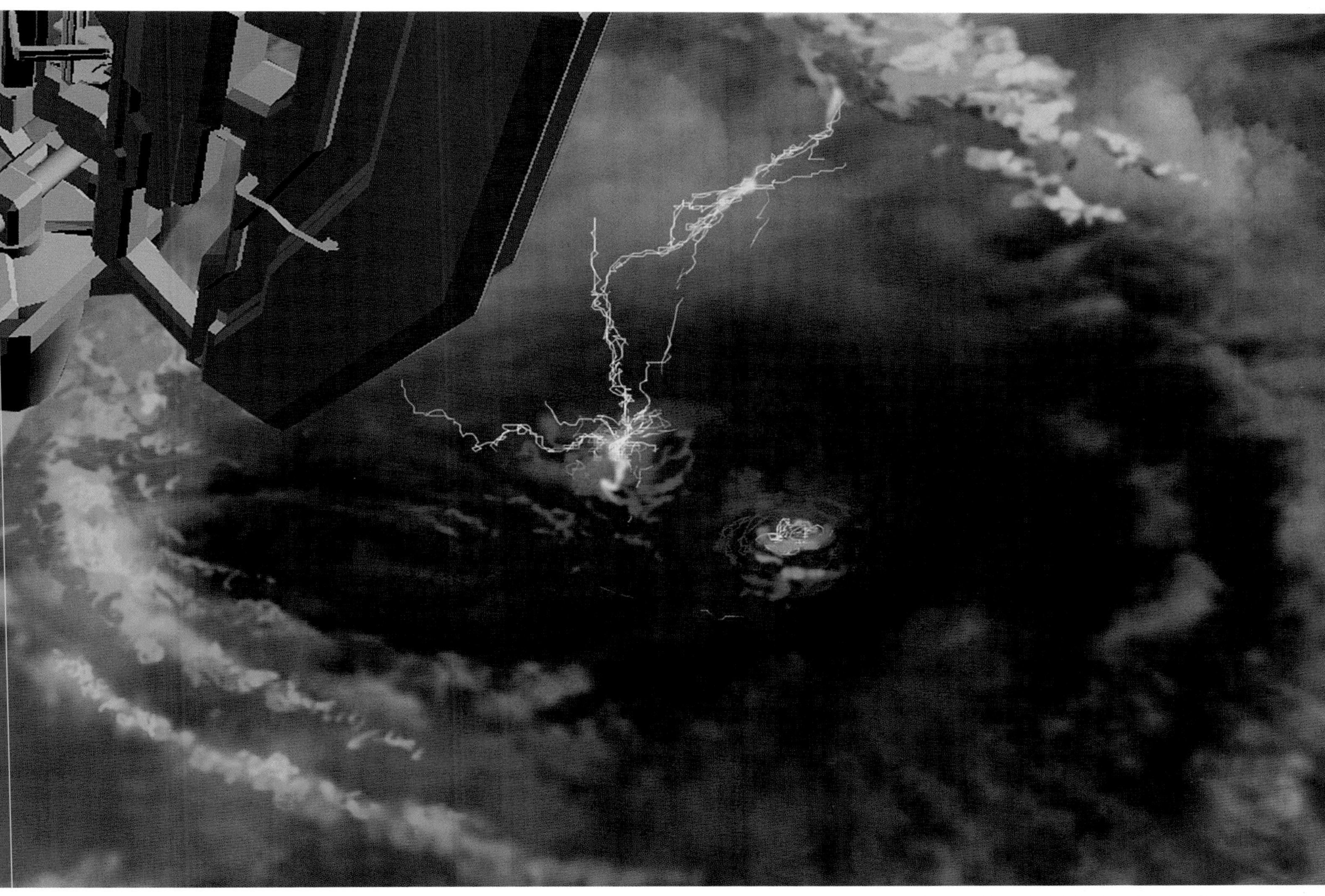

▲ The swirling maelstrom of a gas giant is the perfect backdrop to a vast and mysterious floating Forerunner structure. Art by Eddie Smith.

The work demands a great deal of collaboration between the designers and the artists. Michael Zak, environment artist, explains, "Bungie's open forum style is probably the best part of working here—and is absolutely necessary for us to do our jobs properly. It's tough to socialize in a more traditional corporate environment, but here it was pretty fast and easy to get to know people, form a rapport. In a couple of months at Bungie I probably got to know more people than in an entire year in my last job.

"A comfortable environment, peers you respect, fun work—man, that's nice."

"It's a very diverse group here, in pretty much every aspect of Bungie," explains Michael Wu. "We've got painters, and architects, and industrial designers, and writers. . . . It's interesting to see people pursue games as a legitimate means of expression. It's a growing media, still in its infancy. So that's definitely exciting."

I've seen some really talented people fail to make the transition into this relatively new form," Michael Zak explains. "It's a different mind-set to integrate the traditional methods of

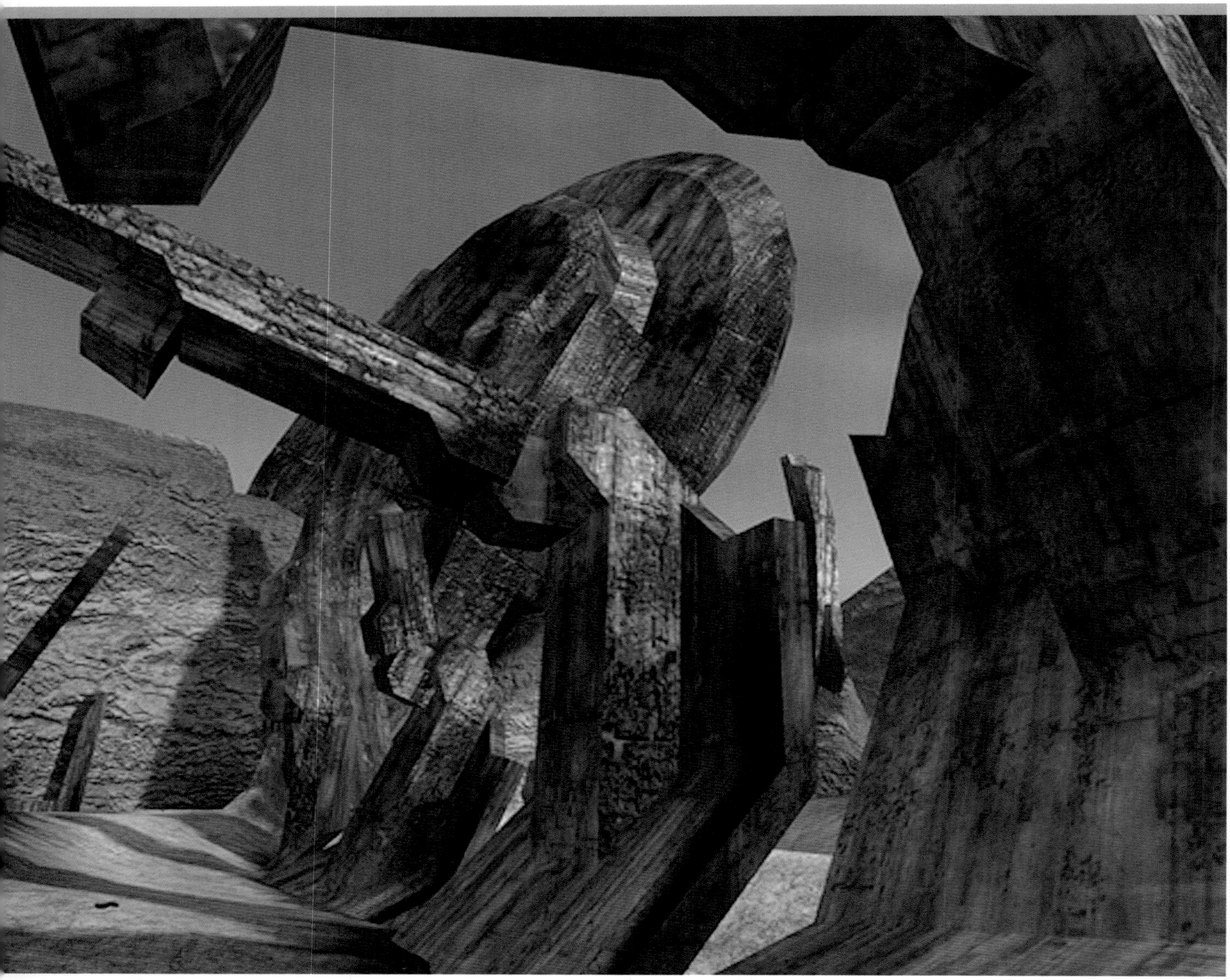

▲ Screen shot of a *Halo 2* multiplayer map, "Burial Mounds."

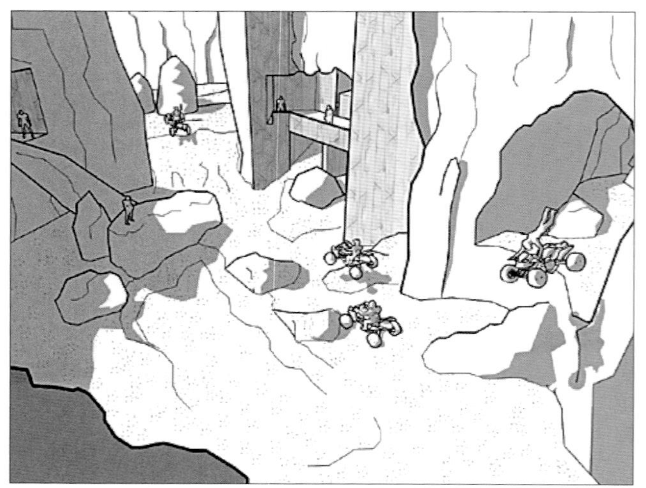

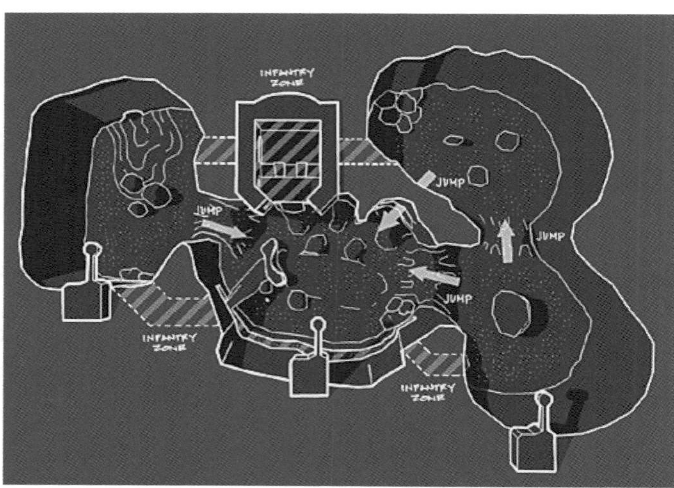

▲ Concept art and overview schematic for the *Halo 2* multiplayer map "Burial Mounds." Artwork by Chris Carney.

painting or modeling and apply them successfully to the process of making a game."

To build the *Halo* games' various otherworldly environments, the artists turn to a variety of sources of inspiration: films, books, other video games, and each other. "I think we all get a lot of our inspiration from within the team," says Michael Wu.

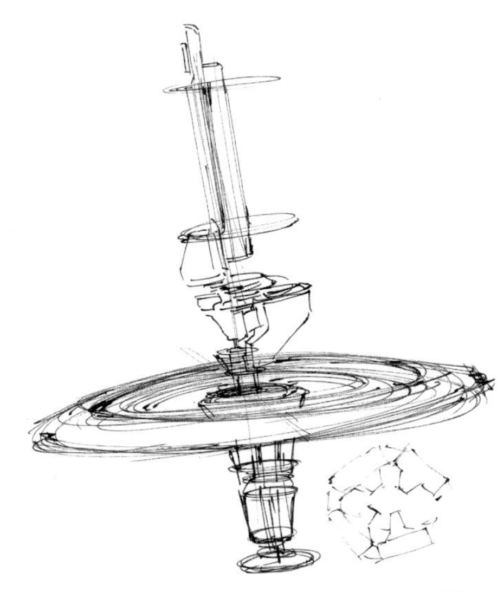

▲▼ Concept art of a human space station by Eddie Smith.

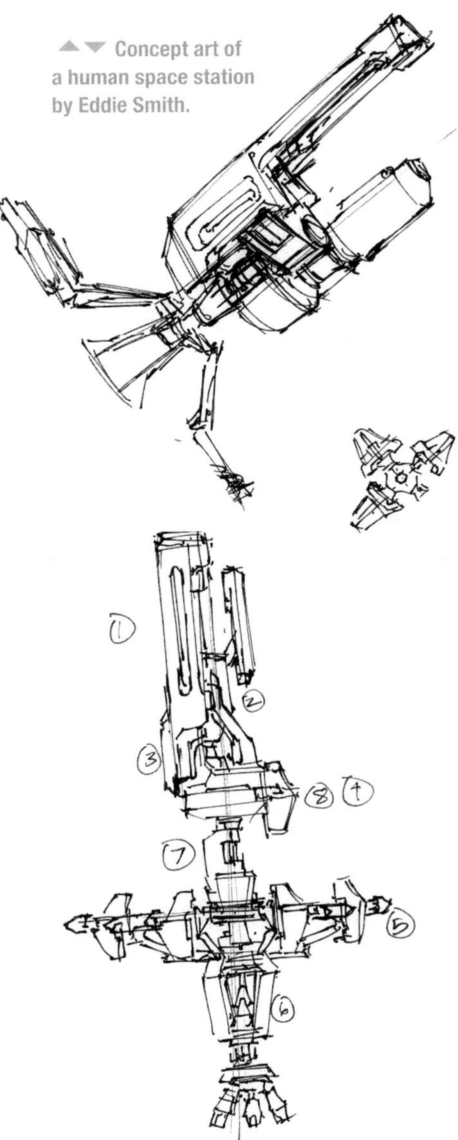

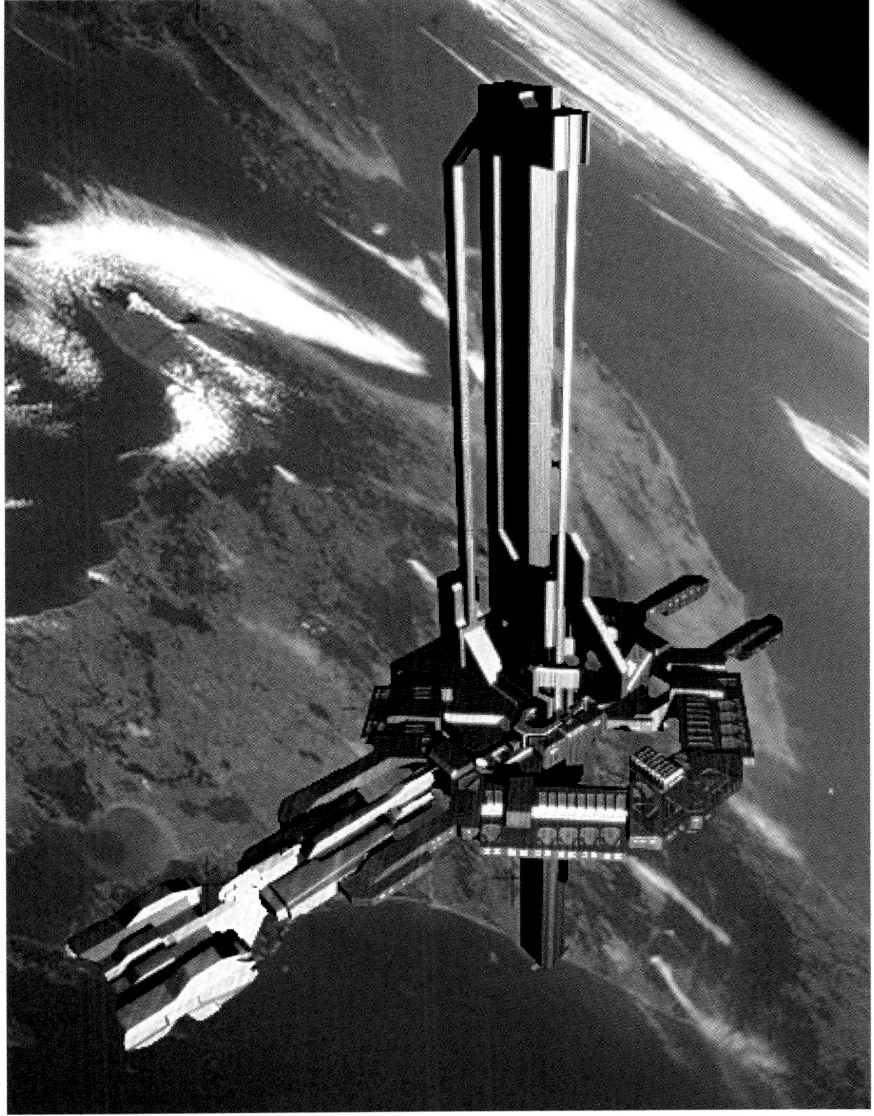

▲ A human space station, as crafted by Paul Russel.

Environment artist Frank Capezzuto agrees. "I pull a lot of inspiration just off our huge library of concept art, models, textures—there's tons of stuff we can look at and go, 'Wow, that's cool, but wouldn't be even cooler *if* . . . "

"I want to make something the guys next to me think is really cool," Wu continues. "But I must say that the fan community that plays the game, and vocally expresses their feelings on the game, have a *huge* impact on my approach to my work. I use fan feedback as a reality check, because they keep you honest. When they don't like something I worked on, it's really a knife in my heart. That kind of thing keeps you going, keeps you plugging away to the point where your eyes hurt, your bones ache. Because you don't want to disappoint them."

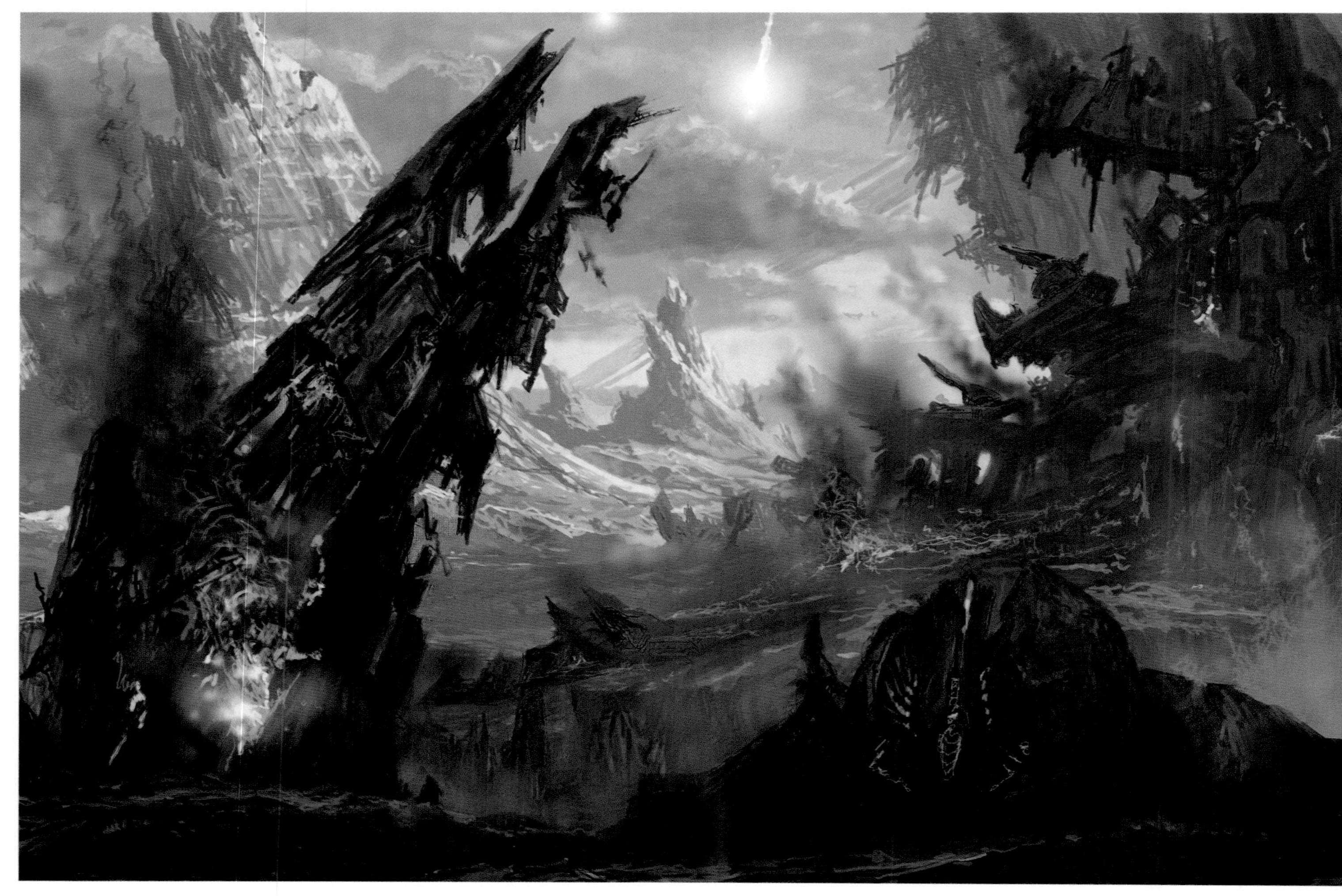

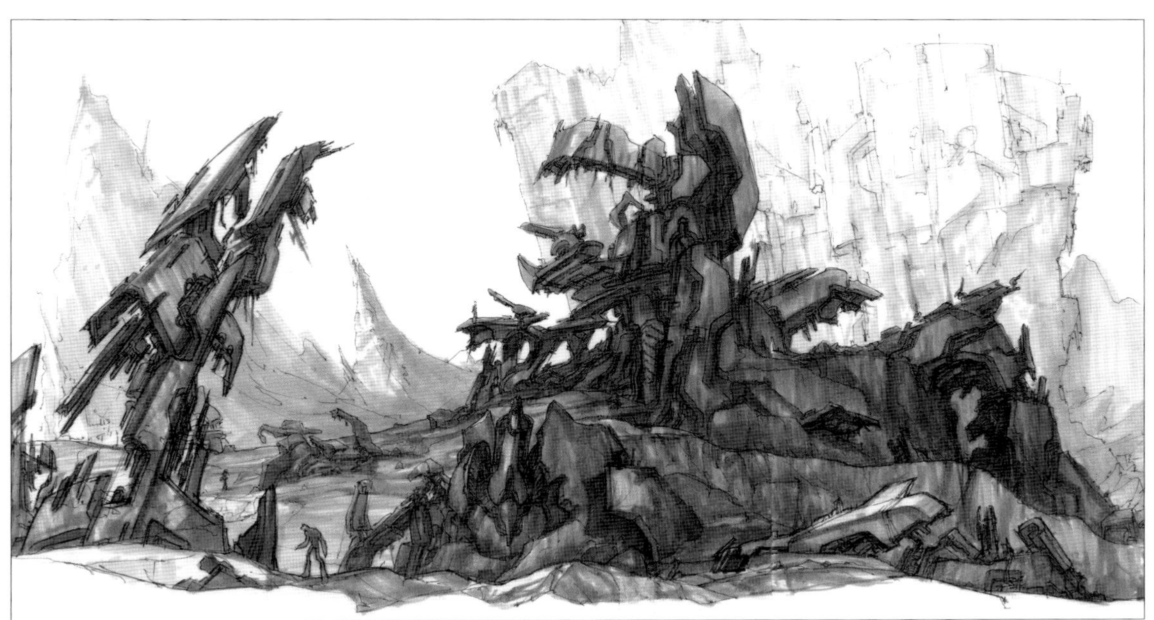

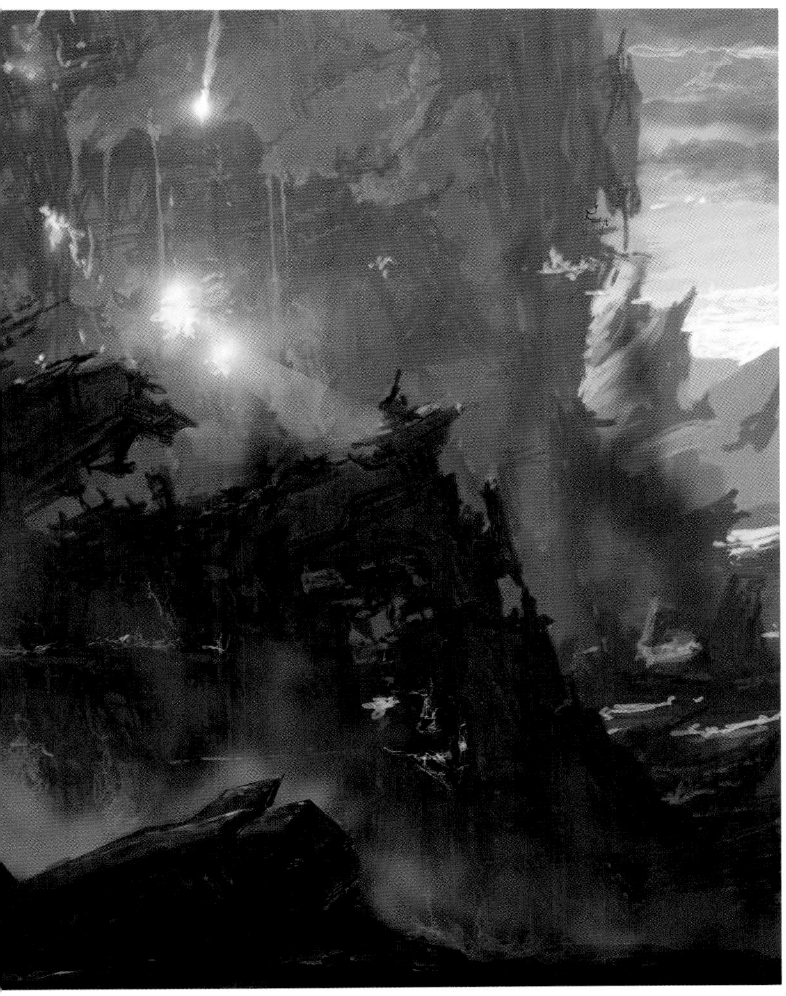

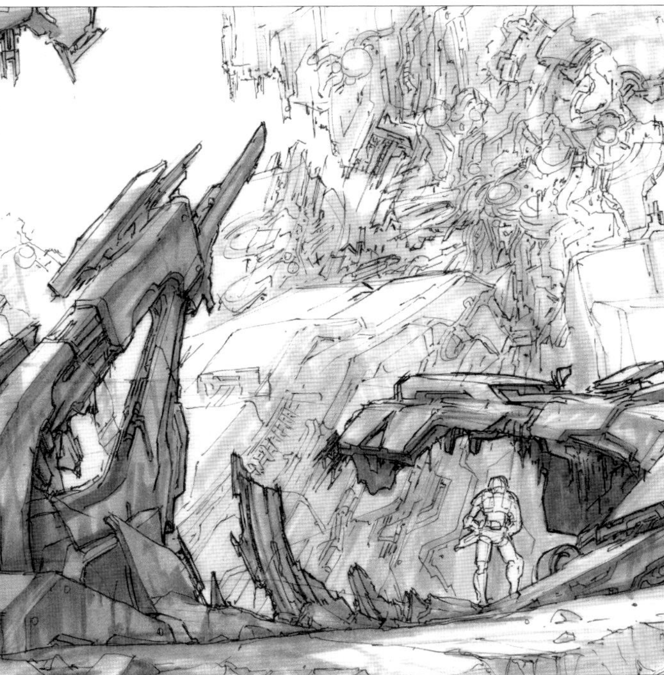

▲ Concept sketches depicting the wreckage of the ring structure Halo. It's on Basis, the moon flanking one side of the ring structure in the first game. Artwork by Eddie Smith.

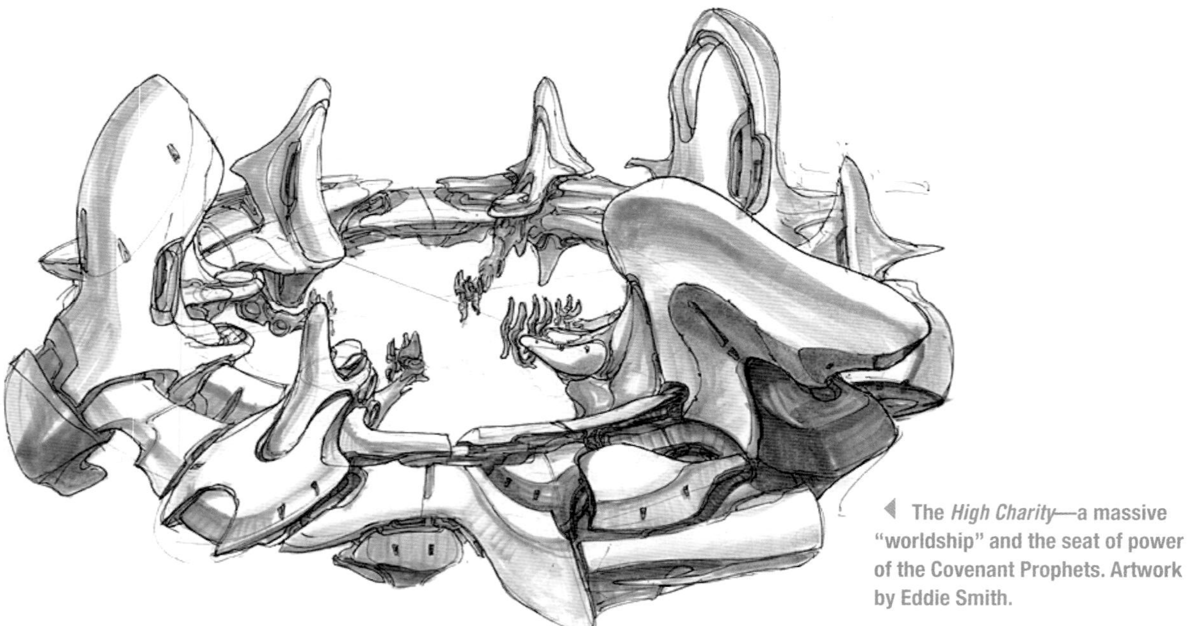

The *High Charity*—a massive "worldship" and the seat of power of the Covenant Prophets. Artwork by Eddie Smith.

This gloomily lit concept of the Council Chamber shows the grandeur, majesty, and perhaps sanctity of the Prophet chambers.

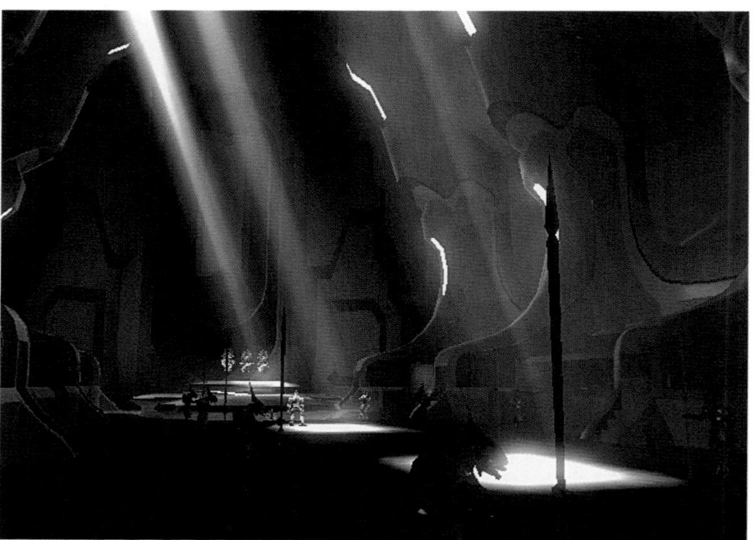

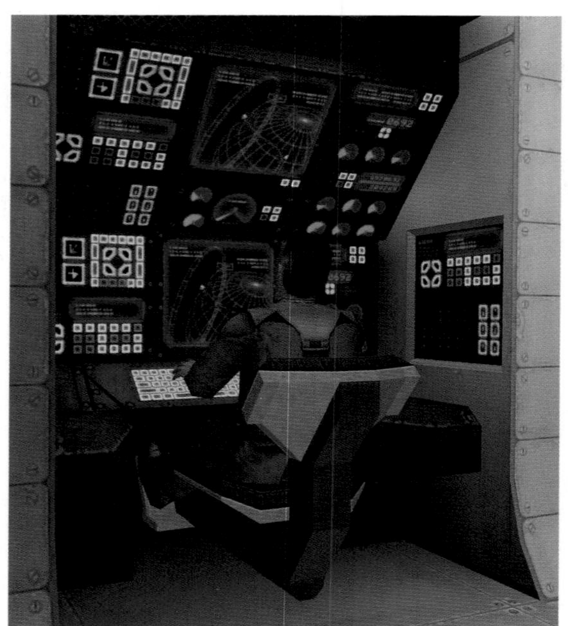

Screen shots of the *Pillar of Autumn*'s bridge, above and right.

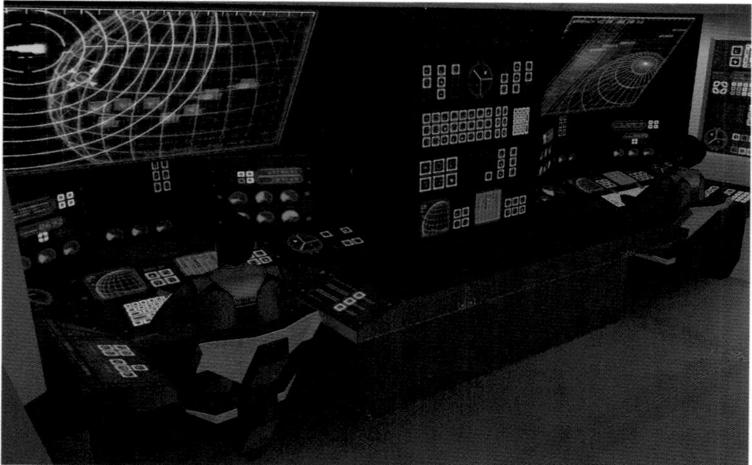

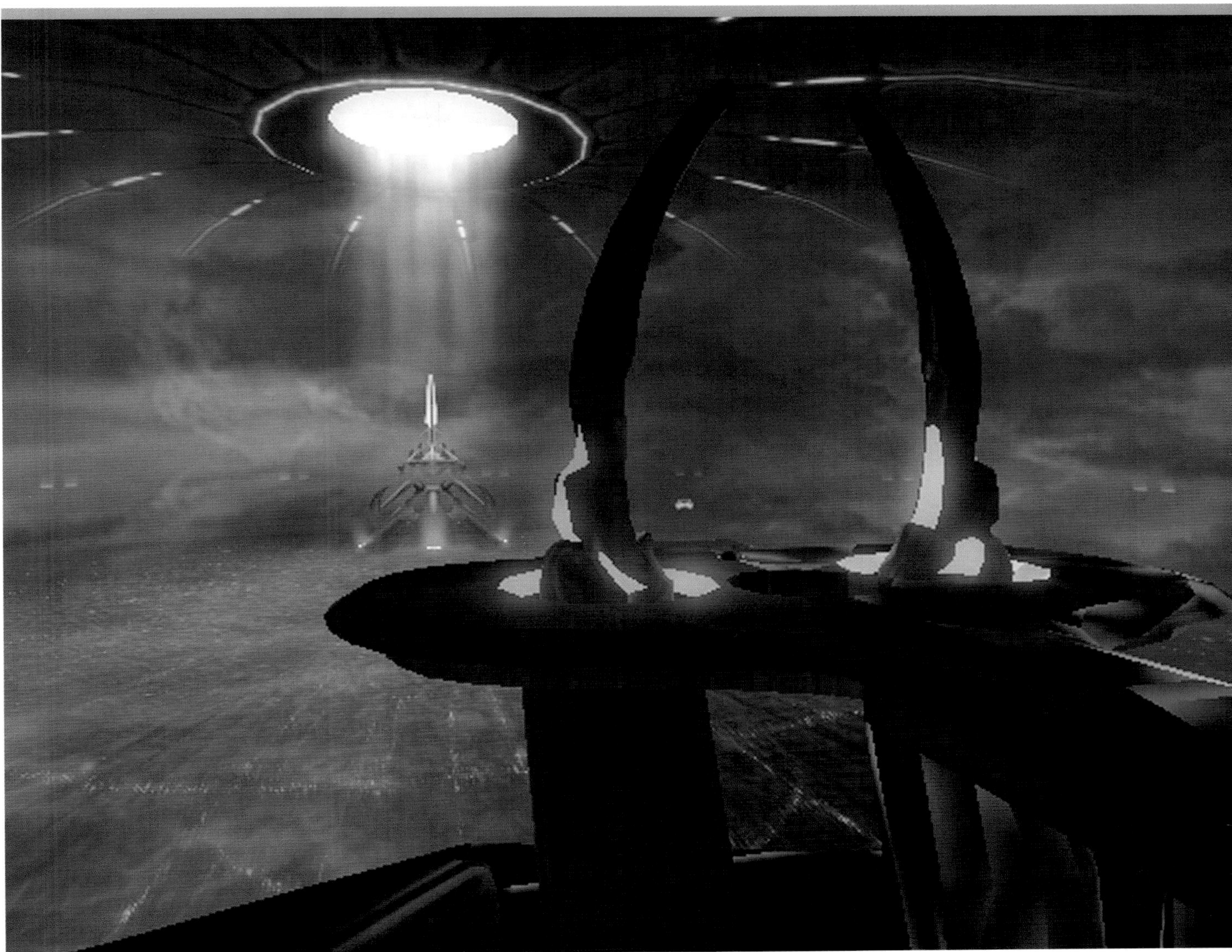

▲ A look inside a mysterious Covenant vessel, *High Charity*. This screen shot was taken early in the *Halo 2* development process.

"I feel completely the opposite, actually," says environment artist Christopher Barrett with a laugh. "Obviously, I'm happy that people love the game, but I don't spend time worrying about stuff like that. My motivation is pretty selfish. What thrills me is the creation of a fully realized, three-dimensional world. When I stay late to create some cool effect—broken beams, or something you can walk under, or through, or into—that's why I do it. It's great that people love it . . . because it supports my habit, which is making these worlds look and feel *real*."

To build the different environments in the game, the environment team determined that there were three "schools" of *Halo* architecture: the functional, industrial look of the human structures (such as the interior of the cruiser, the *Pillar of Autumn*); the sleek, shiny alien interiors of the Covenant; and the enigmatic, cavernous structures of Halo's builders, the Forerunners. "The three schools of *Halo* architecture," Marcus Lehto says, "was really driven by [environment artist] Paul Russel."

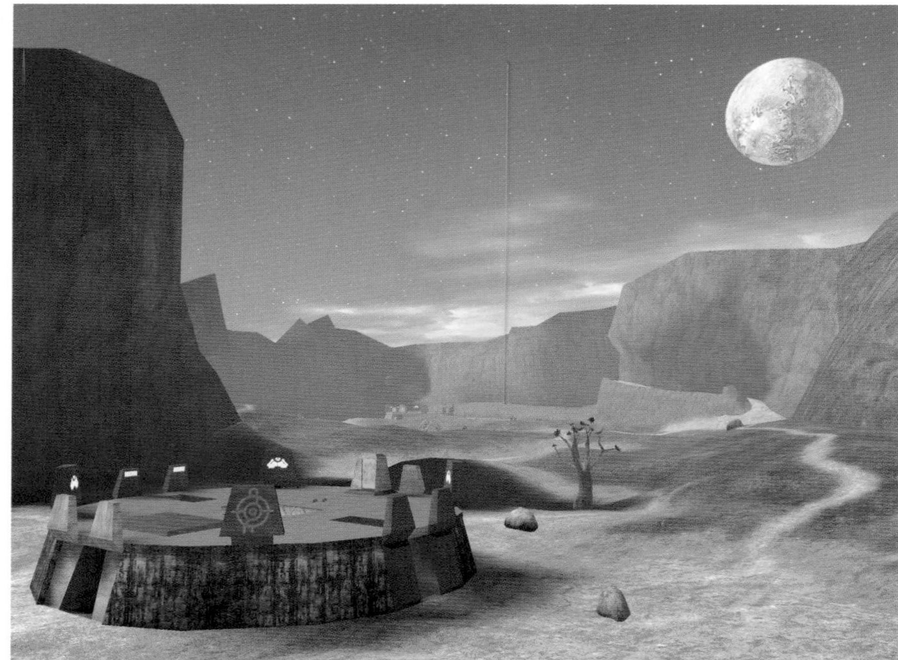

Who'd have thought that a closed-in, arid, and pointless box canyon would become such a classic? This is Blood Gulch.

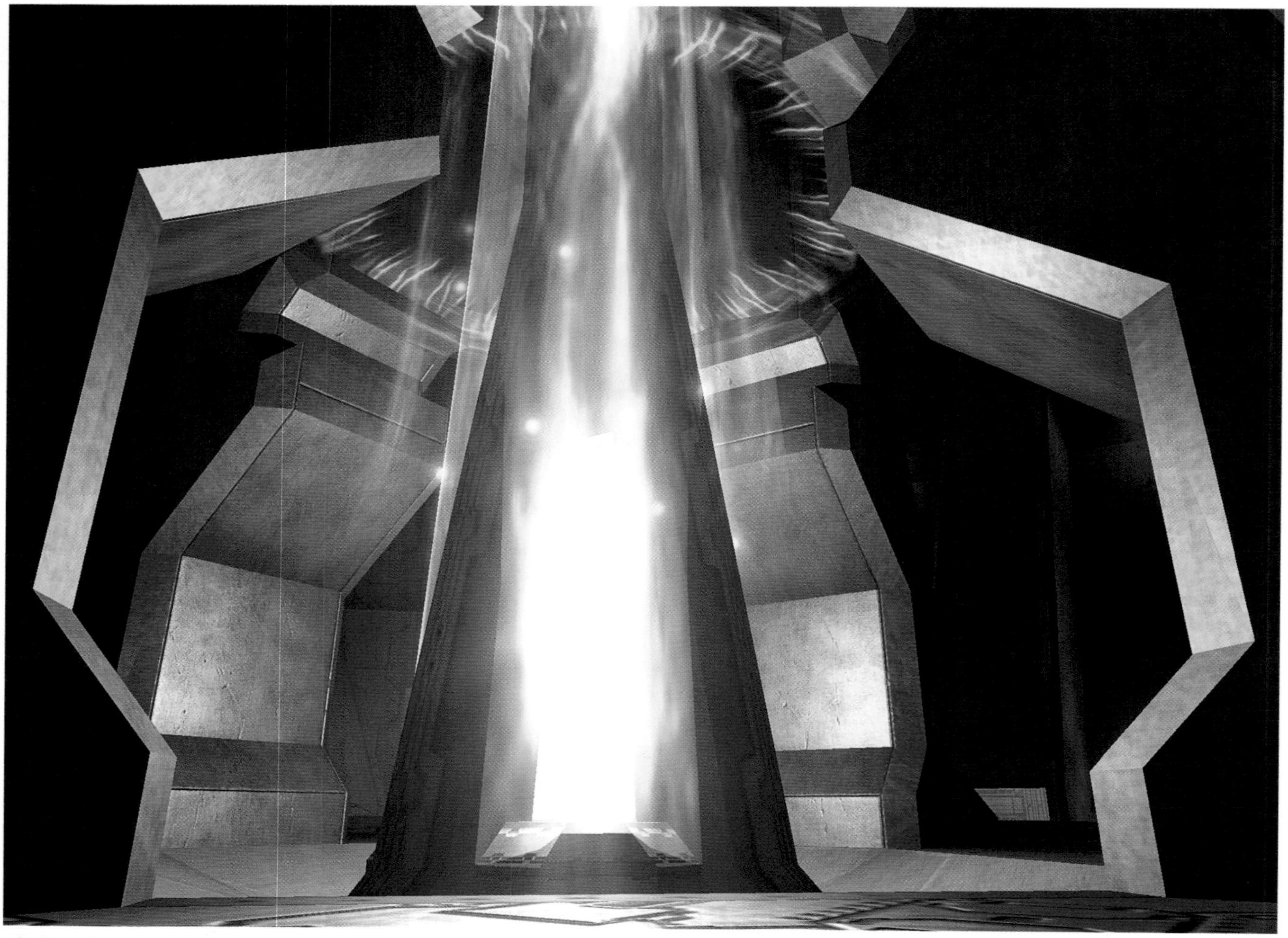

One of several generators one would find in the Forerunner ring structure called Halo.

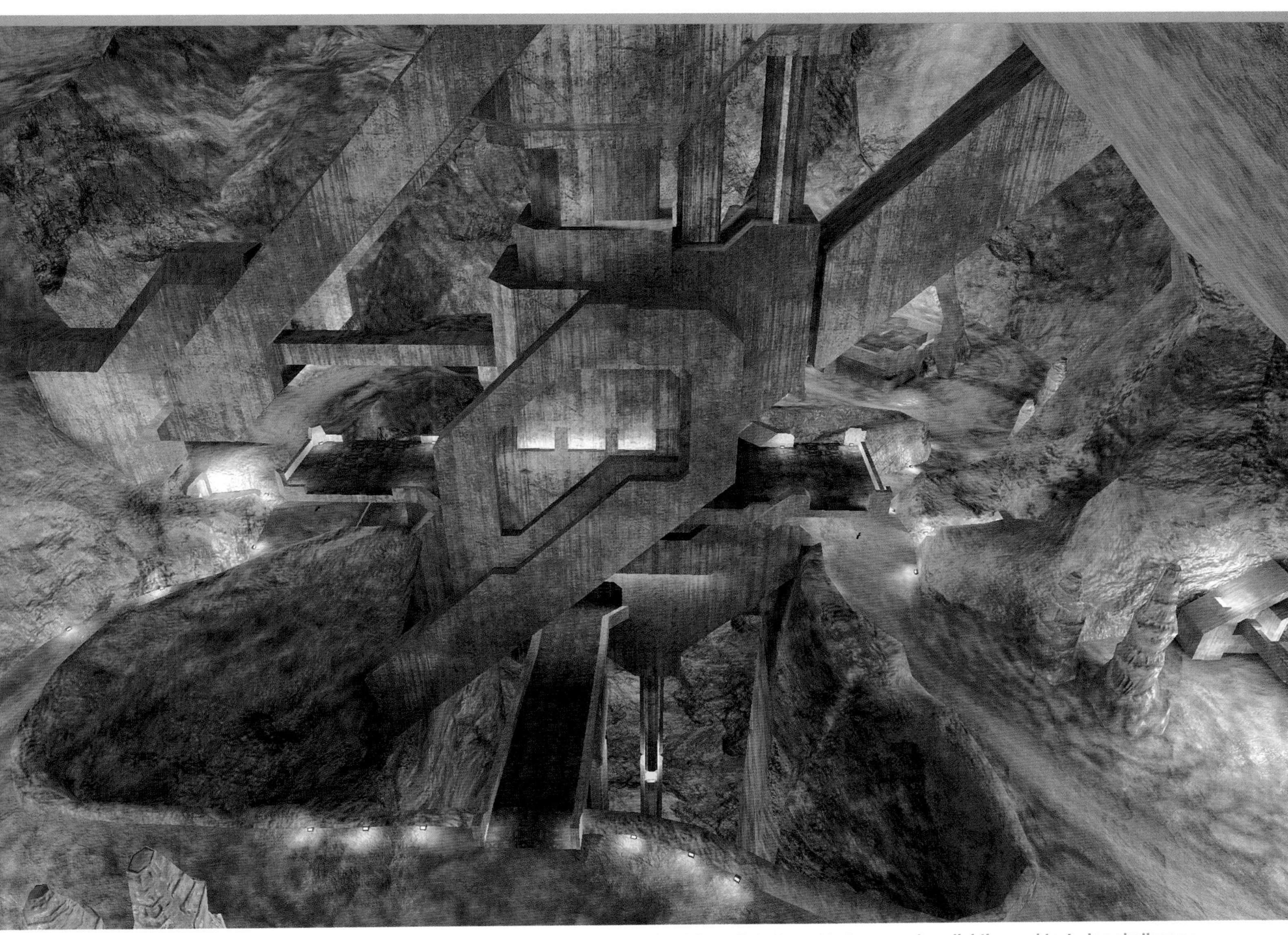

▲ The immense underground spaces of the "Waterworks" multiplayer level from *Halo 2* provided some unique lighting and texturing challenges, but stalactites and stalagmites glitter like real limestone.

A longtime Bungie artist, Paul Russel contributed a great deal to the *Halo* experience . . . including the game's name. "Believe it or not, I came up with the title 'Halo' back in Chicago." Russel chuckles. "I even have the original document that listed all of our working titles. We had something like thirty suggestions, and we couldn't come up with one we liked. Originally, the game was supposed to be set on this hollowed-out planet, but it morphed into the ring design. So I piped up and said, 'What about calling it *Project: Halo*—becauce of the ring?' Which is stupid and obvious, of course, but considering the source . . . " Russel shrugs. "I think Jones still prefers *Red Shift*."

"Everyone remembers it differently; I was *positive* everyone hated it. Someone said that consumers would be confused by the title and mistake it for some kind of religious game, or confuse it with *Messiah*. There was some concern that the word 'halo' doesn't exactly scream 'action.' All valid concerns, now that I think of it. Halo is a pretty stupid title for a game, isn't it?"

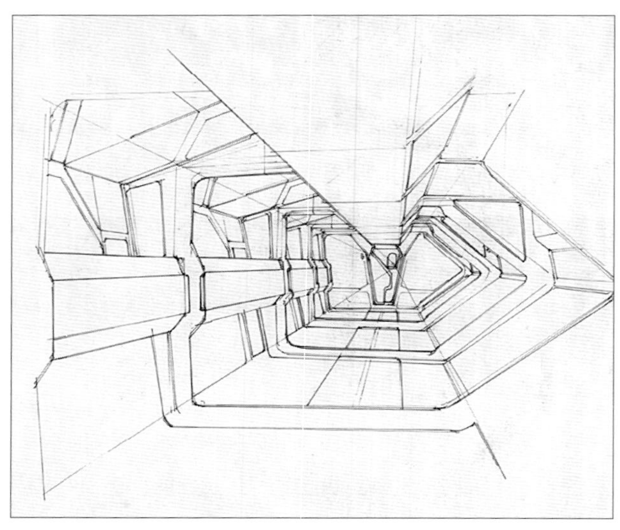

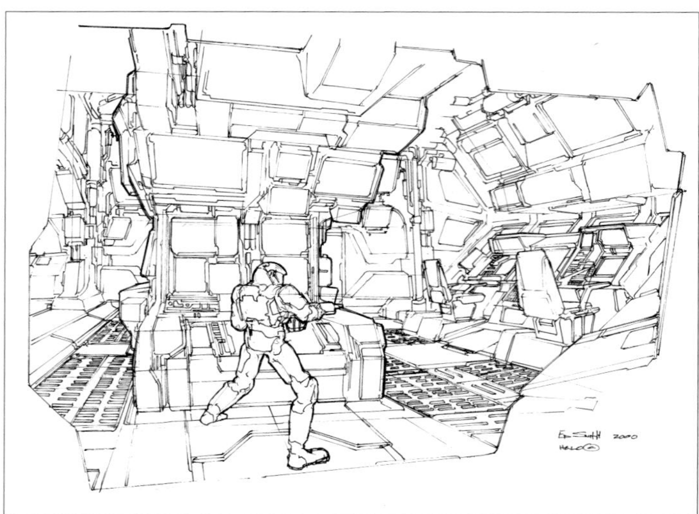

▲ The design team wanted a cramped, claustrophobic feel for "Human" levels (such as the interior of the *Pillar of Autumn*), as seen in these concept sketches by Eddie Smith.

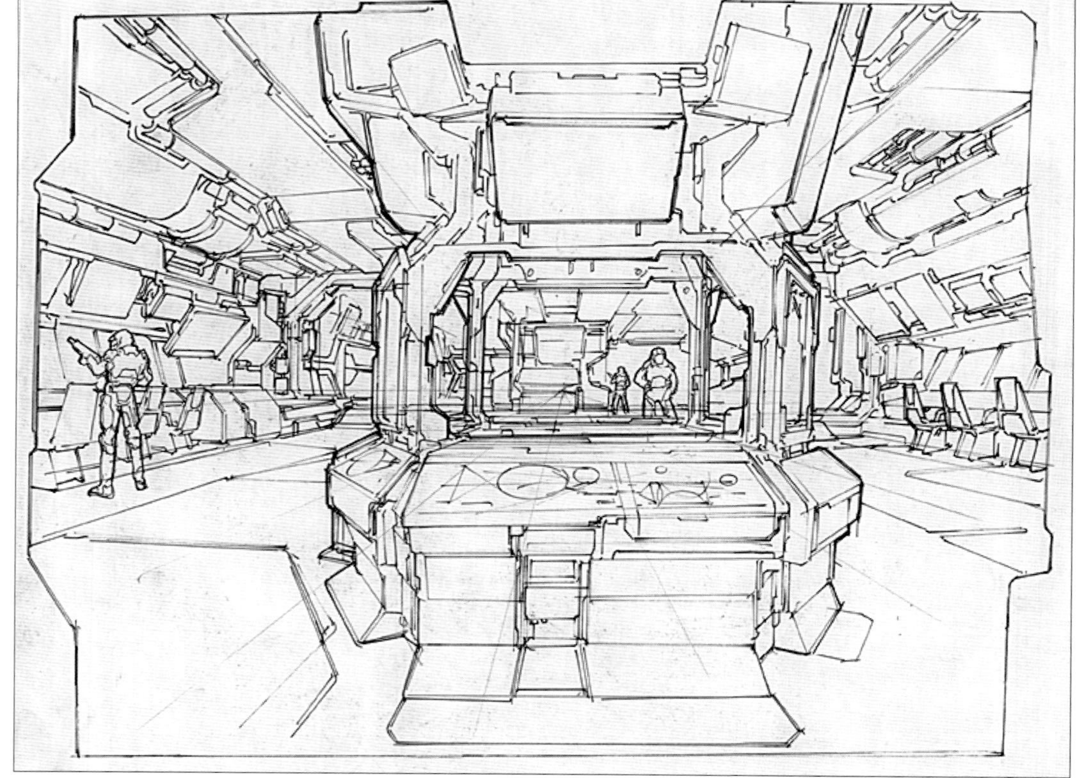

The Pillar of Autumn

The *Pillar of Autumn* is an old, battered human warship, the lone surviving vessel in the aftermath of a critical battle against the Covenant. With the alien enemy in hot pursuit, the *Autumn* stumbles across the ancient construct, known as "Halo."

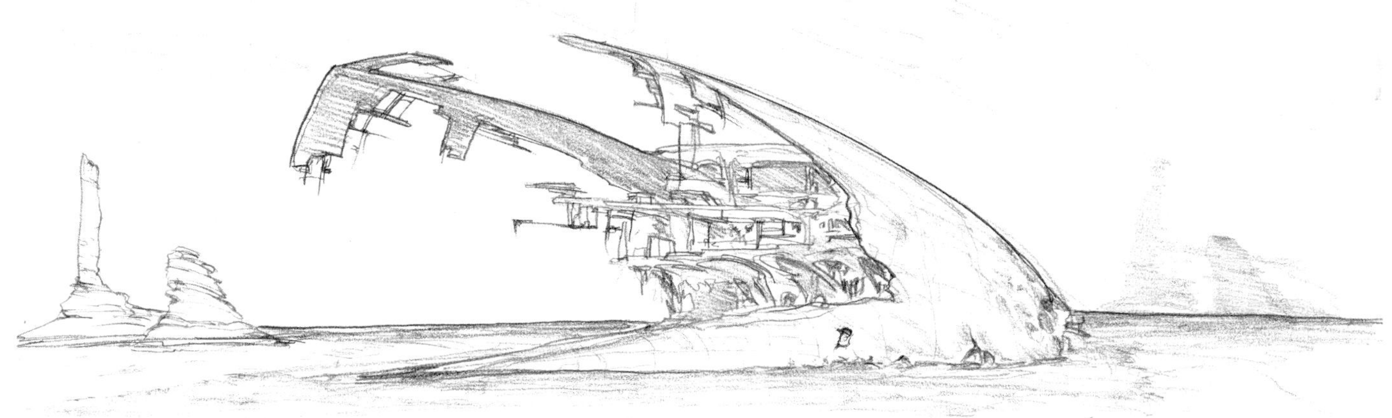

▲ Very early designs for the site of the *Pillar of Autumn*'s crash site on Halo. Concept art by Shi Kai Wang.

The first experience the player has in the first *Halo* game is exploring the *Pillar of Autumn*, so it was absolutely vital that the ship look as believable and interesting as possible. Drink vending machines line one wall near the mess deck; sly jokes can be found on the ship's bulletin boards ("For Sale: Chicago office," for example, a quip about Bungie's move to Redmond, Washington); color-coded arrows point the player to various locations within the ship, much like guide lines in a hospital. All of this detail helps create a believable, functional, lived-in environment.

Environment artist Paul Russel spearheaded the creation of the ship's interiors. "The work I did on the *Pillar of Autumn* came from looking at Ron Cobb's work on *Aliens*," Russel explains. "I won't call it anything cheesy like a 'homage' or anything; Cobb's work informed a lot of what I did on the *Autumn*. It was taking that future industrial look that Cobb did so brilliantly and riffing off of that, without turning it into a blatant swipe.

"The idea was to show things in a really functional way," he continues. "It all looks like it fits together, and the metal is done in these gunmetal greens and pale grays—it looks like something built by human hands."

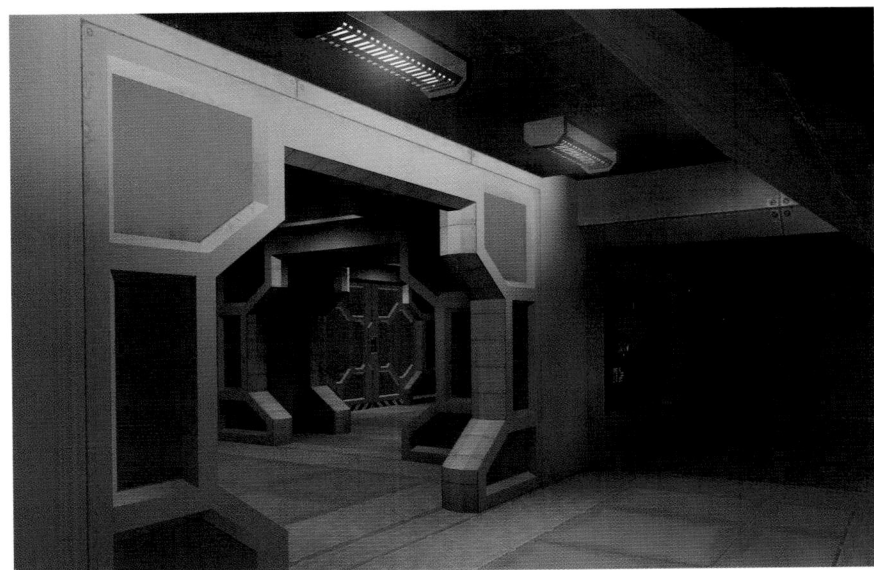

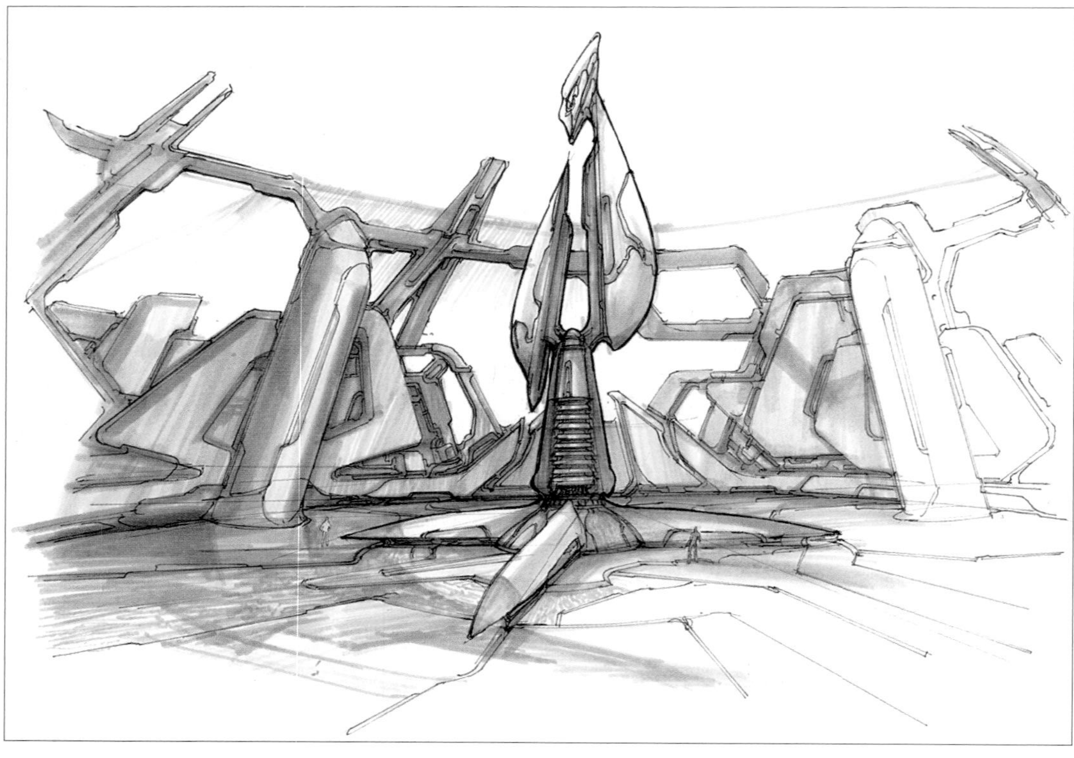

Design sketch of the Control Room on Halo. Art by Eddie Smith.

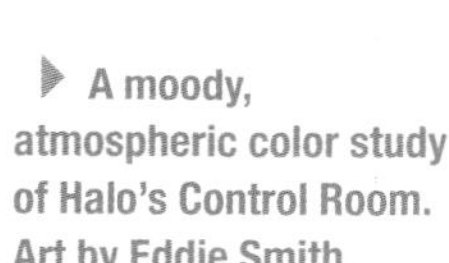

A moody, atmospheric color study of Halo's Control Room. Art by Eddie Smith.

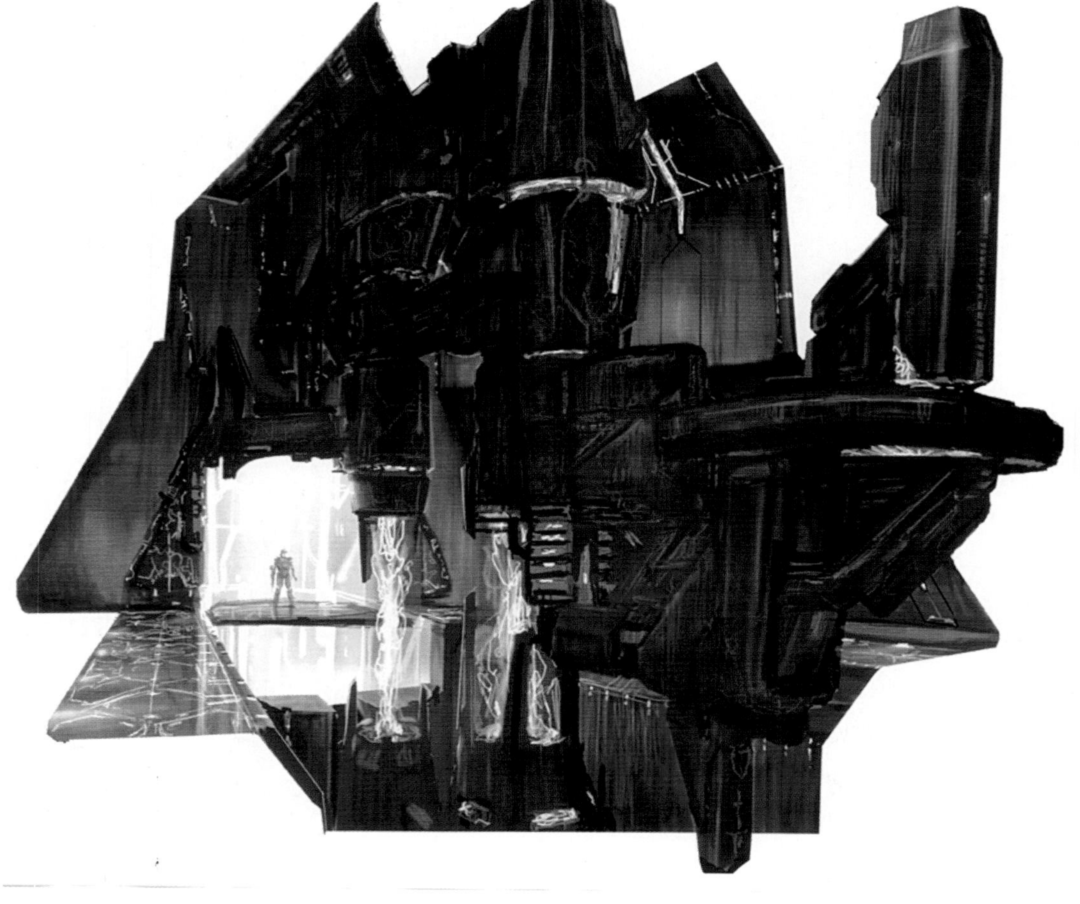

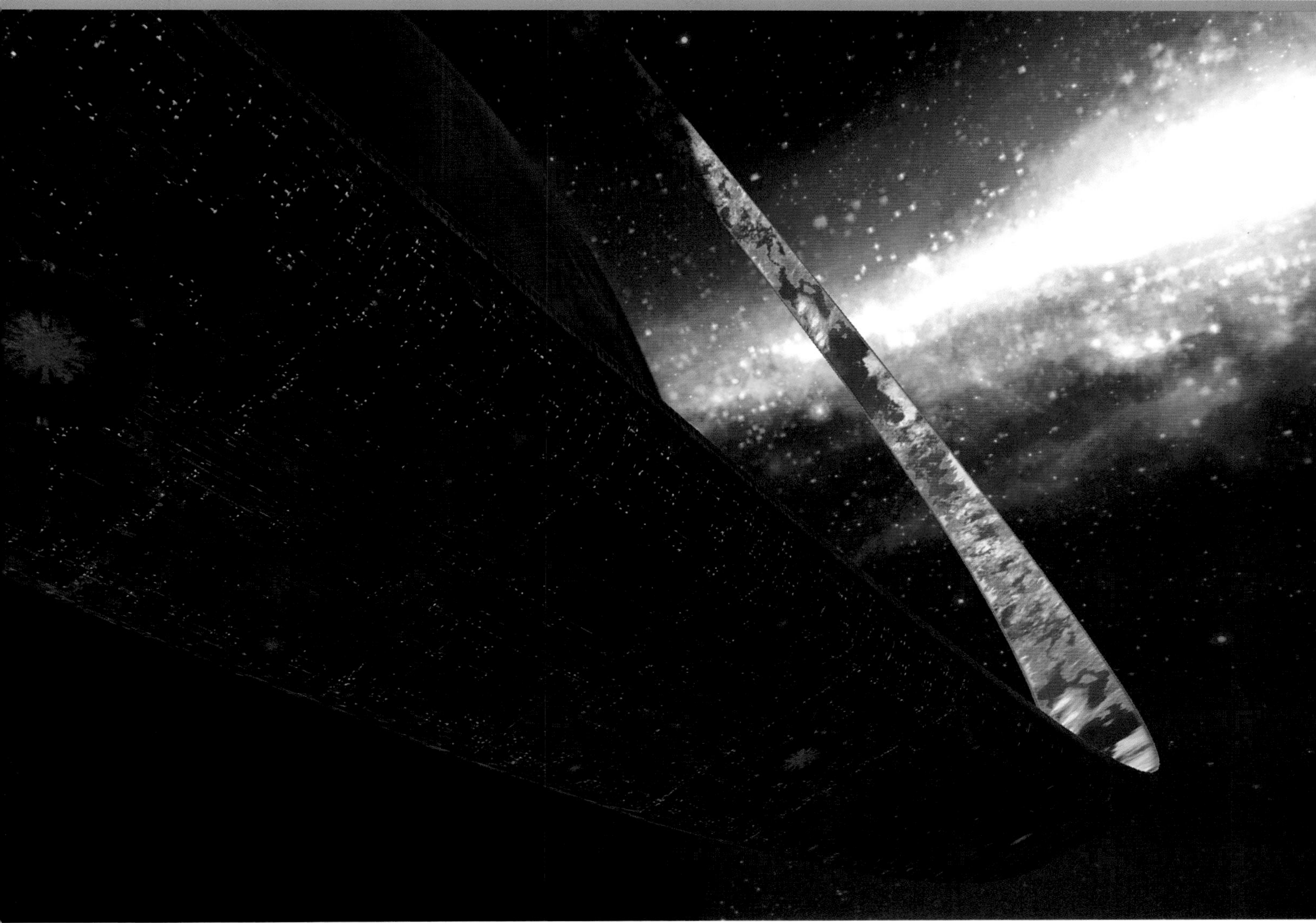

▲ Screen shot from *Halo.*

HALO

Built untold thousands of years ago by a superrace known only as the Forerunners, Halo becomes a pivotal battleground between the humans and the Covenant. The combatants believe that whoever controls Halo will possess a weapon of unimaginable power, enough to end the war. It is the exploration of Halo, and the unlocking of its many secrets, that drives the story.

Halo and the myriad Forerunner structures across its surface required the development of a visual language: the tenets of Forerunner architecture.

"To me, the ring itself was a 'character' in the game—an entity unto itself," says art director Marcus Lehto. "When we started, we had an idea of how the ring functioned, an idea of its scale, but that was about all. We started to come up with the visual language of the Forerunners, and from there we developed a better understanding of Halo."

During the process, noted painter Craig Mullins was tapped to provide matte and concept paintings, to help the environment artists hone their work. "The exterior surface took shape when Craig Mullins, an amazing painter, did some concept paintings," Lehto explains. "They were these amazing images showing the ring in various stages of 'disassembly'—one pristine, one kind of battle damaged, and one with the ring on fire and coming apart. From that we gleaned the surface texture and applied it to the 3-D model of the ring that appears in the game."

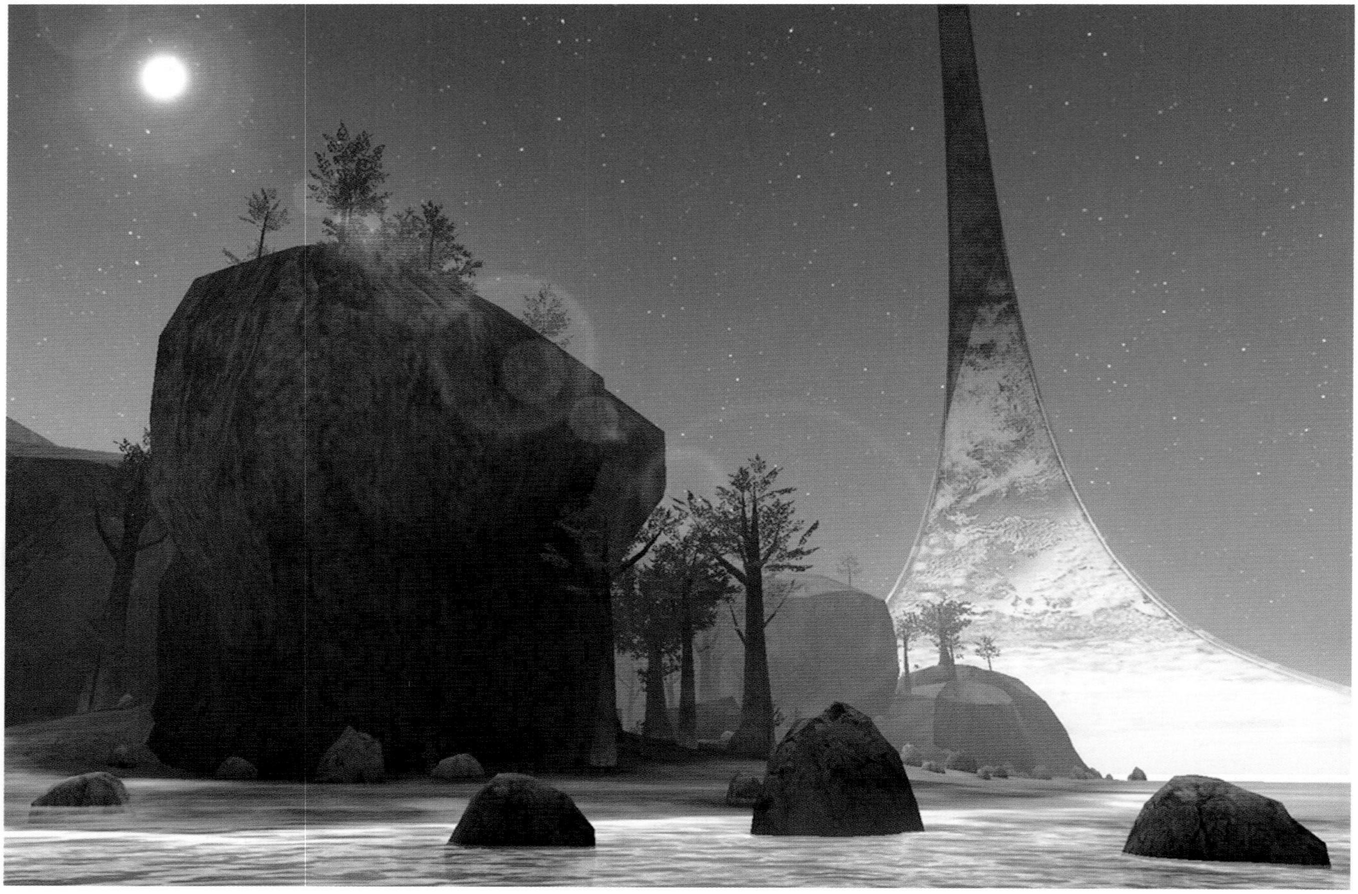

▲ Screen shot from *Halo*.

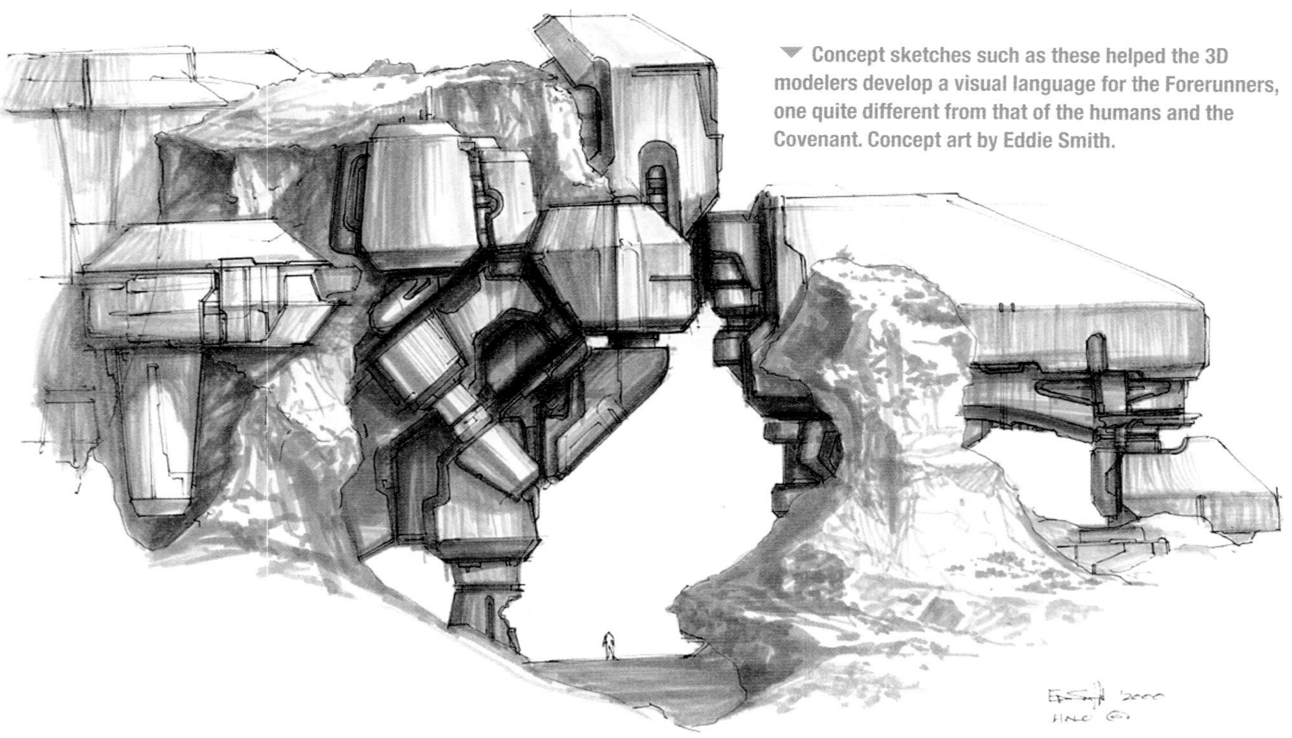

▼ Concept sketches such as these helped the 3D modelers develop a visual language for the Forerunners, one quite different from that of the humans and the Covenant. Concept art by Eddie Smith.

THE SILENT CARTOGRAPHER

"The Silent Cartographer" began as a test map—essentially the "box" everyone threw stuff in to examine; lighting, visibility, objects, effects, and so on.

Used for early demonstrations of the game, "The Silent Cartographer" ended up as one of the most memorable levels in *Halo*.

"In the case of the Forerunners," Marcus Lehto says, "I felt that the structures that we showed on the surface of Halo were simply the tip of the iceberg. The structures themselves were unique in and of themselves, but once you entered them and got below the surface, there was this deep, sprawling architecture filled with increasingly complex machinery."

Crafting the Forerunner visual language was a challenging process, as Paul Russel explains: "Forerunner architecture was created through a lot of trial and error. Back in Chicago, the original stuff was this insane hybrid of Louis B. Sullivan and Aztec. It wasn't until we were something like five months away from 'content complete' that we really made some breakthroughs with the look of Halo's interior structures. A lot of that stemmed from some great concept illustrations by Eddie Smith."

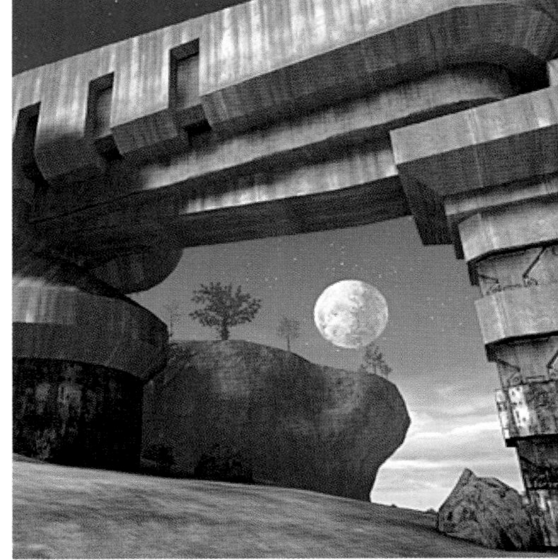

▲ Screen shot from *Halo*.

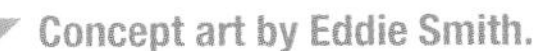

▼ Concept art by Eddie Smith.

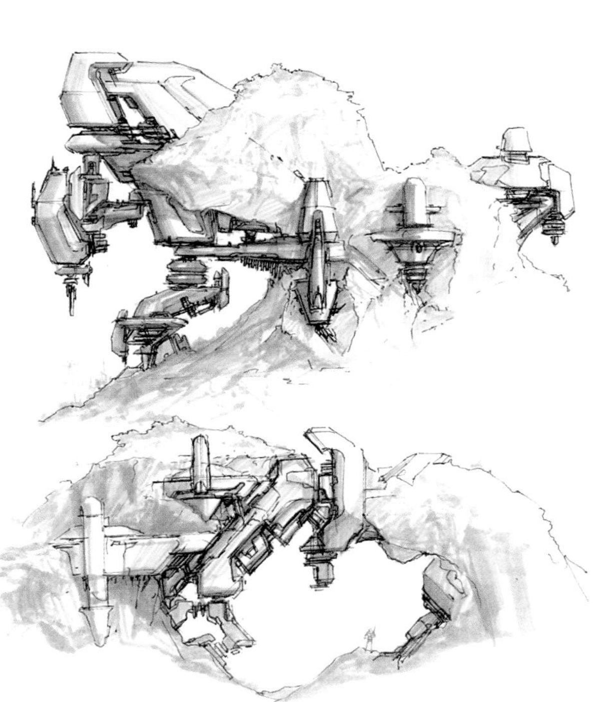

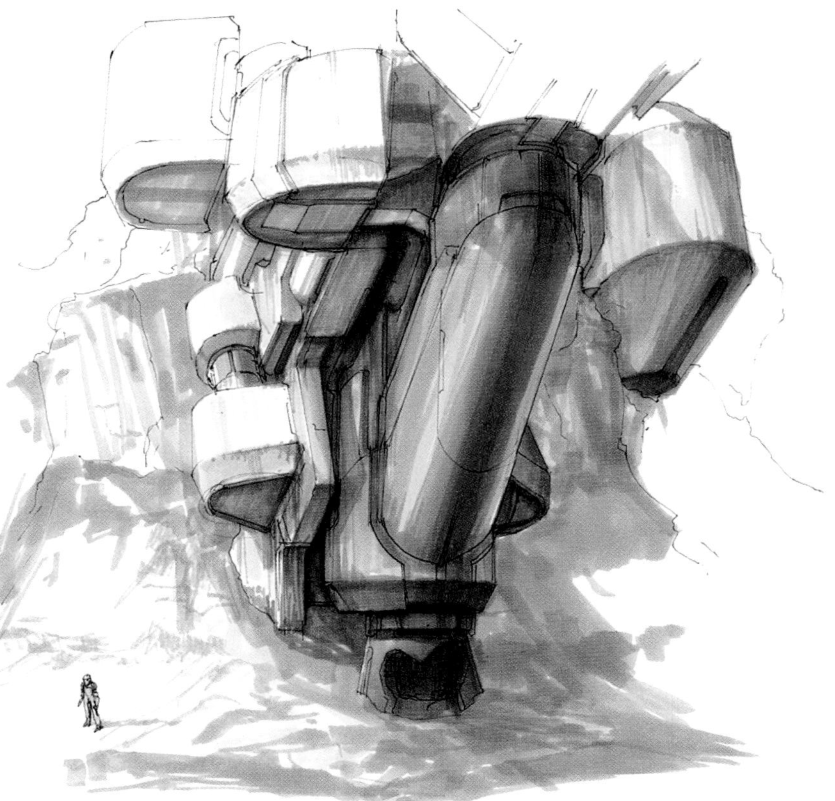

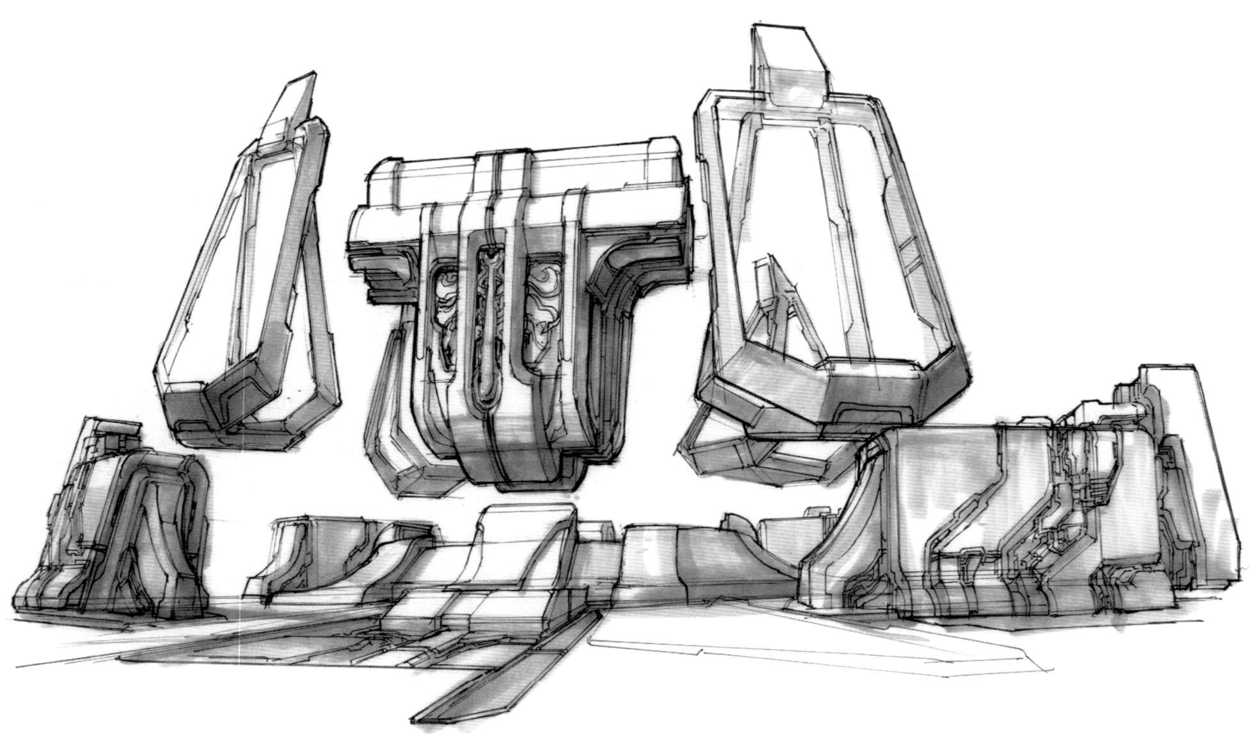

▲ **The seamless solidity of Forerunner architecture is imposing, yet elegant, eschewing details like pipes and wires, and yet it is often delicately inscribed with mysterious decorative patterns. Concept art by Eddie Smith.**

"The Forerunner visual language didn't really come together for me until I worked on the level that became 'The Silent Cartographer' in *Halo*—the 'beach landing' level."

On "The Silent Cartographer" level, the Master Chief and a platoon of Marines engage a Covenant beachhead—complete with ocean surf churning on a realistic sandy beach—and discover a massive underground complex of incredible scope.

"There's all these crazy-looking structures sticking out of the ground and the cliffs in all these strange angles," Russel continues. "But as you enter the buildings, the look of the Forerunner architecture really started to evolve the deeper inside the buildings you went. I just kept improving and refining the more I worked on the level. By the time I hit the bottom, the Forerunner look really gelled."

Artist Eddie Smith—who has done concept art for *Halo* and *Halo 2*, as well as a number of related illustrations—recalls his work on the Forerunner architecture. "When I started doing concept sketches for *Halo*, there wasn't any real mandate or direction . . . I just wanted to give the environment team some kind of starting point," he says. "There was this kind of vague, preconceived notion about how it should all look, but there was nothing concrete.

"The first thing I did was look at the story synopsis, and just started sketching based on what was written on the page. I knew what human and Covenant architecture looked like, so I tried to make the Forerunner concepts different—which suited my style just fine. I like to think of it as this kind of 'streamlined industrial.'"

For *Halo 2*, the artists have the unenviable task of topping their predecessor, of taking the look and feel of Forerunner architecture into new territory, without abandoning the style established by Russel. "The environment artists are taking the Forerunner stuff in a more elaborate direction than we could in *Halo*," Russel says, "which is really exciting—to see what these guys can do."

Environment artist Frank Capezzuto adds: "I had to really adjust to how the Forerunner stuff looks. My design style is very industrial, so my normal instincts to throw in cables and pipes, conduits, boxes, and so on had to be overcome.

"Once I started looking at Forerunner structures as individual sculptures, rather than more conventional buildings, it began to click. It took a while to adjust, but the result is, to me, very appealing aesthetically."

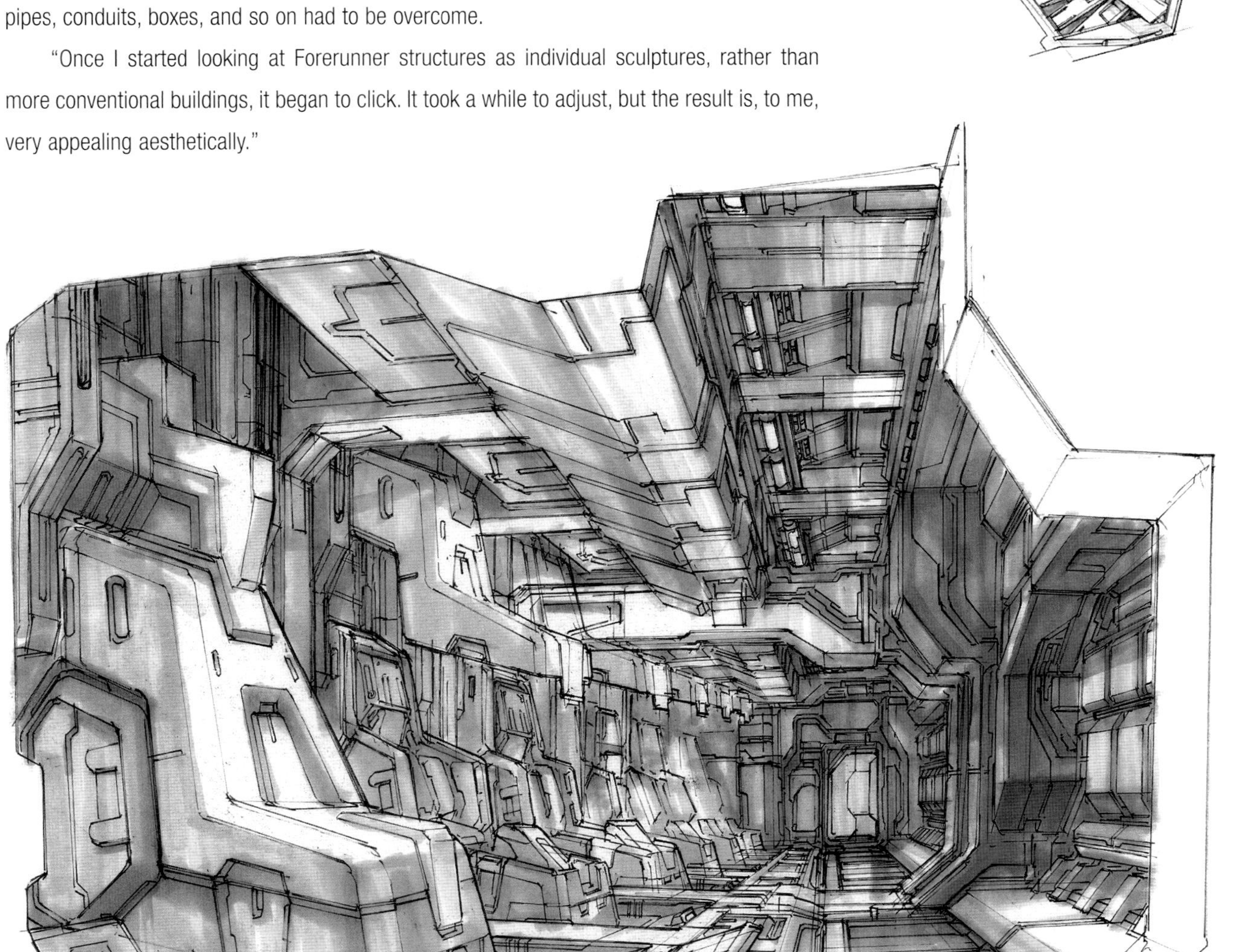

▲ **Concept art by Eddie Smith.**

▲ The "Swamp" level's gloom means that players have to pay close attention to their motion trackers—forcing a gameplay homage to the *Aliens* movie.

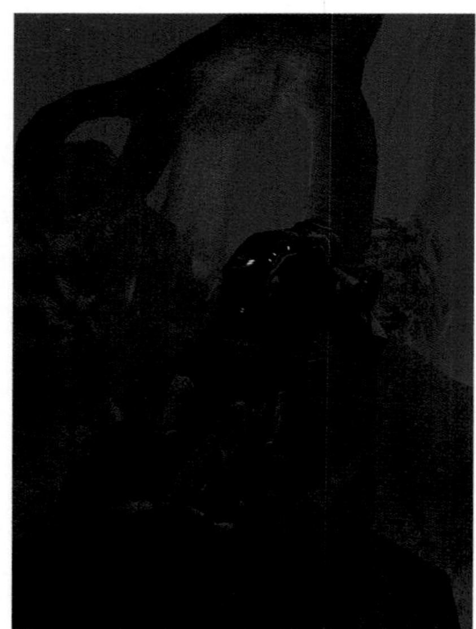

▲ Treating this mangrovelike swamp tree more like a character than an object led to its twisted and menacing aspect.

SWAMPS

In addition to the Forerunner architecture, the Halo construct features a number of different, seemingly natural terrain types: icy glacier fields, verdant grasslands, rolling hills, and even stagnant, vine-choked swamps. Each location type offered up unique challenges that the art team had to overcome.

"For me, probably one of the best parts of working on *Halo* was the 'evil tree,'" environment artist Michael Wu explains. "I was working on the swamp environment, thinking that the player would spend a lot of time in and around these twisted, gnarled trees. I was kind of pulled in late in the process, and there was this constant sense of being underwater—worried about the deadline.

"So I built this tree, and I was panicking a bit because all I had to show for my time thus far was this one tree. Eric Arroyo came in and really helped me out. He treated my evil tree as a character. It was very eye-opening."

Artist Eric Arroyo recalls: "I helped out Michael Wu on the swamp levels. Michael can really build 3D models, but he doesn't draw. So part of the process of building the environment is knowing what to show and what not to, which sketches can really help with.

"So when I came in to help him out, he gave me this incredibly twisted, gnarled tree, a 3D model that was just insanely complex. I had to work with it a lot, so it held up to close scrutiny—since the player would spend a lot of time on and around these trees—without it being so complex that we couldn't manipulate it."

Forerunner swamp structural concept art by Shi Kai Wang.

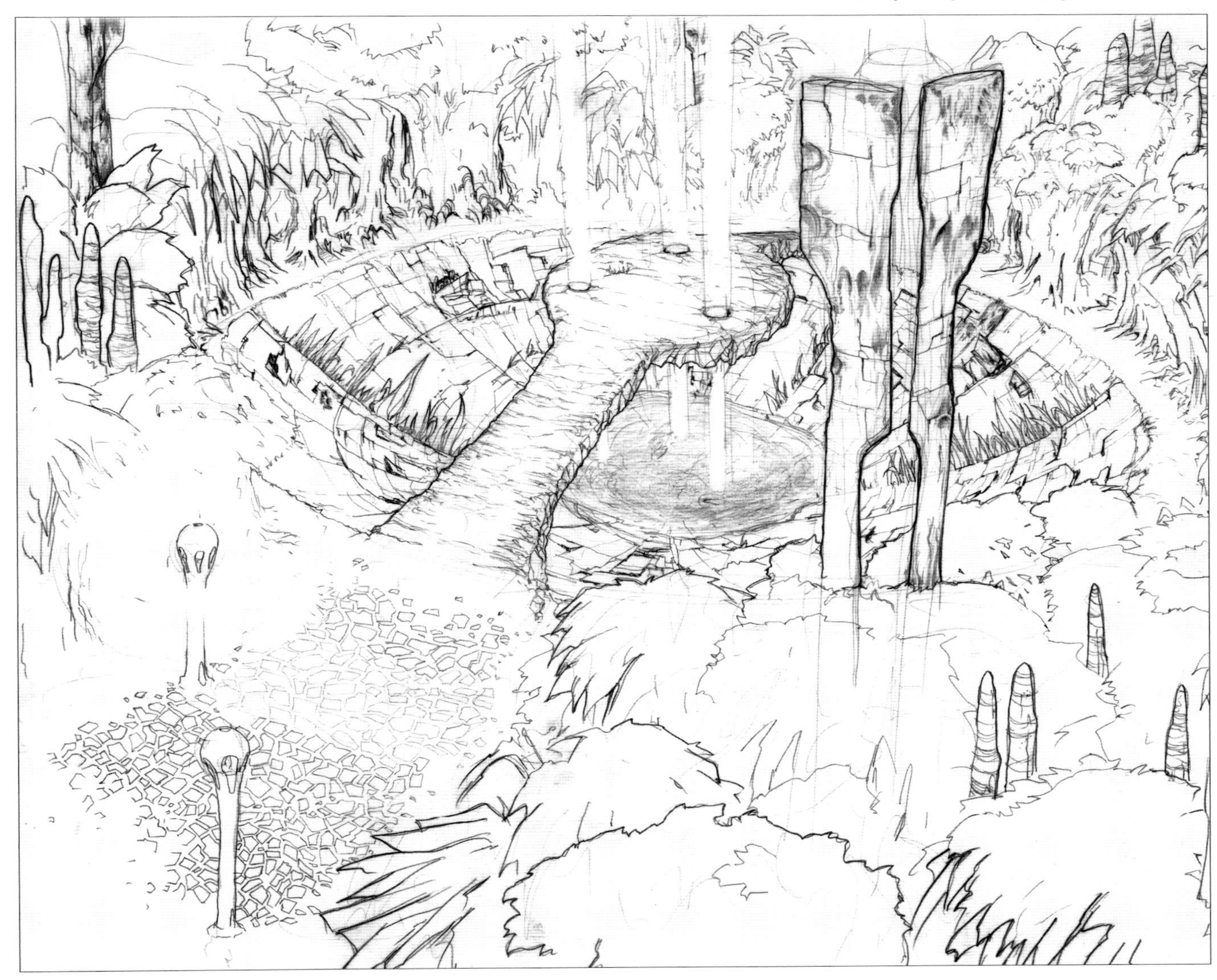

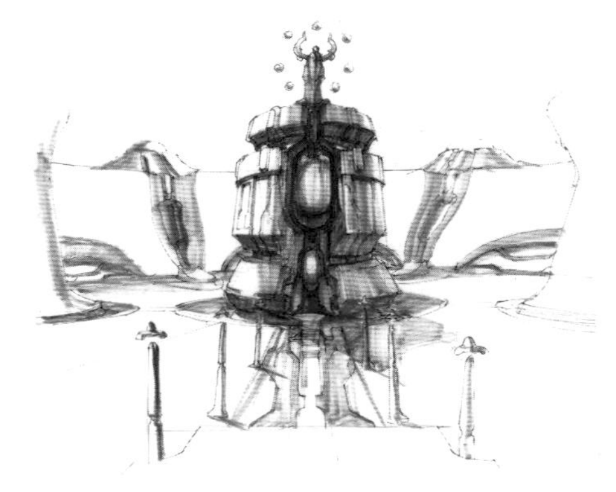

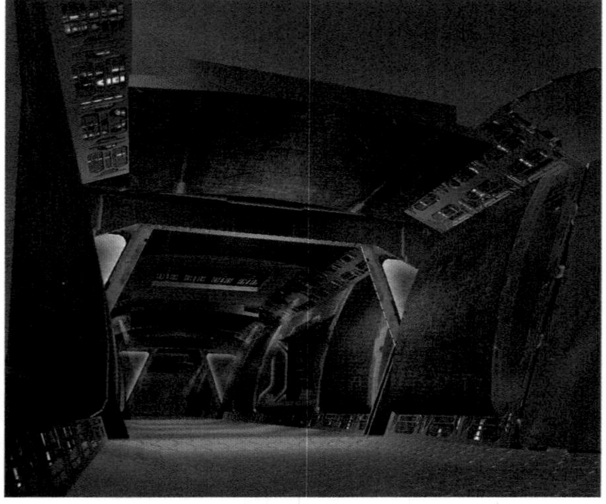

▲ Organic shapes, pearlescent lighting, and occasionally gaudy colors give the Covenant ship *Truth and Reconciliation* an unmistakably alien sheen.

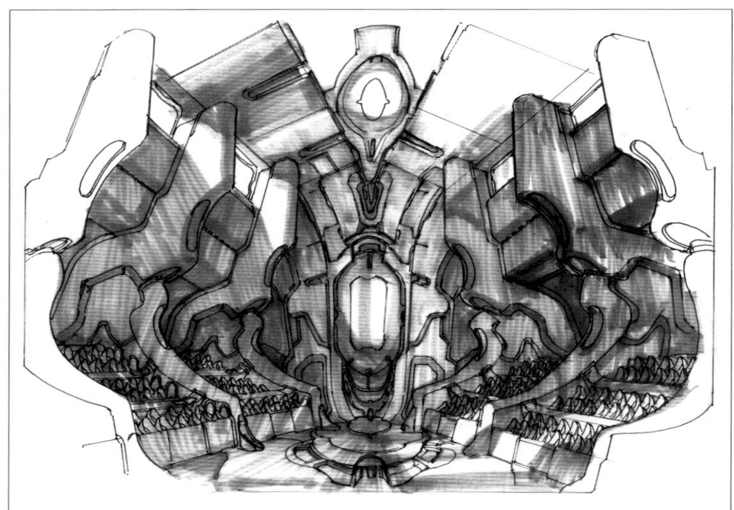

▲ Art by Eddie Smith.

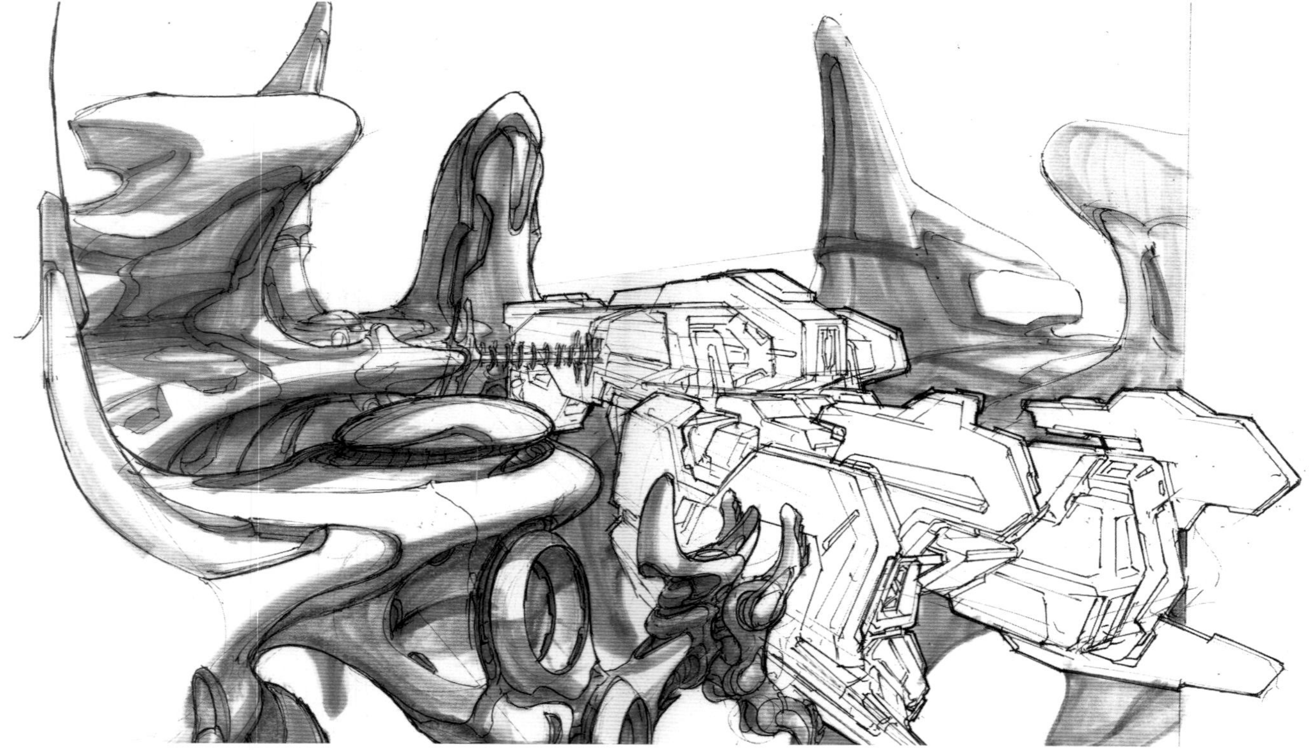

COVENANT ENVIRONMENTS

Halo's primary menace, the deadly alien collective called the Covenant, needed a unique look to differentiate it from the Forerunner environments. The artists decided on sleek, curved, organic-looking structures, all very shiny (to capitalize on the Xbox hardware's graphics processing power).

The color scheme—unlike the subdued Forerunner architecture—was comparatively garish, and a subtle, pearlescent sheen gives Covenant interiors a nearly insectlike appearance.

To showcase the Covenant environments, the game designers sent the Master Chief on a rescue mission into the heart of a Covenant warship, the cruiser known as *Truth and Reconciliation.*

"I worked on the '*Truth and Reconciliation'* level—where the player has to board a Covenant ship," Eric Arroyo says. "The initial plan was to have a ramp that you walk up to get into the alien ship—so the ship itself was supposed to be low to the ground.

"But the ship was so big, we didn't want people to get too close to it—it would have required so much detail. So we came up with the idea of the grav lift—the beam of purple and white energy that whisks you up inside. That way, the ship could hover much higher. Plus, the gravity lift was just so visually interesting.

"That's a great illustration of how the various disciplines interact: The gravity lift solved one problem, and ended up affecting the overall design of the level. That's one of the best things about this project and Bungie in general: the cross-pollination of ideas."

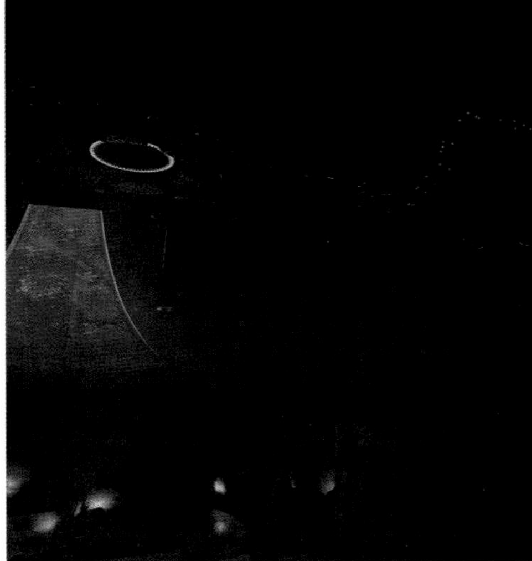

▲ **Covenant technology includes grav lifters on many scales, from the engines of Ghosts to the grav lifter pictured here—big enough to lift vast numbers of people, vehicles, and equipment.**

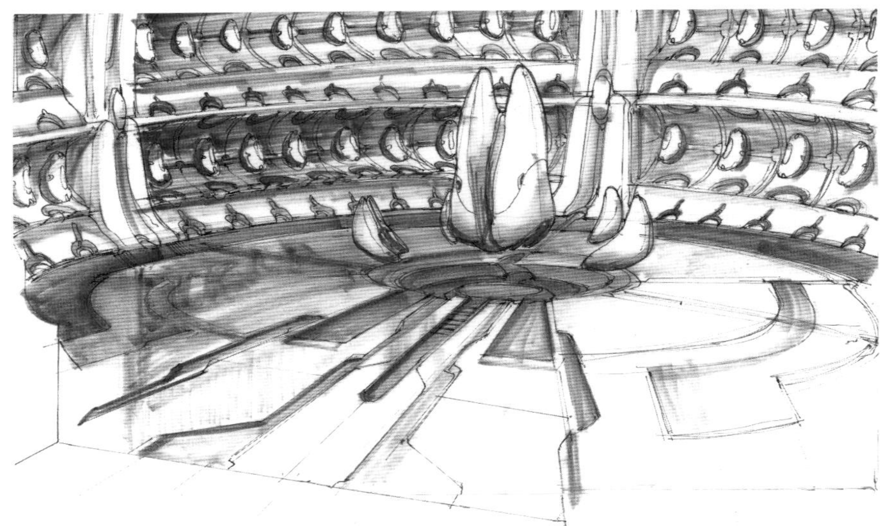

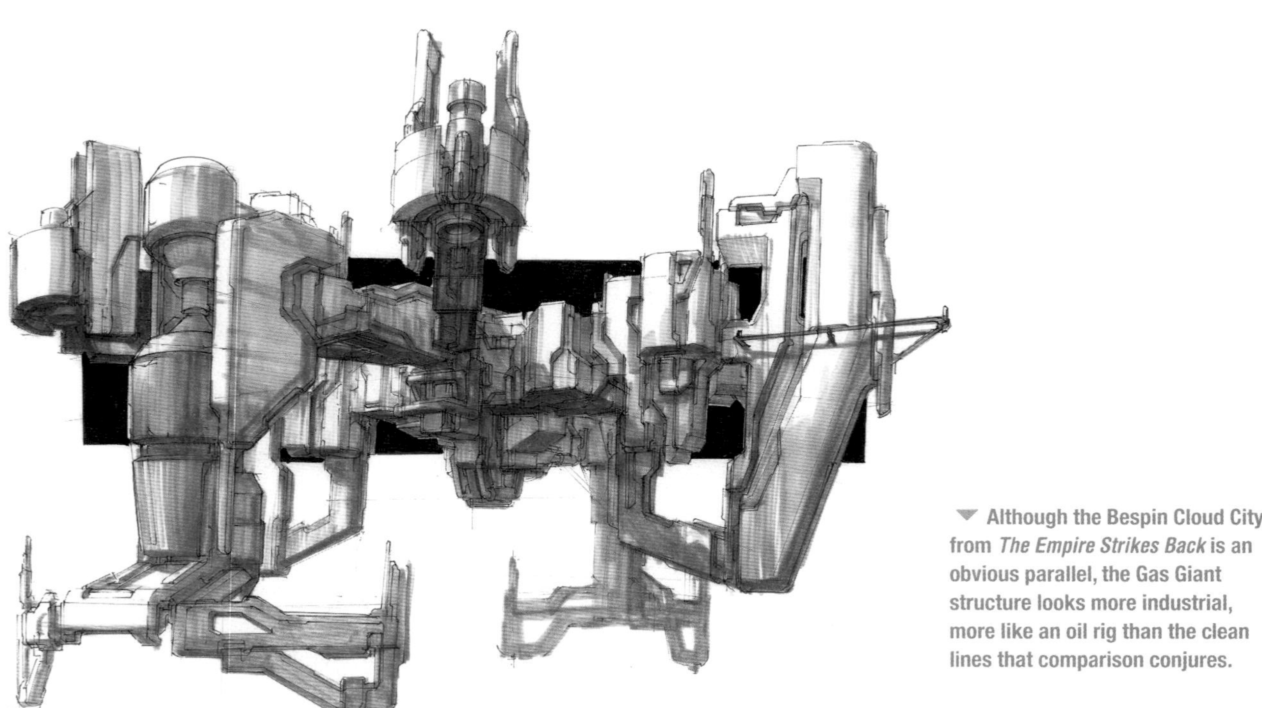

▼ Although the Bespin Cloud City from *The Empire Strikes Back* is an obvious parallel, the Gas Giant structure looks more industrial, more like an oil rig than the clean lines that comparison conjures.

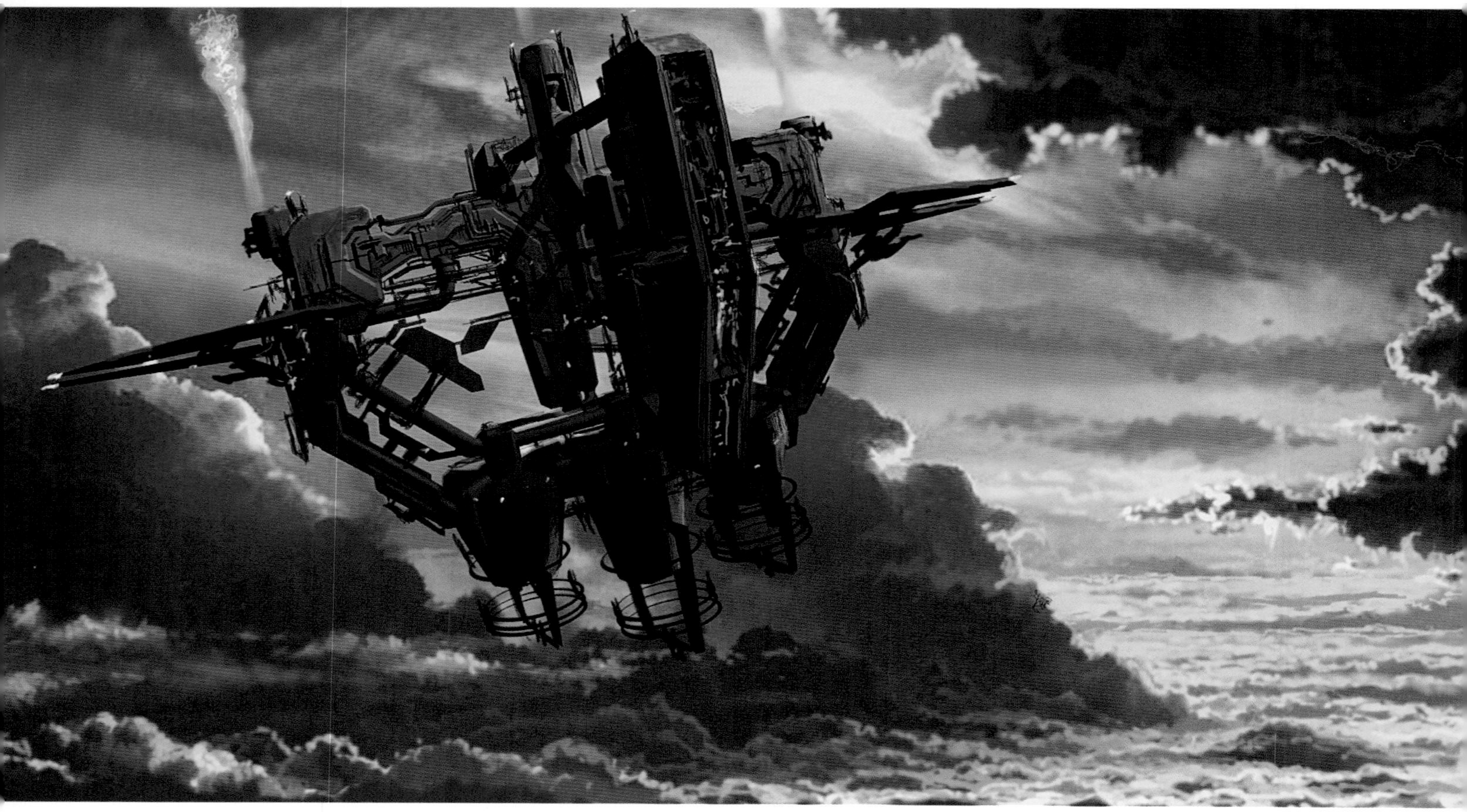

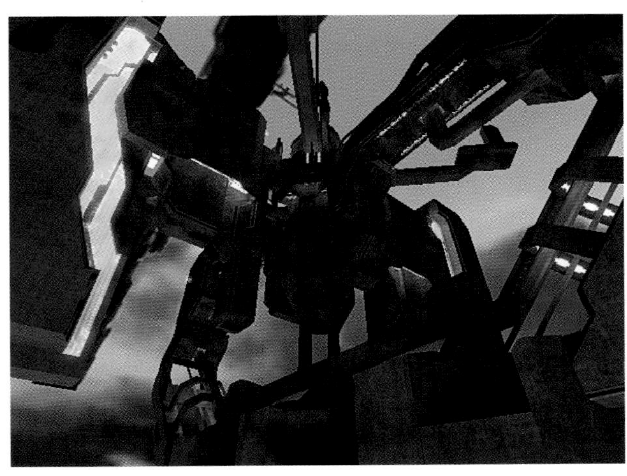

GAS GIANT

The gas mine is one of many suspended in the depths of the Gas Giant Threshold, the planet around which Halo once orbited. However, these facilities predate Halo by thousands of years. More industrial in nature, they operated autonomously for millennia, with only a handful of Sentinels to maintain them.

But when the Flood was first encountered, the Forerunners retrofitted some of these gas mines to study the parasite. Dangling from a support superstructure higher in the atmosphere, the mines could be detached in the event of an outbreak. The Forerunners captured and stored countless specimens in their desperate search for any defense against the Flood.

All that they learned was that more extreme measures would be necessary.

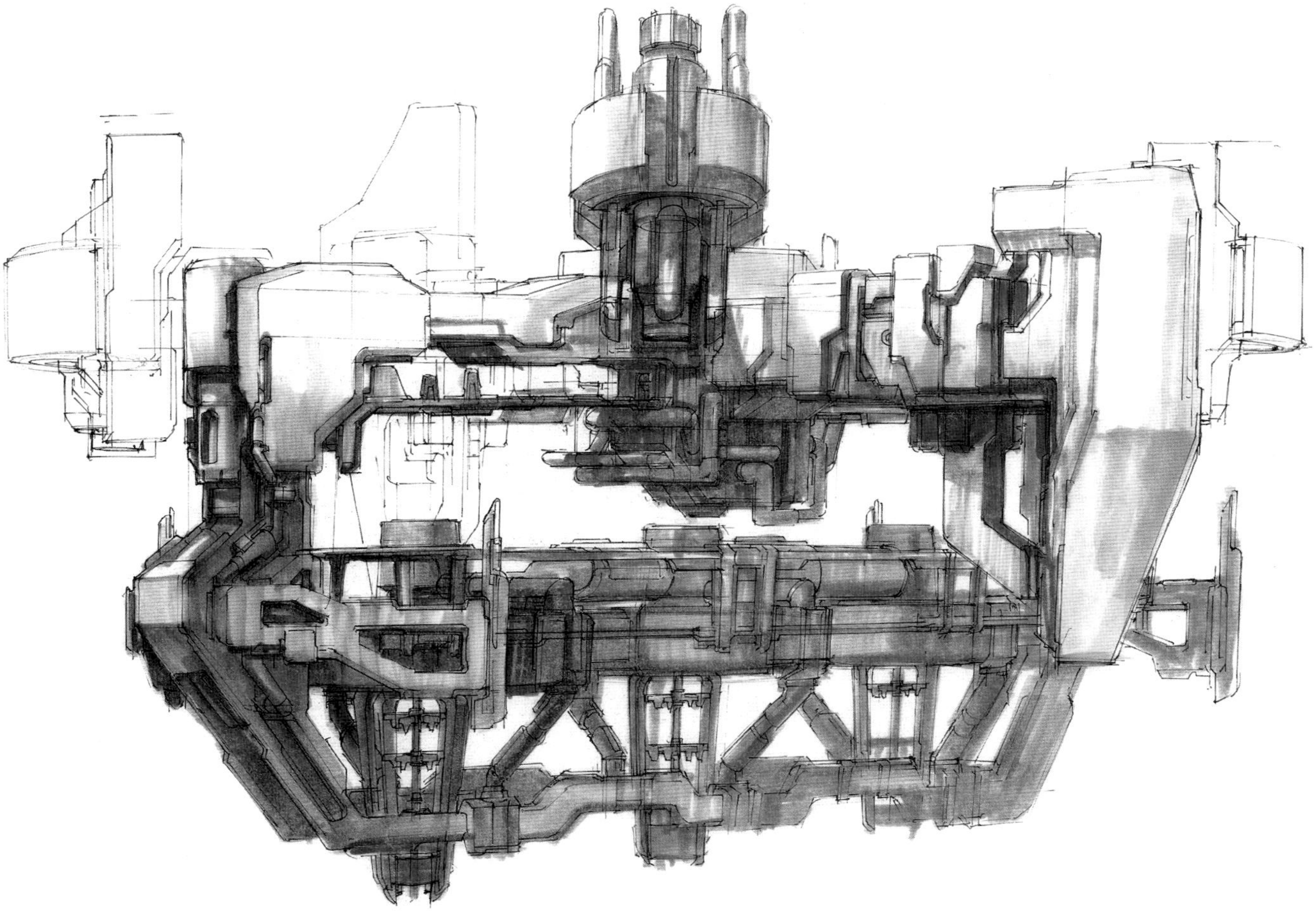

▲ Concept art by Eddie Smith.

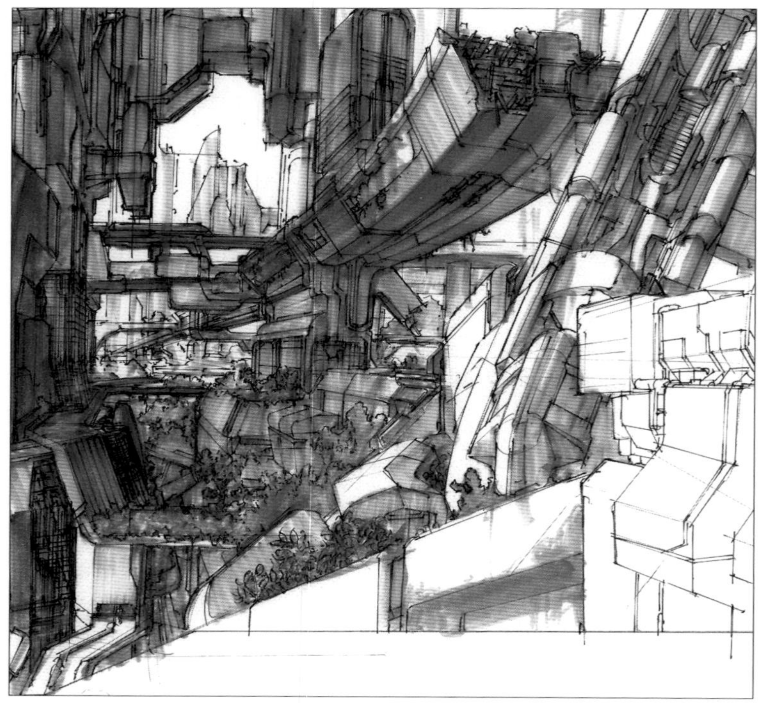

◀ ▼ Early sketches focus on the space tether, the single most visible structure in New Mombasa.

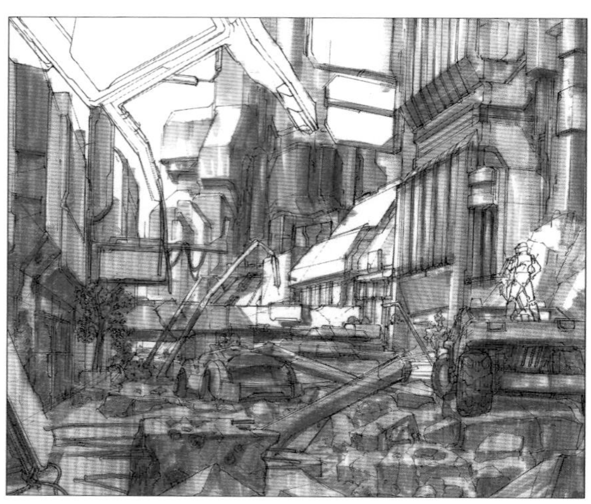

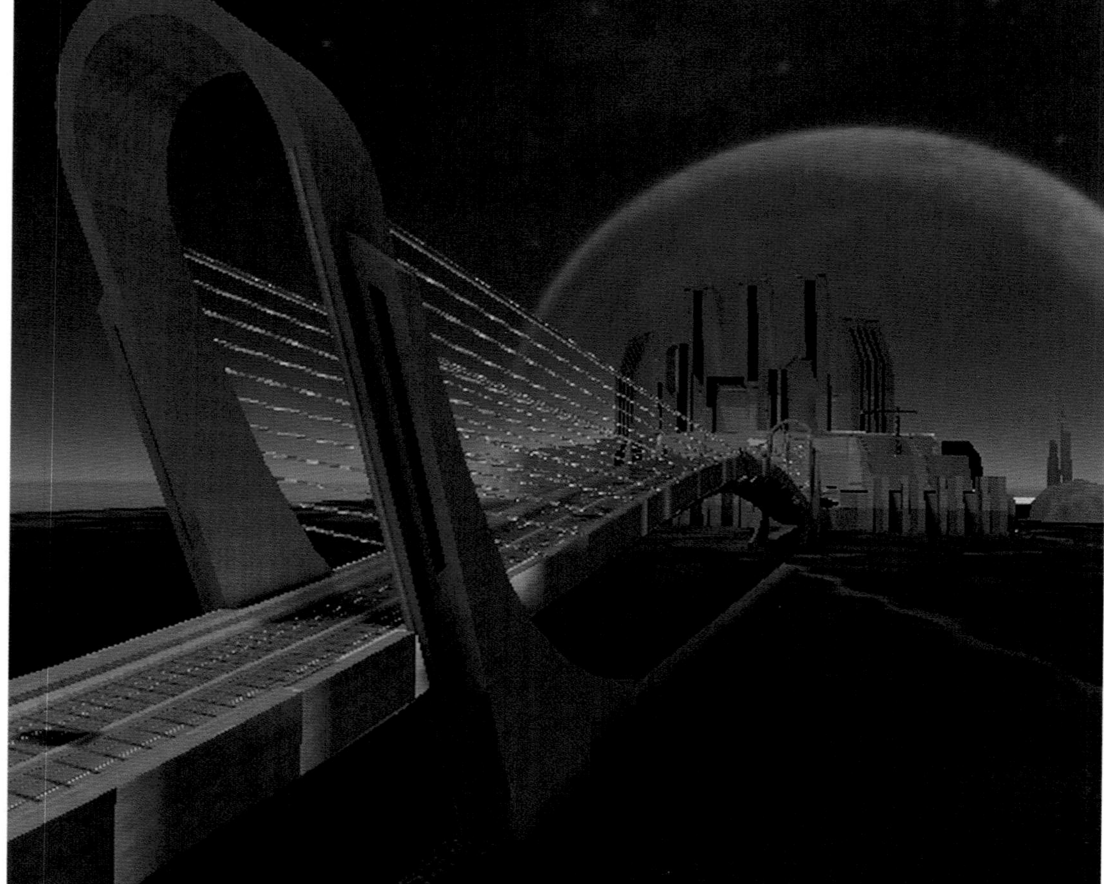

▶ The bridge is as much a location as an object. Major battles take place on this massive suspension structure.

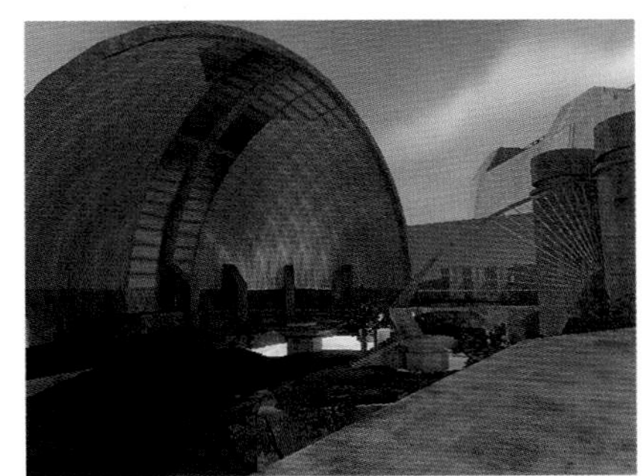

New Mombasa gives way to Old Mombasa, with smaller, warrenlike mazes of streets and alleyways and more traditional takes on African architecture.

NEW MOMBASA

The East African megalopolis of New Mombasa is of course based on a real geographic location. However, this vision of the city as it might appear in 2552 is a far cry from the palm-fringed, hotel-strewn beaches of today's Kenyan coast. In 2552, the location's proximity to the equator makes it an ideal location for a freight- and trade-carrying space "tether," a colossal elevator structure designed to efficiently get manpower and matériel into orbit.

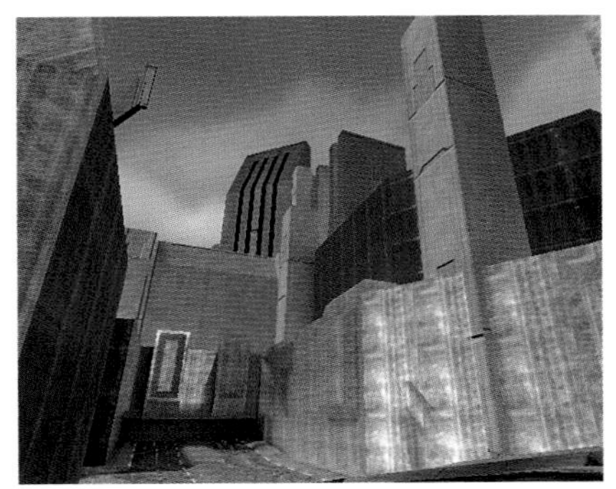

The economic and strategic importance of New Mombasa is reflected in the scale and scope of the city as envisioned by Bungie. Clearly industrial and practical, the city is still strewn with parks, gardens, and other more bucolic and attractive structures. Far from the distopian visions seen in movies like *Blade Runner* and *The Fifth Element*, New Mombasa incorporates attractive, practical architecture with a clean, expressive aesthetic.

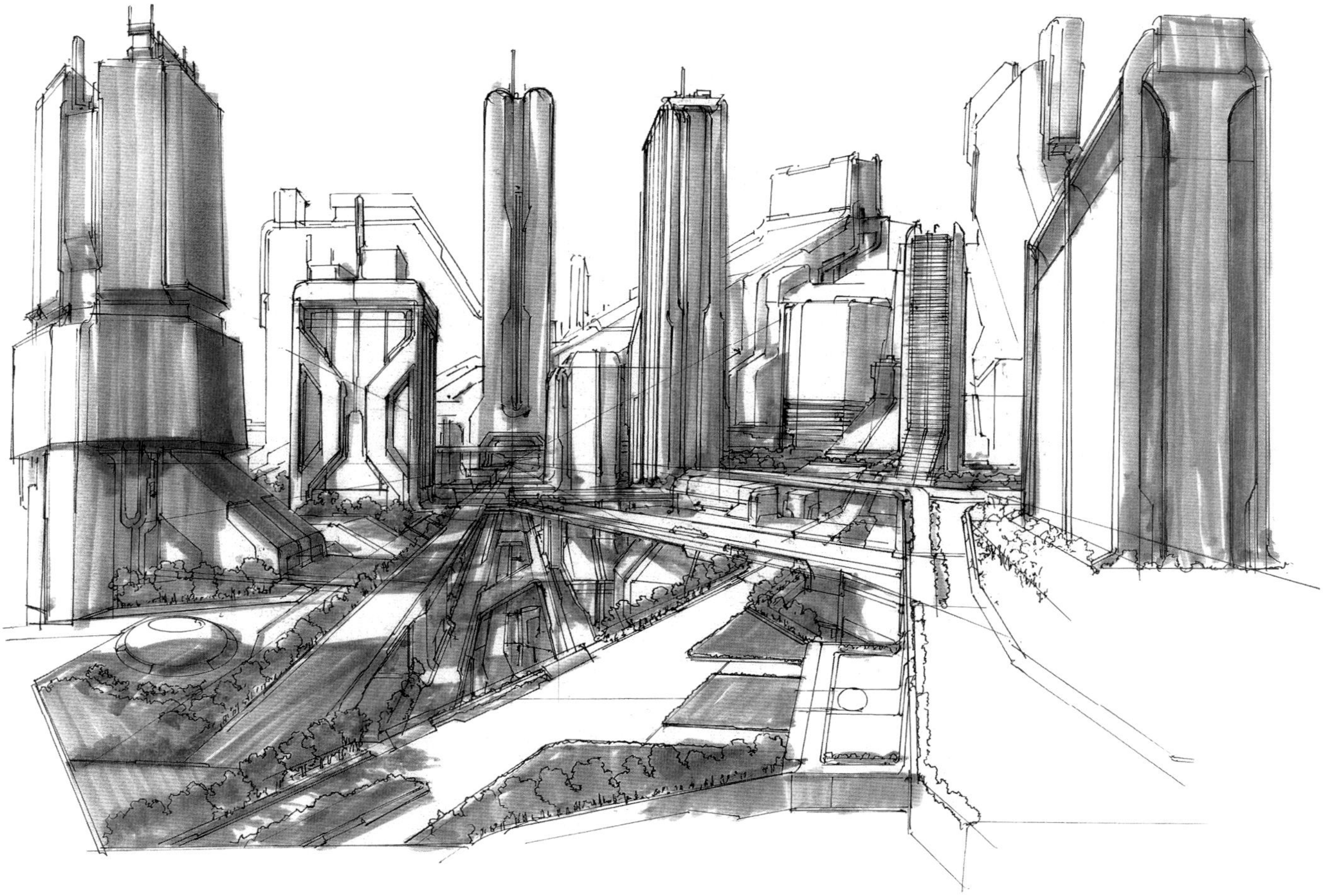

HUMAN ARCHITECTURE

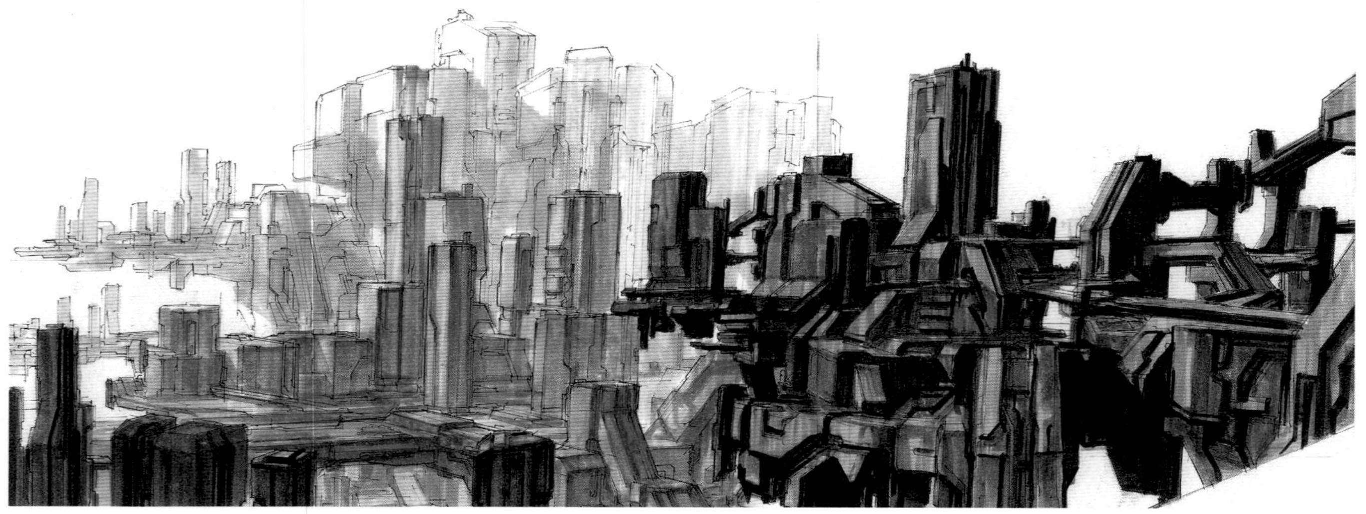

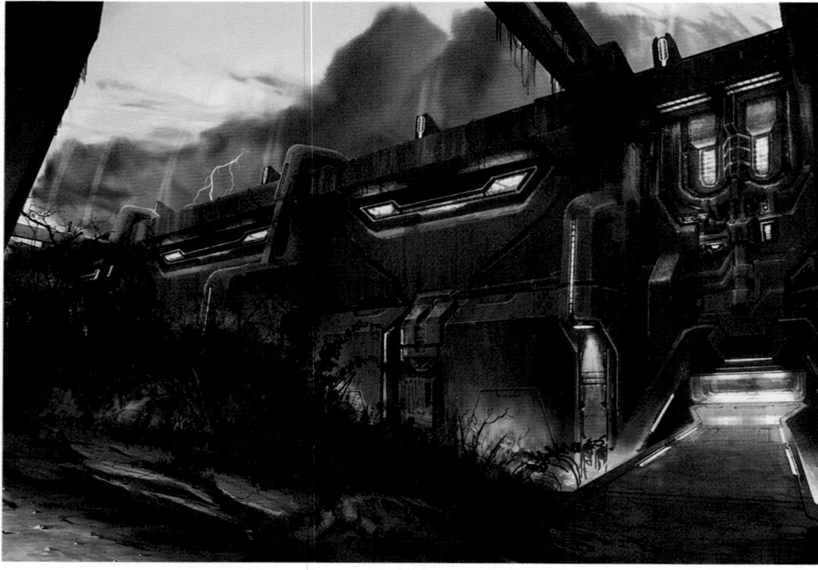

▲ This concept painting does an excellent job of showing how architecture makes little attempt to blend with the landscape, and yet still somehow complements it.

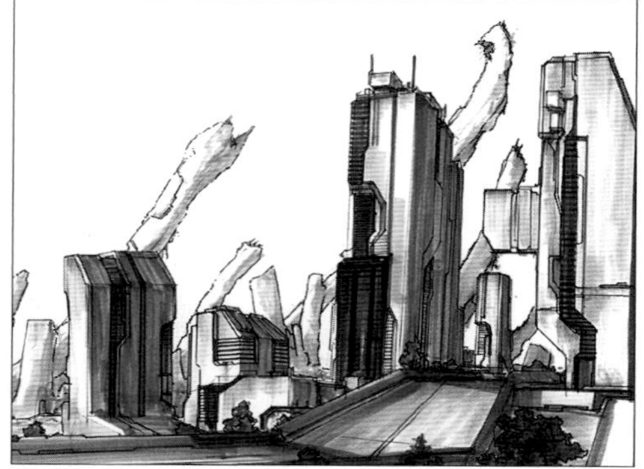

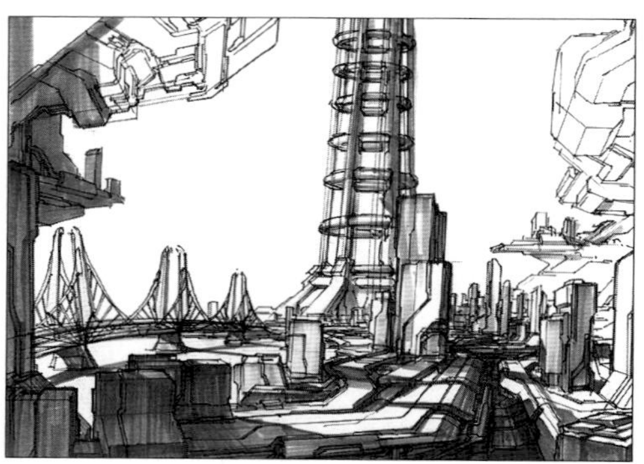

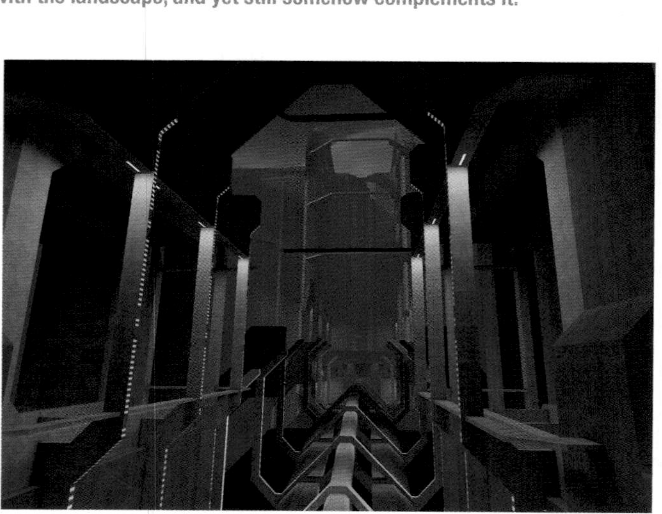

◀ This gallery-like transit corridor plays host to a vehicle as big as some other games' entire levels. Screen shot from early development of *Halo 2*.

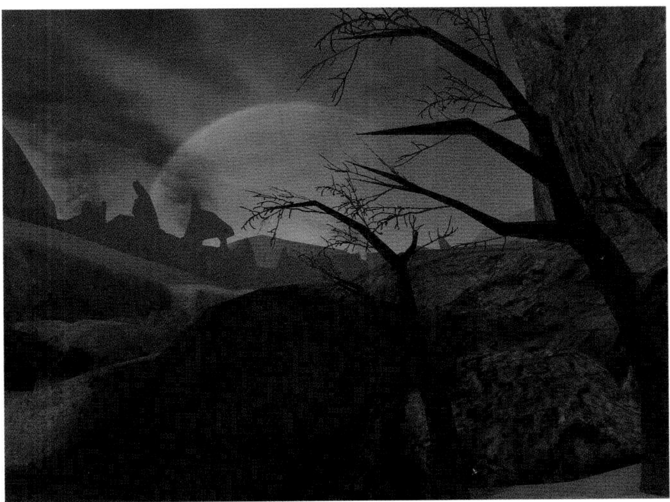

Early screen shot of Sentinel Wall. Note the use of fog and lighting to create mood.

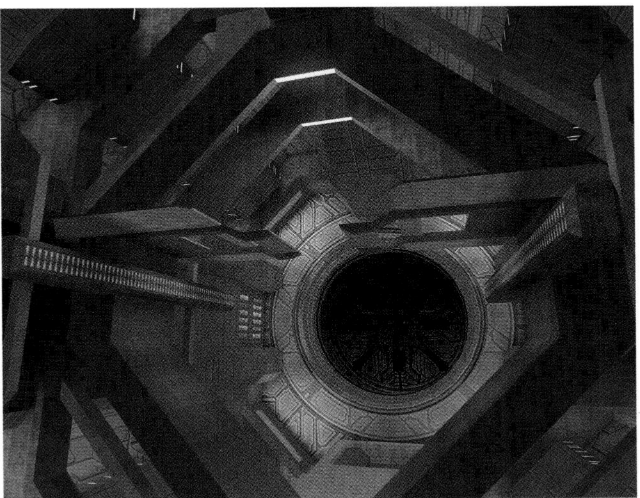

A screen shot like this gives virtually no sense of scale. The environments need characters and objects to give them spatial context.

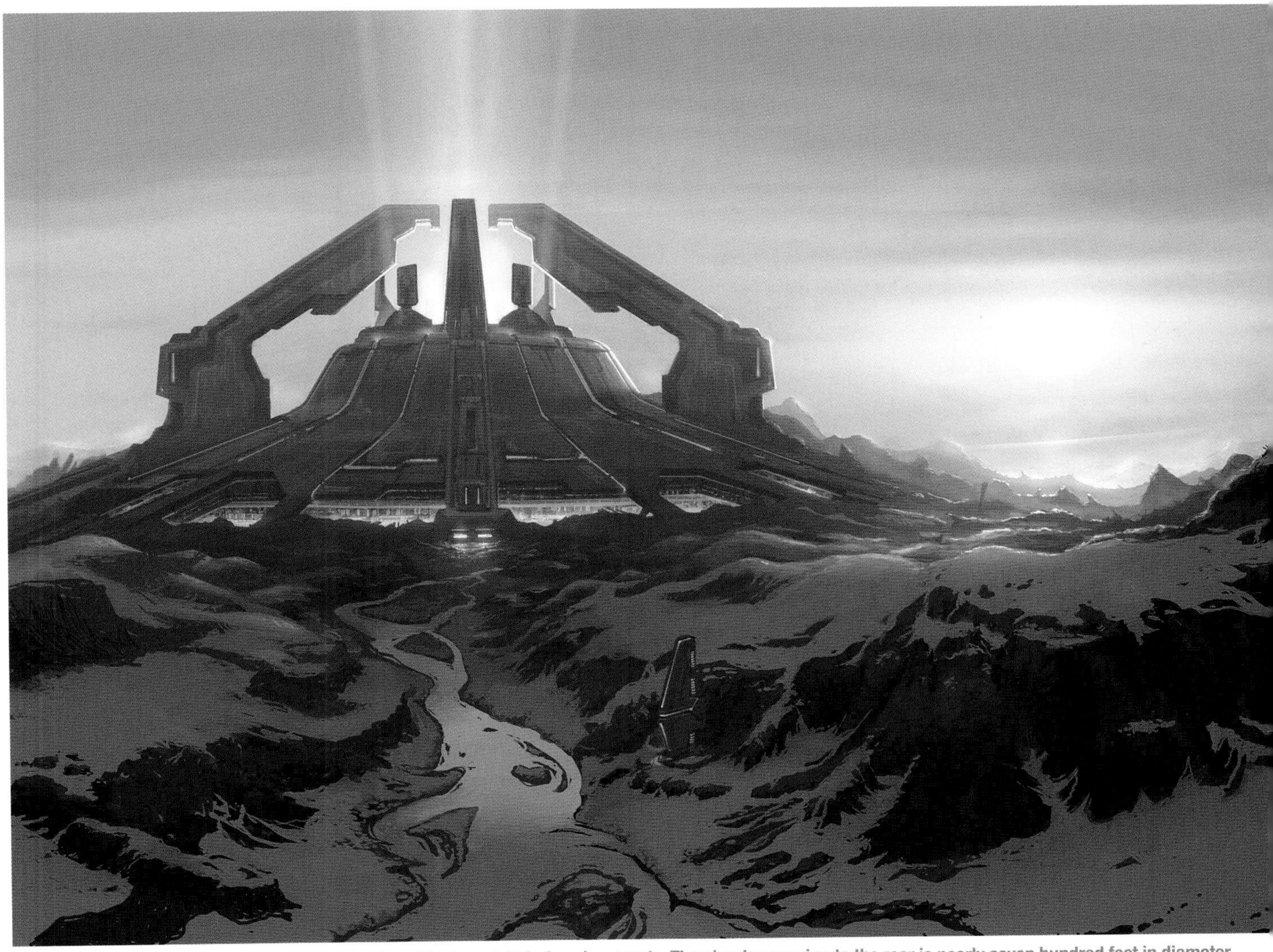

The space shown in the above screen shot is not typical of *Halo 2* environments. The circular opening to the rear is nearly seven hundred feet in diameter.

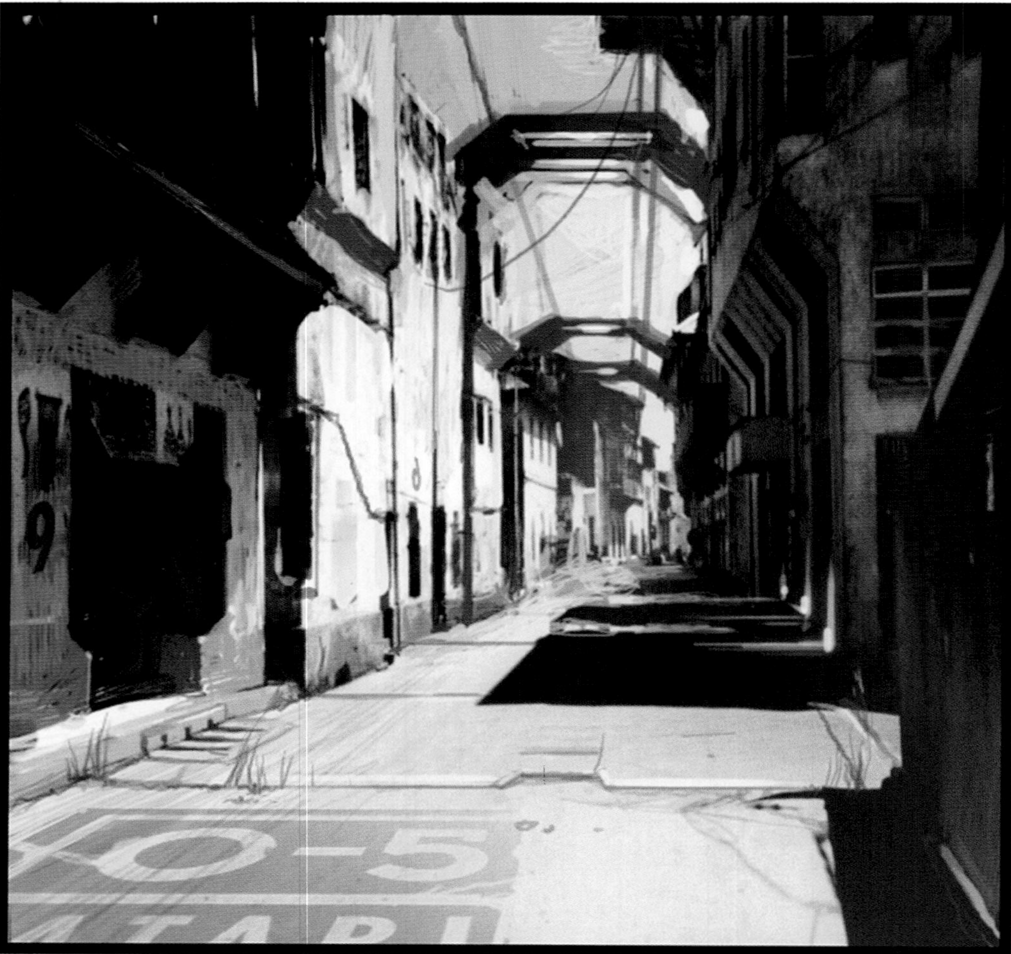

▲ Human environments are the most familiar looking but, in a way, require more thought. Concept painting by Chris Barrett.

▶ The vast space station is one of the first places you'll explore in *Halo 2*.

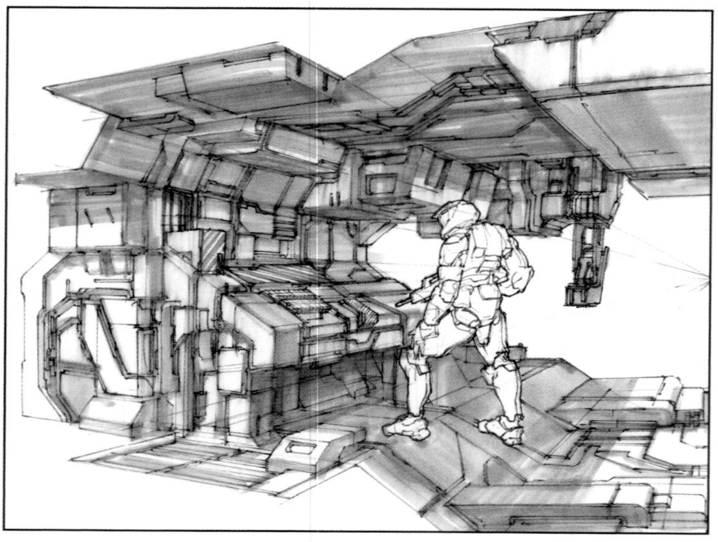

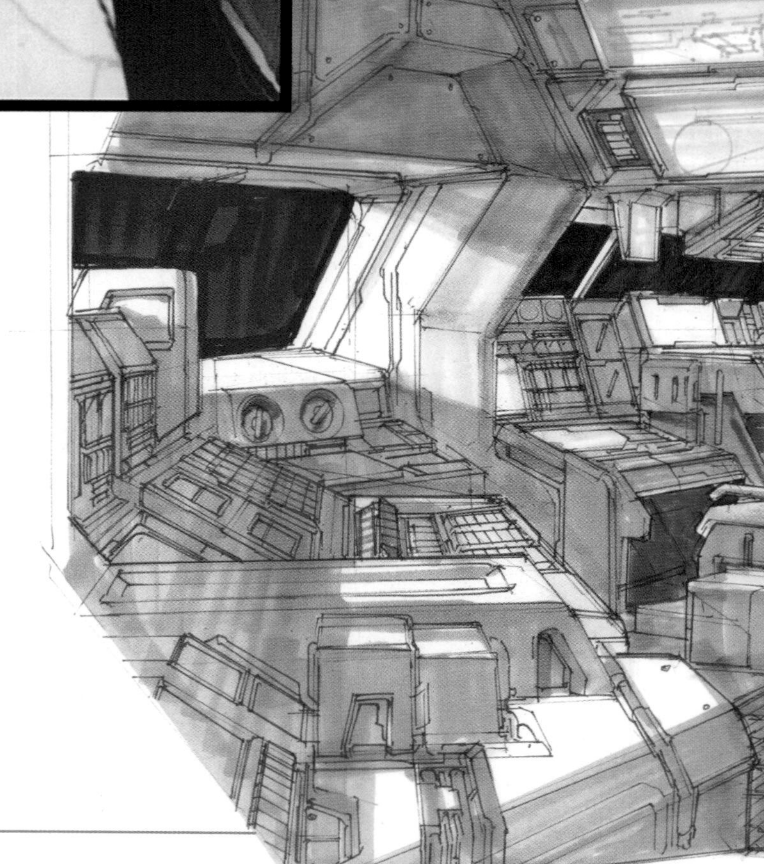

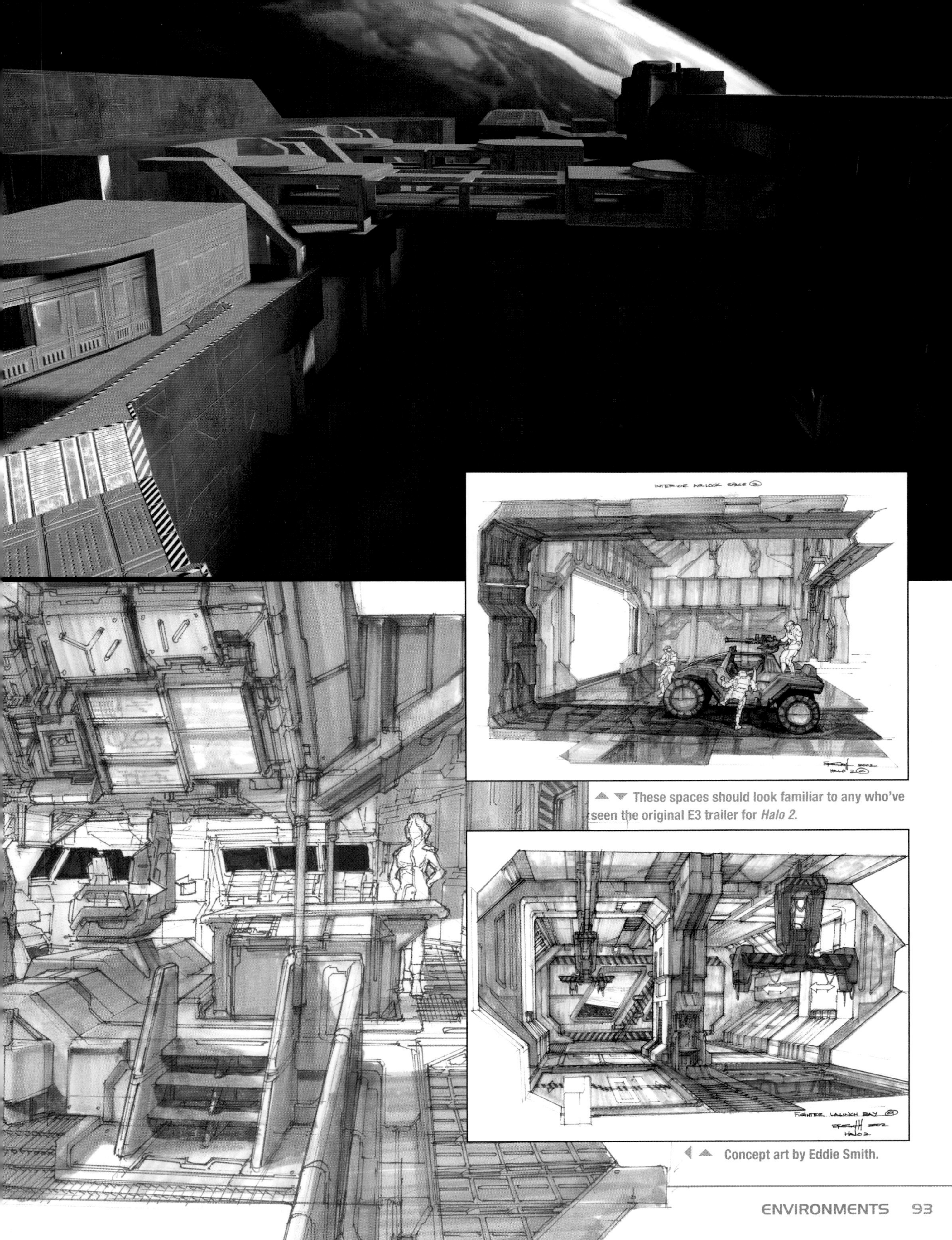

▲▼ These spaces should look familiar to any who've seen the original E3 trailer for *Halo 2*.

◀▲ Concept art by Eddie Smith.

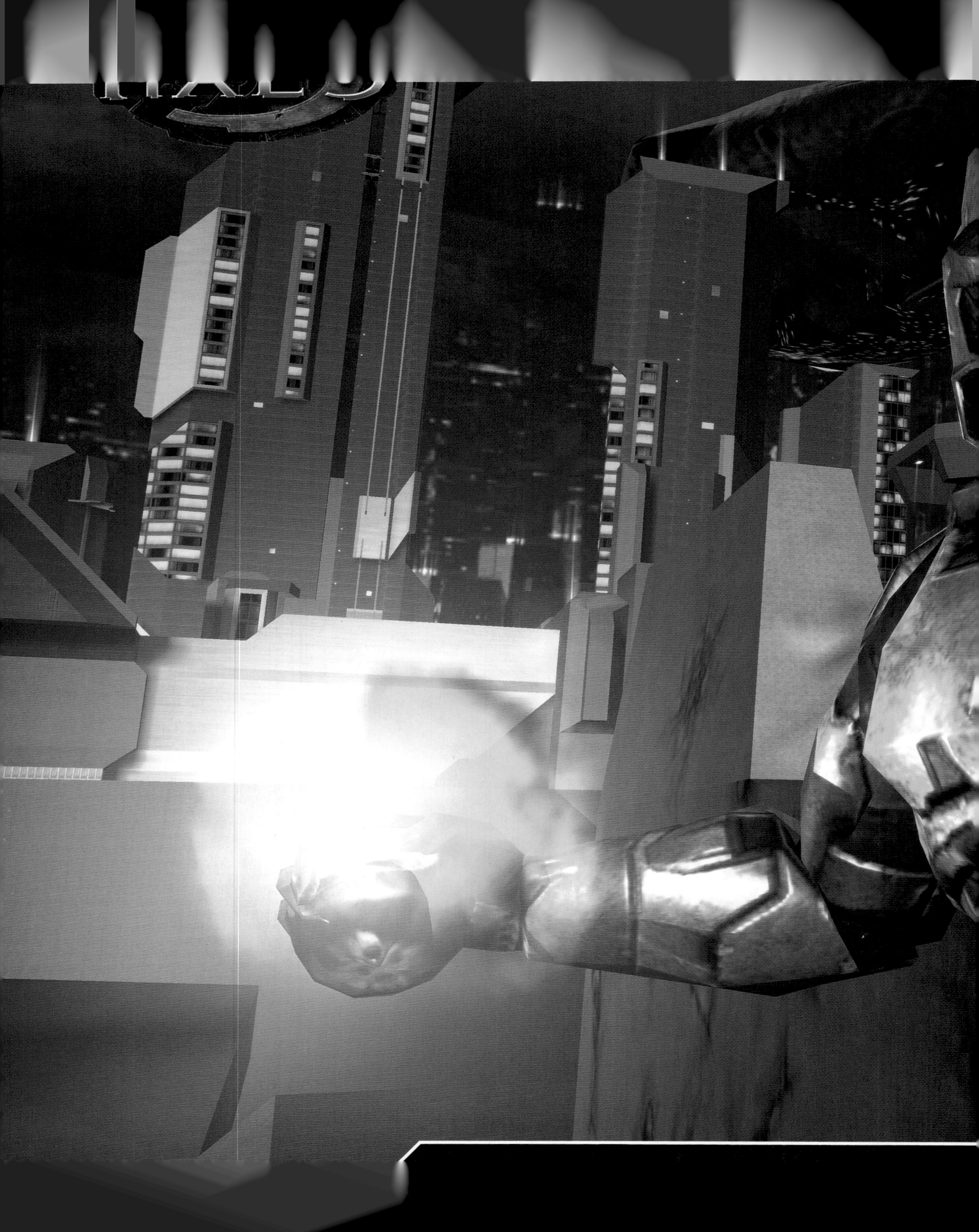

WEAPONS AND GEAR

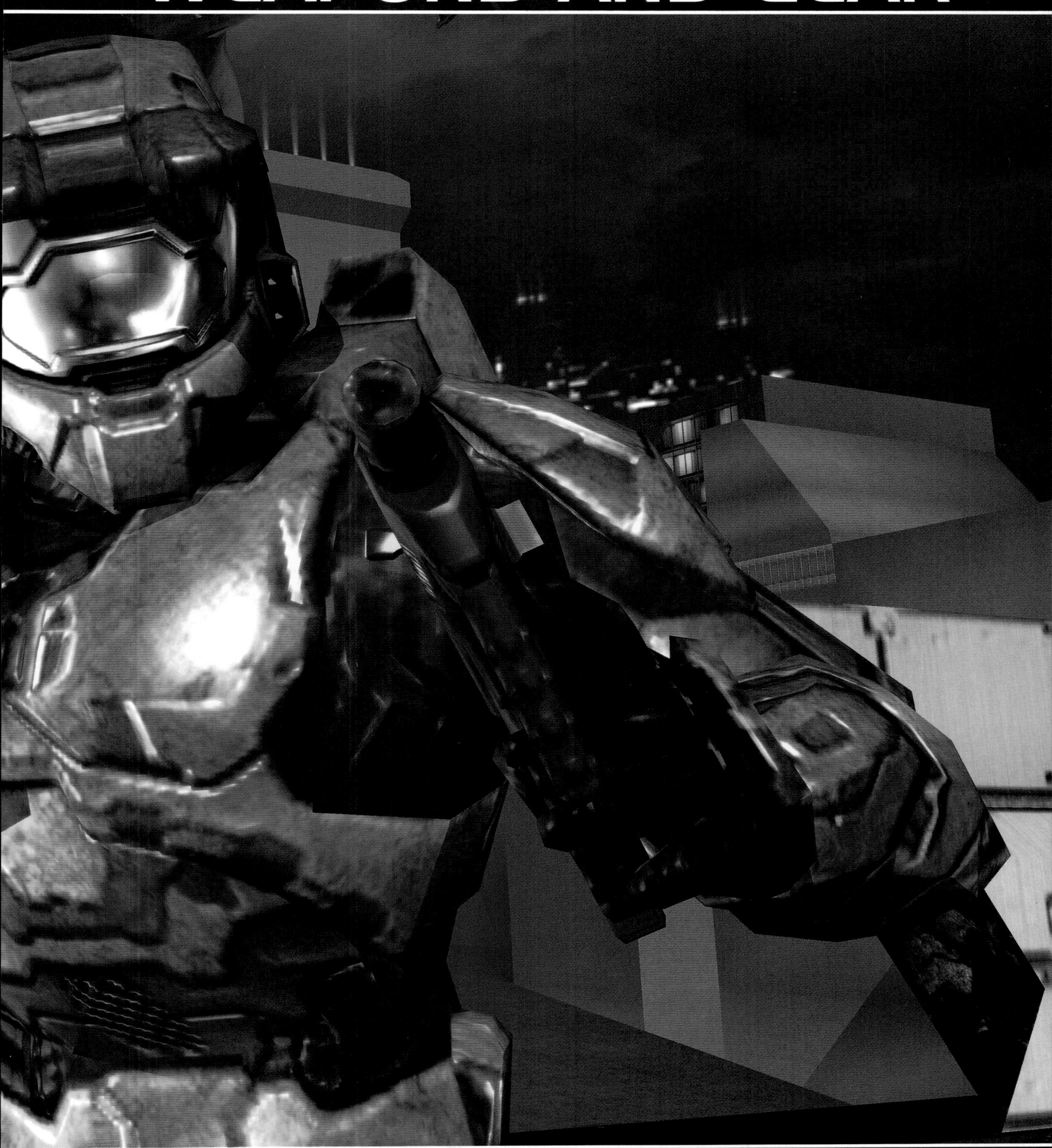

"'Contact. All teams stand by: enemy contact, my position.'

The Chief snaked the fiber-optic probe up and over the three-meter-high stone ridge. When it was in place, the Chief linked it to his helmet's heads-up display.

On the other side he saw a valley with eroded rock walls and a river meandering through it . . . and camped along the banks as far as he could see were Covenant Grunts.

These Grunts were unusually well armed: needlers, plasma pistols, and there were four stationary plasma cannons. Those could be a problem.

One other problem: There were easily a thousand of them."

—Excerpt from
Halo: The Fall of Reach
by Eric Nylund.

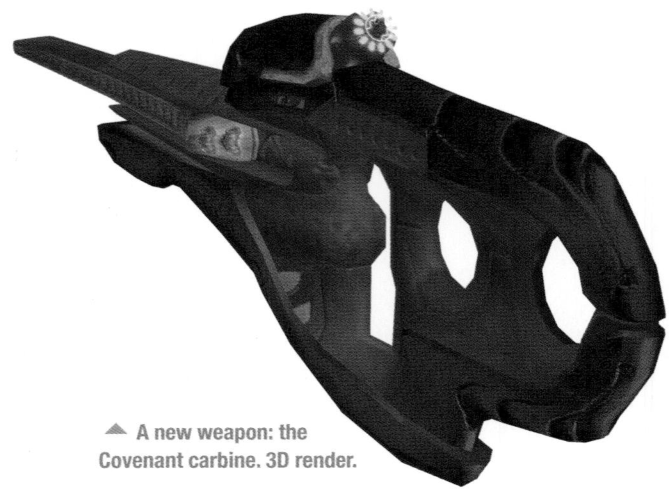

▲ A new weapon: the Covenant carbine. 3D render.

Along with compelling characters and imaginative environments, *Halo* required a collection of interesting and believable weapons—a necessary component to any successful "first person shooter" (FPS). Since *Halo* is set in a far-flung future, the design team had to concoct a futuristic arsenal, but still make it recognizable and intuitive to contemporary eyes.

Travis Brady, 3D artist and modeler, explains, "This group is a great source of all kinds of information. There are guys who know all sorts of obscure details that help us refine our designs, and send us along new paths we might not have considered."

HUMAN WEAPONS

Robt McLees was intrigued by the task of developing the humans' weaponry for the game. "Back in the early days of development on *Halo*," he says, "the game was an RTS (real-time strategy game). The first version of the assault rifle was built, but it didn't need to be super-detailed or anything. When we switched gears and started developing *Halo* as a first-person shooter we had a silhouette that we all liked, but it was basically a cardboard box. So I got to work cramming a bunch of detail into that silhouette. Over time, the assault rifle evolved into what it is now.

"Back then, I was pretty much the only person familiar with firearms at Bungie, so it was a constant battle to make the weapons look like they could actually work, as opposed to just

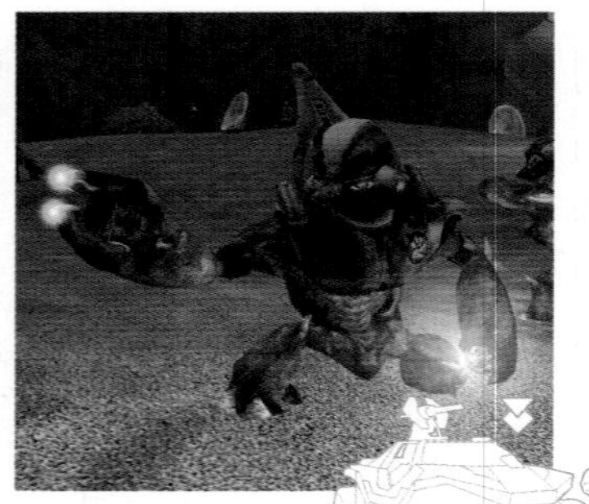

▲ A Grunt major with plasma pistol and armed plasma grenade.

▲ Art by Dave Candland.

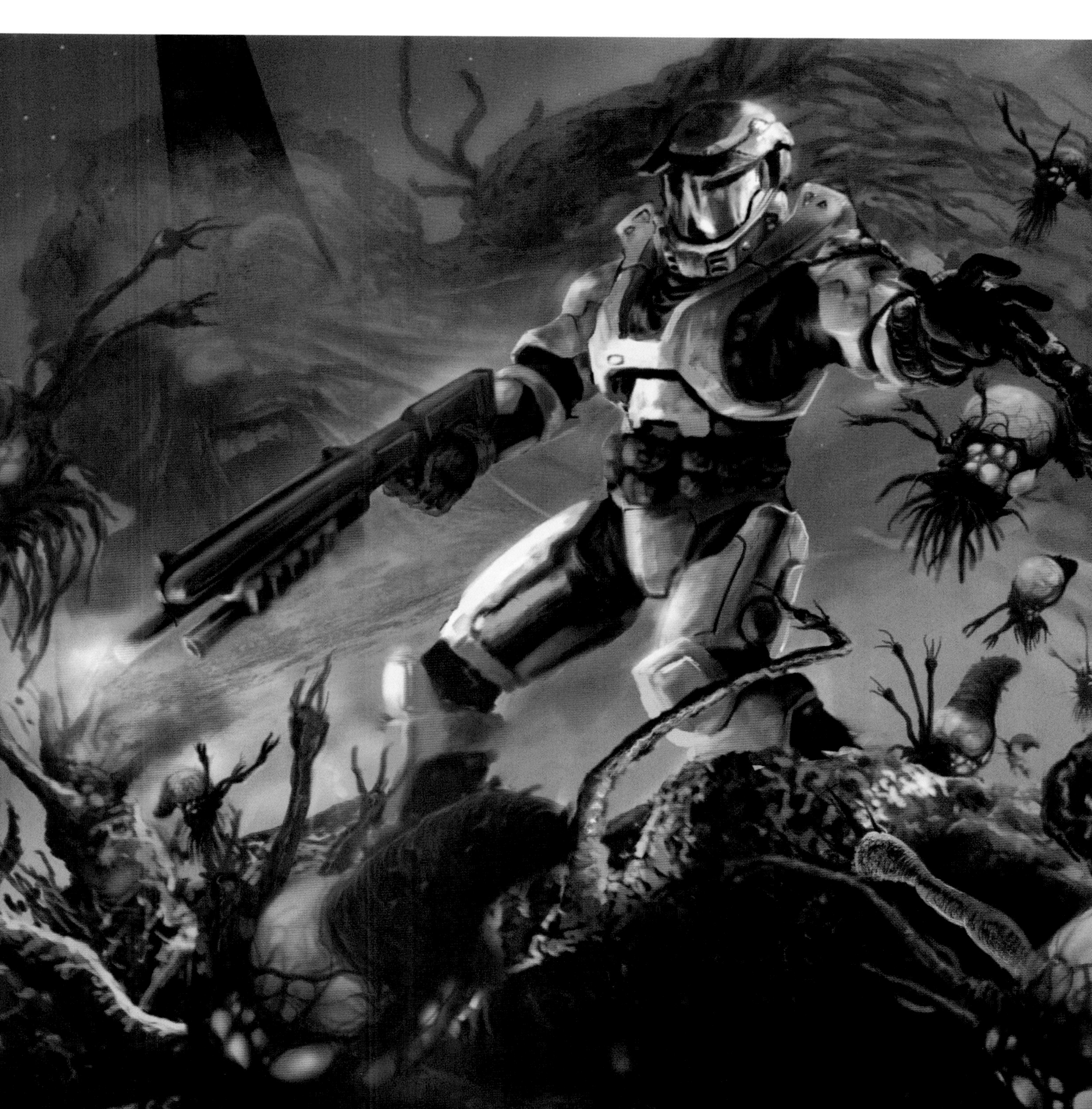

The shotgun was the best weapon against the Flood in close quarters. Art by Eddie Smith and Lorraine McLees.

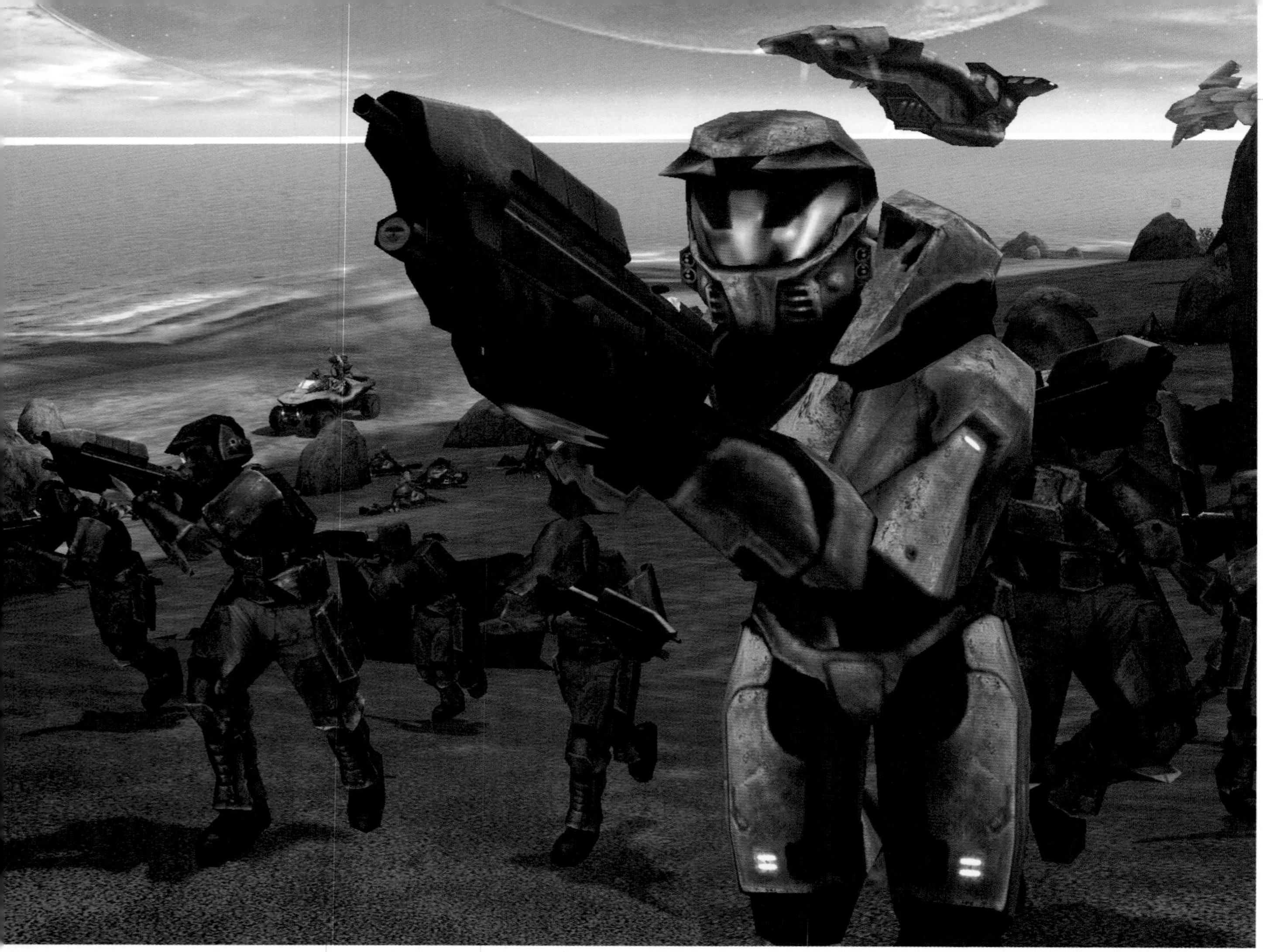

▲ Master Chief and a squad of Marines storm a beach in this scene from *Halo*.

'look cool.' I agonized for a long time just to make sure the assault rifle design had enough room for bolt travel."

This attention to detail prompted McLees to draft thumbnail descriptions of each weapon he designed—complete with caliber, features (such as the assault rifle's digital ammunition counter), and even slang terms that Marines in the game could use during the game.

▼ In *Halo 2*, you'll be able to simply trade guns with your allies by walking up to them and hitting "X" to exchange.

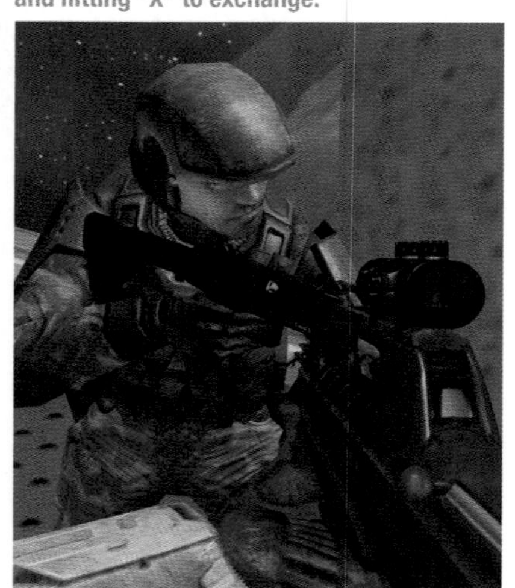

ASSAULT RIFLE

The assault rifle is one of the most distinctive in the game. Also known as the MA5B Individual Combat Weapon System (or MA5B-ICWS), it features a digital ammunition counter that functions during play, and a compass that provides relative bearing from the player's starting point.

Robt McLees applied his knowledge of firearms to the design, reworking its ergonomics and overall look until he had crafted the final version.

McLees's familiarity with the subject matter had one unintended consequence, however: During *Halo*'s development a firearms manufacturer developed a cutting-edge military assault rifle that bore a striking resemblance to McLees's design. "I don't know when the images of the FN2000 appeared, but I didn't see them until three or four months after the game shipped,"

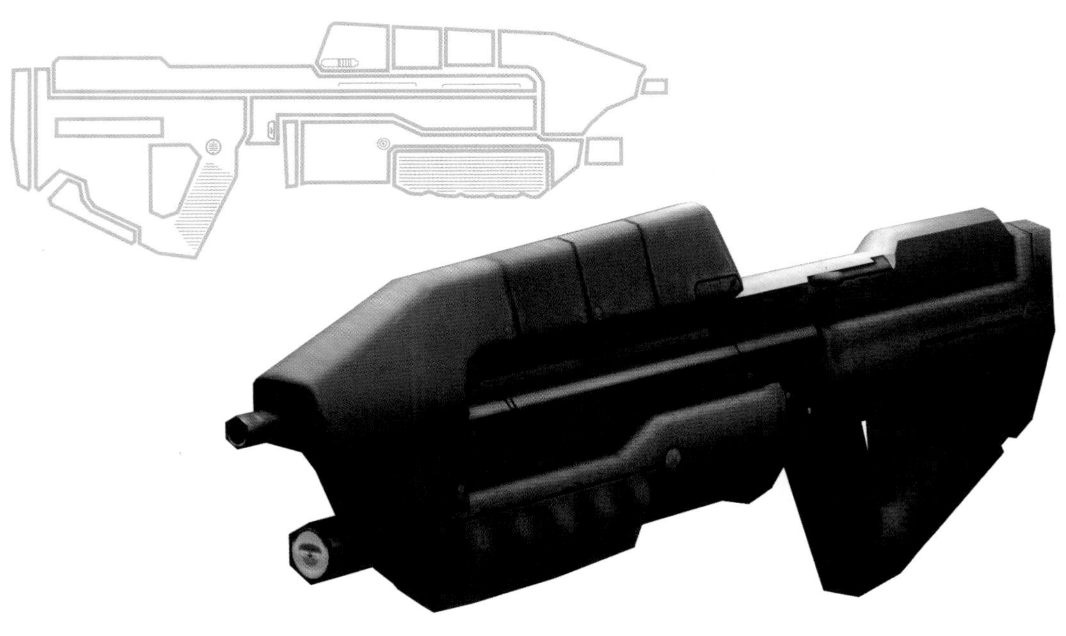

Robt McLees's rendition of the assault rifle proved eerily prescient—Robt spotted a real-life rifle looking almost identical just a few months later.

McLees says. "And I thought, 'Oh, *great*. Now everyone's going to think I swiped the design from Fabrique Nationale.' It was surreal to see how close the *Halo* assault rifle was to its real-world counterpart . . . and it was all totally by accident."

PISTOL

The M6D Personal Defense Weapon System is the standard sidearm of human military personnel. The M6D (also called an HE pistol, due to the weapon's standard explosive ammunition) is compact, and very accurate.

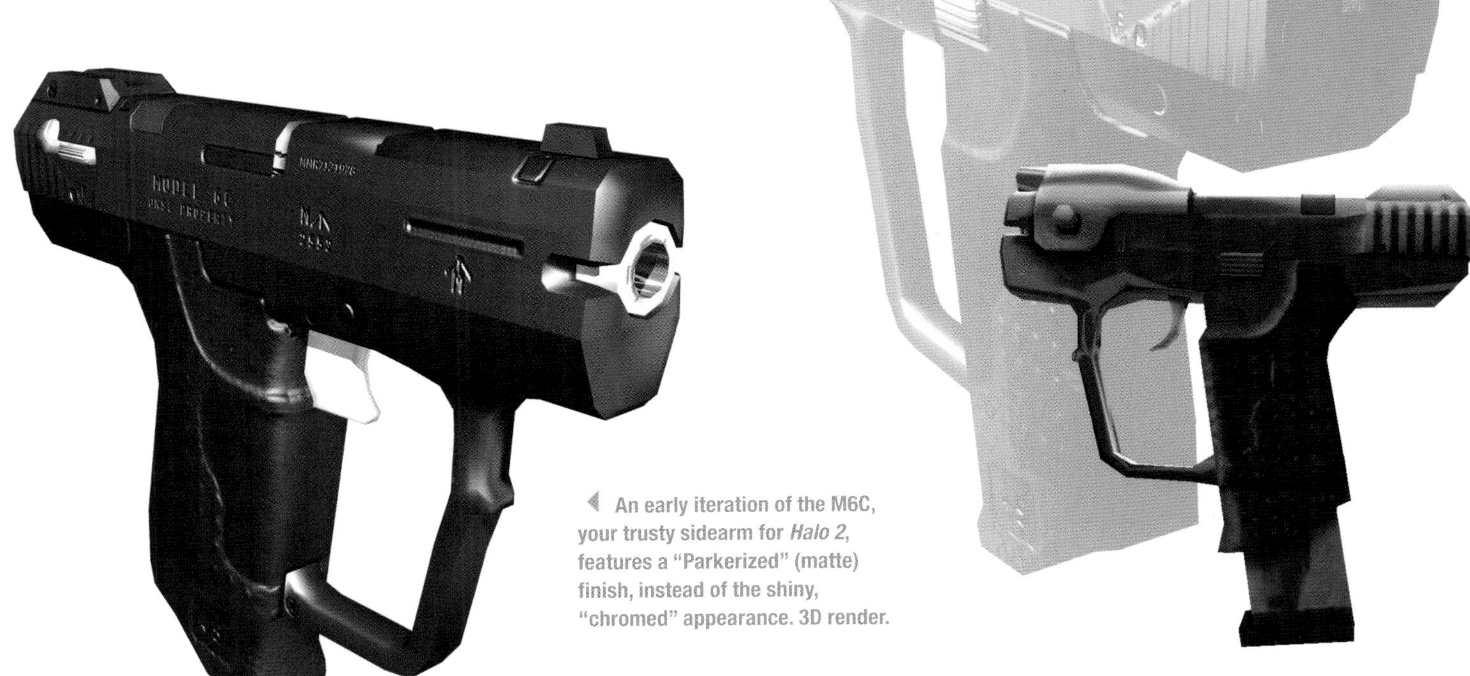

An early iteration of the M6C, your trusty sidearm for *Halo 2*, features a "Parkerized" (matte) finish, instead of the shiny, "chromed" appearance. 3D render.

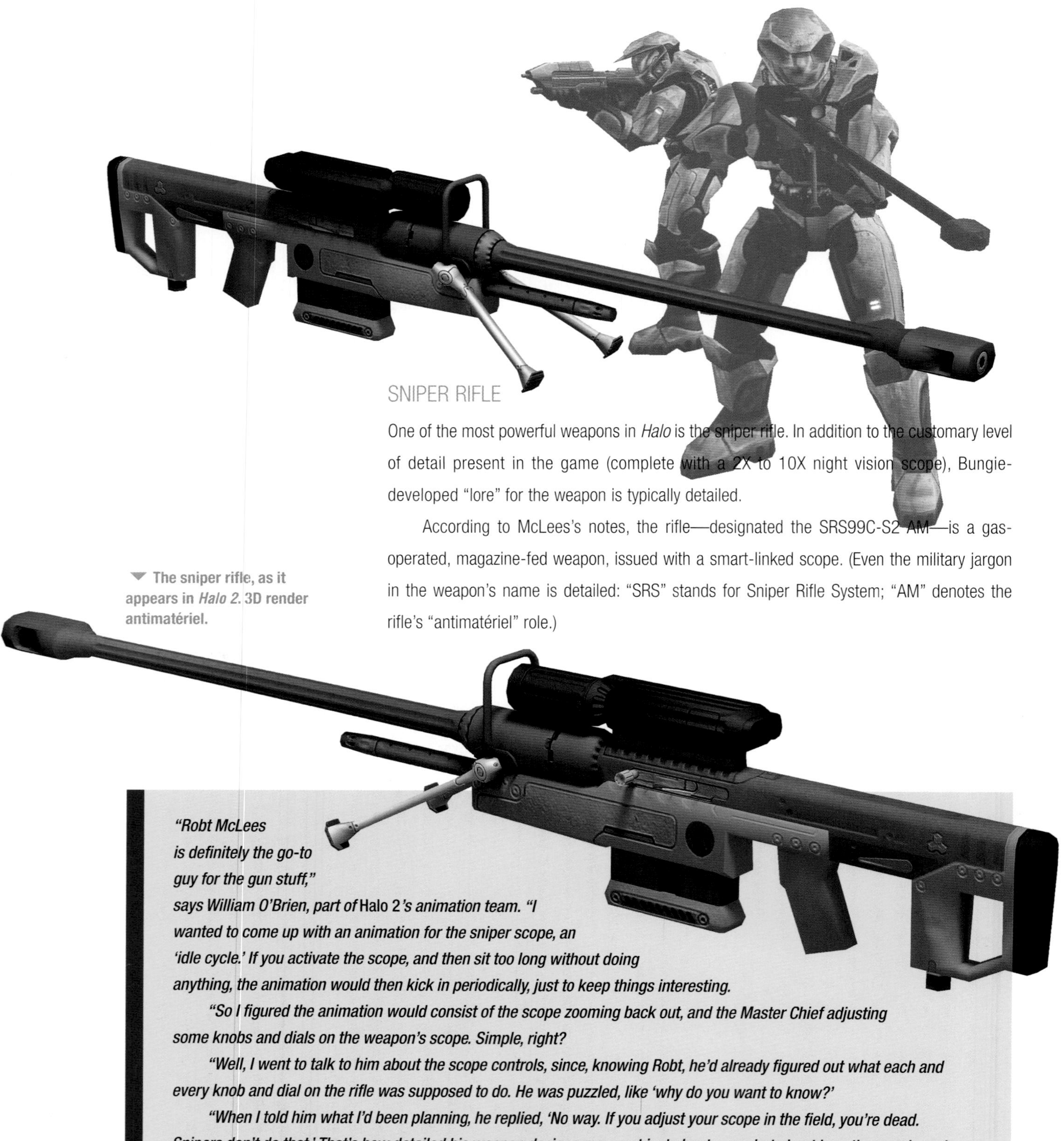

SNIPER RIFLE

One of the most powerful weapons in *Halo* is the sniper rifle. In addition to the customary level of detail present in the game (complete with a 2X to 10X night vision scope), Bungie-developed "lore" for the weapon is typically detailed.

According to McLees's notes, the rifle—designated the SRS99C-S2 AM—is a gas-operated, magazine-fed weapon, issued with a smart-linked scope. (Even the military jargon in the weapon's name is detailed: "SRS" stands for Sniper Rifle System; "AM" denotes the rifle's "antimatériel" role.)

▼ The sniper rifle, as it appears in *Halo 2*. 3D render antimatériel.

"Robt McLees is definitely the go-to guy for the gun stuff," says William O'Brien, part of Halo 2*'s animation team. "I wanted to come up with an animation for the sniper scope, an 'idle cycle.' If you activate the scope, and then sit too long without doing anything, the animation would then kick in periodically, just to keep things interesting.*

"So I figured the animation would consist of the scope zooming back out, and the Master Chief adjusting some knobs and dials on the weapon's scope. Simple, right?

"Well, I went to talk to him about the scope controls, since, knowing Robt, he'd already figured out what each and every knob and dial on the rifle was supposed to do. He was puzzled, like 'why do you want to know?'

"When I told him what I'd been planning, he replied, 'No way. If you adjust your scope in the field, you're dead. Snipers don't do that.' That's how detailed his weapon designs are—not just about guns, but about how they work, and how a sniper would fire them. Amazing."

ROCKET LAUNCHER

One of the more unusual designs for human weapons is the rocket launcher ("officially" designated the M19 SSM, but more commonly referred to as the "Spanker"). Essentially, the weapon is a double-barreled rocket launcher. When one rocket is fired, the magazine tube rotates, placing the second round into firing position.

The nickname "Spanker" refers to the writing found on the launcher's magazine box, which reads "SPNKr"—a nod to an older Bungie title, *Marathon*. (The rocket launcher in *Marathon* bore the same name.)

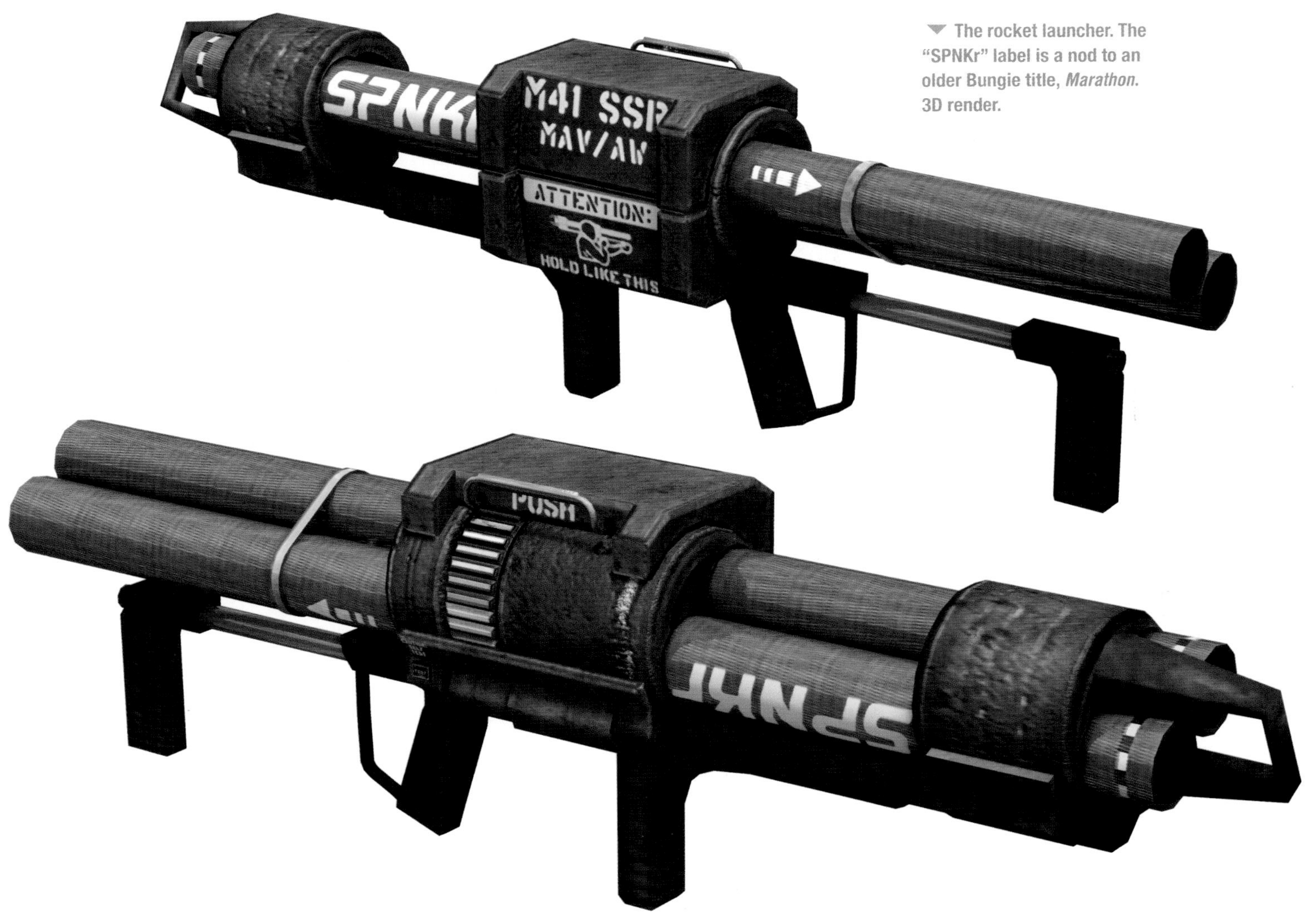

▼ The rocket launcher. The "SPNKr" label is a nod to an older Bungie title, *Marathon*. 3D render.

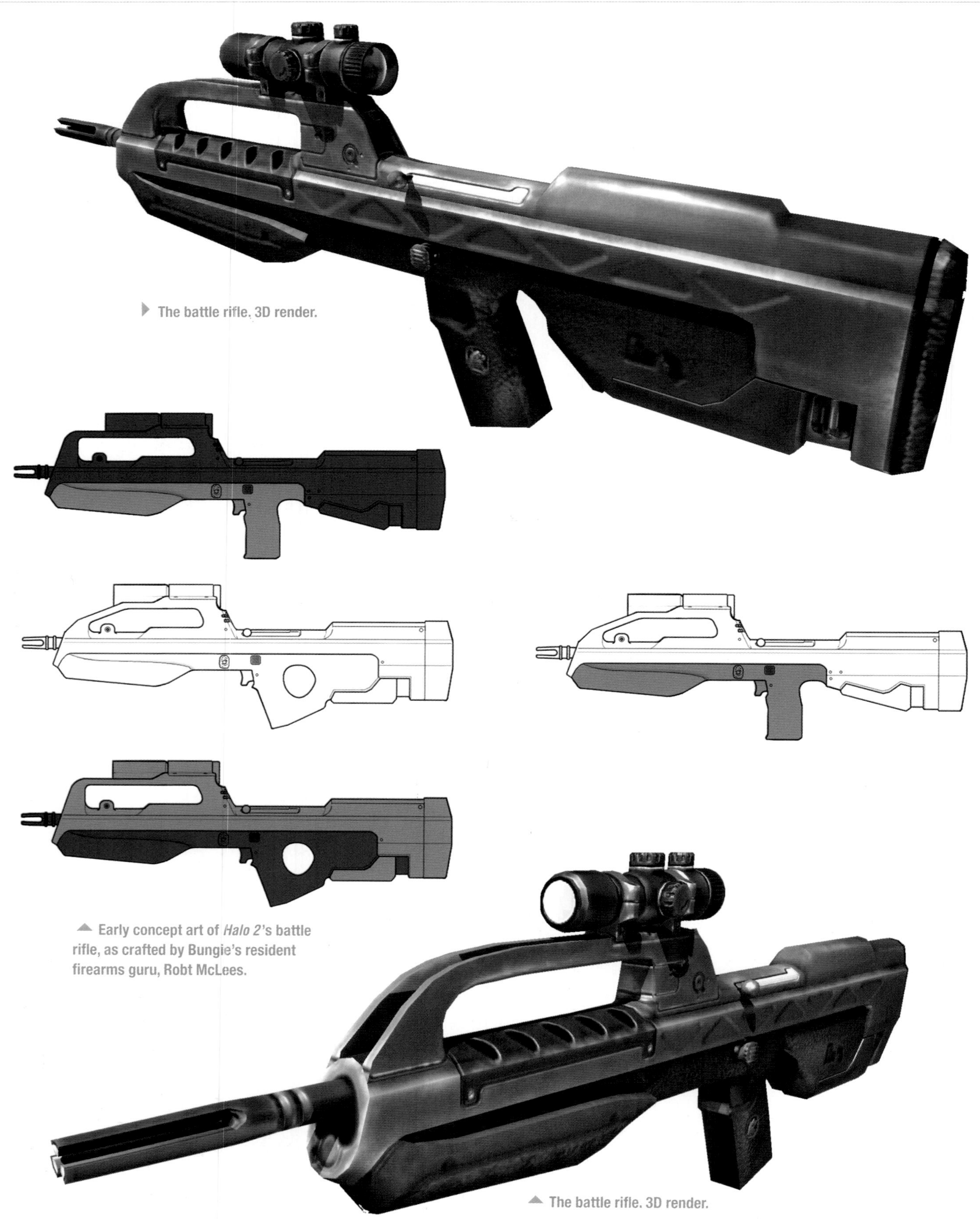

▸ The battle rifle. 3D render.

▲ Early concept art of *Halo 2*'s battle rifle, as crafted by Bungie's resident firearms guru, Robt McLees.

▲ The battle rifle. 3D render.

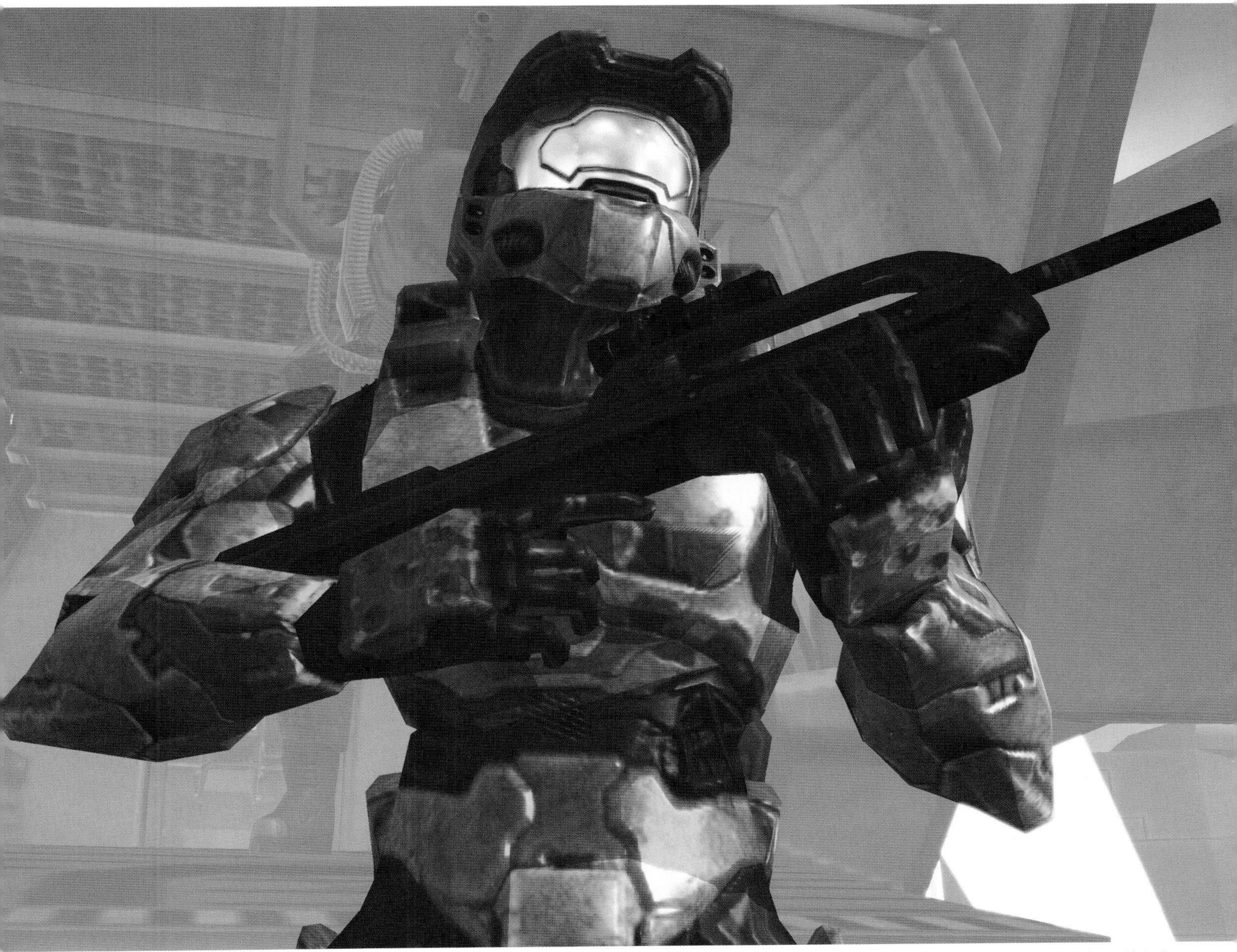

▲ The Master Chief prepares for war. Screen shot from *Halo 2.*

BATTLE RIFLE

A new weapon for *Halo 2*, the battle rifle is a stripped down, almost skeletal version of the assault rifle. It has a longer barrel, a scope, and is more accurate (though with a smaller ammunition capacity). "The battle rifle fires a heavier, harder-hitting round than the assault rifle," McLees explains, "and it is also a semiautomatic weapon so it has a lower rate of fire. It is also far more accurate than the AR. Basically, I designed it to look like the smarter, more useful cousin of the assault rifle.

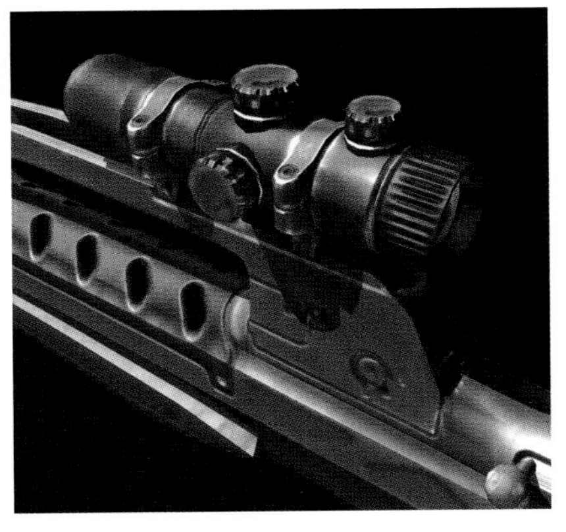

"In *Halo*, the pistol behaved more like a rifle than the assault rifle, and the assault rifle behaved like a submachine gun. Now we have a rifle that behaves like a rifle, an SMG that behaves like an SMG, and a pistol that behaves like a pistol. Basically I initiated a 'throw off the shackles of FPS conventions' party and just about everybody showed up."

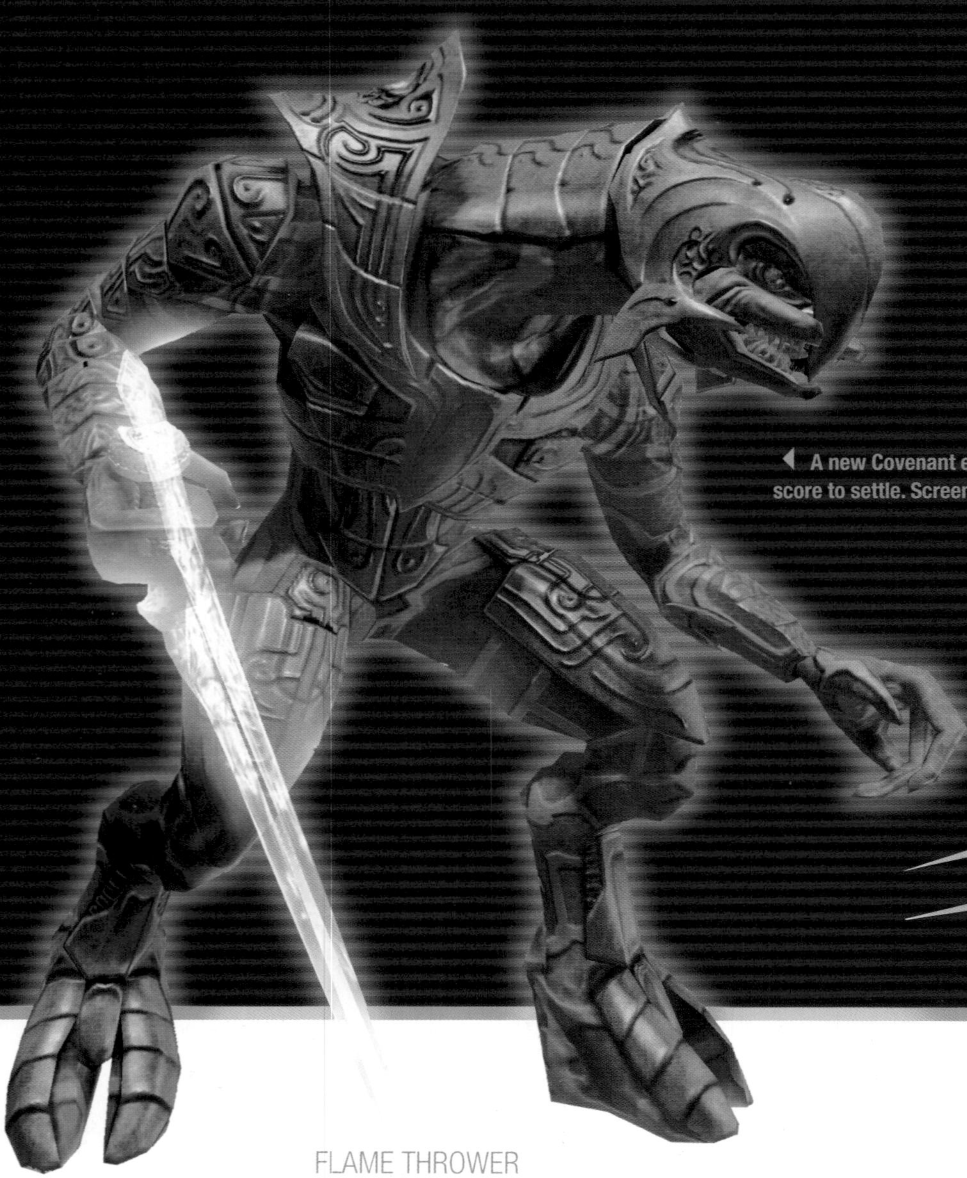

A new Covenant enemy with a personal score to settle. Screen capture from *Halo 2*.

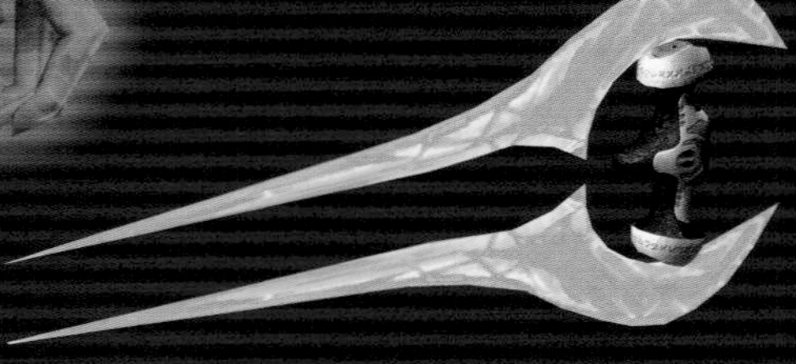

Covenant energy sword.

FLAME THROWER

Originally intended to appear in the first *Halo* game on the Xbox, the flame thrower (or, more martially, the M7057 Defoliant Projector) was cut from the game due to time constraints.

Fortunately for fans, the flame thrower was included in the subsequent PC and Macintosh releases of *Halo*. Sadly, the flame thrower won't be seen in *Halo 2*.

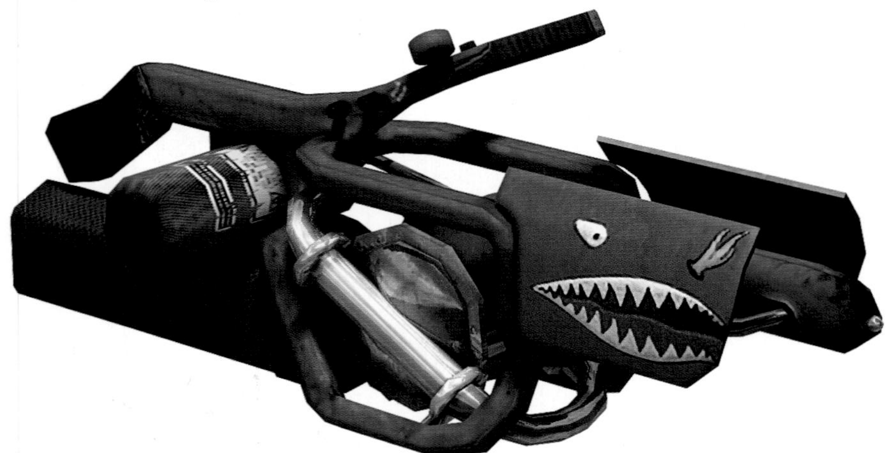

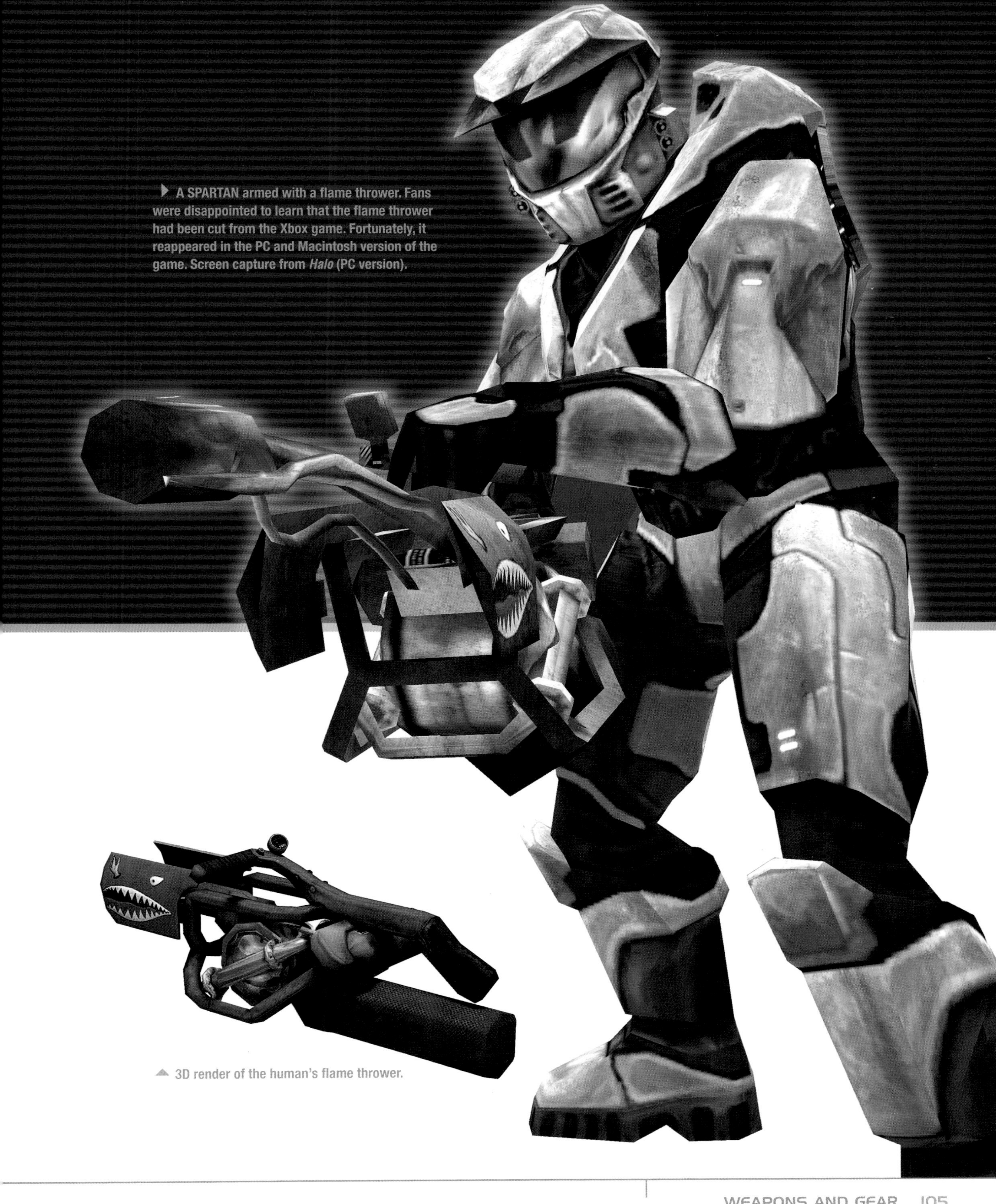

A SPARTAN armed with a flame thrower. Fans were disappointed to learn that the flame thrower had been cut from the Xbox game. Fortunately, it reappeared in the PC and Macintosh version of the game. Screen capture from *Halo* (PC version).

3D render of the human's flame thrower.

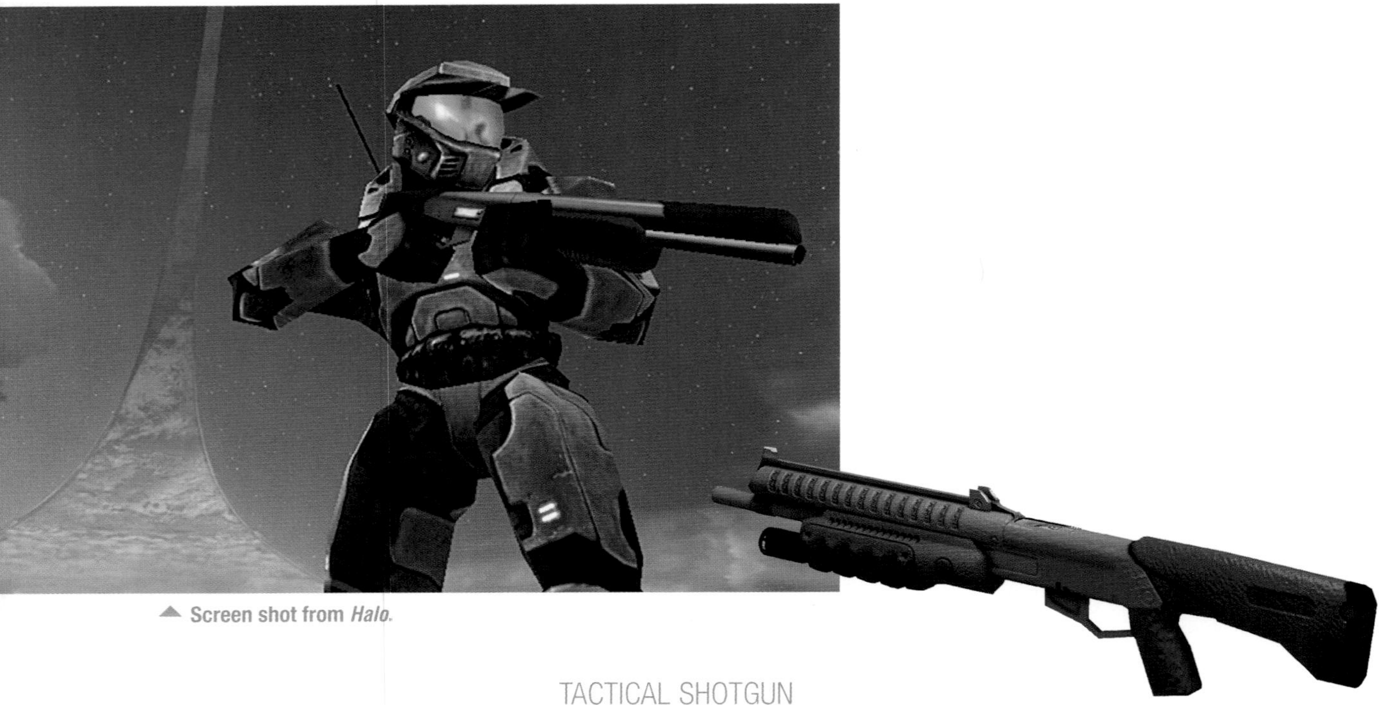

▲ Screen shot from *Halo*.

TACTICAL SHOTGUN

The shotgun (a.k.a. the M90 Close Assault Weapon System) would appear on cursory inspection to be the most conventional of the human weapons featured in the game.

However, the M90 has an unusual placement for its magazine tube; typical shotguns require the shooter to load shotgun shells into a magazine tube that runs below the barrel. The M90's magazine tube runs along the top of the gun, *above* the barrel. To reload the shotgun, shells are inserted along the weapon's top.

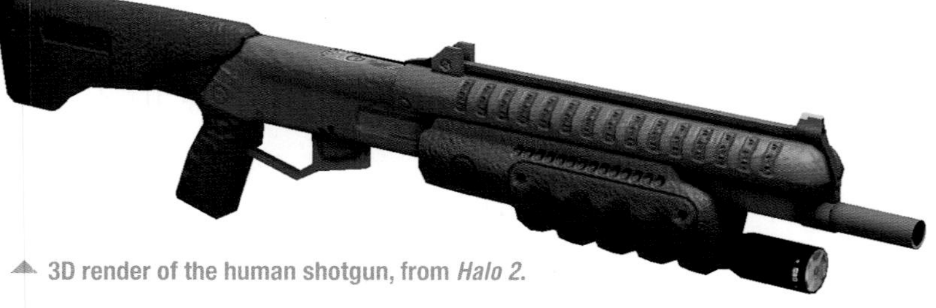

▲ 3D render of the human shotgun, from *Halo 2*.

Part of the process of designing new weapons for use in the game is research. There are volumes of material printed concerning firearms and their function—but nothing beats practical experience. "Definitely the highlight of working on Halo 2 *was the trip we took to South Carolina," artist Robt McLees says. "We got to hang out with several members of the U.S. Special Forces. They demonstrated weapon handling and tactical movement—it was really fun and they are great guys, but the best part was near the end of the day.*

"I got a chance to fire a fully automatic and sound-suppressed Heckler & Koch MP5SD, but the weird thing was I didn't want to 'bullet-hose' the thing. Lieutenant Colonel Mark, our host, told me my shooting was, and I quote, 'Awesome. Very good. Good shooting.'

"That was great. Just the highest praise."

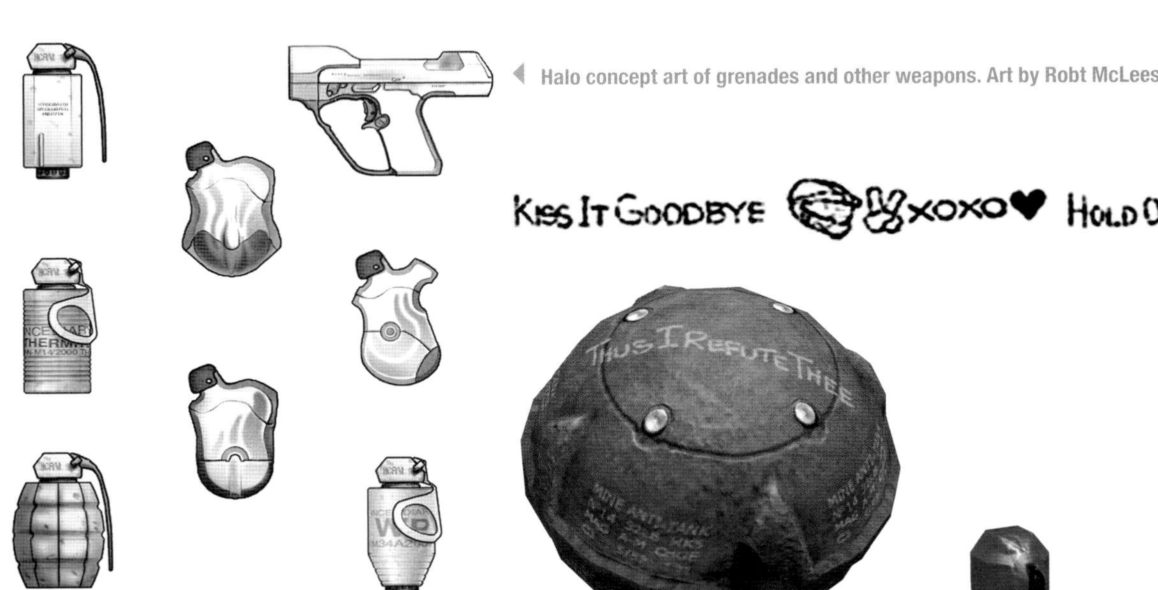

Halo concept art of grenades and other weapons. Art by Robt McLees.

Alternate looks for human grenades were explored. In the end, the pineapple style won out.

GRENADES AND EXPLOSIVES

Even items as simple as grenades needed to undergo a thorough design process. In the case of human explosive ordnance, the items needed to be both recognizable to contemporary audiences and futuristic enough to exist in *Halo*'s fictional 2552.

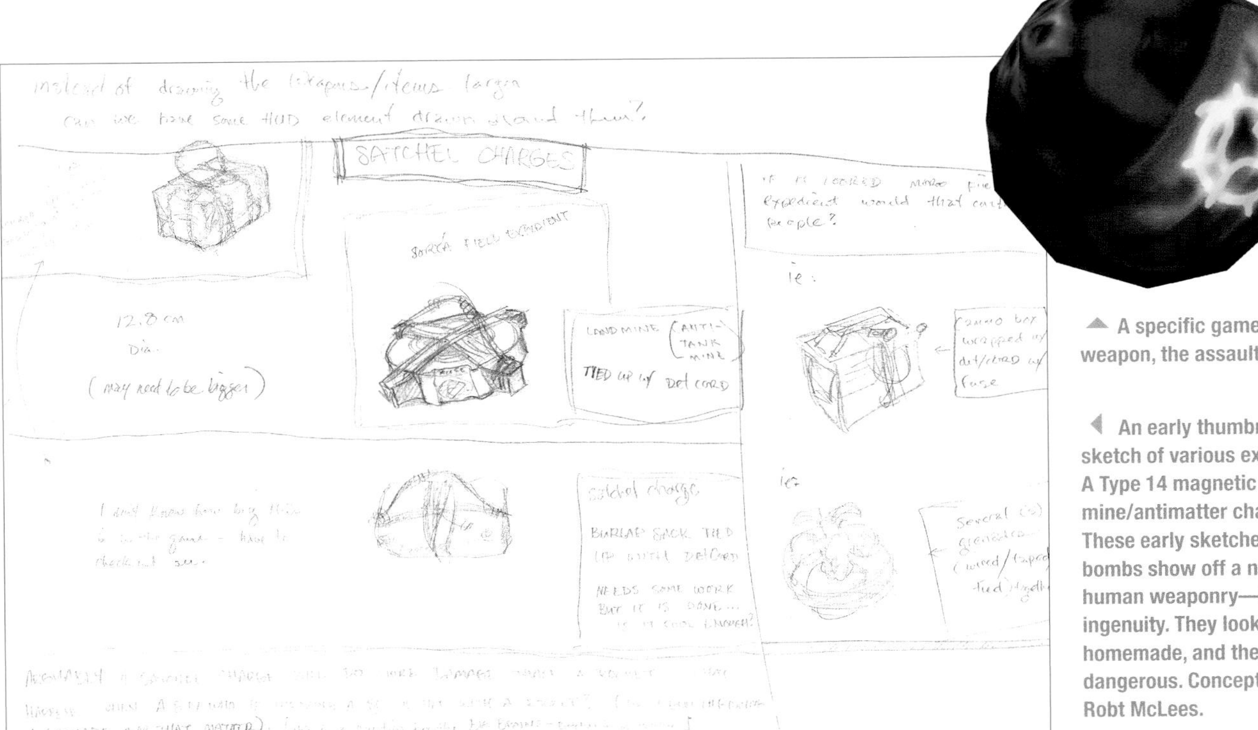

A specific gametype weapon, the assault bomb.

An early thumbnail sketch of various explosives. A Type 14 magnetic antitank mine/antimatter charge. These early sketches for bombs show off a new side to human weaponry—handmade ingenuity. They look homemade, and they look dangerous. Concept art by Robt McLees.

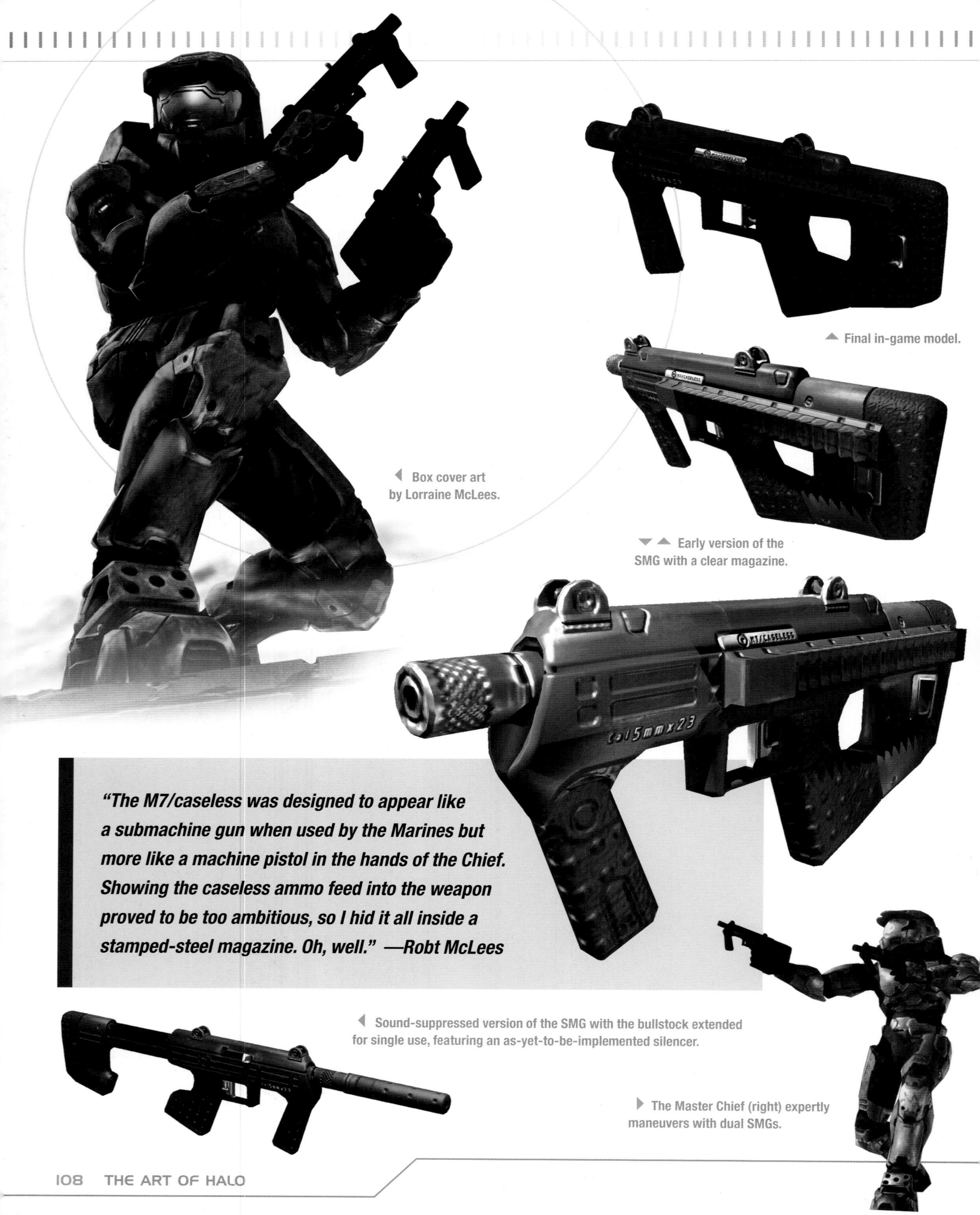

Box cover art by Lorraine McLees.

Final in-game model.

Early version of the SMG with a clear magazine.

"The M7/caseless was designed to appear like a submachine gun when used by the Marines but more like a machine pistol in the hands of the Chief. Showing the caseless ammo feed into the weapon proved to be too ambitious, so I hid it all inside a stamped-steel magazine. Oh, well." —Robt McLees

Sound-suppressed version of the SMG with the bullstock extended for single use, featuring an as-yet-to-be-implemented silencer.

The Master Chief (right) expertly maneuvers with dual SMGs.

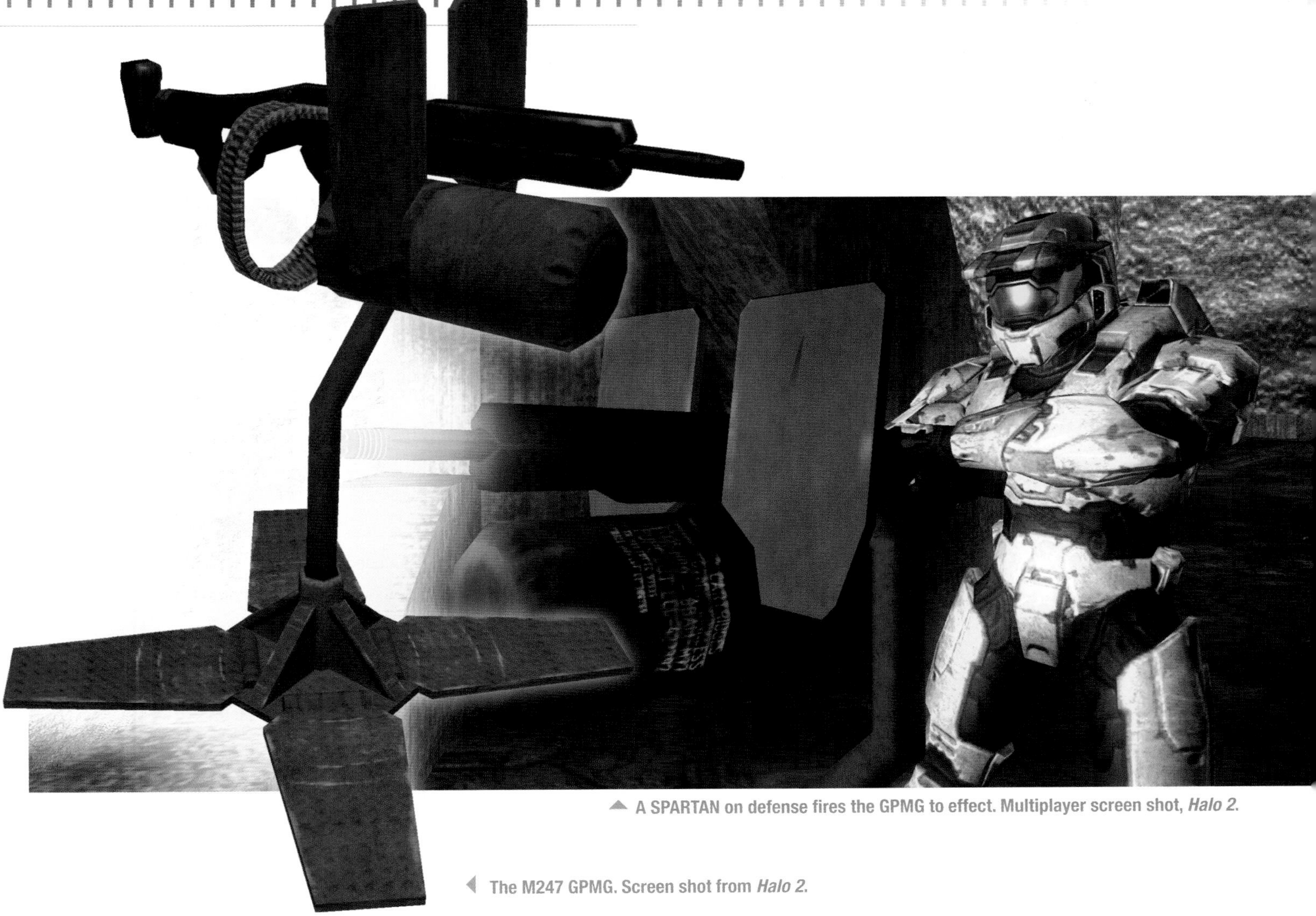

▲ A SPARTAN on defense fires the GPMG to effect. Multiplayer screen shot, *Halo 2*.

◀ The M247 GPMG. Screen shot from *Halo 2*.

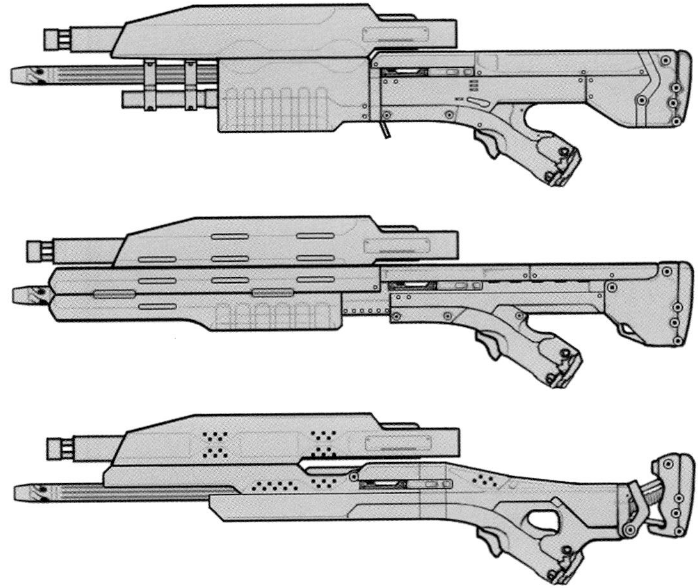

▲ Concept by Robt McLees for the M247 GPMG, shown here with 25mm grenade launcher.

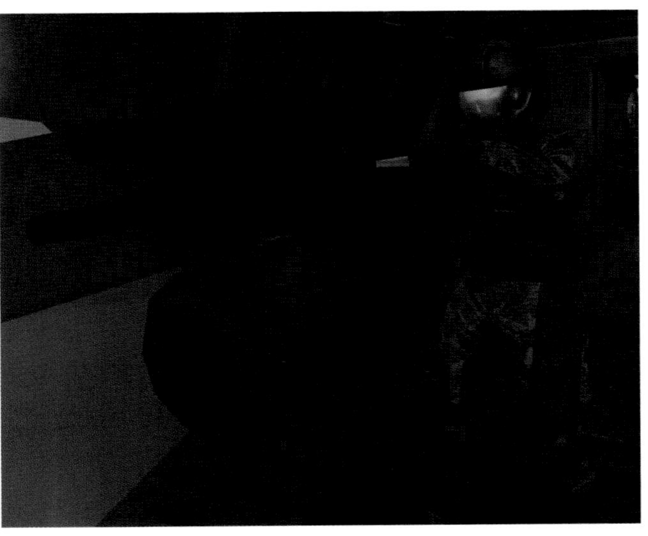

▲ A crew chief mans a bulkhead-mounted M247 GPMG from the back of a Pelican ready to provide covering fire. Screen capture from the *Halo 2* E3 2003 build.

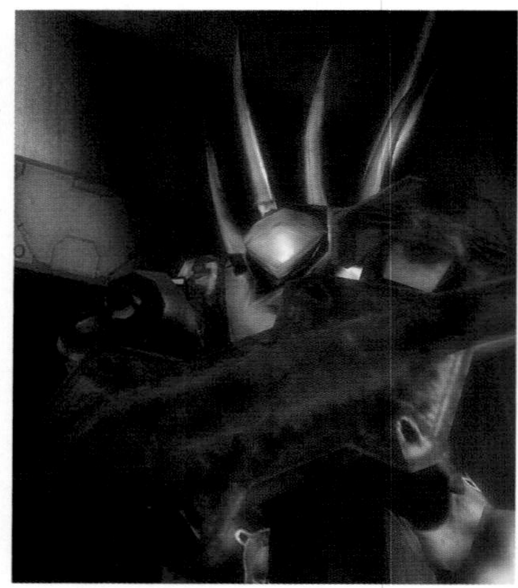

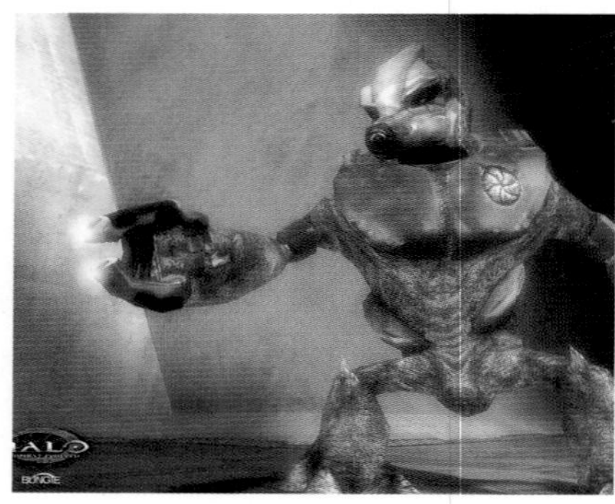

▲ Atmospheric images of a Hunter (top) and Grunt (below), featured on the Bungie.net website.

COVENANT WEAPONS

Another artist, Shi Kai Wang, developed much of the unusual alien weaponry of the Covenant. Whereas McLees needed to develop weaponry that was distinctly human, Shi Kai worked with McLees to create devices that were distinctly alien—but still recognizable to human audiences.

"I studied industrial design in college," Shi Kai says. "Immediately after I graduated, I started work at a video game company that was working on a science fiction game similar to some of the stuff in *Halo*—it was called *Esoteria* by Mobeus Designs. The game never really took off, but I was intrigued by a lot of those kinds of concepts, and it always stuck with me.

"Later on, when I got to interview with Bungie, I saw the kinds of stuff they were working on, and just knew this was what I wanted to do, too. Plus, the work environment was a lot like college—where you're surrounded by talented people who believe in themselves and what they are doing. That was great."

PLASMA PISTOL

The Plasma Pistol—designed by Robt McLees—is roughly equivalent to a human handgun. It fires packets of supercharged energy at a target, inflicting burn damage.

The weapon can be overcharged, however—storing up power for several seconds before

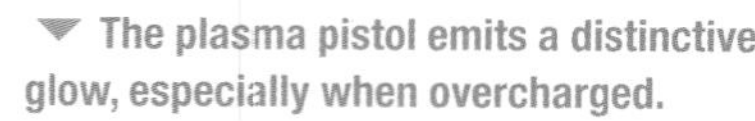

▼ The plasma pistol emits a distinctive glow, especially when overcharged.

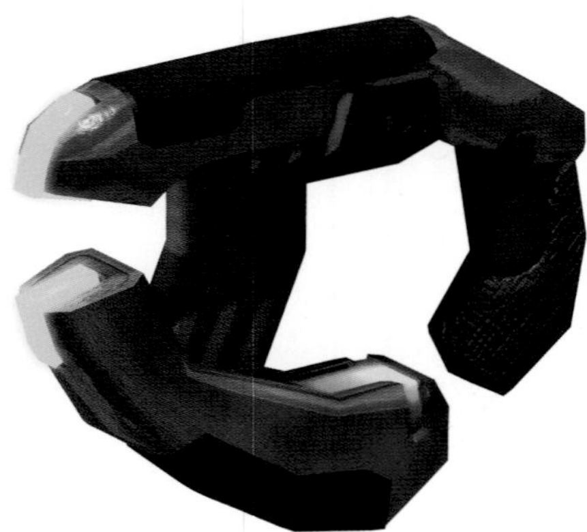

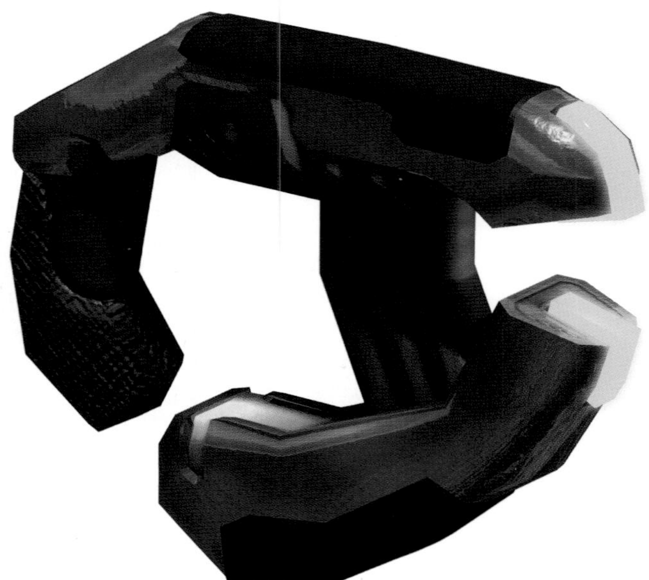

discharging a massive blast at the target. This overcharging is not without risks; the weapon overheats and requires several seconds to cool down. Overcharging dramatically reduces the lifespan of the pistol's power core.

A red SPARTAN demonstrates proper dual-wielding posture with twin plasma pistols.

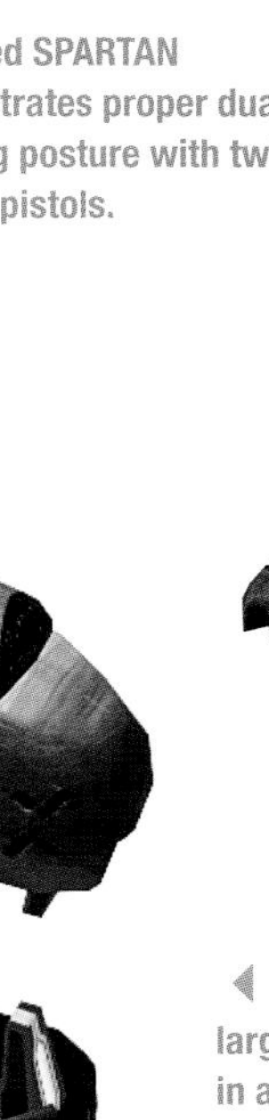

The plasma rifle is surprisingly large and looks almost pistol-sized in an Elite's big hands.

PLASMA RIFLE

The plasma rifle is the main infantry weapon of Covenant forces. The distinctively shaped weapon fires a bolt of energy.

Additionally, the plasma rifle is capable of full-automatic fire, delivering a withering hail of energy blasts in seconds.

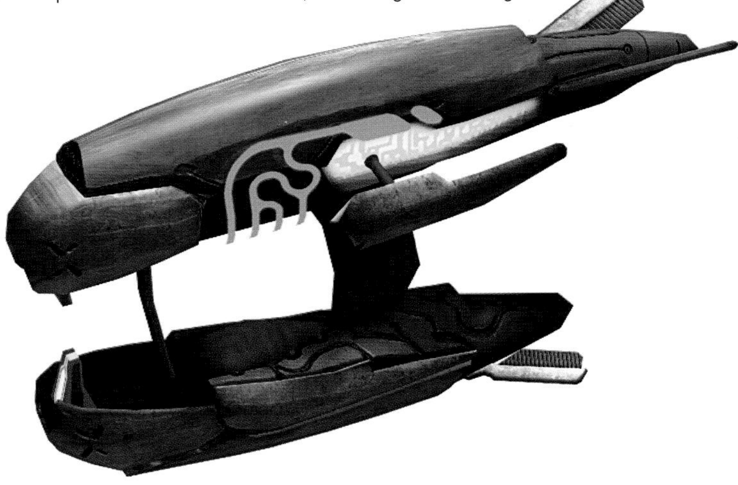

Probably the most commonly encountered Covenant weapon, the plasma rifle fires a rapid stream of superheated plasma.

FUEL ROD GUN

The fuel rod gun (also designed by Robt McLees) is an energy weapon that is used by Covenant Hunters; the weapon is integrated directly into Hunter armor (though versions are mounted on some Covenant vehicles or built as stationary, fixed emplacements).

Veteran Grunts are often equipped with a man-portable version of the fuel rod gun. This weapon is equipped with a dead man's switch—it overloads and explodes if the operator dies.

Fuel rod guns are also mounted as a secondary blast on Covenant Banshee fliers.

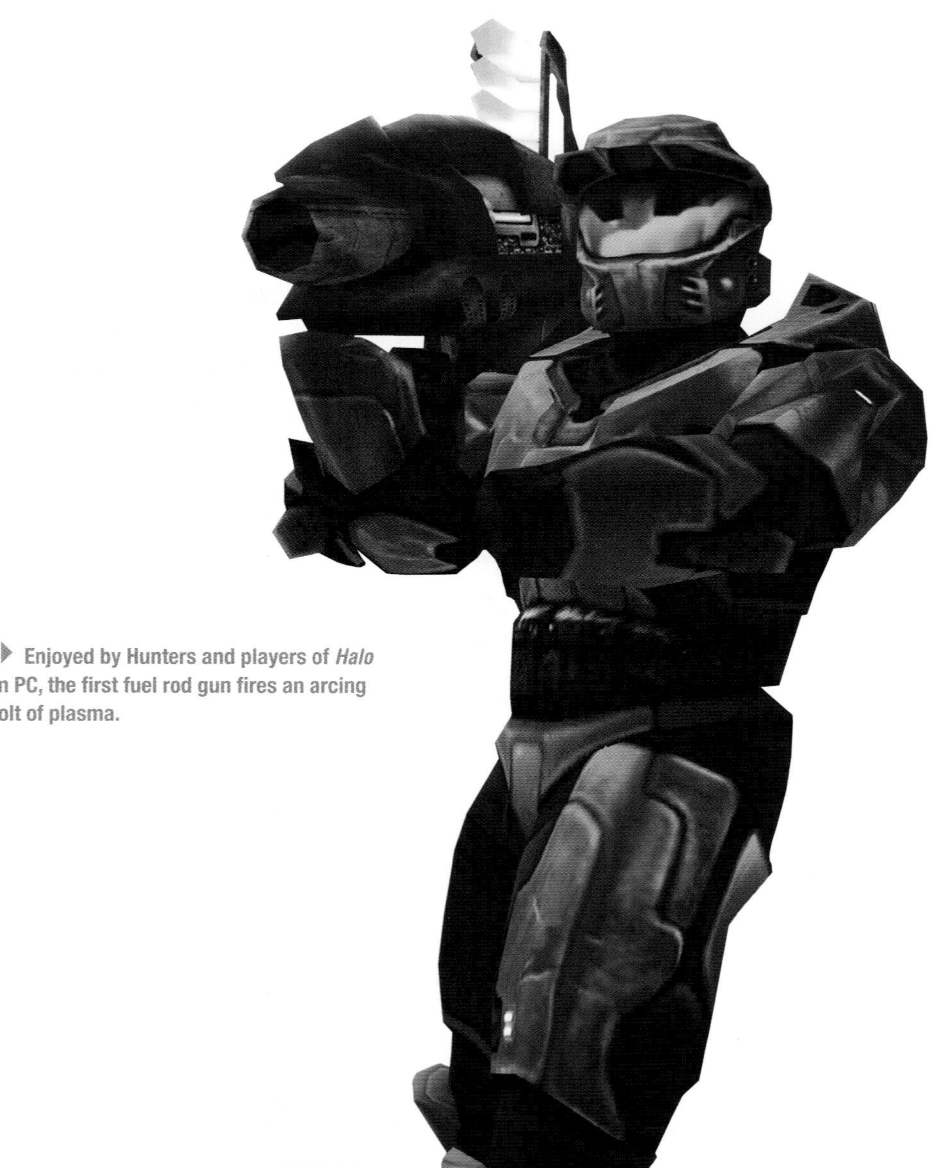

Enjoyed by Hunters and players of *Halo* on PC, the first fuel rod gun fires an arcing bolt of plasma.

NEEDLER

The Covenant needler is an unusual projectile weapon that fires long, glowing "needle" rounds that resemble glowing purple shards of glass. The needles impale soft targets (including human body armor, and certainly unarmored humans), and explode after inflicting puncture damage. The weapon is very quiet, and to date, human scientists are unsure what propels the needles.

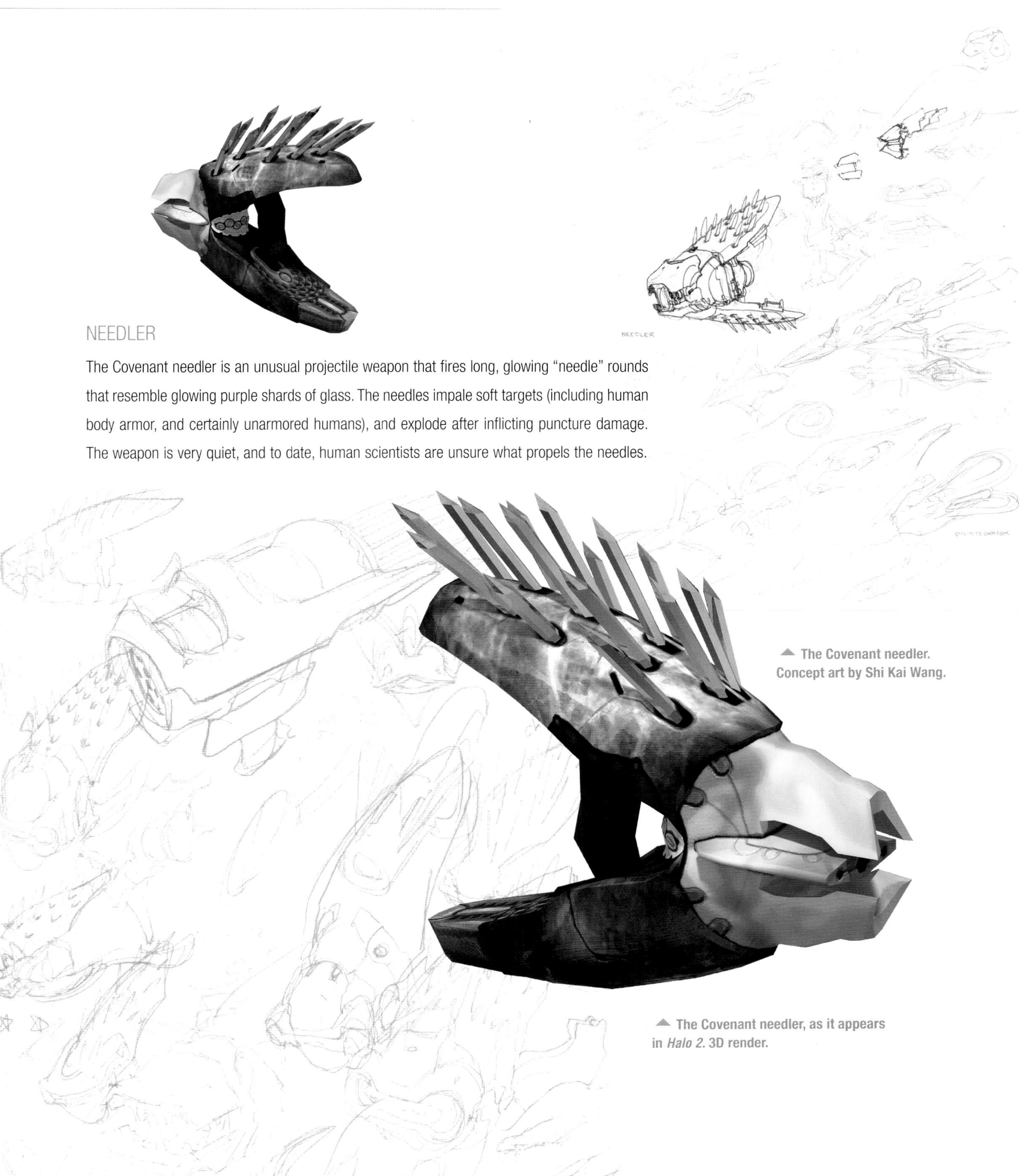

▲ The Covenant needler. Concept art by Shi Kai Wang.

▲ The Covenant needler, as it appears in *Halo 2*. 3D render.

> *"When we hit the point where the game content was complete, and the game went into beta testing, we came in and just* played," *Shi Kai Wang recalls. "I remember coming in really happy. After months of this incredibly grueling schedule, it was really exciting to see the stuff we'd done on the screen, working."*

"SHADE" STATIONARY PLASMA TURRET

Covenant ground forces often employ stationary energy weapon turrets to strengthen defensive positions.

Shades fire a series of rapid-fire plasma "pulses" from the tribar energy emitter. The beams flash a brilliant purple-white and inflict tremendous damage.

The gunner sits in the "ball" section, directly behind the energy emitter. The ball in turn floats on an antigrav cushion located in the wide, claw-footed tripod mounting structure.

The turret rotates a full 360 degrees, and can be employed against aerial and ground targets.

The Shade turret blurs the lines between architecture, weaponry, and vehicles.

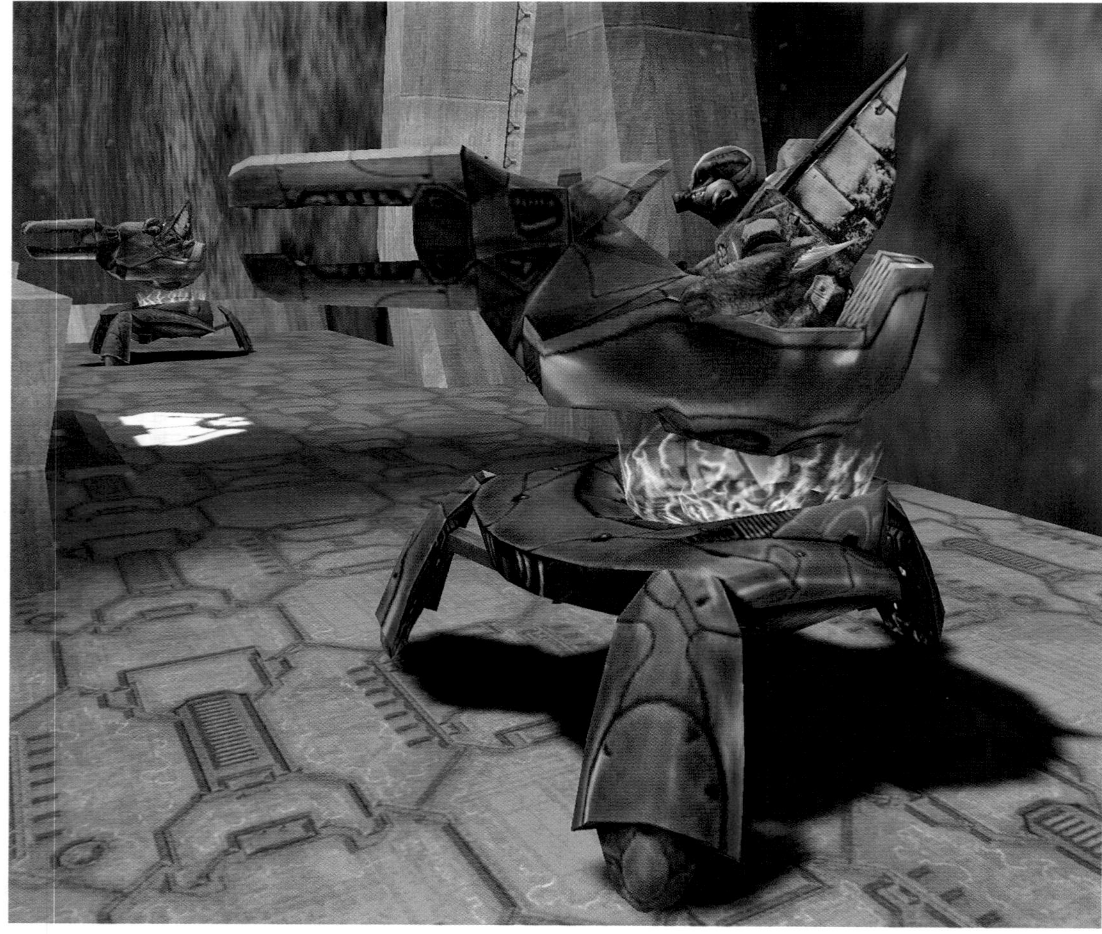

Shade plasma turrets are indisputably Covenant in appearance but can be manned by human gunners. Screen capture from *Halo*.

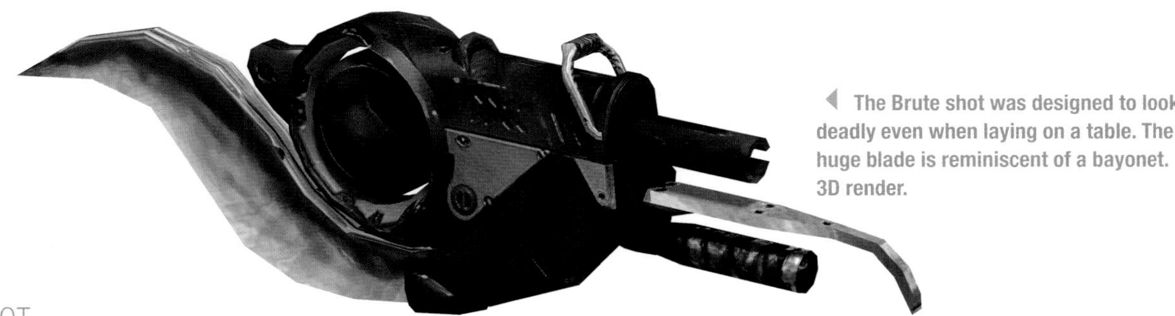

The Brute shot was designed to look deadly even when laying on a table. The huge blade is reminiscent of a bayonet. 3D render.

BRUTE SHOT

The Brute shot seems destined to become one of the defining weapons in *Halo 2*. It was created to match its owner, the Brute. Massive, gorilla-like aliens require primitive-looking, viscious guns, and the Brute shot captures that aesthetic perfectly. It looks almost too dangerous to hold, with its curving stock-mount blade and gaping, grenade-launching barrel. Introducing *flavors* from the varying Covenant species is as important as any broad design aesthetic for the Covenant.

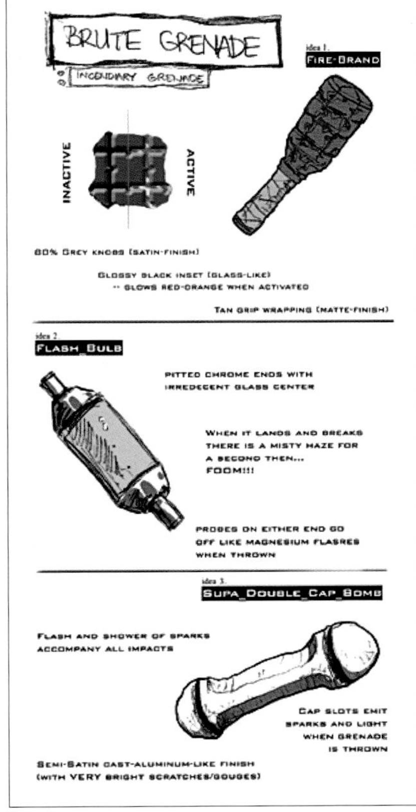

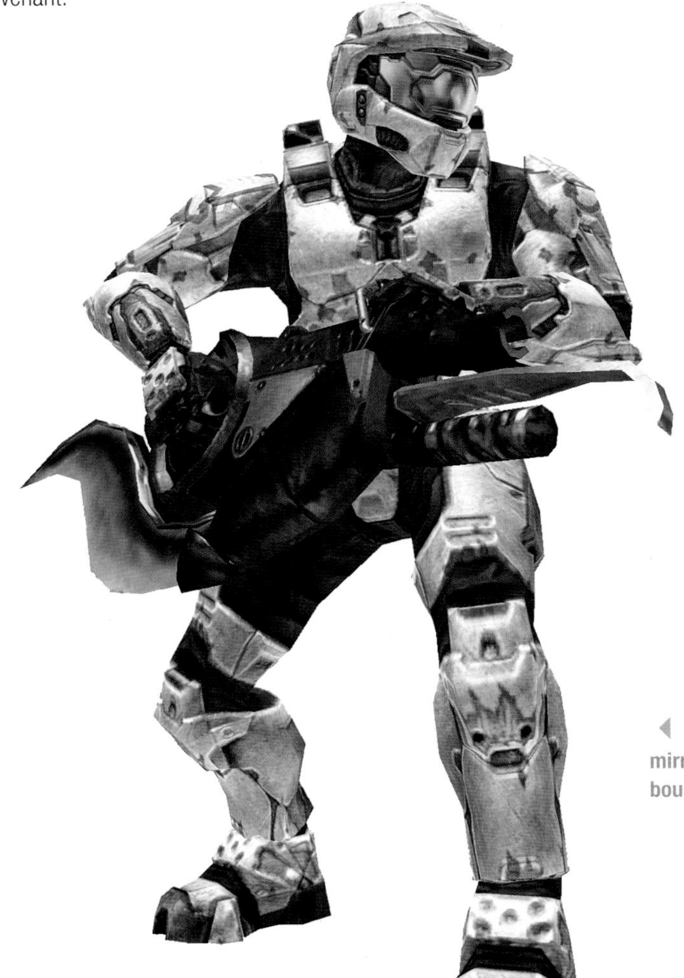

The Brute shot's physical appearance is mirrored in its action—the gun fires bouncing, devastating grenades.

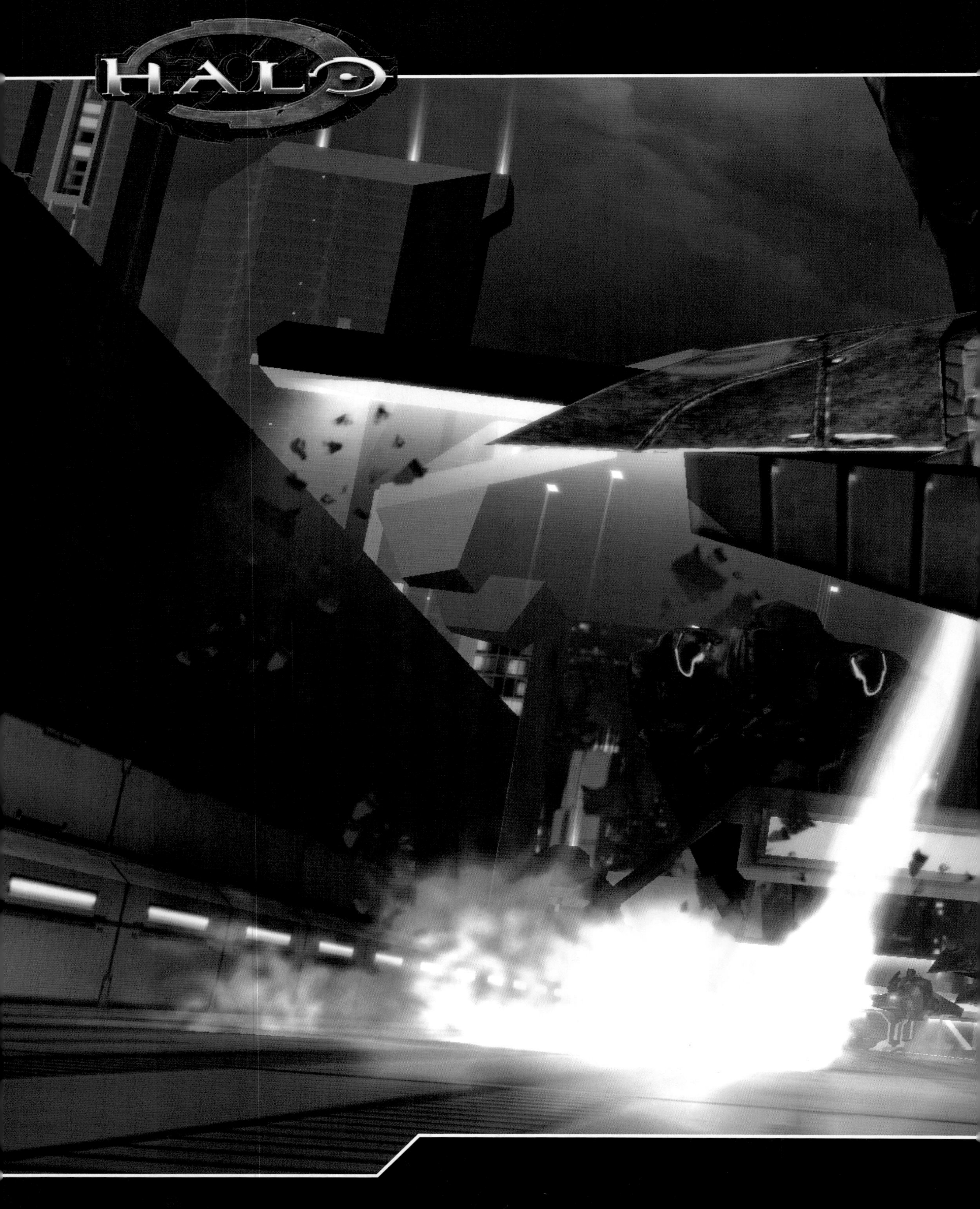
HALO

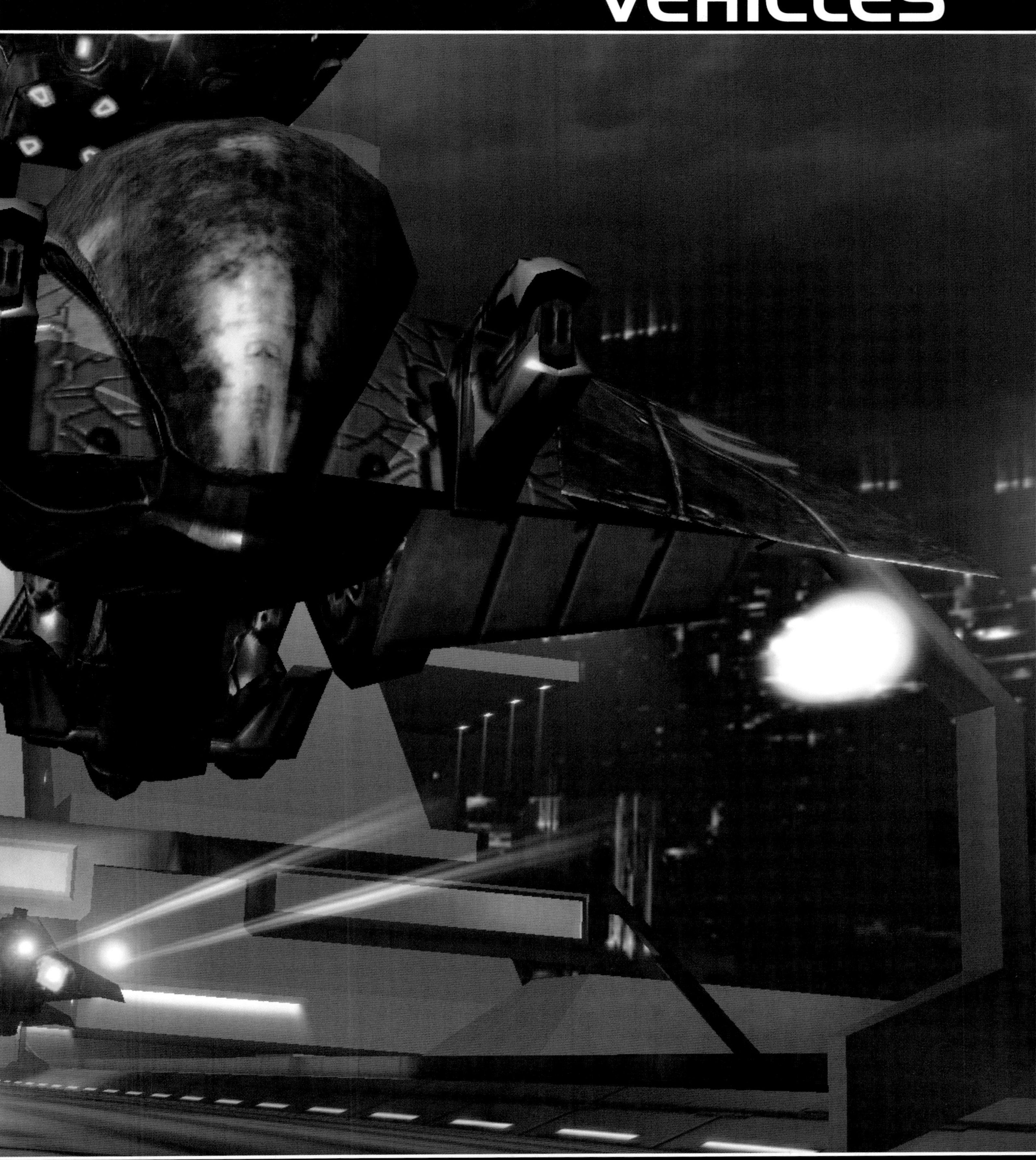

"Faster!" Corporal Harland shouted. "You want to die in the mud, Marine?"

"Hell no, sir!" Private Fincher stomped on the accelerator and the Warthog's tires spun in the streambed. They caught, and the vehicle fishtailed through the gravel, across the bank, and onto the sandy shore.

Harland strapped himself into the rear of the Warthog, one hand clamped onto the vehicle's massive 50mm chain gun.

Something moved in the brush behind them—Harland fired a sustained burst. The deafening sound from "Old Faithful" shook the teeth in his head. Ferns, trees, and vines exploded and splintered as the gunfire scythed through the foliage . . . then nothing was moving anymore.

—Excerpt from
Halo: The Fall of Reach
by Eric Nylund.

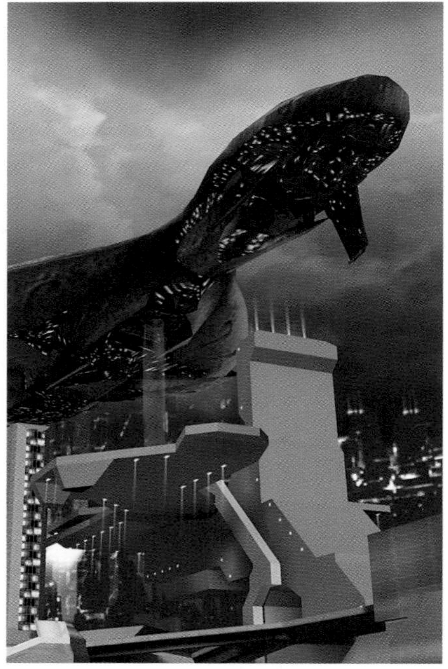

A Covenant Cruiser. Screen shot from *Halo 2*.

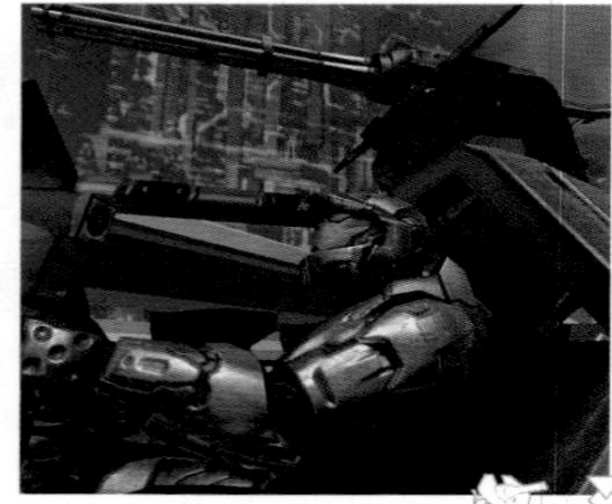

A close-up of the Warthog shows off vehicle and character detail.

Vehicles play an important role in *Halo*—and mark a departure from the norm for the genre of first-person shooter games.

Though several FPS games have included vehicles, they were handled in a fairly rudimentary way (often running on scripted "rails" through a particular level, and offering limited, or even no, control to the player). Along with *Halo*'s ability to allow the player to seamlessly make the transition between interior and exterior environments, the inclusion of a wide variety of vehicles for the player to control was one of the features that made the game stand out.

To develop the vehicles, the artists began with concept sketches, which were refined and redrawn several times. "I was inspired by all sorts of sources," says art director Marcus Lehto. "I tend to absorb a lot of what I see, in movies, on TV. When I see something visually interesting in a film, it's like 'Wow, if we could do *that* and translate it into a game . . .'"

After the concept sketches were accepted, 3-D artists would begin building models—along with the texturing, bump mapping, and light mapping.

According to Lehto, "The basis for everything we put in the games is realism. We try and make things look tangible and real to the player, so that they can latch on to them and believe in them, and immerse themselves into the game as completely as possible."

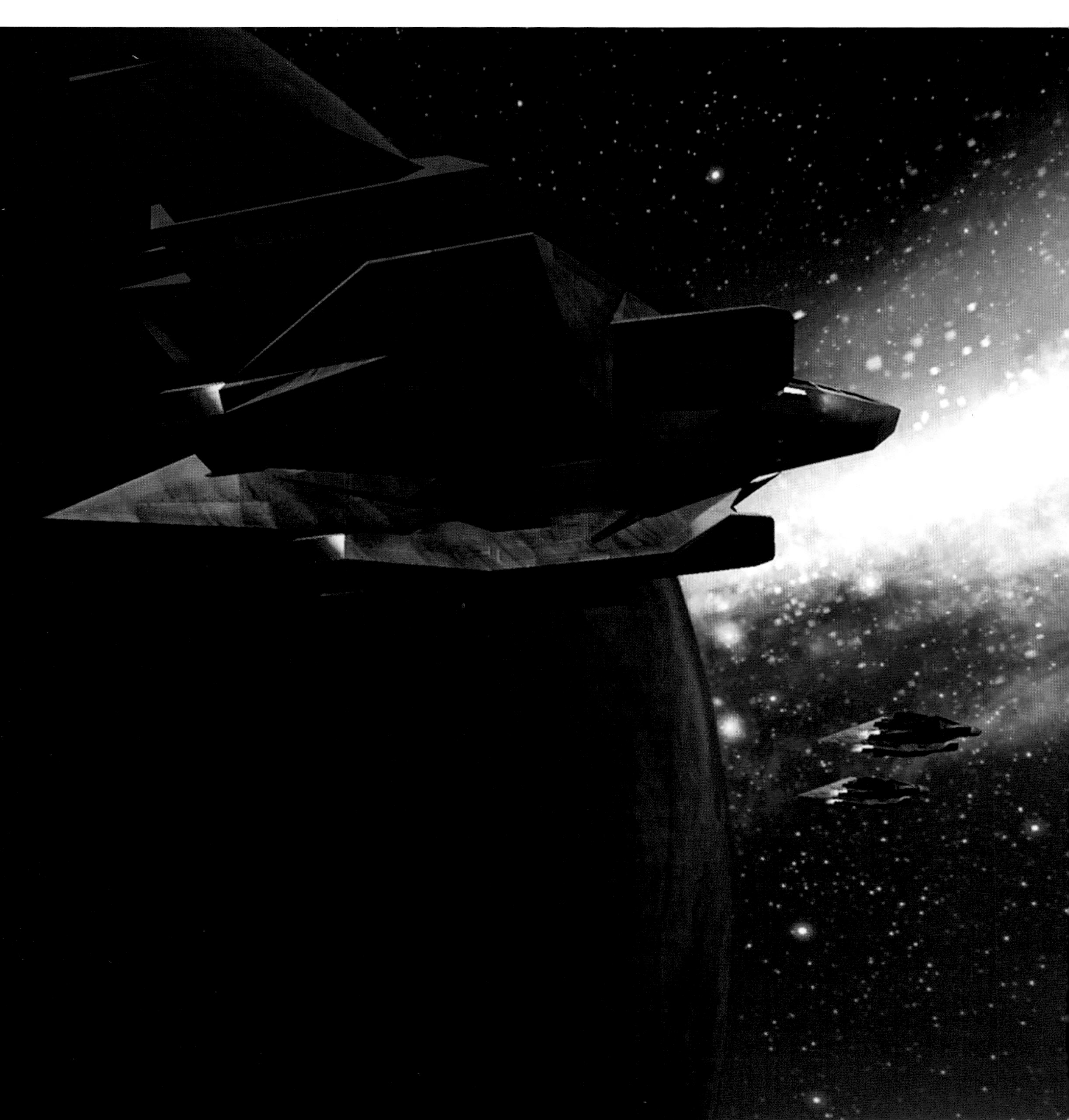

▲ A flight of Longsword heavy fighters on patrol. Though they appear only briefly on screen, these vehicles play an important role in *Halo*'s story: The Master Chief's escape from Halo depends on the angular spacecraft.

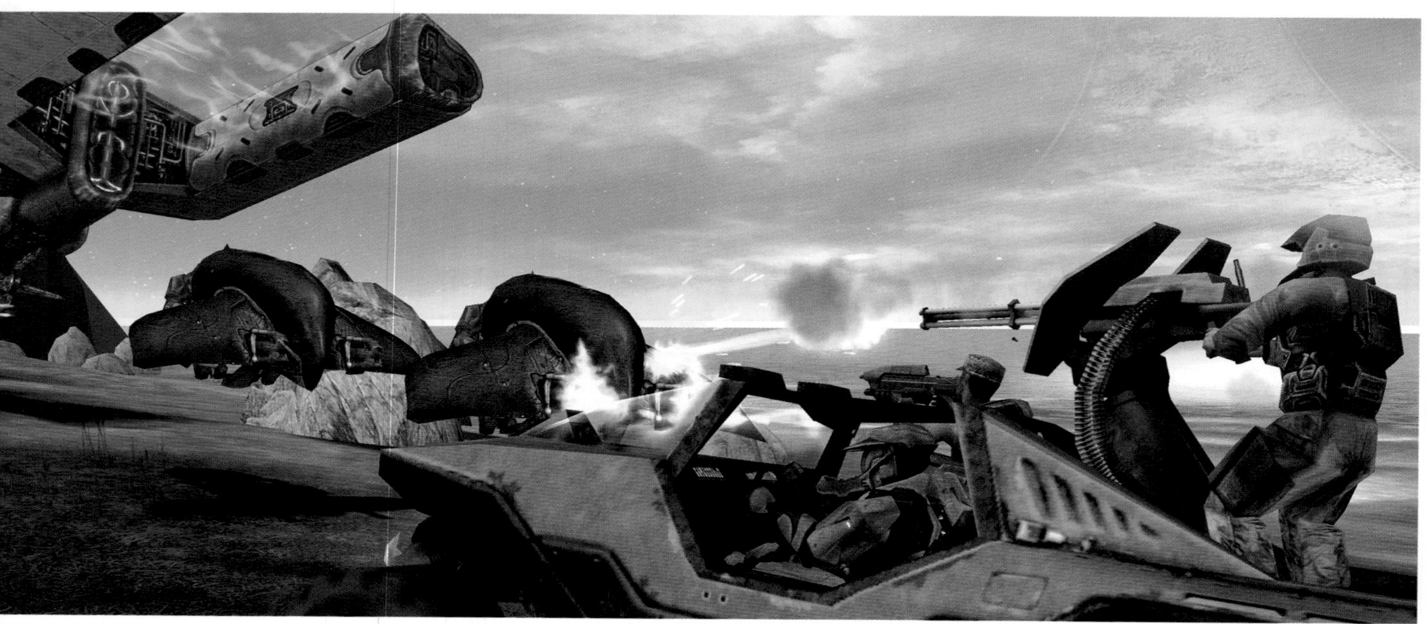

▲ This panoramic screen shot from *Halo* shows off early vehicle-on-vehicle combat, a motif that is repeated throughout the game.

HUMAN VEHICLES

Marcus Lehto, Eric Arroyo, and Eddie Smith spearheaded the creation of the humans' vehicles. "Human vehicles were designed to be very functional and utilitarian—the aliens got all the really sleek stuff," says Lehto. "But it was so much fun to design the vehicles, and make them look like something you'd just want to drive around, and crash into stuff, and mow through Covenant ranks."

▲ A greater knowledge of the Xbox's capabilities allows the team to add things like vehicle damage. The M12G1 Warthog LAAV is seen here in one of its damaged permutations.

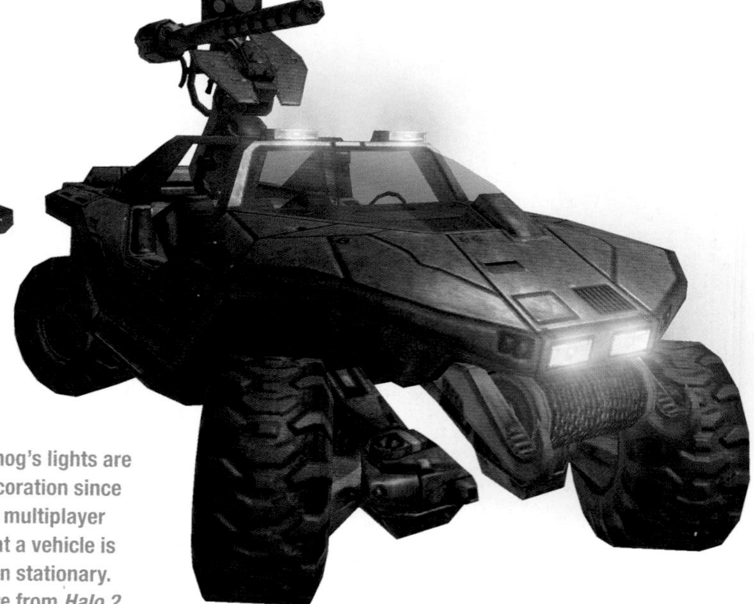

▶ The Warthog's lights are more than decoration since they can alert multiplayer opponents that a vehicle is occupied when stationary. Screen capture from *Halo 2*.

WARTHOG

The Warthog—a four-wheel-drive military "jeep"—is the first vehicle the player encounters. The M12 Light Reconnaissance Vehicle is fast, and can carry two additional Marine passengers: one riding shotgun and another manning the massive chain gun mounted in the rear of the vehicle.

For *Halo 2*, several variants of the Warthog were considered—and a civilian version was briefly glimpsed on a billboard during a scene from a demonstration "movie" developed for *Halo 2*.

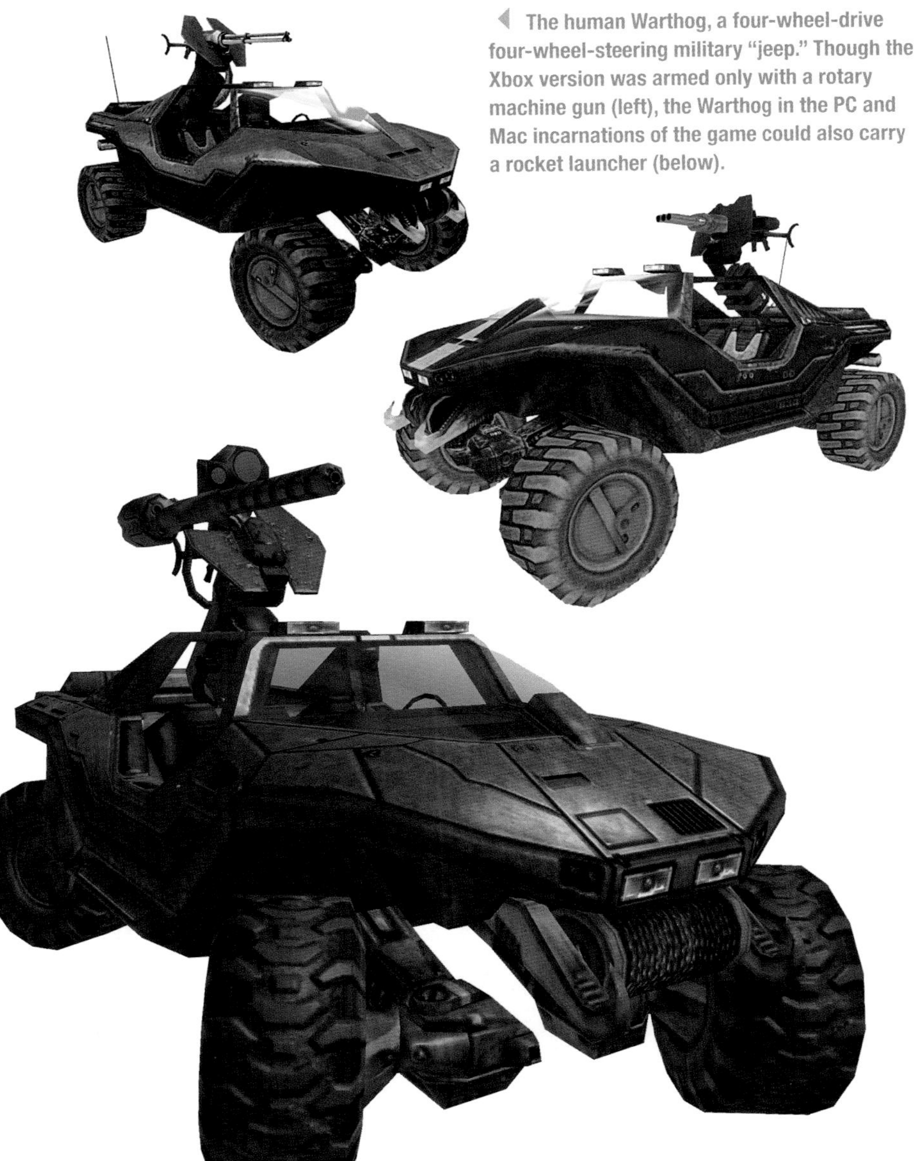

◀ **The human Warthog, a four-wheel-drive four-wheel-steering military "jeep." Though the Xbox version was armed only with a rotary machine gun (left), the Warthog in the PC and Mac incarnations of the game could also carry a rocket launcher (below).**

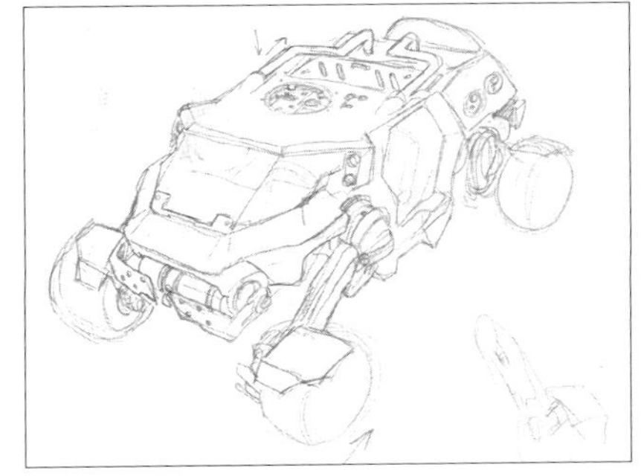

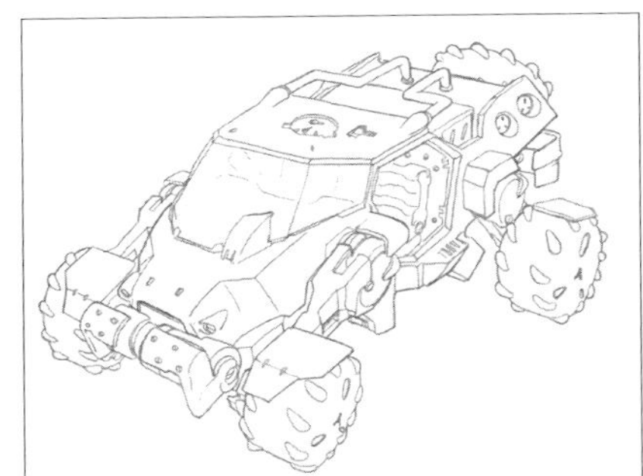

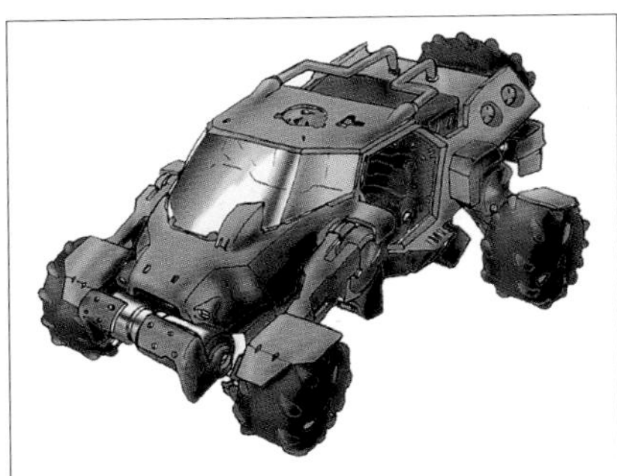

▲ **When developing the vehicles for the game, the designers wanted above all to create things that would be fun to drive. Nowhere is that more apparent than in these designs for the Warthog. Concept art by Shi Kai Wang.**

"SCORPION" TANK

The "Scorpion" tank (a.k.a. the M808B Main Battle Tank) is a massive, lumbering behemoth, armed with a powerful 90mm cannon, and a chain gun similar to the Warthog's. The Scorpion's treads are mounted on a unique independent suspension system, which allows it to move quickly over uneven terrain.

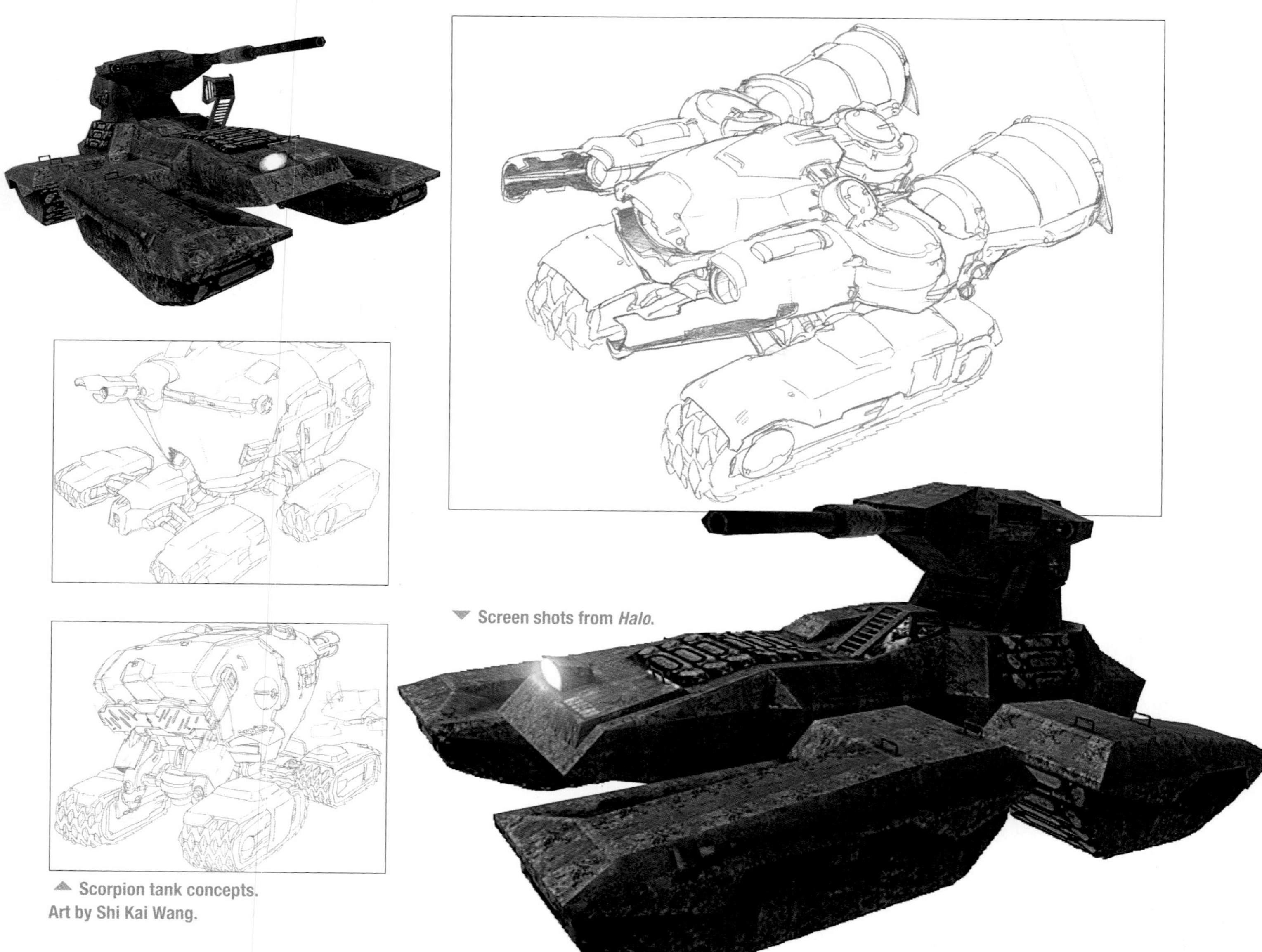

▲ An early concept of the Scorpion tank by Marcus Lehto.

▲ Scorpion tank concepts. Art by Shi Kai Wang.

▼ Screen shots from *Halo*.

PELICAN

The standard method of deploying people from orbit to ground is the D77-TC Troop Carrier—the "Pelican." The Pelican is capable of vertical takeoff and landing.

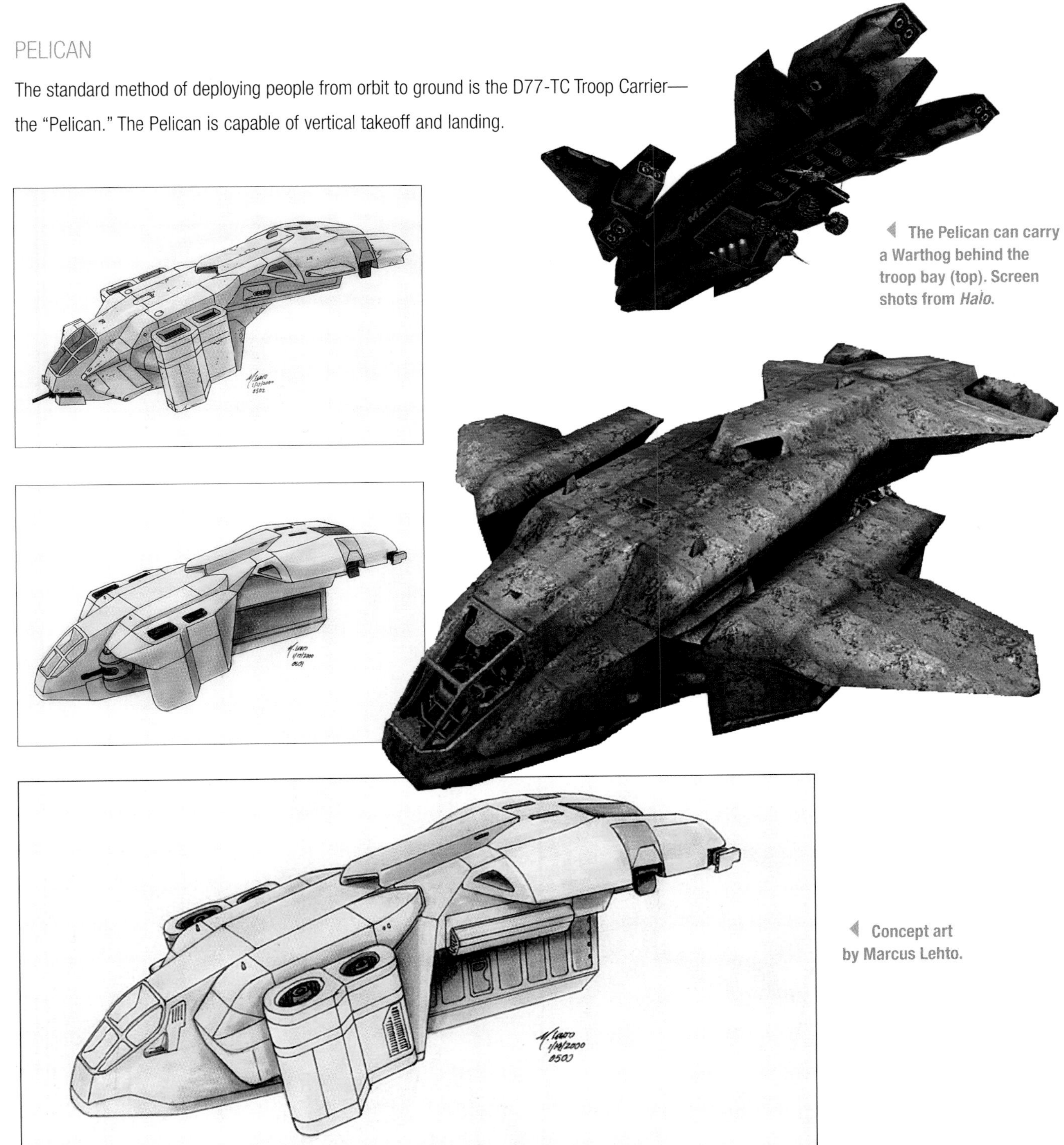

The Pelican can carry a Warthog behind the troop bay (top). Screen shots from *Halo*.

Concept art by Marcus Lehto.

▸ The Longsword fighter, featured very briefly, still underwent many design iterations—showing the need to make sure each aspect of the universe is cohesive and "correct."

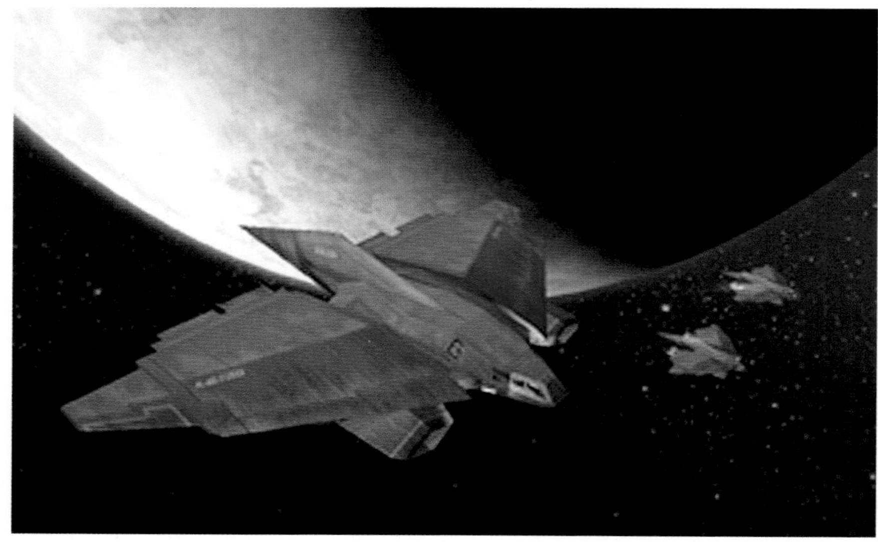

▾ The *Pillar of Autumn*'s final resting place is dramatically illustrated in this concept by Shi Kai Wang.

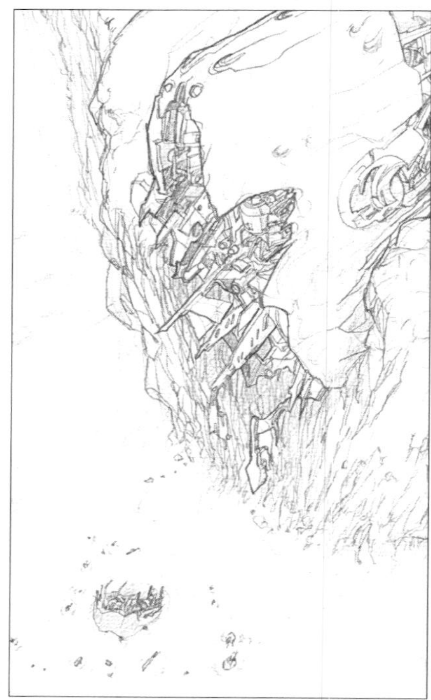

LONGSWORD FIGHTER

The Longsword (which acts as a fighter-bomber) is heavily influenced by modern stealth fighter designs such as the F-117, and stealth bombers, like the B-2. Though this vehicle is sighted only briefly in *Halo*, and is not a vehicle the player can control, the Longsword still underwent a series of design iterations.

▾ *Pillar of Autumn* screen shot from *Halo*.

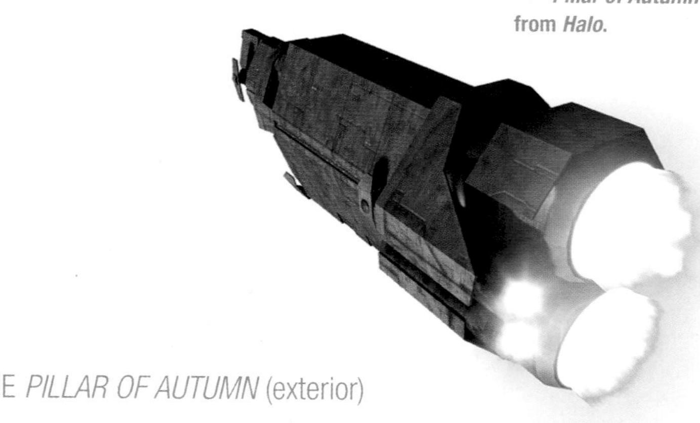

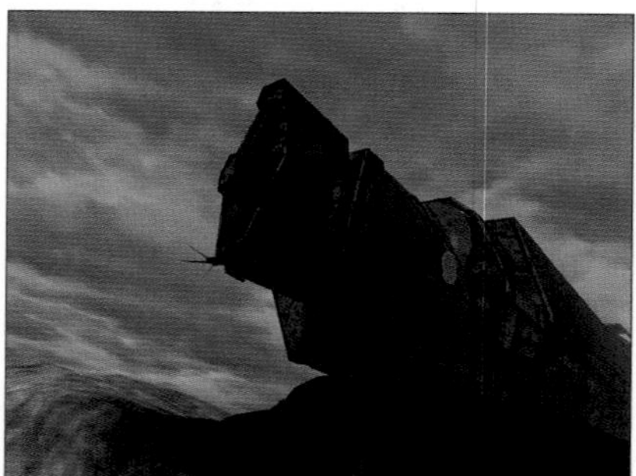

▴ Screen shot of the site of the *Autumn*'s crash on Halo.

THE *PILLAR OF AUTUMN* (exterior)

The last surviving vessel from the humans' doomed stand at Reach, the *Pillar of Autumn* is the vehicle that brings the Master Chief to the mysterious ring-shaped world, Halo. While Paul Russel provided the interior designs of this battered, battle-weary cruiser, the ship's exterior was created by artist Lorraine McLees. "My involvement with *Halo 1* was almost incidental, past the work I was doing on the visual identity/branding stuff. No one was working on the *Pillar of Autumn* exterior design because everyone was so busy. Robt [McLees] felt that by the time we got around to it, it'd be too late, and the result would be substandard, due to time constraints.

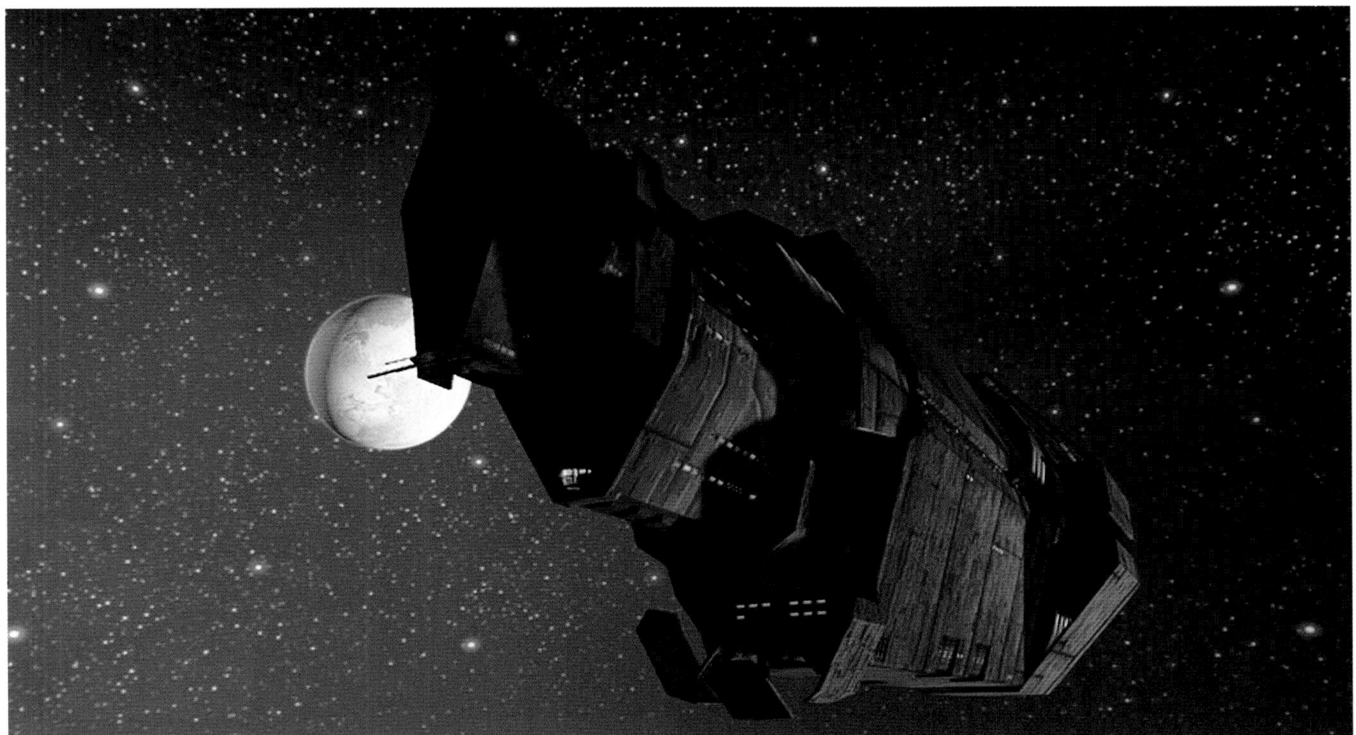

▲ The *Pillar of Autumn* is a classic massive spaceship following in the footsteps of the Imperial *Star Destroyer*, and even *Battlestar Galactica*.

"So, I talked to Jaime Griesemer and Marcus Lehto, and they told me the *Pillar of Autumn* needed to look specifically human—but at that point the only examples I had to work from were a boat design (which got cut from the game), the weapons, and the Warthog.

"I did a handful of sketches, and the guys really liked the one that was reminiscent of the assault rifle's shape. Marcus thought it looked proportionally small, though, so I ended up extending the ship about three hundred percent, making it longer than it was tall."

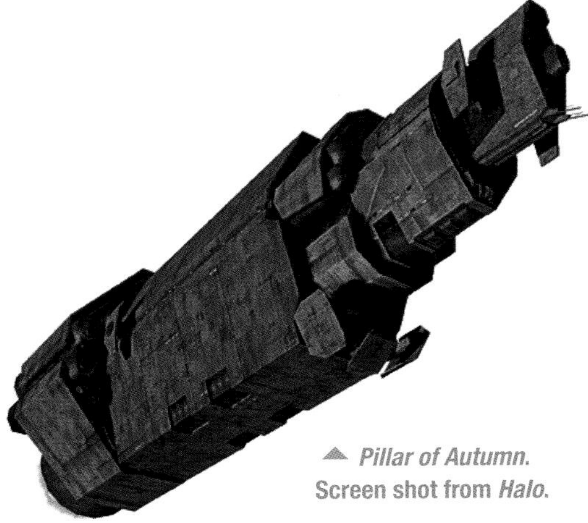

▲ *Pillar of Autumn*. Screen shot from *Halo*.

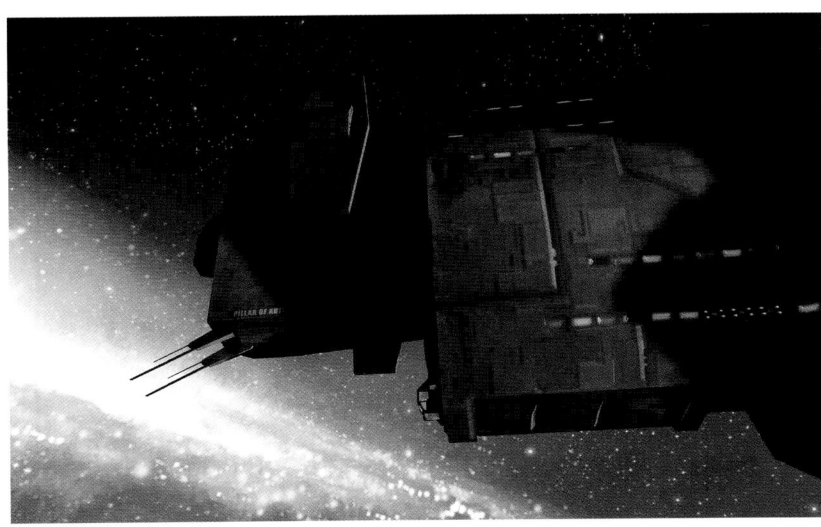

◀ This moodily lit shot shows off the overhanging sections and intersecting planes of the huge craft.

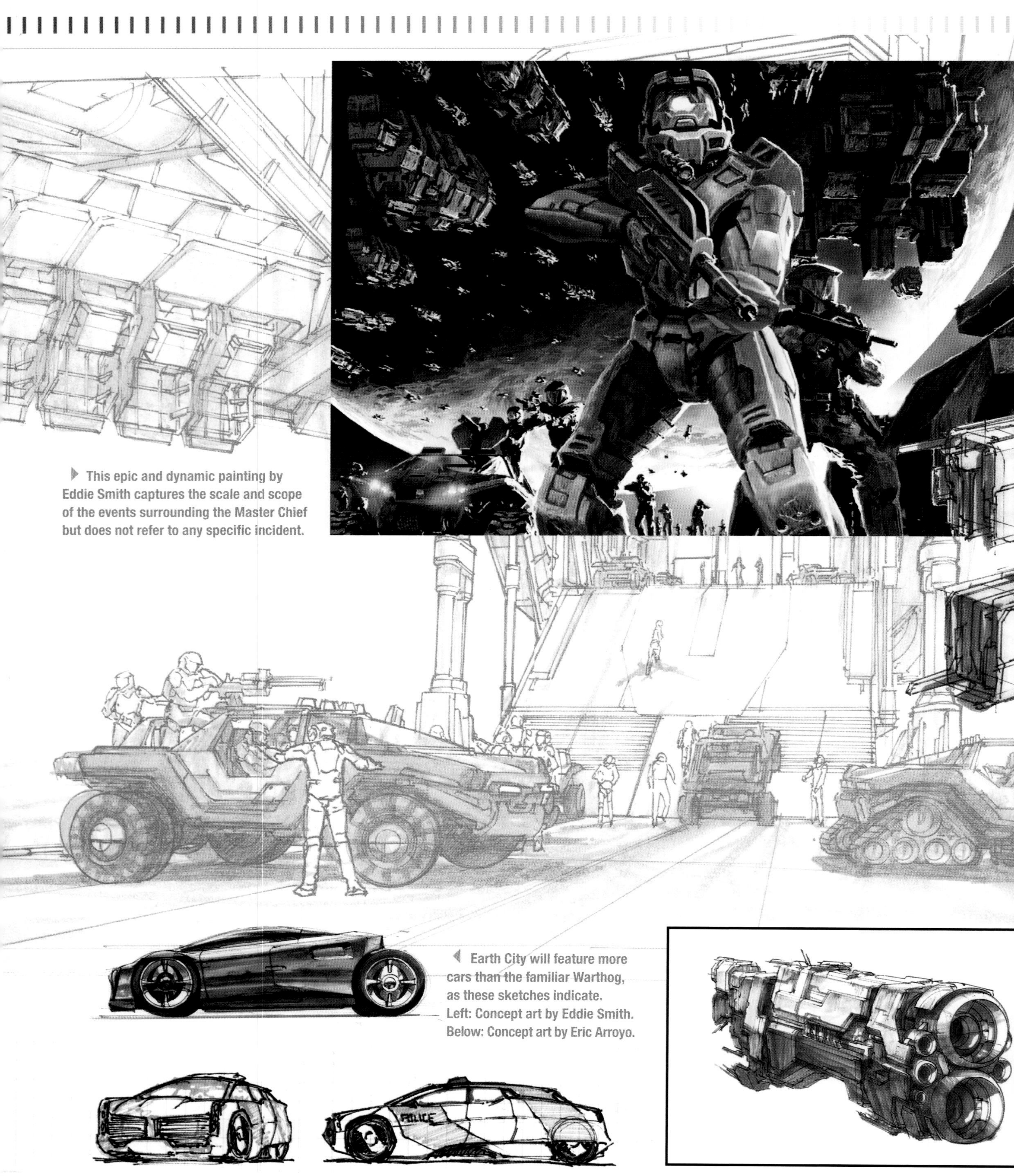

This epic and dynamic painting by Eddie Smith captures the scale and scope of the events surrounding the Master Chief but does not refer to any specific incident.

Earth City will feature more cars than the familiar Warthog, as these sketches indicate. Left: Concept art by Eddie Smith. Below: Concept art by Eric Arroyo.

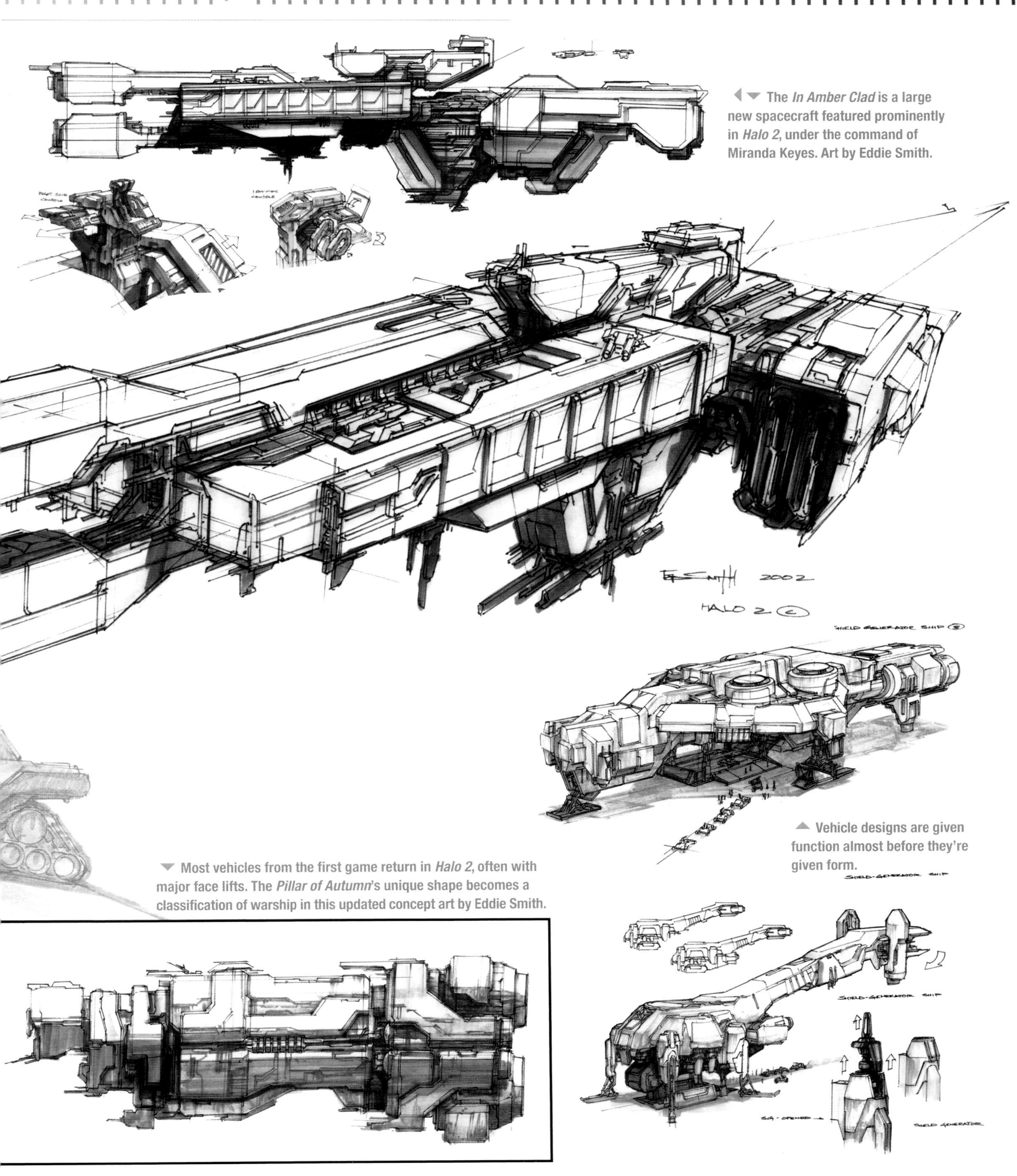

◀ ▼ The *In Amber Clad* is a large new spacecraft featured prominently in *Halo 2*, under the command of Miranda Keyes. Art by Eddie Smith.

▲ Vehicle designs are given function almost before they're given form.

▼ Most vehicles from the first game return in *Halo 2*, often with major face lifts. The *Pillar of Autumn*'s unique shape becomes a classification of warship in this updated concept art by Eddie Smith.

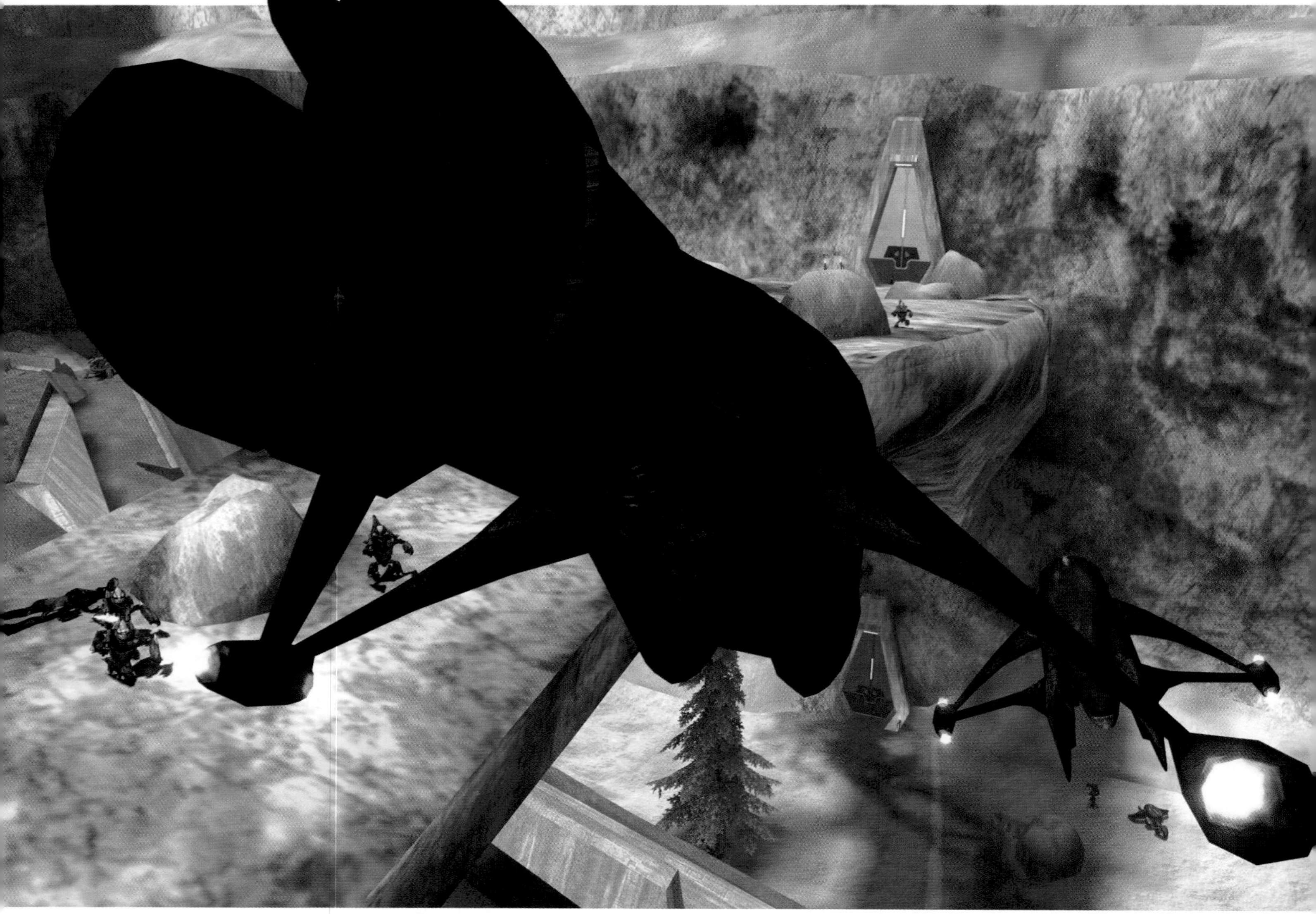

COVENANT VEHICLES

BANSHEE

The Banshee is the Covenant's low-altitude attack craft, favored by the Elites for the role of air support during ground operations. Highly maneuverable, it is armed with two plasma cannons and a fuel rod gun. It's low flight ceiling (estimated between 100 and 300 meters) makes it vulnerable to antiaircraft guns and well-armed infantry.

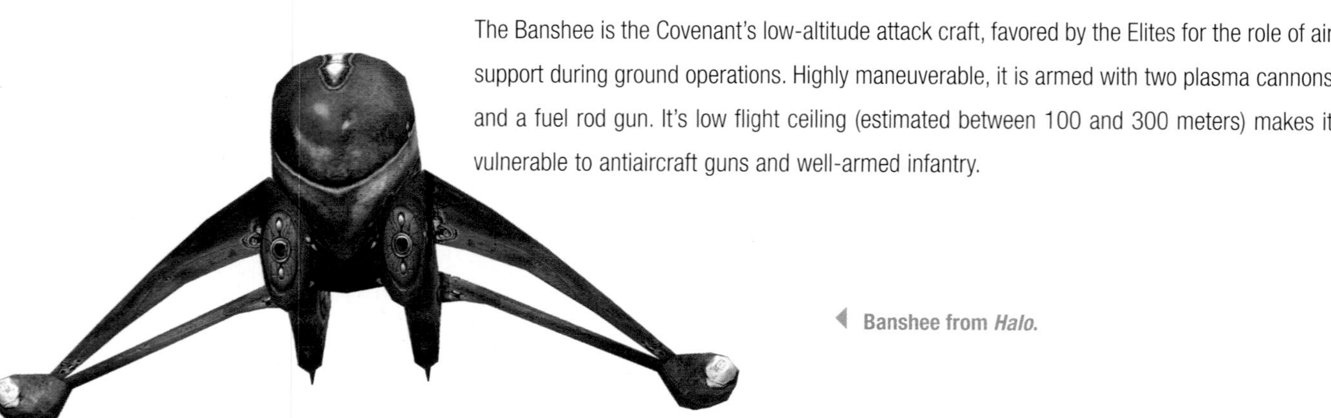

Banshee from *Halo*.

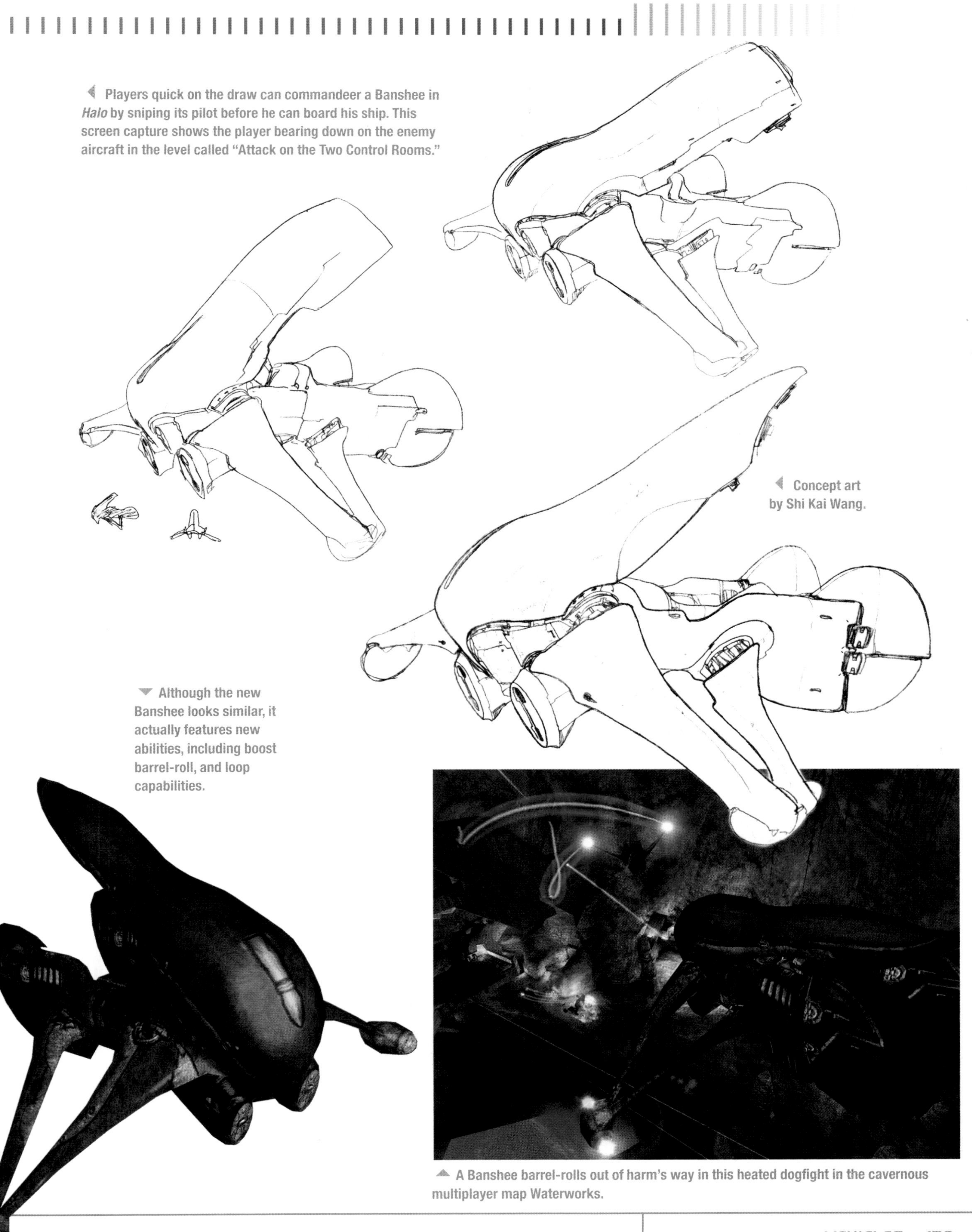

◀ Players quick on the draw can commandeer a Banshee in *Halo* by sniping its pilot before he can board his ship. This screen capture shows the player bearing down on the enemy aircraft in the level called "Attack on the Two Control Rooms."

◀ Concept art by Shi Kai Wang.

▼ Although the new Banshee looks similar, it actually features new abilities, including boost barrel-roll, and loop capabilities.

▲ A Banshee barrel-rolls out of harm's way in this heated dogfight in the cavernous multiplayer map Waterworks.

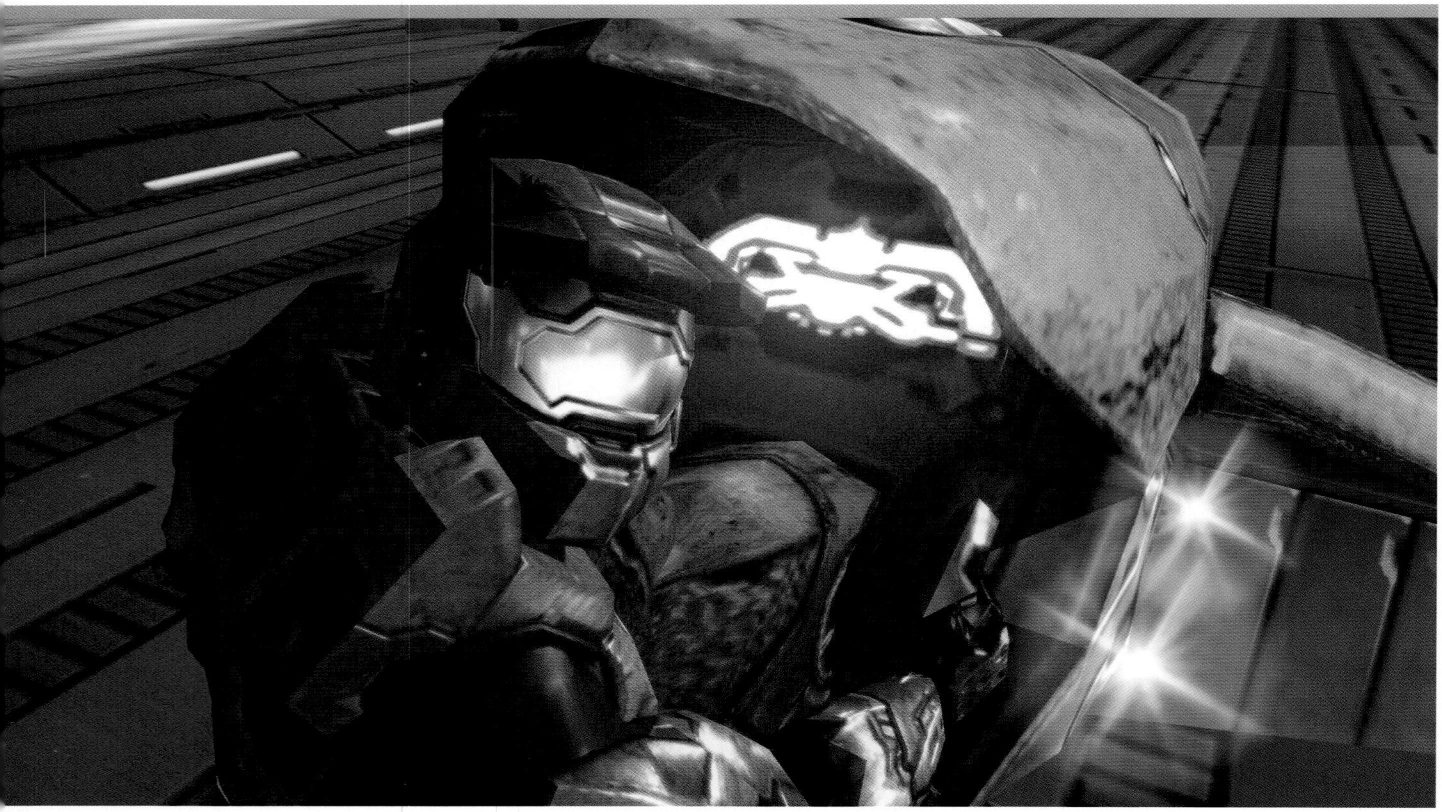

▲ The Master Chief at the controls of the *Halo 2* Ghost, complete with new, more detailed fascia and instrumentation. Screen shot from the *Halo 2* E3 2003 demo.

GHOST

The Ghost is a one-man hover vehicle primarily used in a scouting and close infantry support role. The Ghost hovers low to the ground and moves very quickly. It possesses minimal armor and a pair of plasma cannons. Speed and agility are the Ghost's primary assets on the battlefield.

Although similar in some respects to many single-person transport systems, the Ghost takes it aesthetic cues from the insect world, with smooth, lustrous surfaces reminiscent of beetle wings and casings. It's these iridescent coleopteran surfaces that place it clearly in the Covenant realm. Its grav-lifter engine effects were invisible in the first game—although in *Halo 2* they benefit from an ethereal particle system, and a very dynamic and brilliant "boost effect."

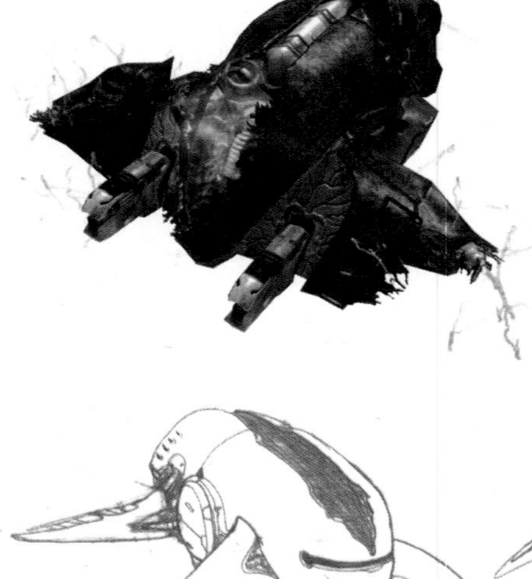

▼ A battle-damaged Ghost from *Halo 2*.

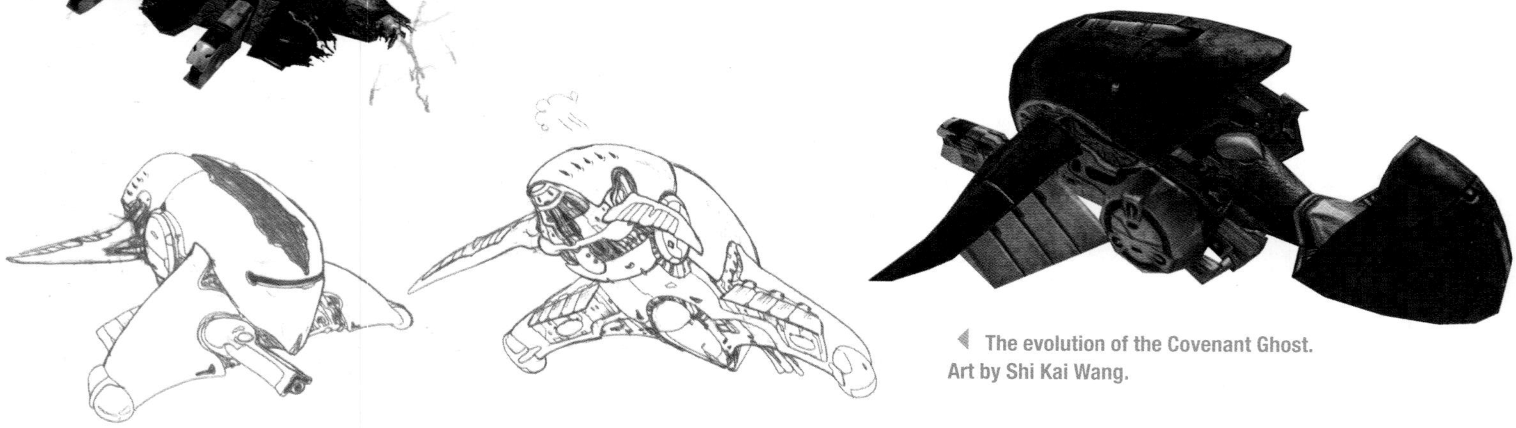

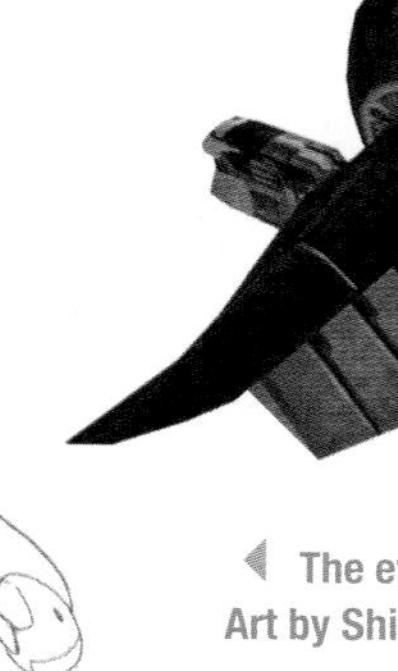

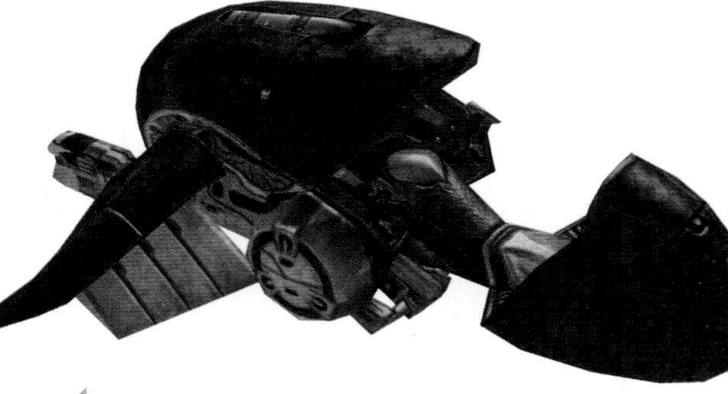

◀ The evolution of the Covenant Ghost. Art by Shi Kai Wang.

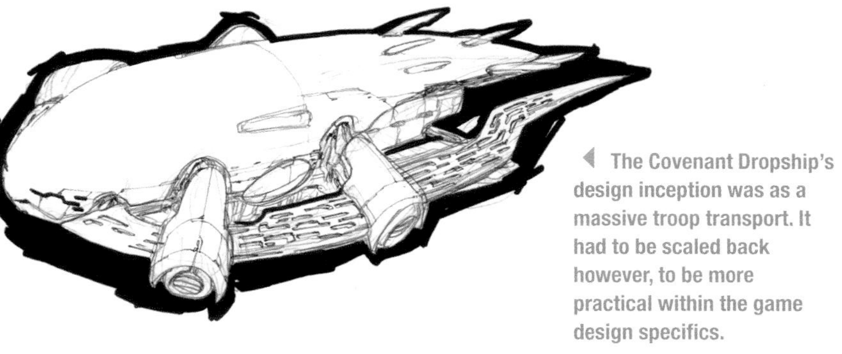

The Covenant Dropship's design inception was as a massive troop transport. It had to be scaled back however, to be more practical within the game design specifics.

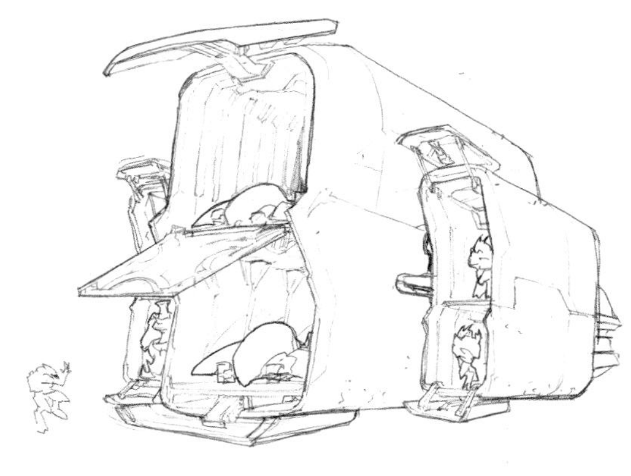

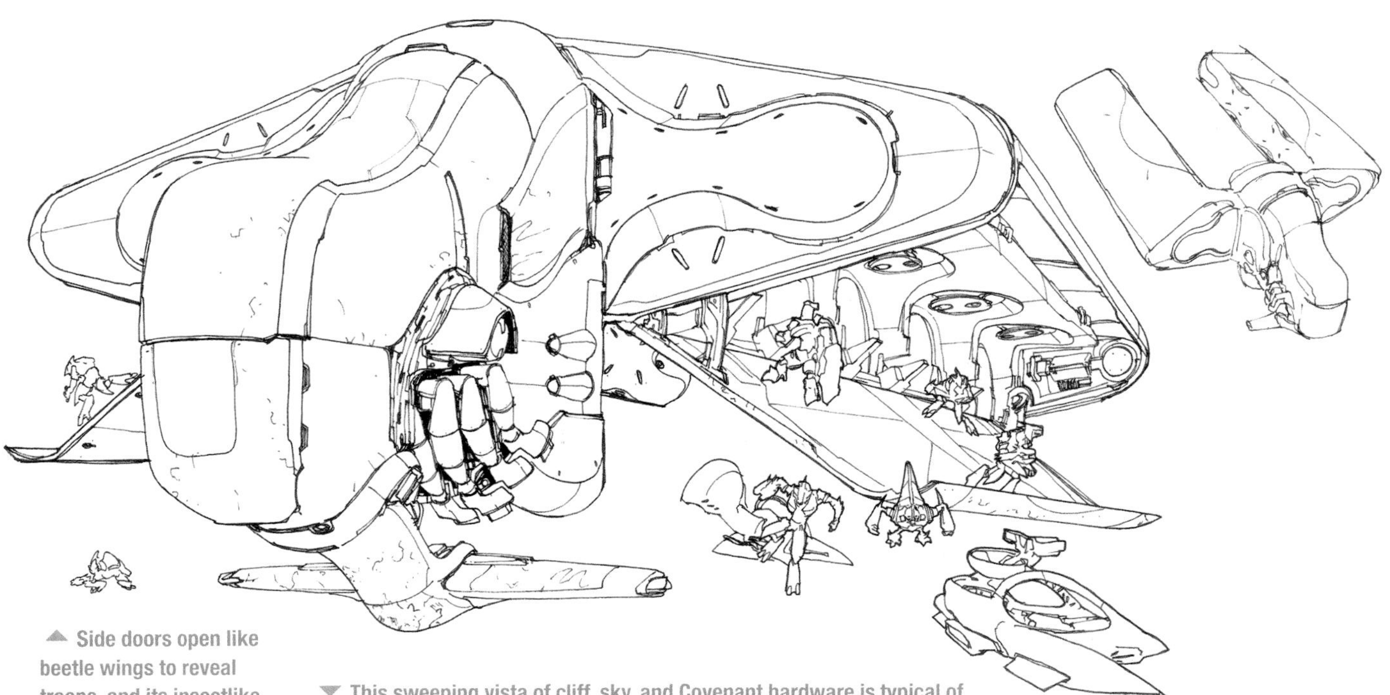

Side doors open like beetle wings to reveal troops, and its insectlike appearance make it a dramatic arrival during its many in-game scenarios. Artist Lorraine McLees notes, "It has the coolest rear-end of all the Covenant ships."

This sweeping vista of cliff, sky, and Covenant hardware is typical of the memorable moments encountered early in the game.

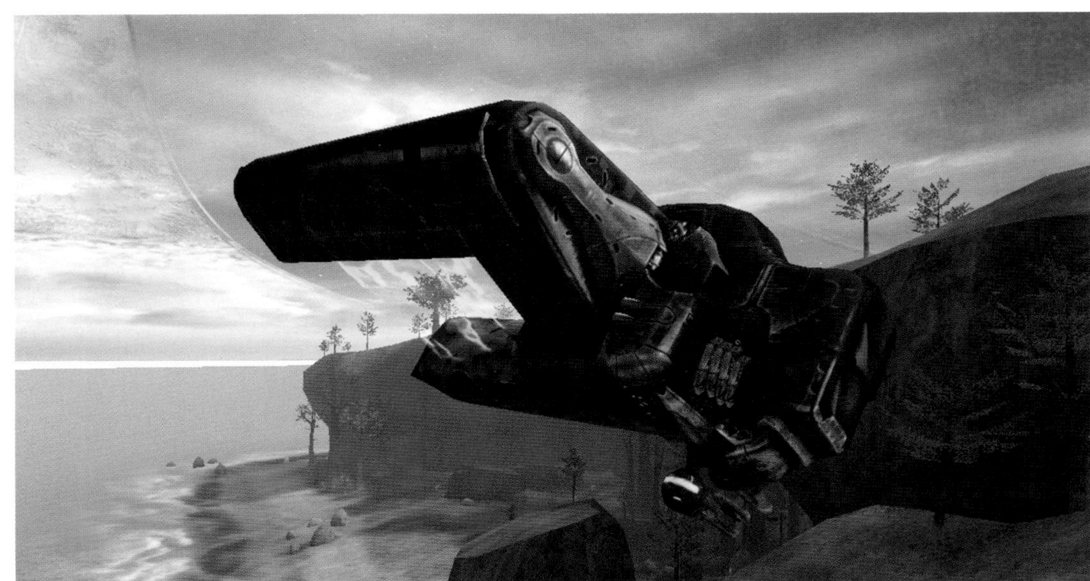

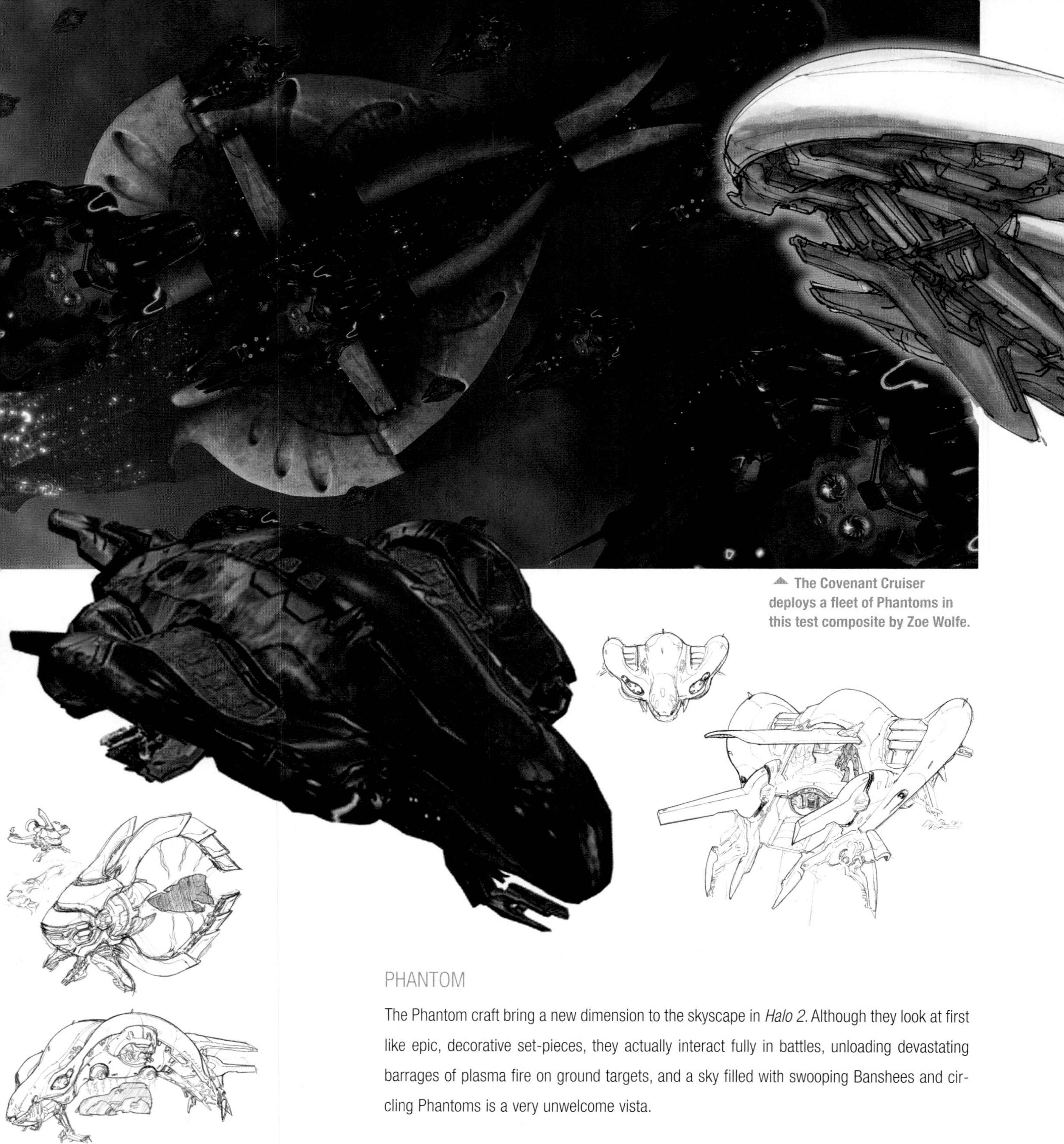

▲ The Covenant Cruiser deploys a fleet of Phantoms in this test composite by Zoe Wolfe.

PHANTOM

The Phantom craft bring a new dimension to the skyscape in *Halo 2*. Although they look at first like epic, decorative set-pieces, they actually interact fully in battles, unloading devastating barrages of plasma fire on ground targets, and a sky filled with swooping Banshees and circling Phantoms is a very unwelcome vista.

▲ The Phantom was designed to be big enough to carry a Wraith tank into combat. The manner in which it would fly, deliver its cargo, and land were all taken into consideration during the design phase. The Phantom craft manages to combine squat bulk with swooping, curving lines to create an airborne presence that looks heavy, menacing, and still somehow sleek. Art by Shi Kai Wang.

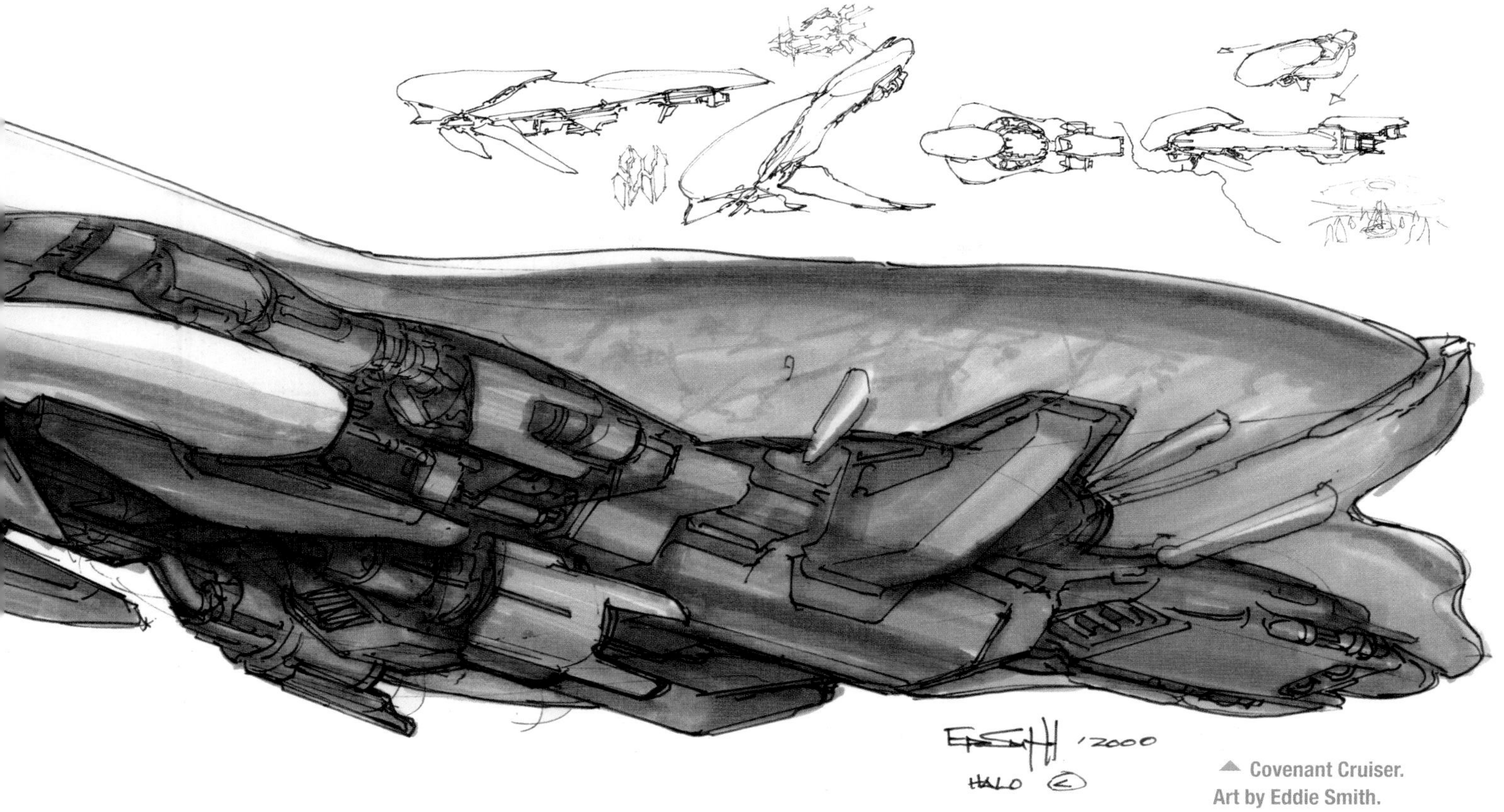

▲ Covenant Cruiser. Art by Eddie Smith.

COVENANT CRUISER

The sheer scale of the Cruiser had to be evident in its swooping curves and sleek lines. Making it graceful, bulky and menacing were all design challenges. Like all Covenant hardware, it's organic in the sweep and form of its lines, and the Cruiser borrows heavily from aquatic themes—part whale, part squid.

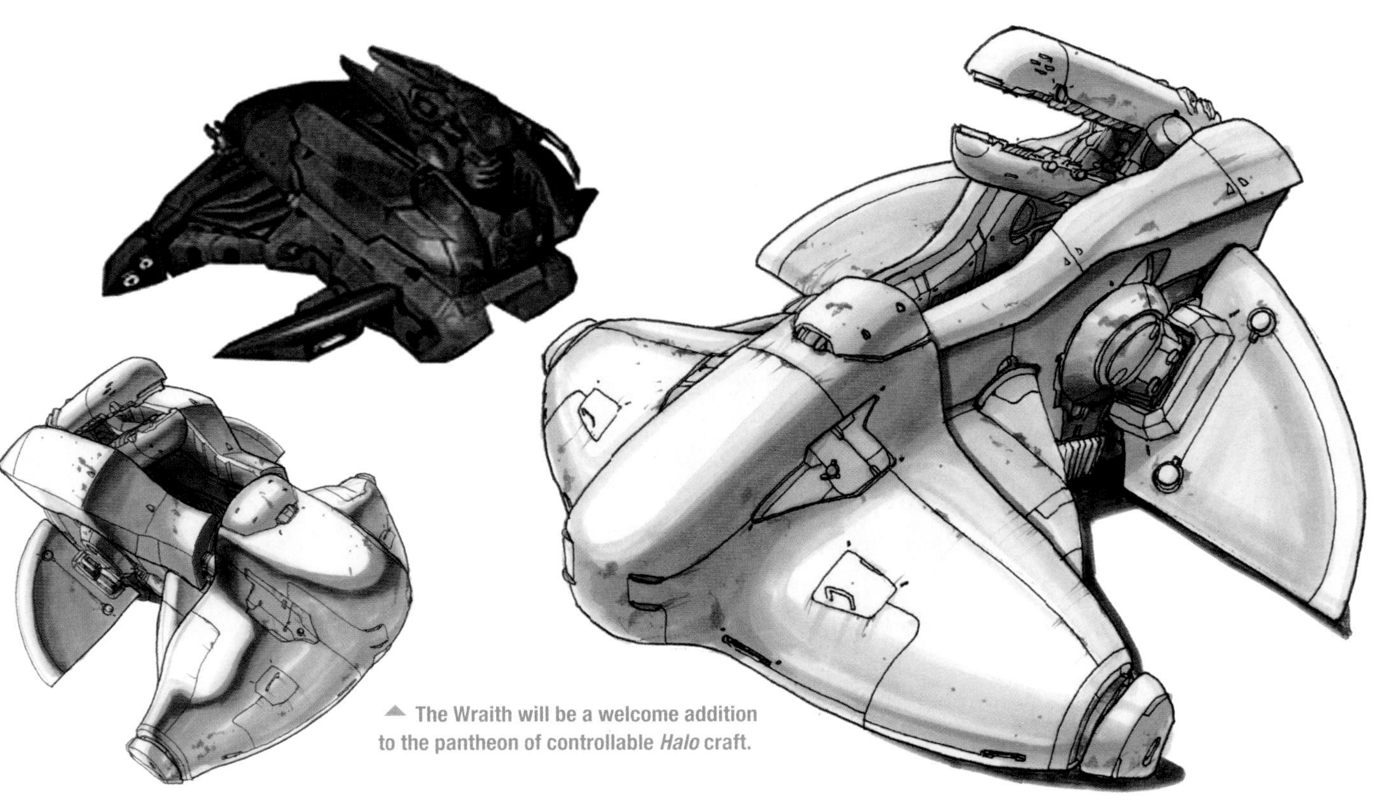

▲ The Wraith will be a welcome addition to the pantheon of controllable *Halo* craft.

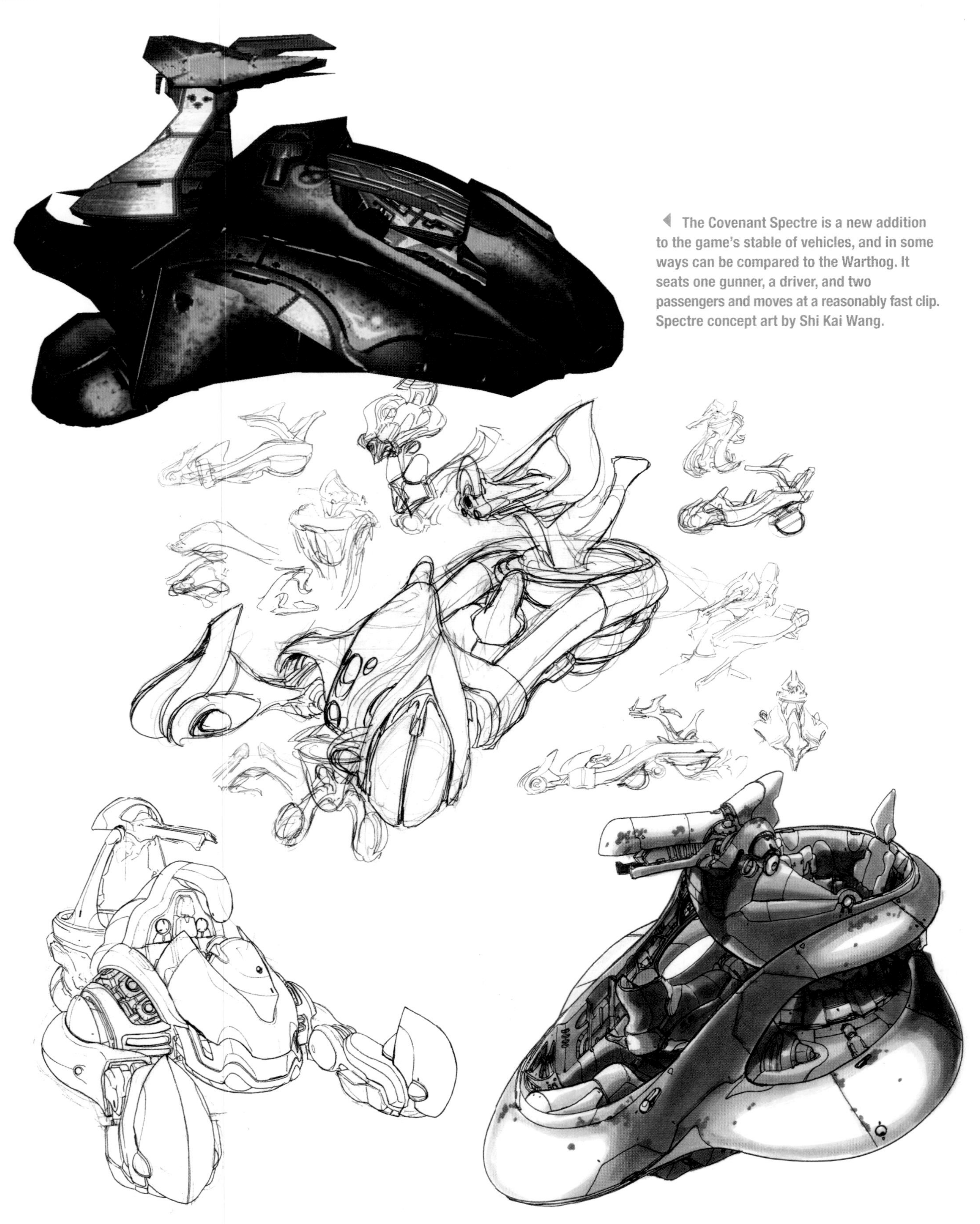

The Covenant Spectre is a new addition to the game's stable of vehicles, and in some ways can be compared to the Warthog. It seats one gunner, a driver, and two passengers and moves at a reasonably fast clip. Spectre concept art by Shi Kai Wang.

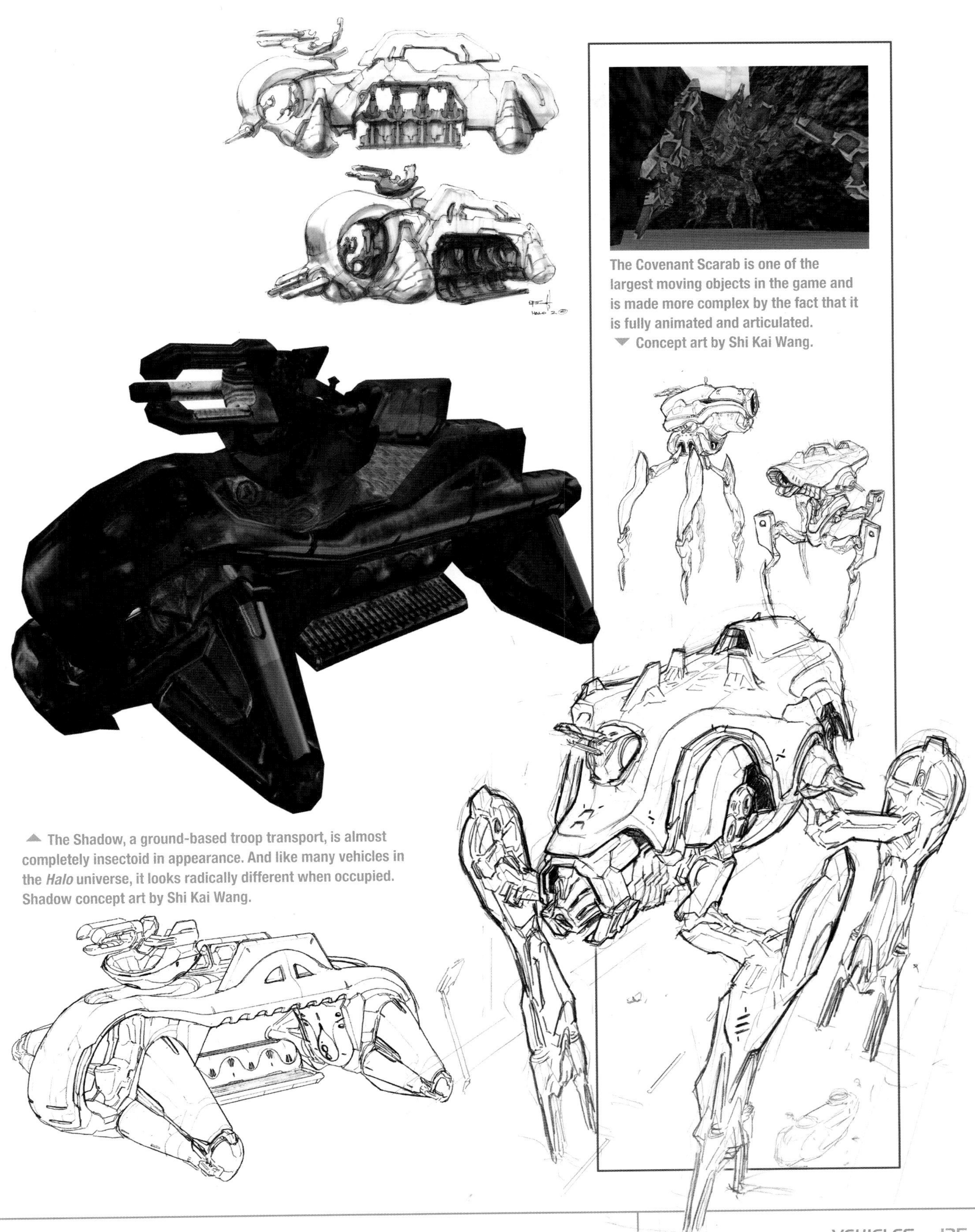

The Covenant Scarab is one of the largest moving objects in the game and is made more complex by the fact that it is fully animated and articulated.

▼ Concept art by Shi Kai Wang.

▲ The Shadow, a ground-based troop transport, is almost completely insectoid in appearance. And like many vehicles in the *Halo* universe, it looks radically different when occupied. Shadow concept art by Shi Kai Wang.

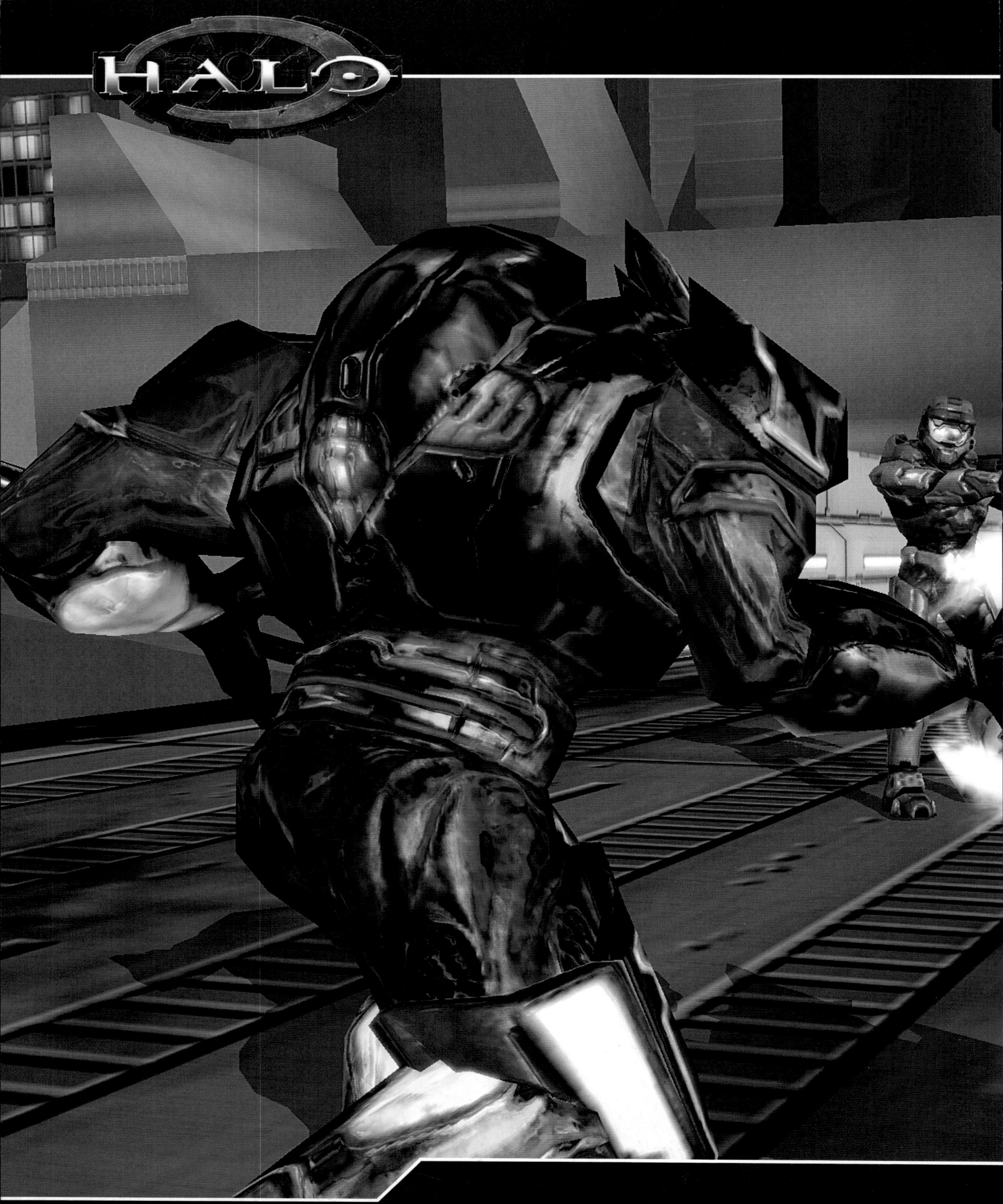
HALO

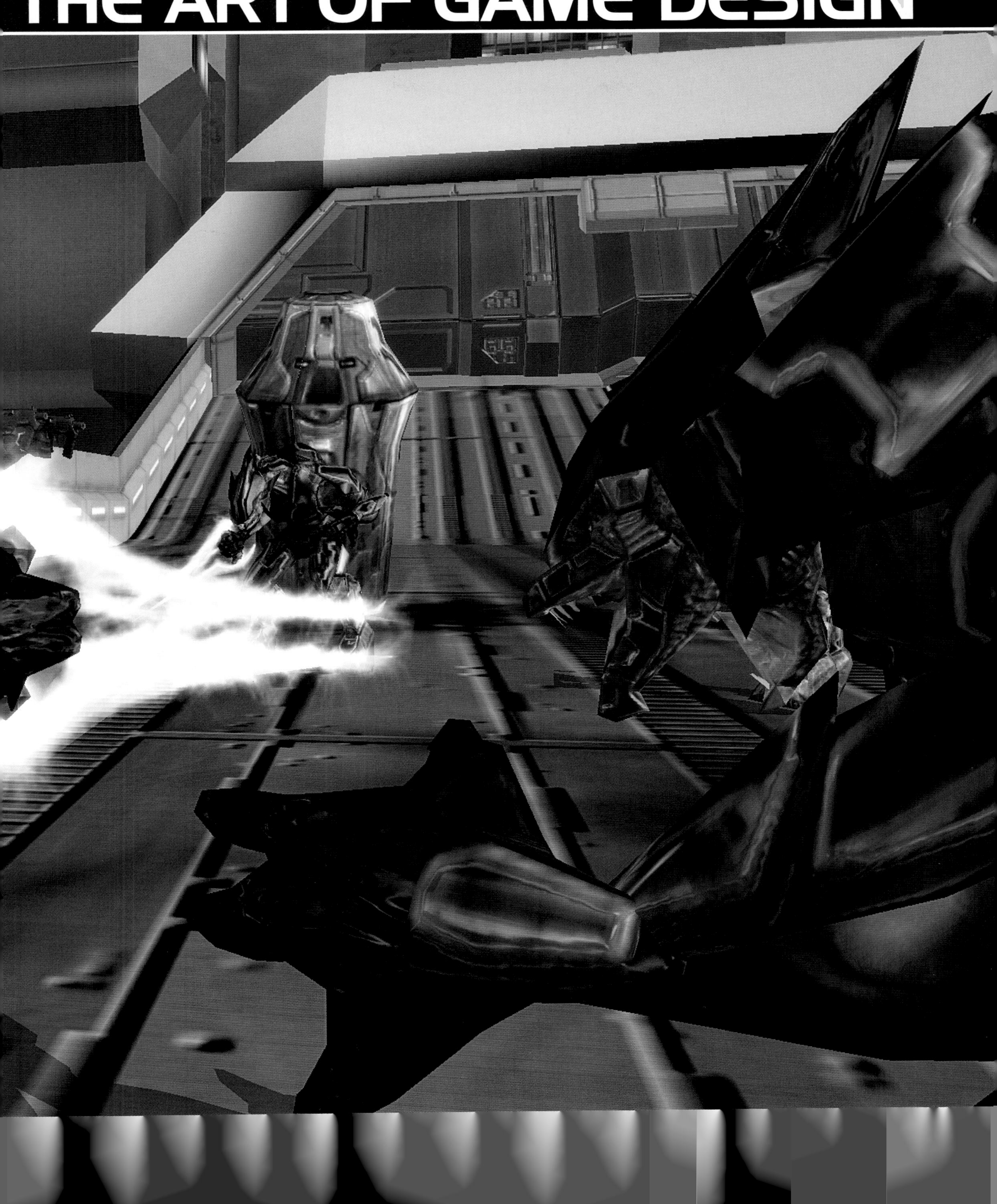

It was time to get off the Truth and Reconciliation. As Covenant troops ran hither and yon, the recently freed Marines armed themselves with alien weapons and linked up with the rest of the rescue team. Keyes and Cortana convened a quick council of war. "While the Covenant had us locked up here, I heard them talking about the ring world," Keyes said, "and its destructive capabilities. . . . [They] kept saying, 'whoever controls Halo controls the fate of the universe.'

"That's bad news," he continued. "If Halo is a weapon, and the Covenant gains control of it, they'll use it against us. Who knows what power that would give them?

"Chief, Cortana, I have a new mission for you. We need to beat the Covenant to Halo's control room."

"No offense, sir," the Master Chief replied, "but it might be best to finish this mission before we tackle another one."

—Excerpt from *Halo: The Flood* by William C. Dietz.

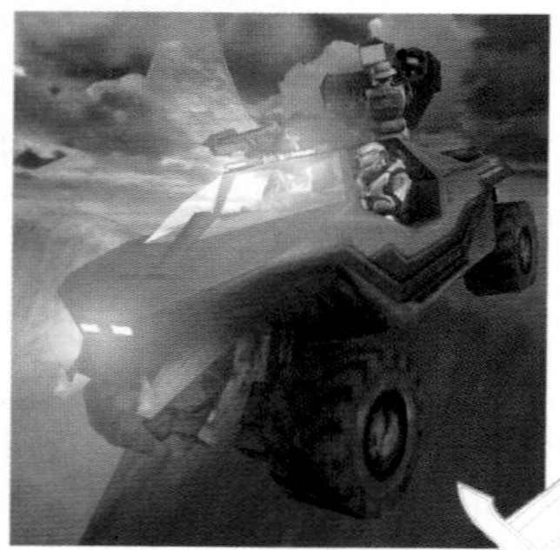

▲ Pre-Xbox *Halo* screen shot.

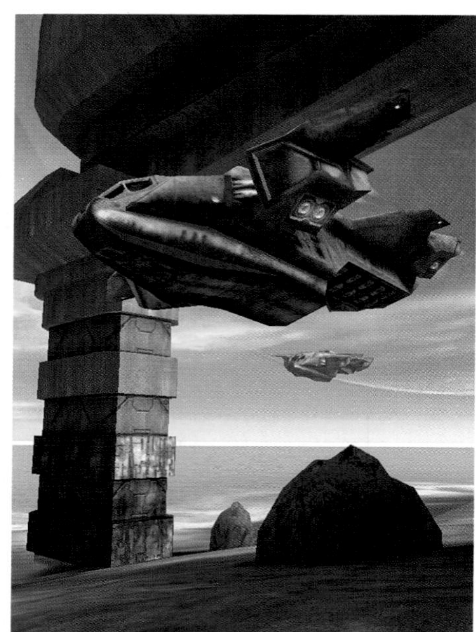

The integration of character design, lifelike animation, compelling story, thrilling game play, rich sound and music, and breathtaking environments is vital to the success of a game. The various Bungie teams work together closely to make sure each aspect of the game is executed properly and achieves the overall vision of the game design.

THE DEVIL IS IN THE DETAILS

Eric Arroyo explains how even the smallest details present challenges. "There's some really deep thought and effort that goes into such seemingly minor things . . . like the space crate. [Game designer] Jaime Griesemer and [lead designer for *Halo*] John Howard told me, 'We need a crate, but *no boxes*.' Every first-person shooter has boxes everywhere, to hide bad guys behind, or hold extra ammo, or whatever.

"The designers were adamant that we didn't include the boxes, but needed something to basically fill that role. So my instructions were to build something that *looks* like a box, *acts* like a box, but *isn't* a box. One that looks good on its side, or upside down, or whatever. 'Oh,' they said, 'it also has to be extremely low resolution.'

"I just shook my head, and said," Arroyo laughs, "'I'm going to go away for a while.'"

Artist Lorraine McLees was faced with a more gruesome challenge, however. "One of the things I did for *Halo* was the skull used in the 'Oddball' multiplayer mode," she explains.

One of the public's first looks at *Halo* came in the November 1999 issue of *Computer Gaming World*.

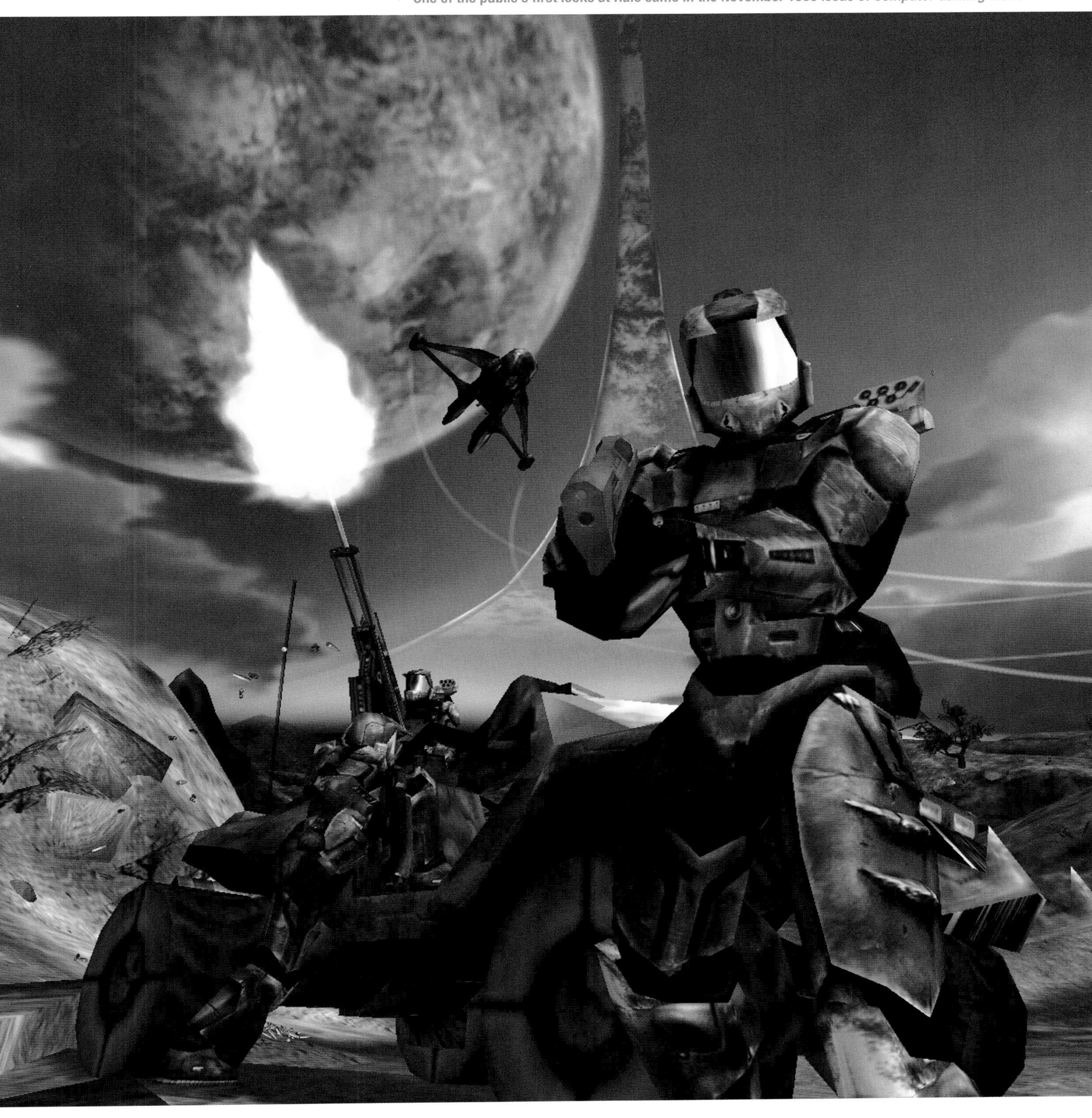

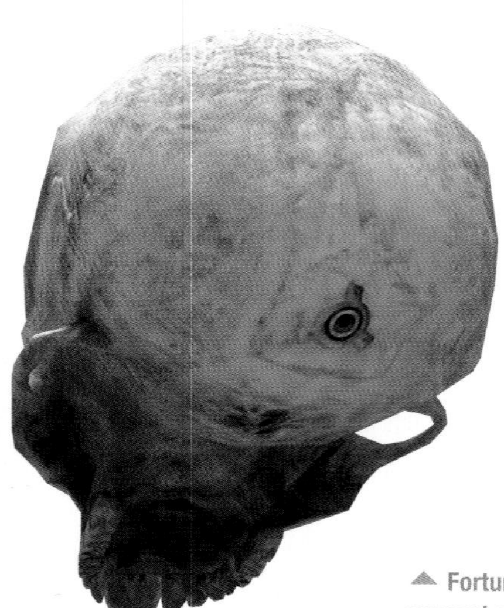

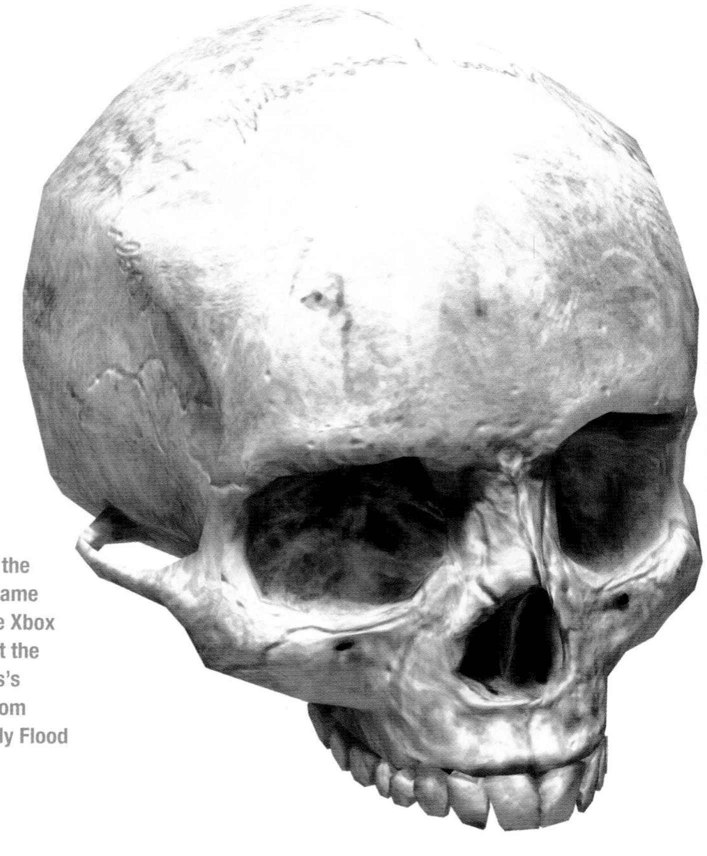

Fortunately, the removal of the flame thrower from the Xbox game meant that the texture for Keyes's skull changed from charred to merely Flood tainted.

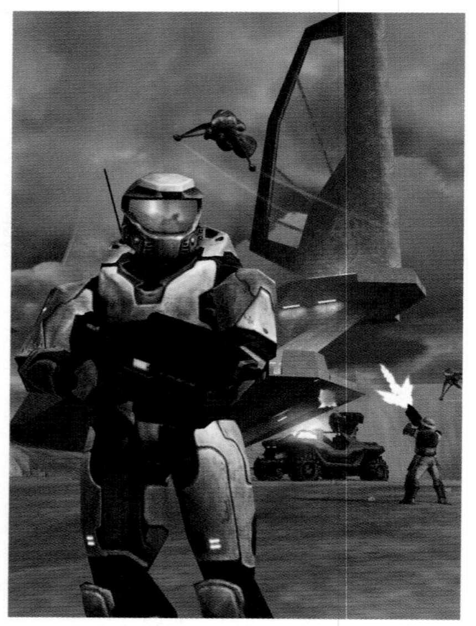

Screen shot from *Halo*.

In "Oddball," players vie for possession of a skull. The player who holds the ball for the longest period of time wins. "One night, during crunch, I was waiting for Robt [McLees], so we could go home, but he had a few things left on his plate to do. I asked if there was anything I could take on so we could get at least an hour or two of sleep.

"It turned out that he'd finished UV mapping the skull, and it just needed to be textured. I ended up redoing the UVs and started doing the preliminary texture, thinking that he'd take over anytime. I was just supposed to be pitching in a little bit, but a couple of days later, the producer on *Halo* was asking me for an ETA. And I thought, 'Oh, so this is mine, now?' I'd inherited the job."

Originally, the skull was supposed to appear in the single-player campaign as well. In one scene, the *Pillar of Autumn*'s fearless commanding officer, Captain Keyes, is absorbed by the alien menace, the Flood. In order to accomplish an important goal, the Master Chief was required to retrieve the fallen captain's neural implants . . . located within Keyes's skull.

"The plan was to use the flame thrower to burn the skull out of the mass of Flood," McLees says, "which meant that the texture had to be burned, as well. Robt looked at a ton of reference pictures—burn victims, and so on—so I didn't have to. It was pretty gruesome research.

"Unfortunately," she continues, "I did my job too well. No one could even look at the thing, it was so realistic and hideous. I was like, 'Does it *have* to be burned?'"

Fortunately, the removal of the flame thrower from the Xbox game meant that Keyes's charred skull didn't make it into the game.

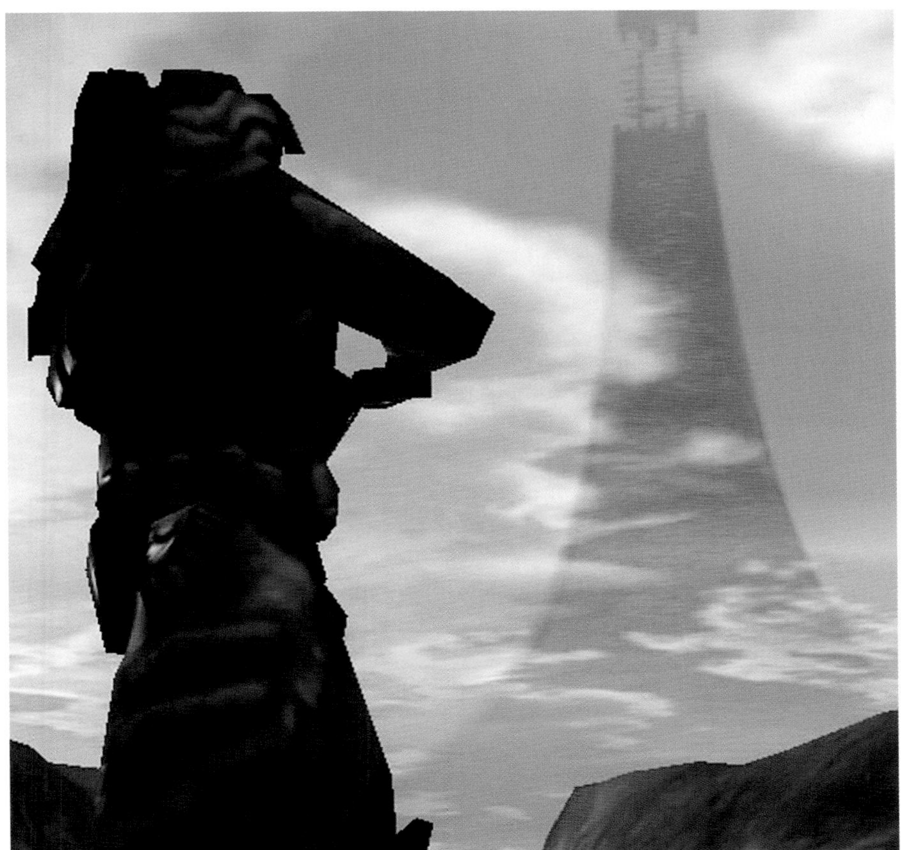

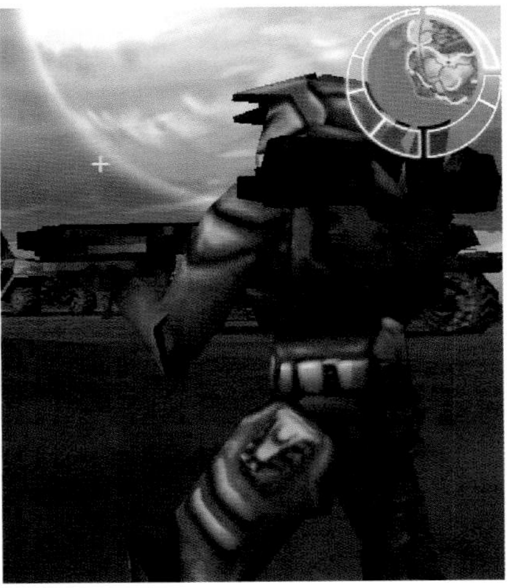

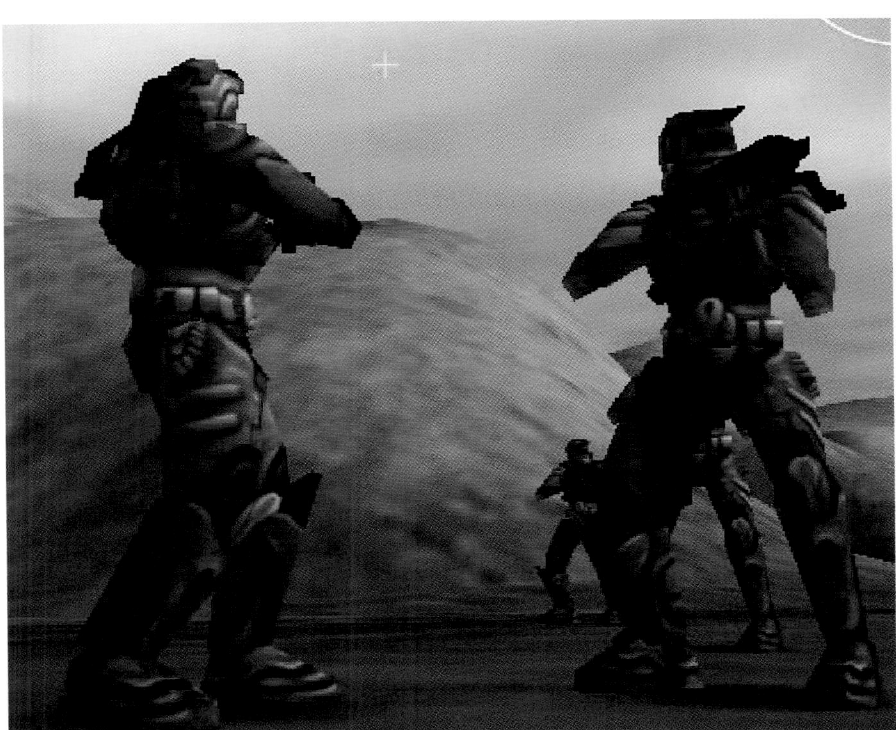

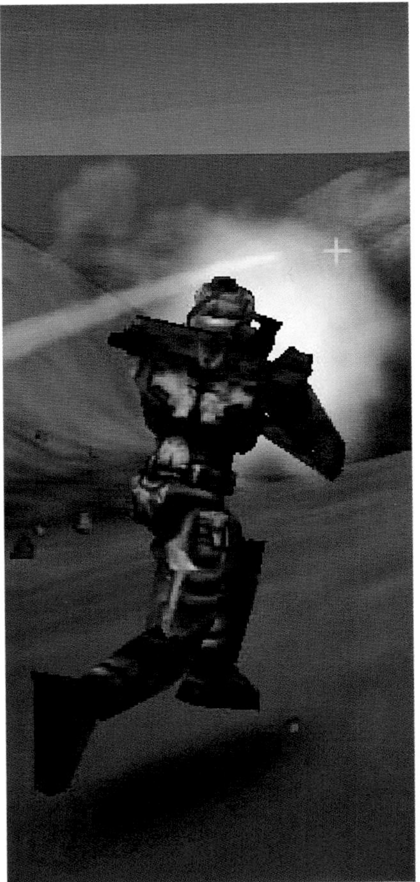

▲ These screen shots are from *Halo*'s very early stages. Note the damaged and decaying ring (upper left) and the navigation interface's similarity to the *Marathon* logo (upper right).

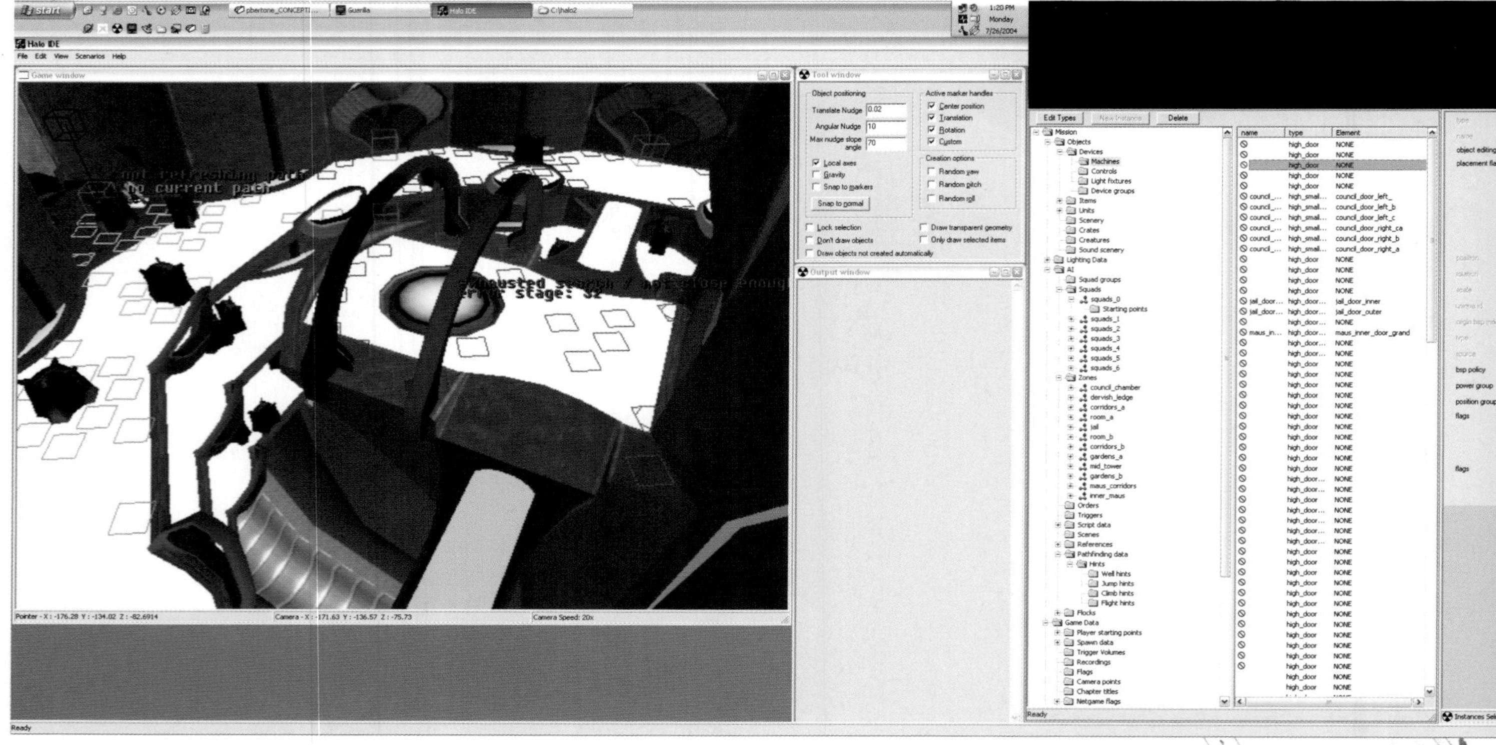

Bungie designed its own tools for the game design, including Guerilla and Sapien. They may not be pretty in themselves, but they allow the designers to quickly tweak and tune game elements.

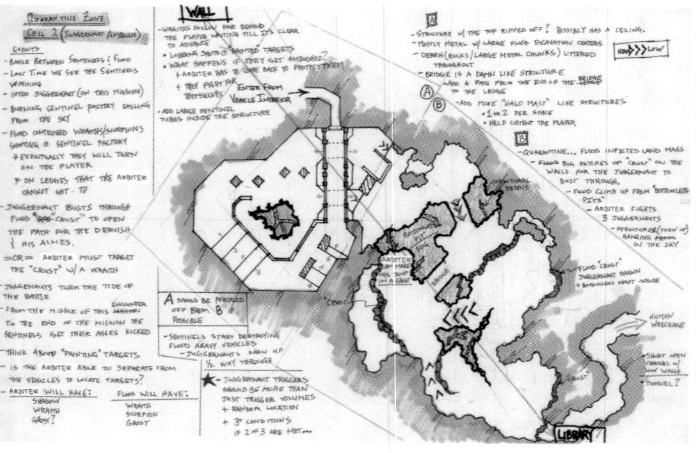

Bungie developed a unique tool set for creating missions and building levels. When a character or item that is assigned an artificial intelligence (AI) to govern its behavior is placed in a level, this interface allows the designer to see what the character is thinking.

Single-player maps are, by necessity, annotated with detailed information about the scenarios and gameplay types that take place in them.

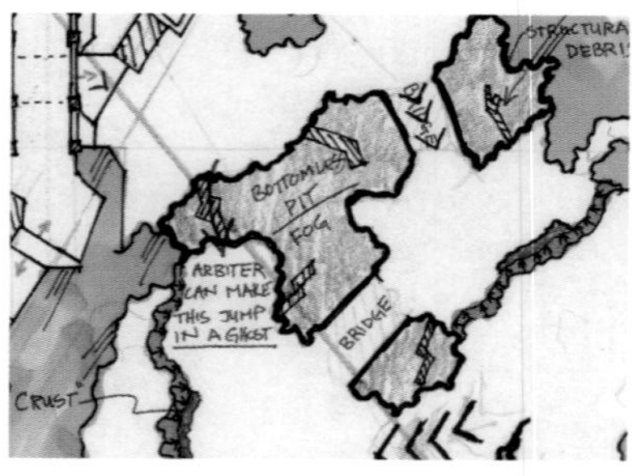

This close-up view of a single-player map sketch shows the preliminary pathway the game designer had in mind for the encounter.

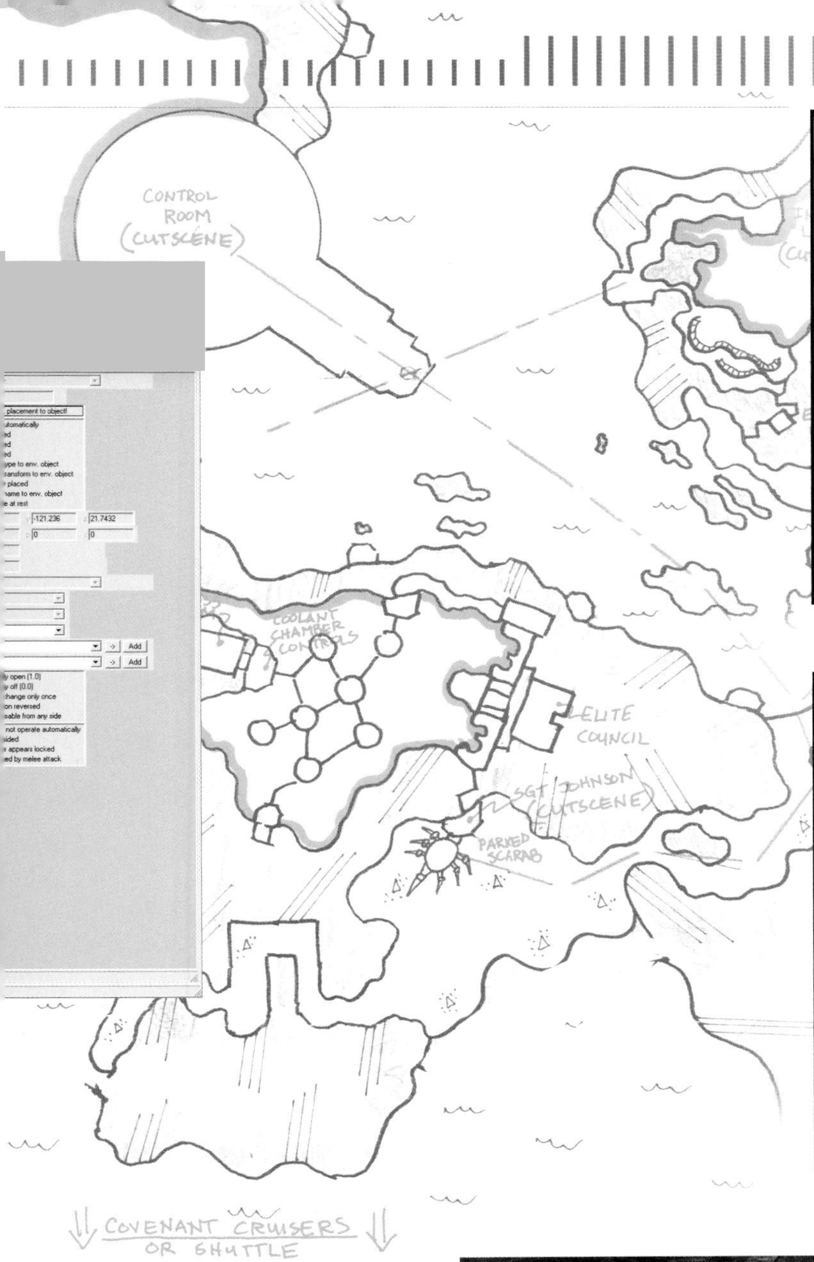

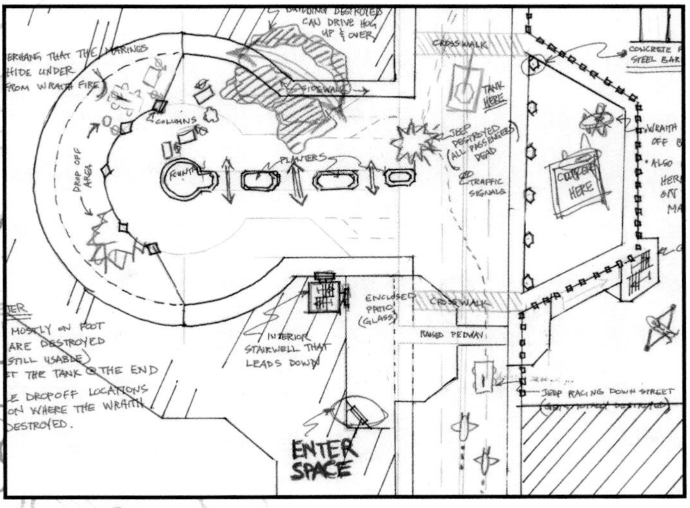

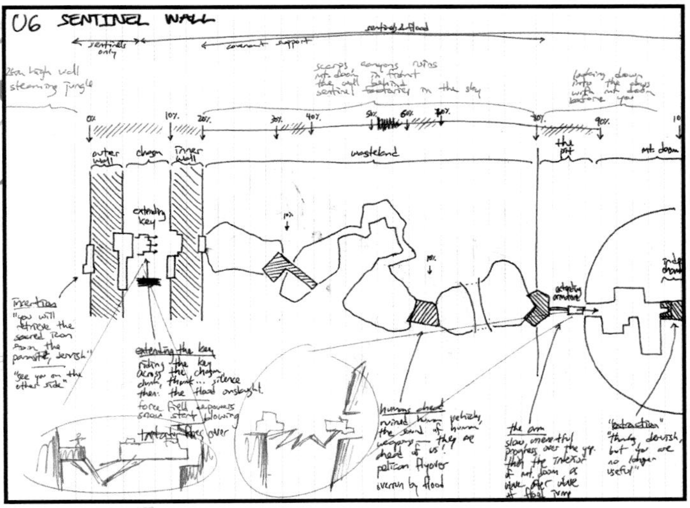

▲ The simple sketch of the "Sentinel Wall" level belies the complexity of its geometry and the number of gameplay factors involved.

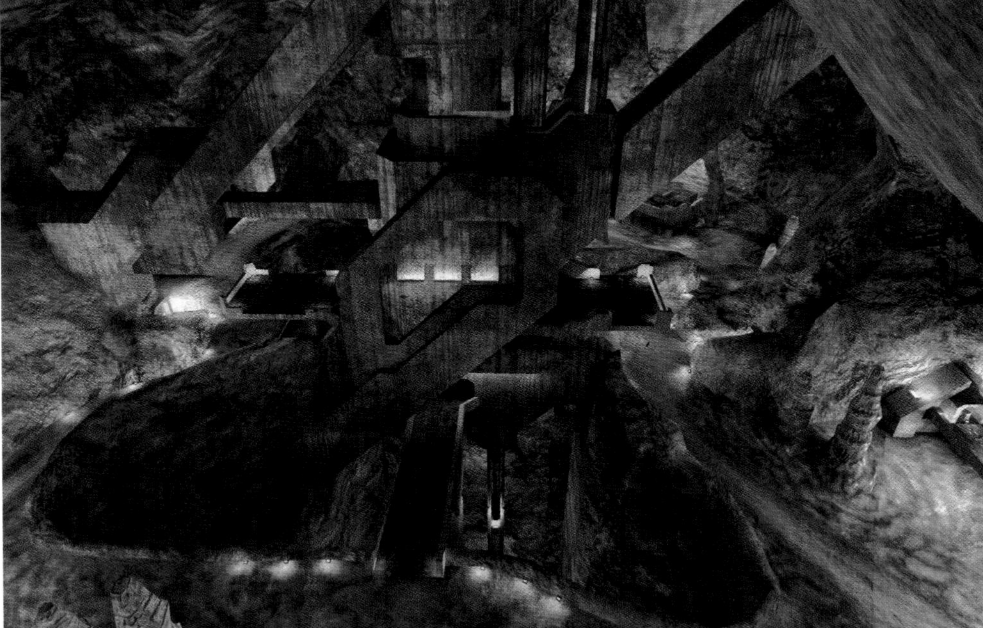

▶ Waterworks' blend of scale and complexity should prove attractive to team-based gamers. The underground locale provided lighting challenges.

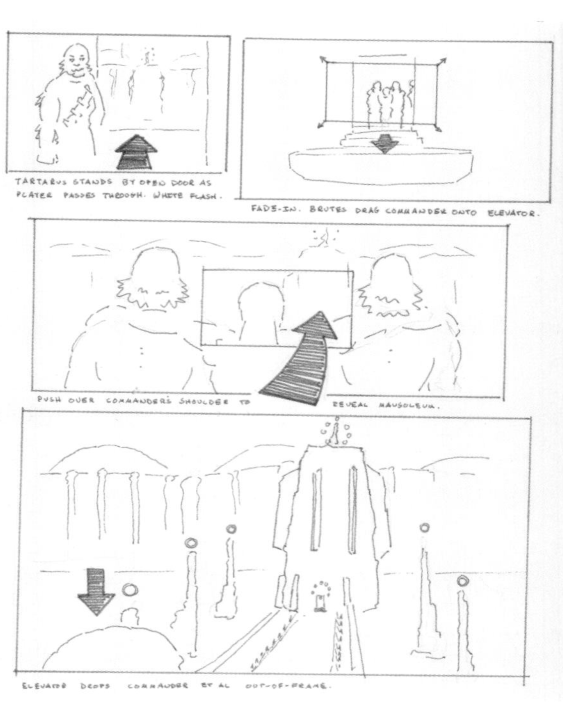

▸ This storyboard takes us through the "making" of the Arbiter—a key moment in the *Halo 2* drama. Storyboards by Joseph Staten.

CINEMATICS AND AUDIO

▾ Storyboarding helps everyone. Really. It helps animators know what to expect, it lets programmers know what needs to be done, and it lets artists concentrate on textures, geometry, and objects and work on detailing the necessary pieces. These, inked by Lee Wilson, help set the mood and tone, as well as the specifics of the action and camera angles. In this instance, the situation being described is just about the most important single cinematic in the game.

One of the key methods of telling the Halo story during game play is the use of "cinematics"—custom-designed animation segments that allow the player to watch the plot unfold. Joseph Staten, Bungie's director of cinematics, explains: "Creating our in-game cinematics is an involved process.

"Obviously, we start by brainstorming, throwing out all the crazy ideas we have and want to include. My job is to put them all down on paper—including rough dialogue. From there, I

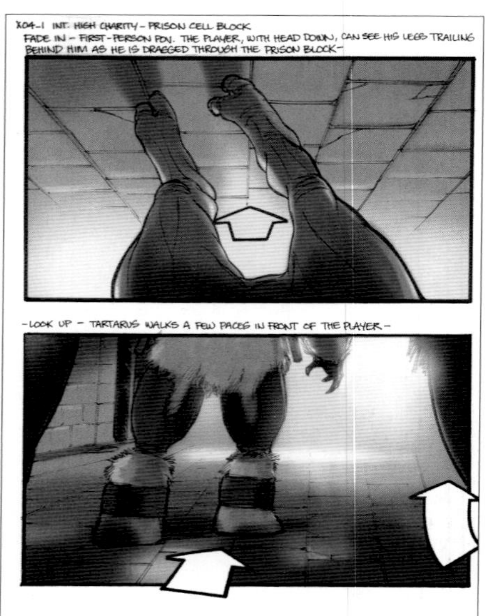

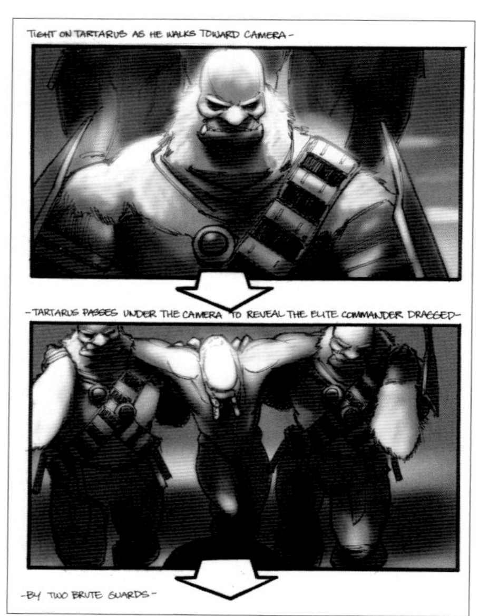

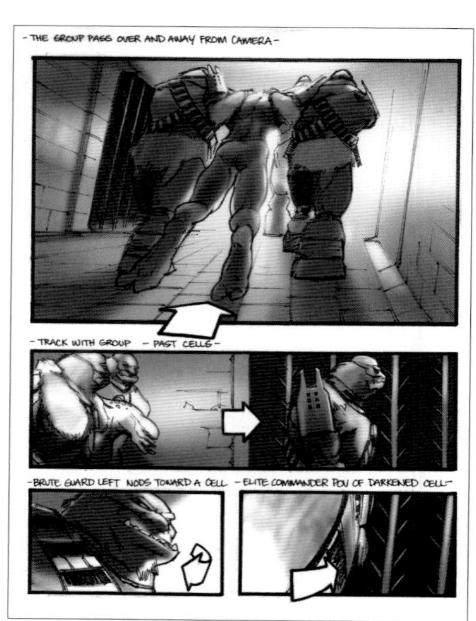

sit down with the environment artists and animators and try and integrate the story with what they're doing.

"After that process is under way, I start sketching out very crude storyboards for as many scenes as I can, usually about half of the overall script. We have to map these to the individual missions in the game, and from there we can refine the top-level dialogue."

Of course, this effort is merely preliminary. Once the basics of the missions are hammered out and a rough plot arc is established, Staten's work intensifies. "At this point, I have to develop a shooting script, and submit it to the team for feedback. Then, once it's firmed out, I send it to Lee Wilson, a freelance storyboard artist."

The process of releasing the script "into the wild" for commentary can be harrowing. Since Bungie's dynamic fosters input on virtually every aspect of the game's creation, the amount of feedback can be overwhelming. "There's a lot of good stuff that comes from folks' comments, but it's difficult to give solid, qualitative comment to words on a page. You need a thick skin to do it, but it makes us better at what we do—sending any kind of art through the Bungie cauldron just improves the whole thing."

At this stage, Staten modifies each scene as needed, and works with artist CJ Cowan to create "videomatics"—rough versions of the individual scenes to be animated. Finally, those pieces are refined and tested in the game's engine, and from there, into final production.

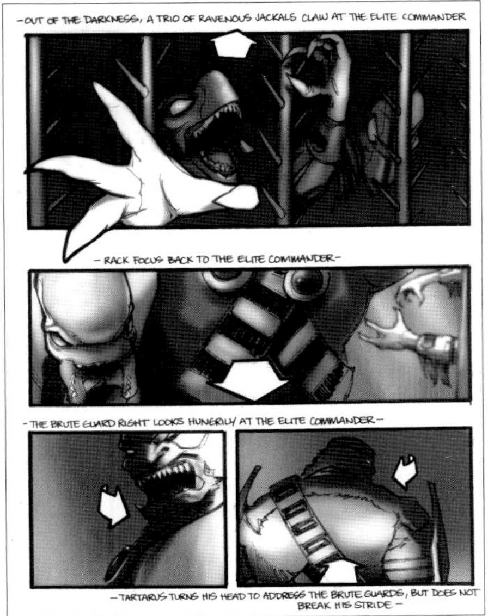

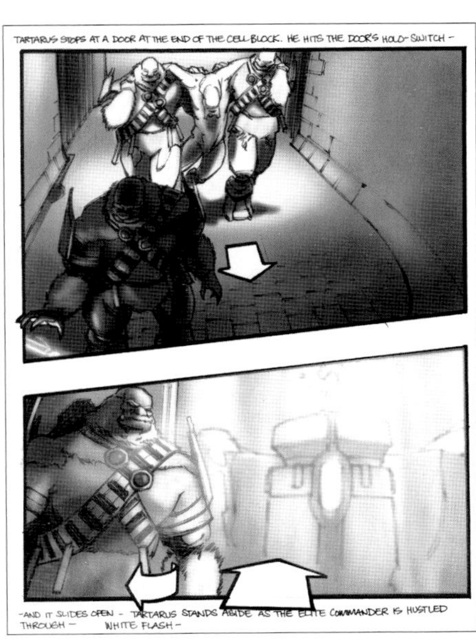

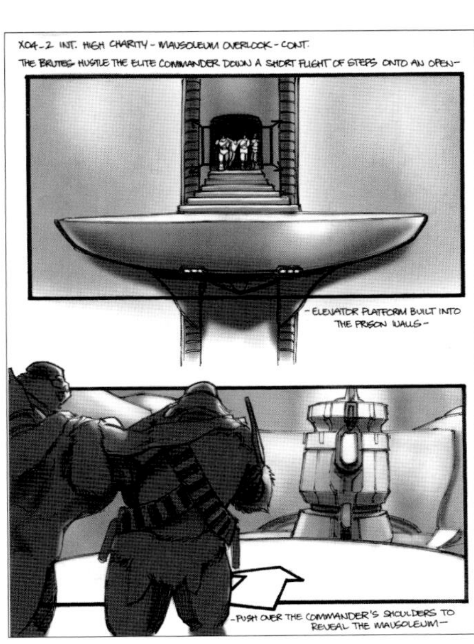

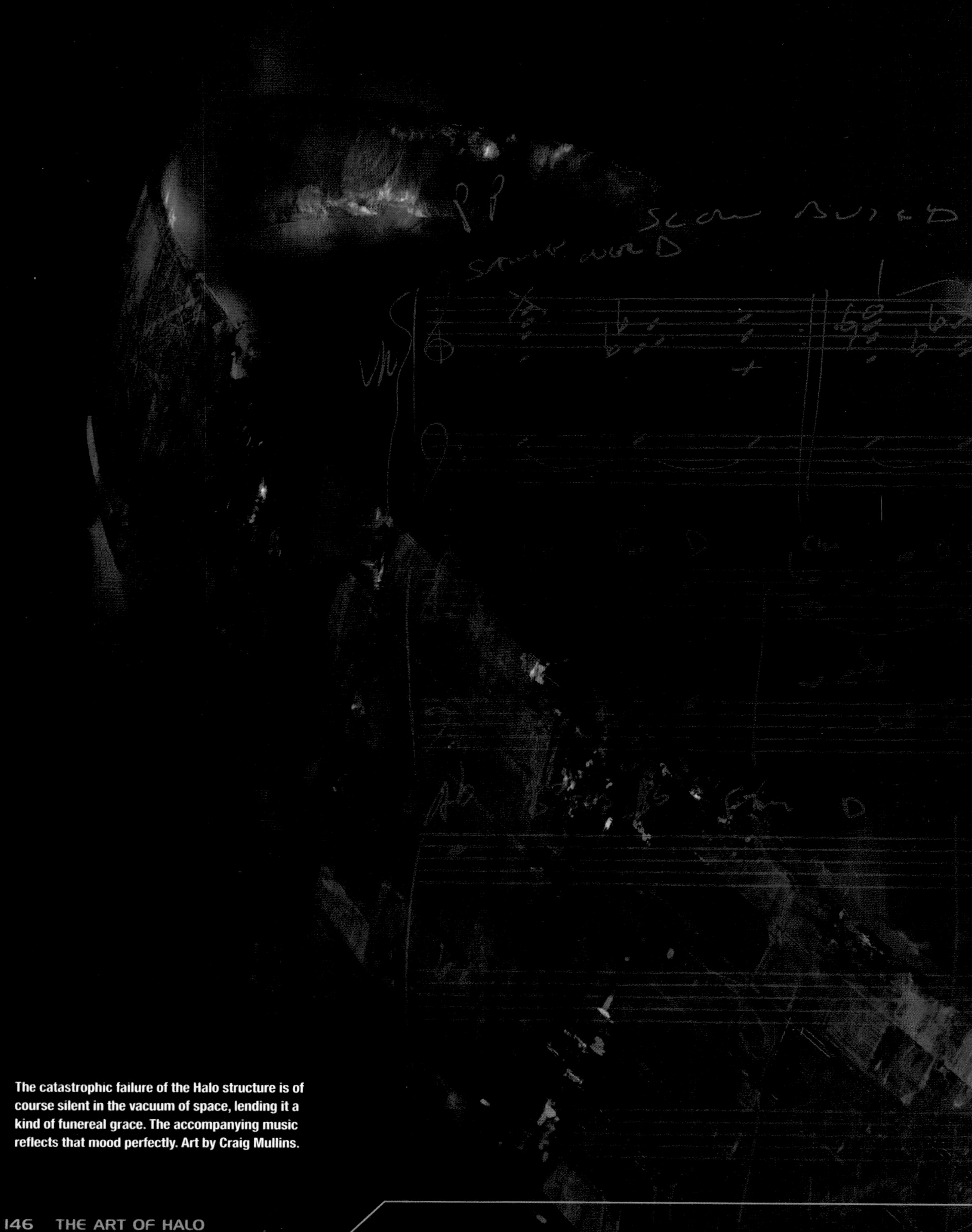

The catastrophic failure of the Halo structure is of course silent in the vacuum of space, lending it a kind of funereal grace. The accompanying music reflects that mood perfectly. Art by Craig Mullins.

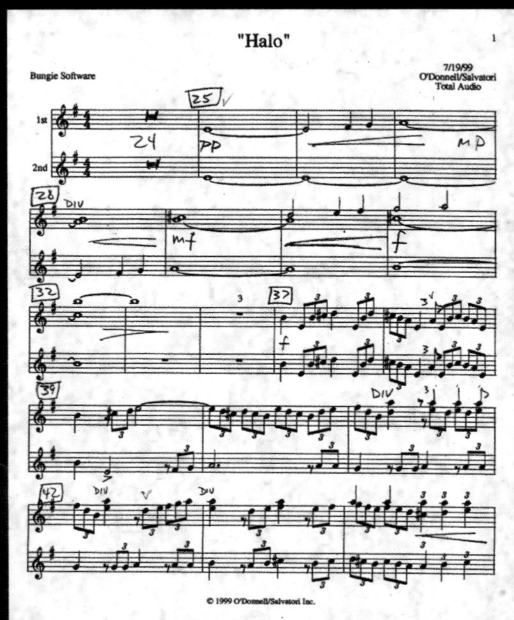

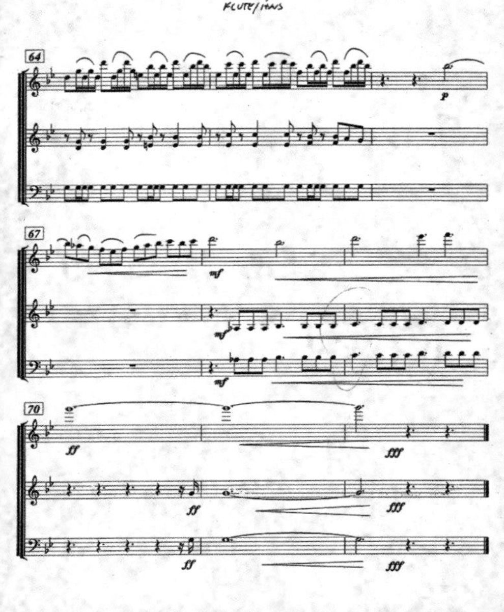

" Before he became a full-time composer and sound director, Marty O'Donnell worked his way through graduate school as a house painter. He was the guy who would be called in once a house had been built. Walls and woodwork can't be painted and varnished until the carpenters are done, so the house wasn't really ready until he was finished.

"Halo was sort of like that, and so was Halo 2—until O'Donnell was finished, the game wasn't yet complete.

"The musical score and sound effects are the final elements that help bring the game to life, making the experience of playing the game more than just a visceral romp through a virtual space."

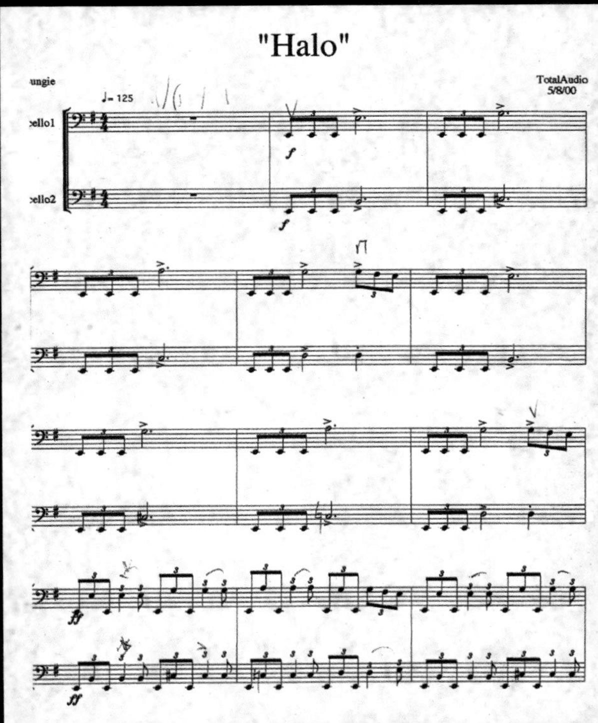

ANIMATION STUDY

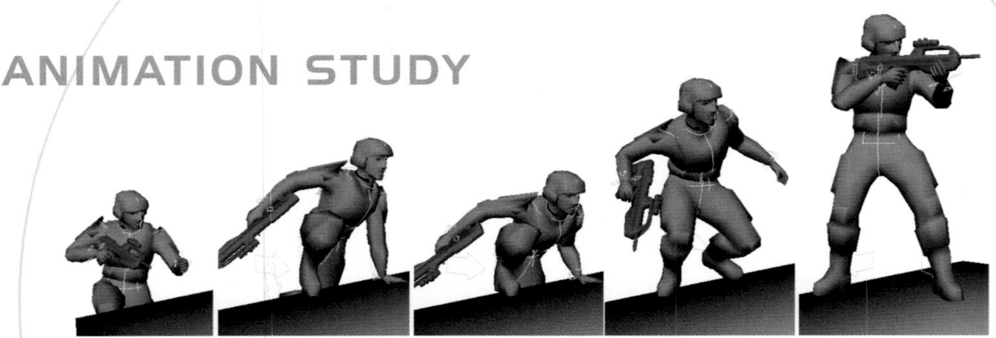

A UNSC Marine exhibits climbing behavior with a neat and natural vault.

It's hardly unique to *Halo*, but the tight bond between AI behavior and animation was further cemented for the sequel. Although animation is more fluid and detailed than before, and there are simply more characters, the main reason that there's so much more animation is that the additional characters also *do* a lot more.

A SPARTAN model boards a Ghost piloted by a rival in multiplayer. There are multiple variations for this one action.

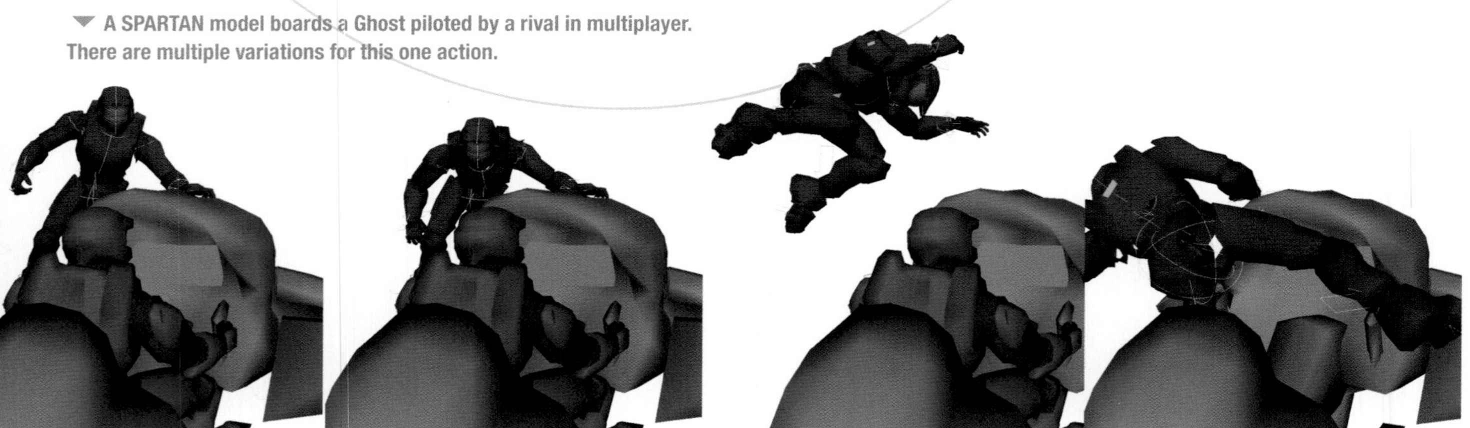

The new Hunter is much more fluidly animated, but sharp-eyed players will notice that it's 25 to 30 percent larger, too. Animation has been changed and improved to better reflect the sheer bulk of these creatures.

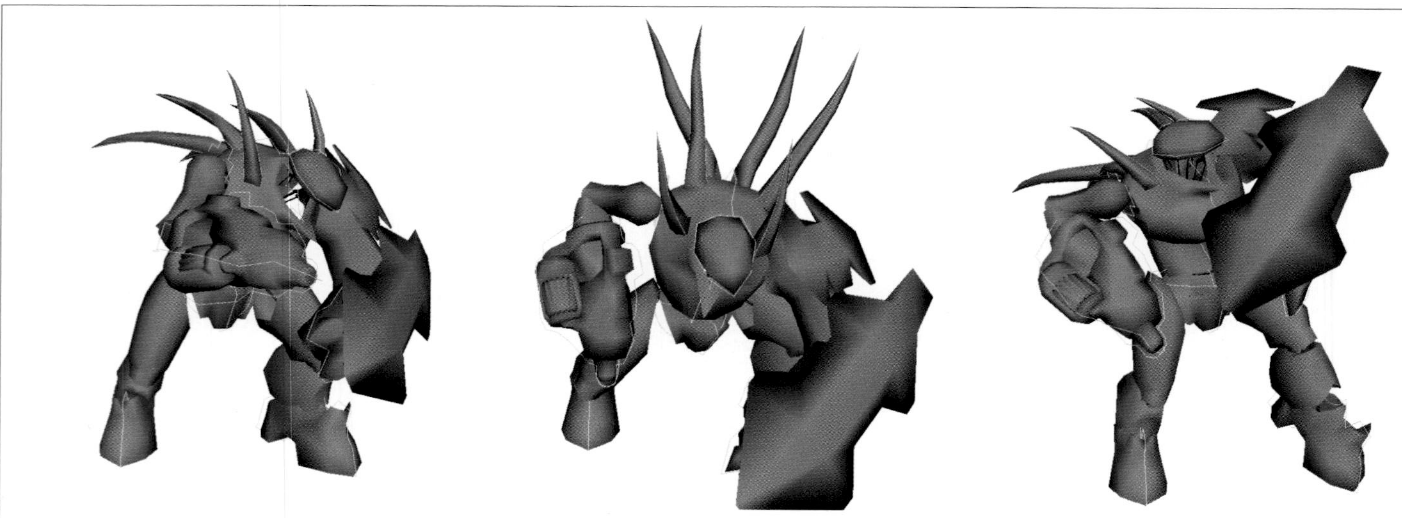

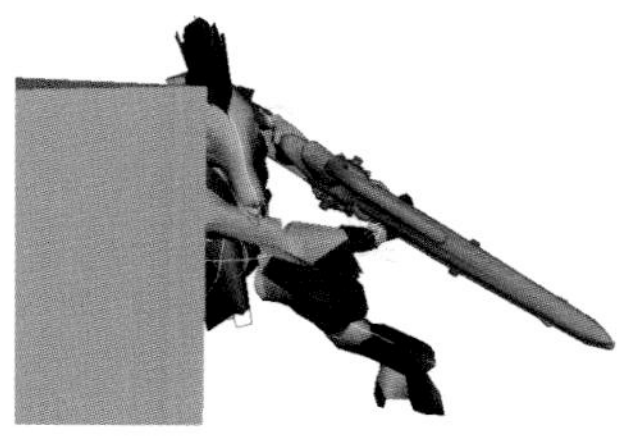
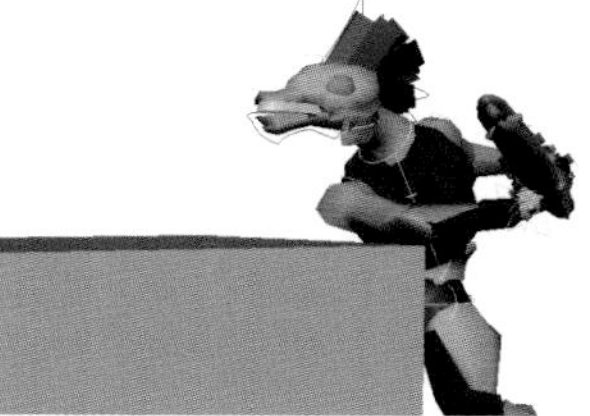
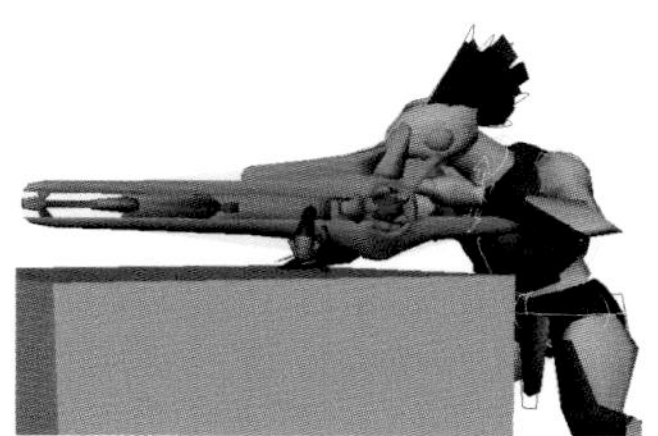

A Jackal demonstrates his ability to take cover.

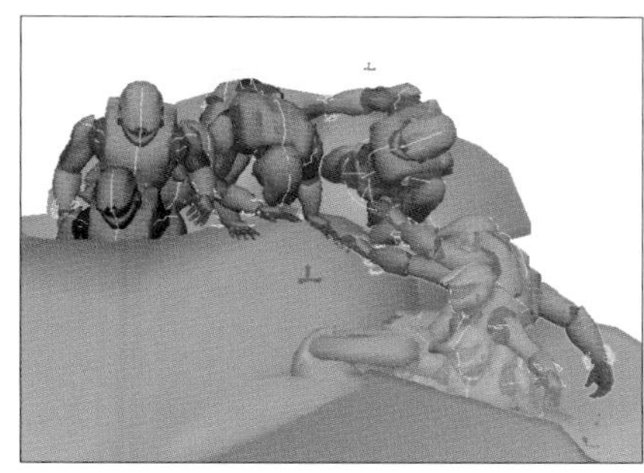

Master Chief hops nimbly into the partially enclosed confines of a Wraith, one of the new vehicles featured in single- and multiplayer modes.

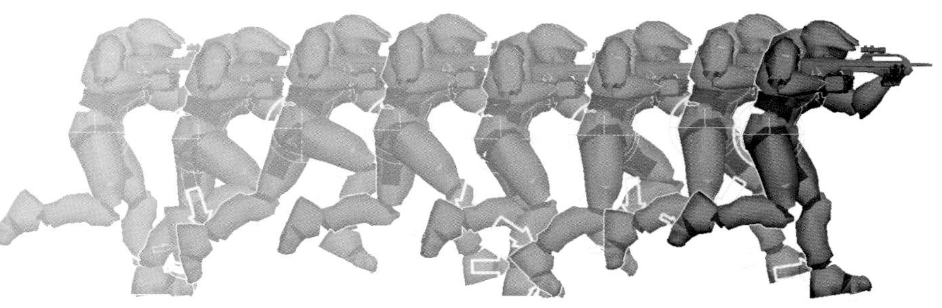

Transitional animations better illustrate Master Chief's move from walk to run and back to walk again.

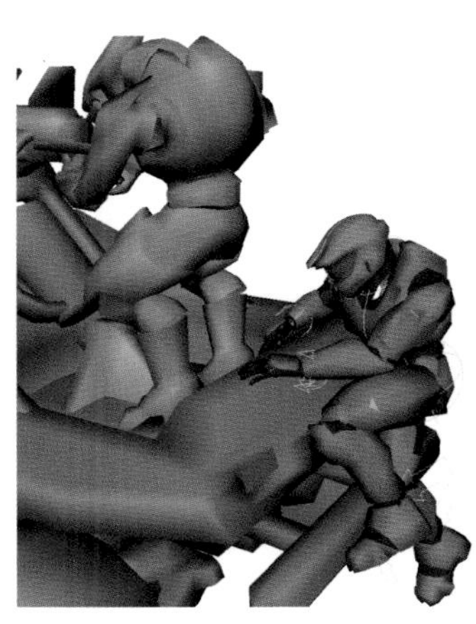
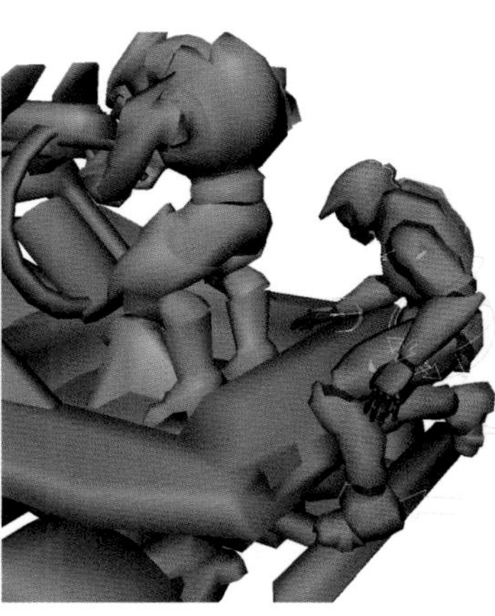
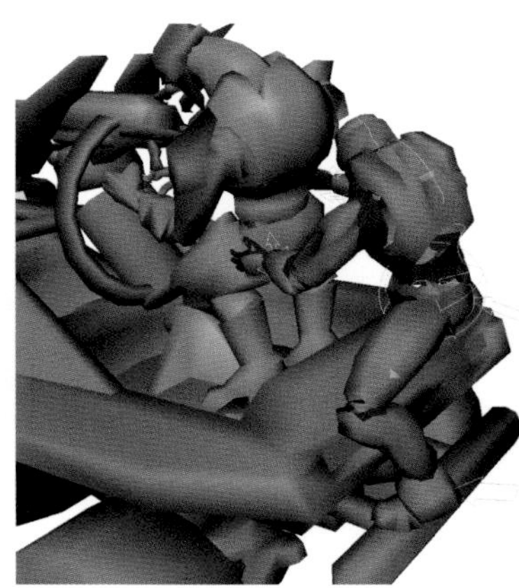

Master Chief can board in campaign and multiplayer modes. Here he takes an Elite out of a turreted vehicle.

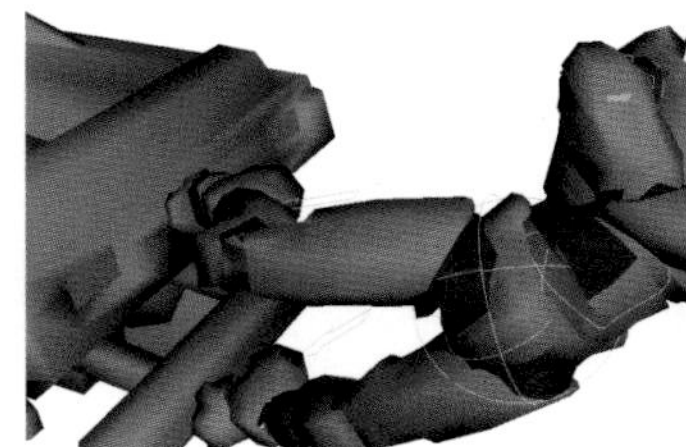

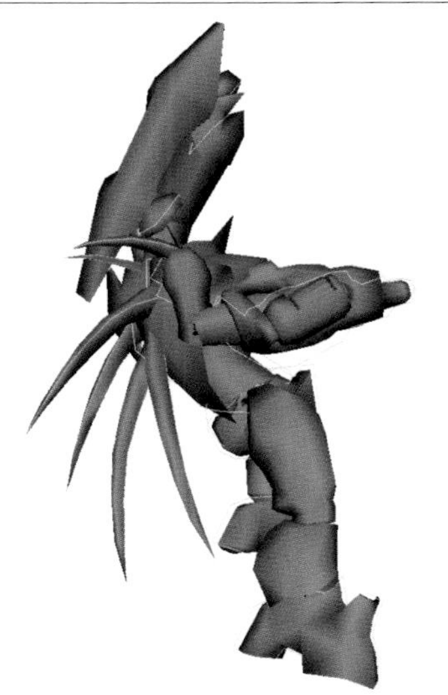
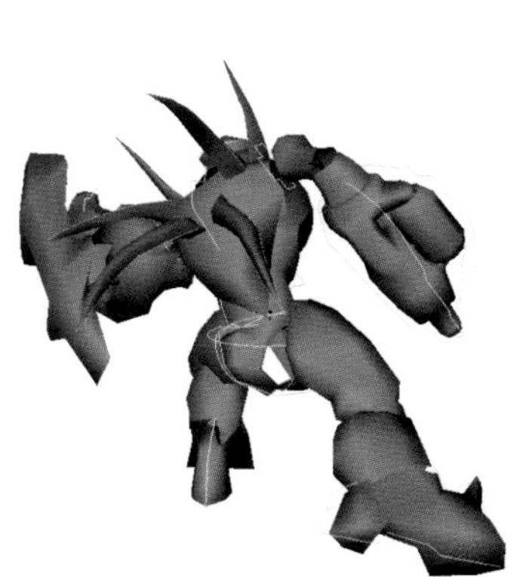
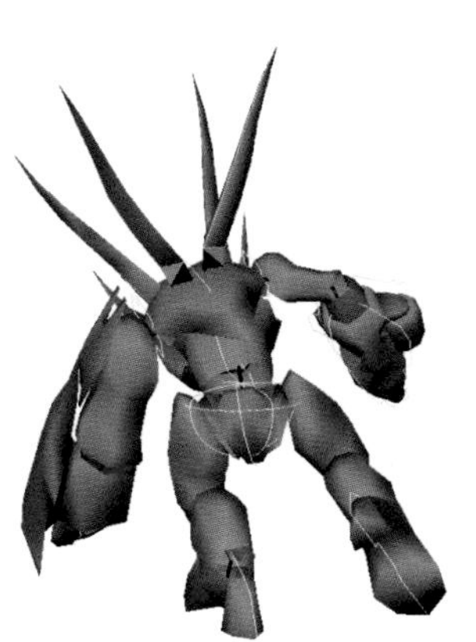
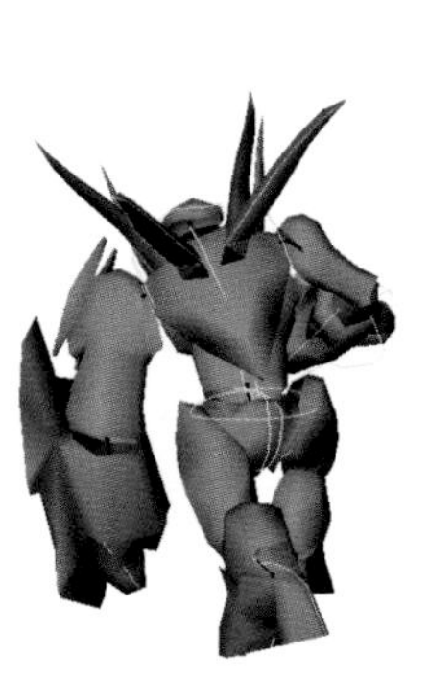

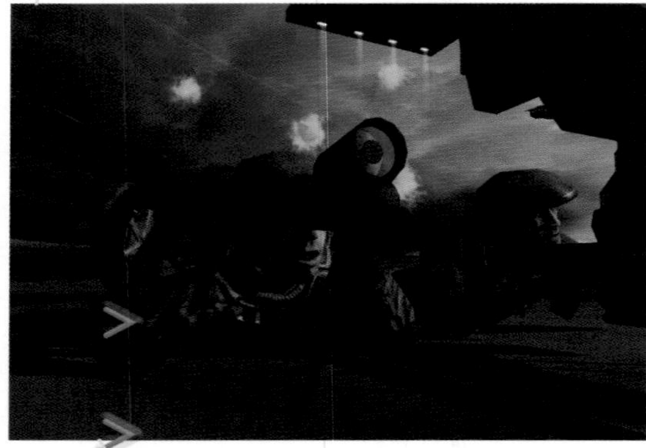

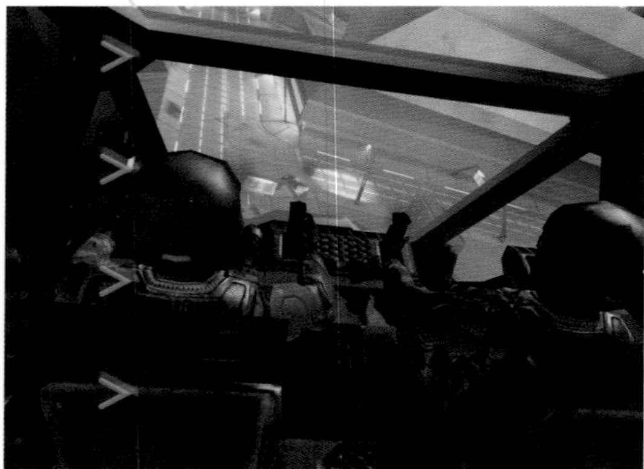

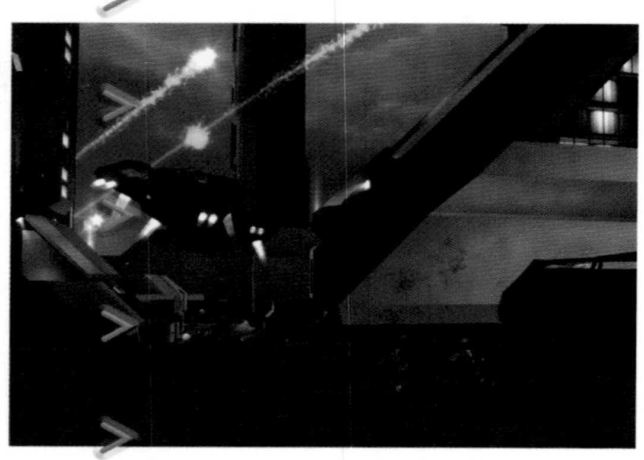

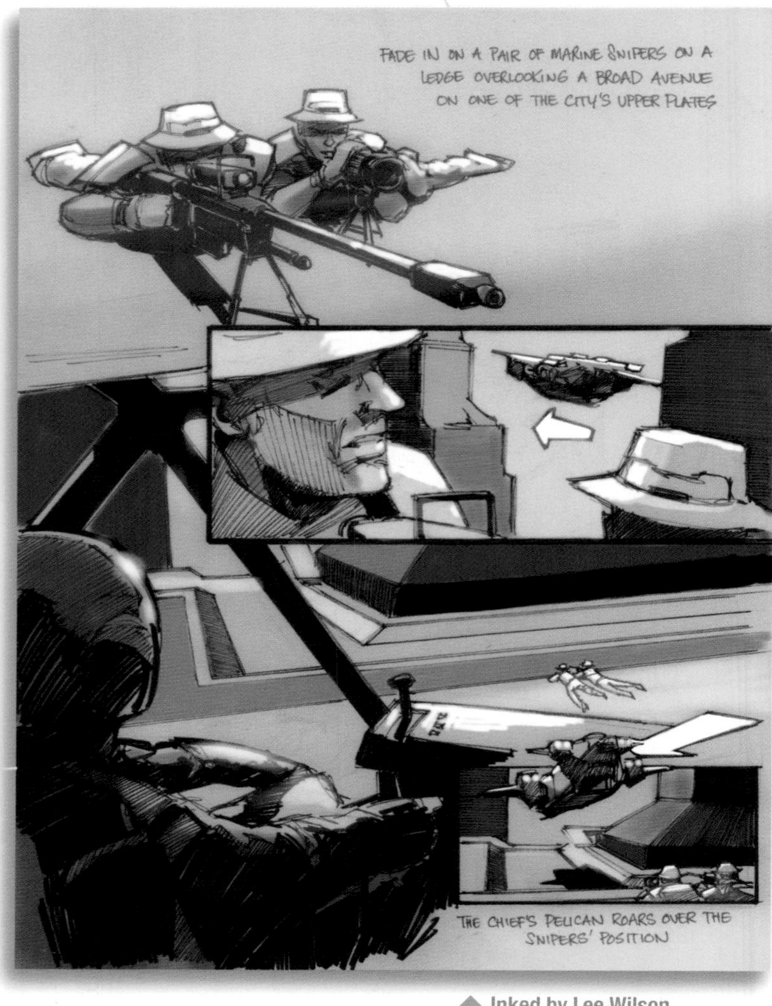

▲ Inked by Lee Wilson.

The cinematic scripts, written by director of cinematics Joseph Staten, differ wildly in purpose and structure from the AI character dialogue, but the flavor of the dialogue remains the same. These particular script fragments have been altered dramatically since their use in the original E3 launch demo. These cinematics introduced a battle on Earth that remains but has been dramatically and noticeably altered since then.

> SPOTTER:
Immediate. Grid kilo-2-3 is hot.
> Recommend mission abort.

> PILOT:
Roger recon.

> PILOT:
It's your call,
> Sarge.

> SERGEANT JOHNSON:
We're going in.

▶ Inked by Lee Wilson.

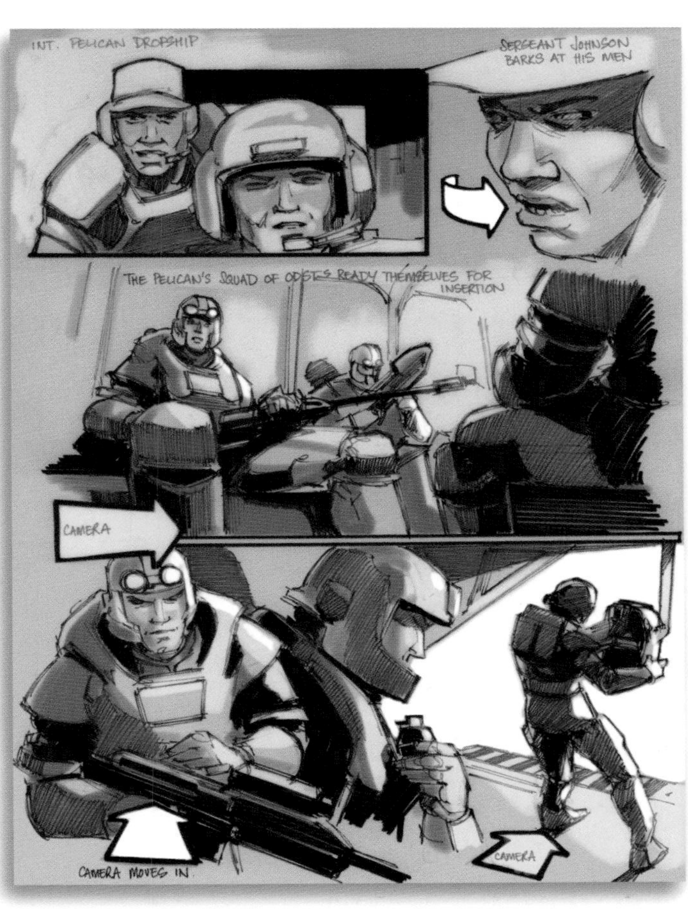

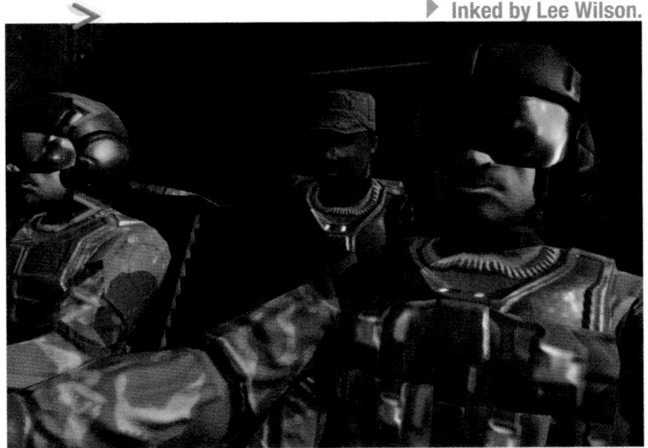

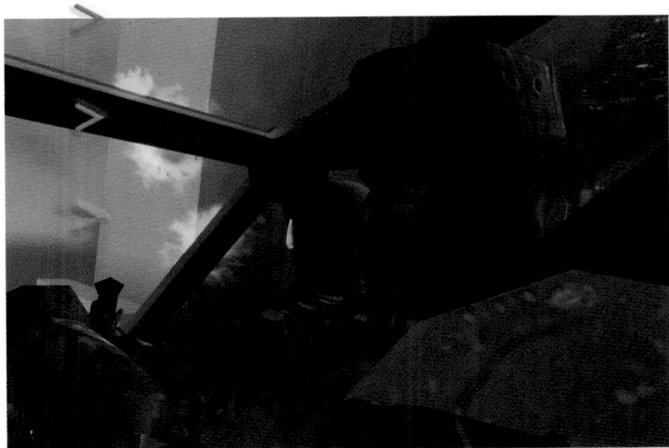

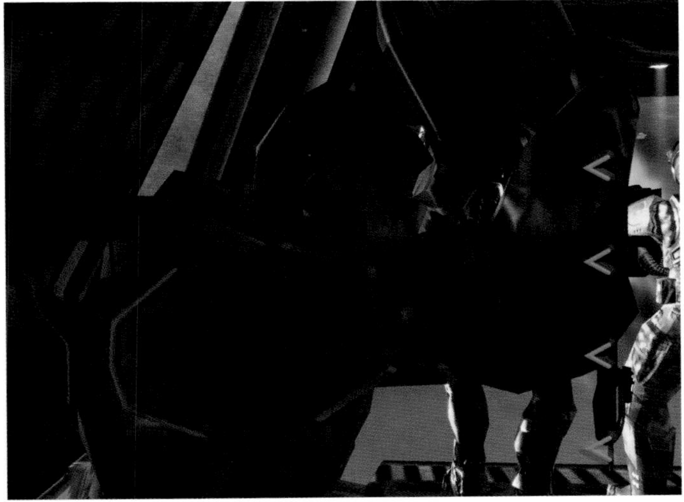

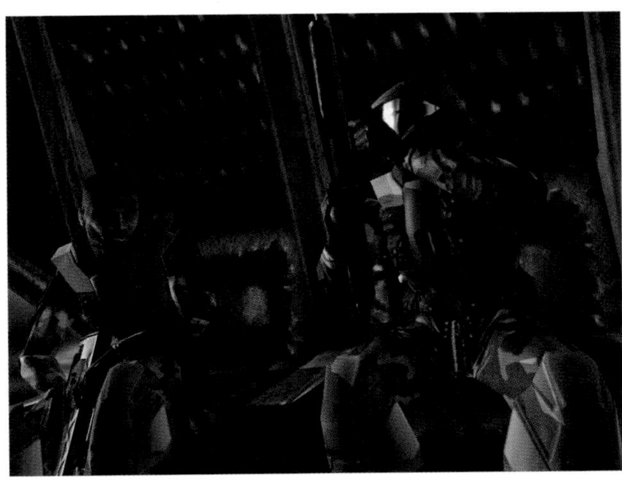

SERGEANT JOHNSON: <
Get tactical,
Marines! <

Inked by Lee Wilson.

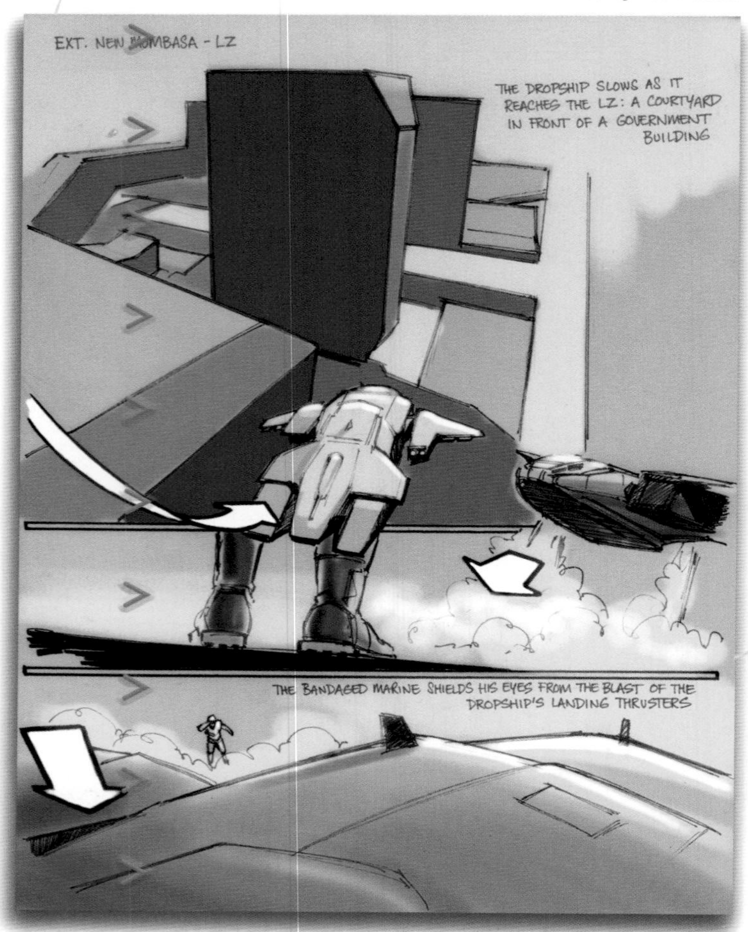

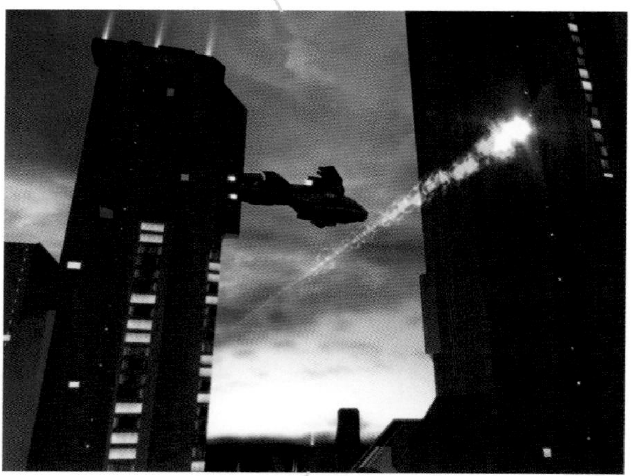

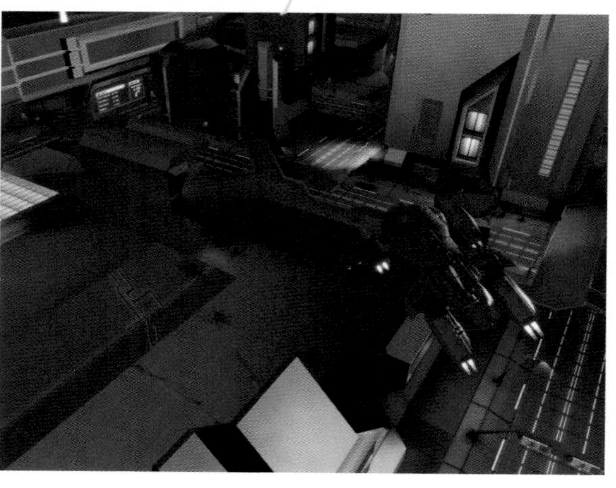

CORTANA:
Covenant ground forces own this city.

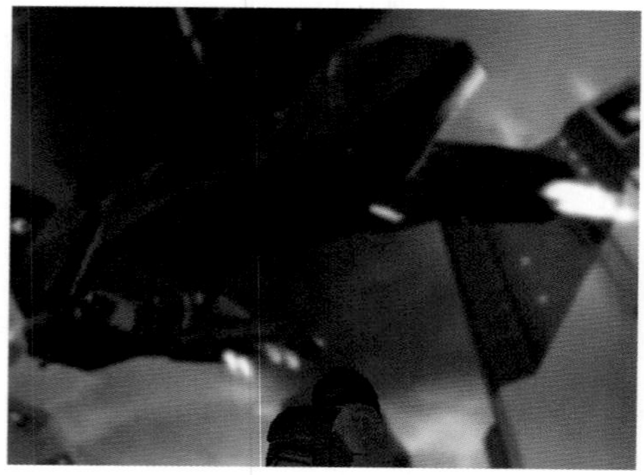

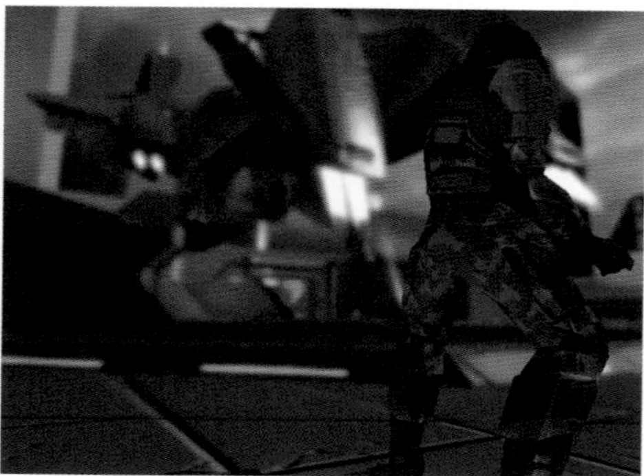

CORTANA:
We'll need to deal with them before we can kill that cruiser.

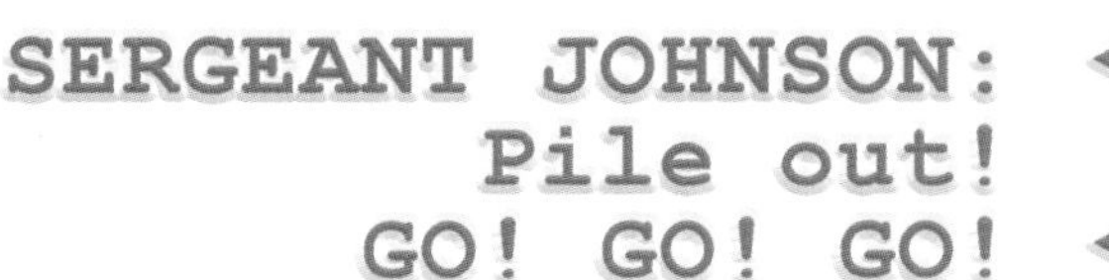

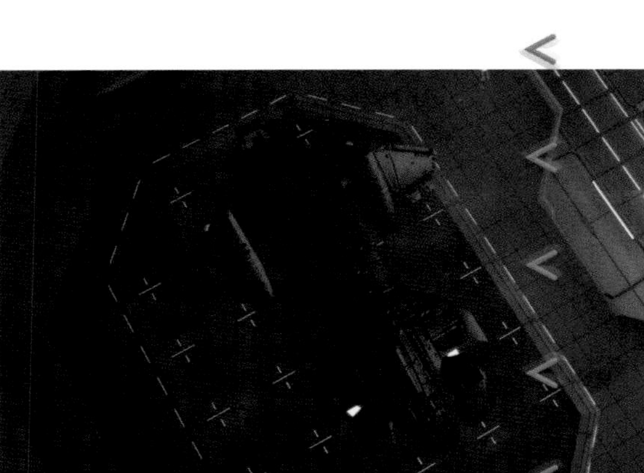

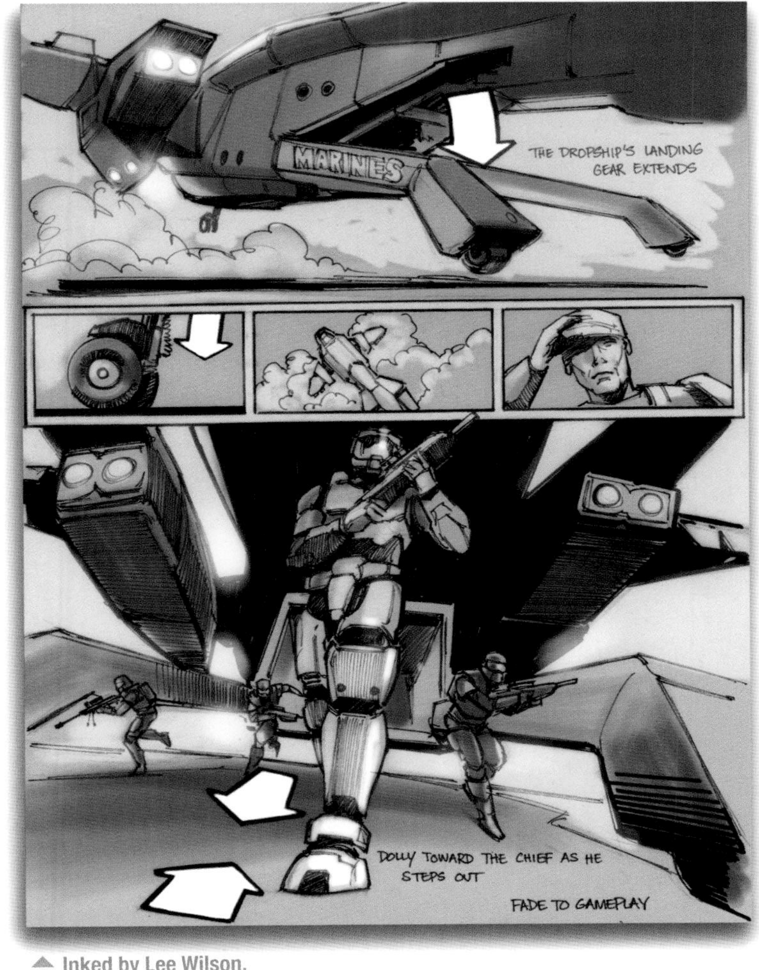

▲ Inked by Lee Wilson.

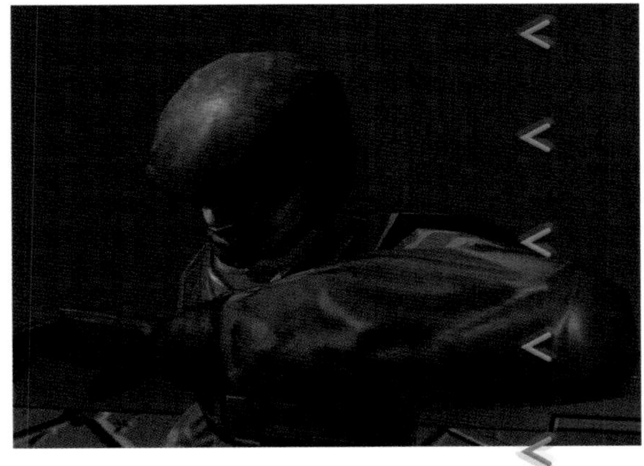

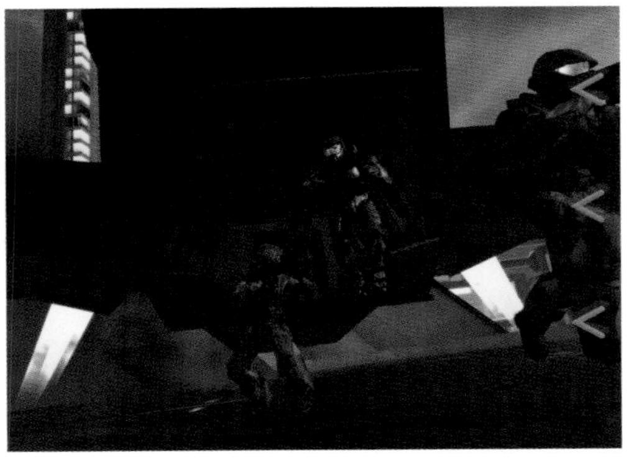

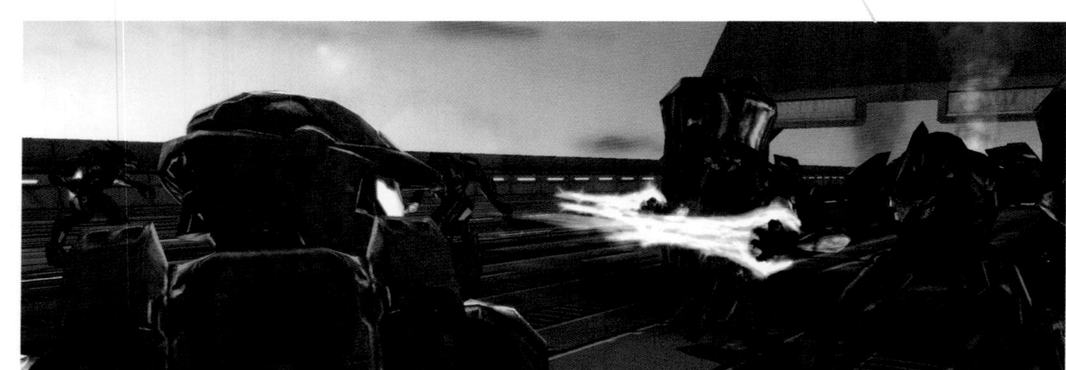

> CORTANA:
Bingo! There's the cruiser.

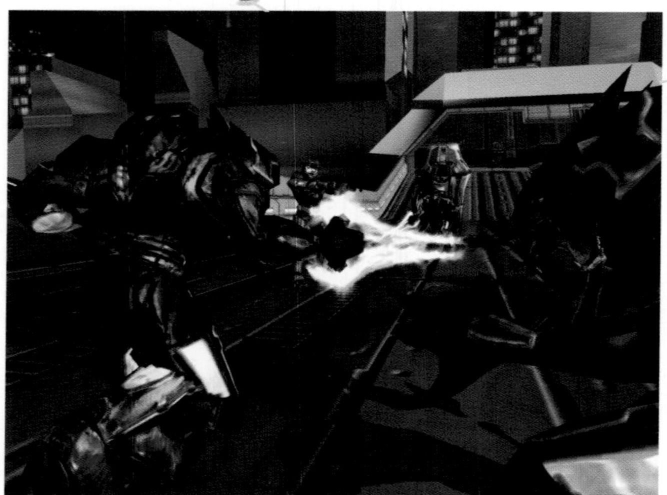

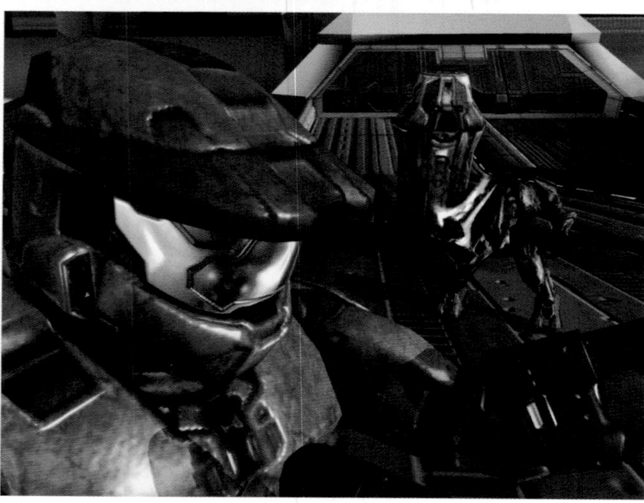

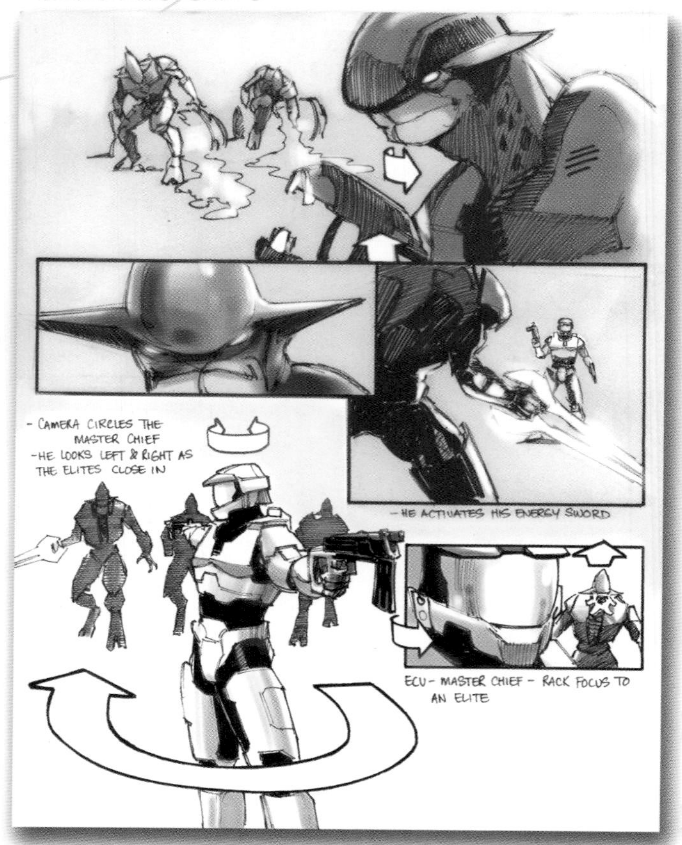

▲ Inked by Lee Wilson.

CORTANA: >
Now all you have
to do is... >

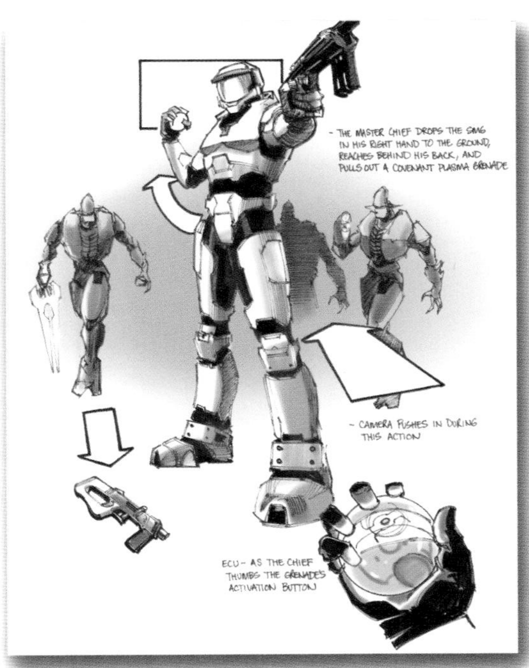

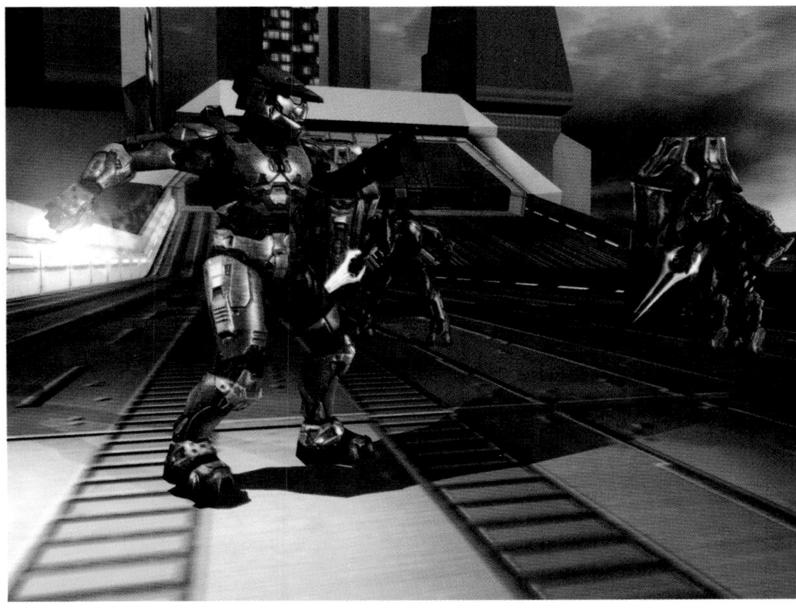

▲ Inked by Lee Wilson.

> **CORTANA:**
> **Betcha can't stick it.**

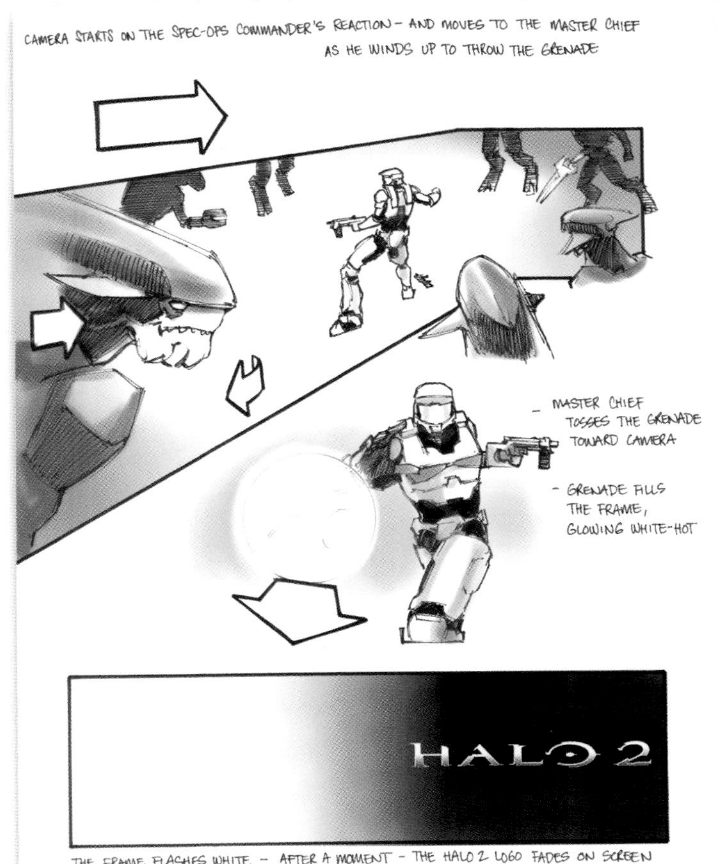

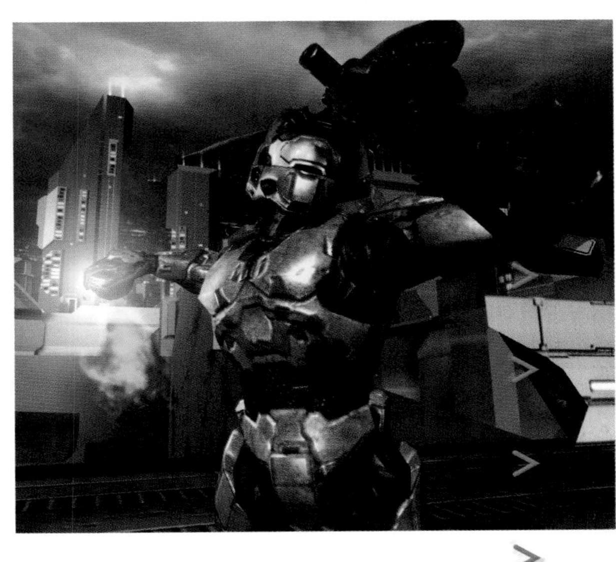

◀ Inked by Lee Wilson.

MASTER CHIEF:
You're on!

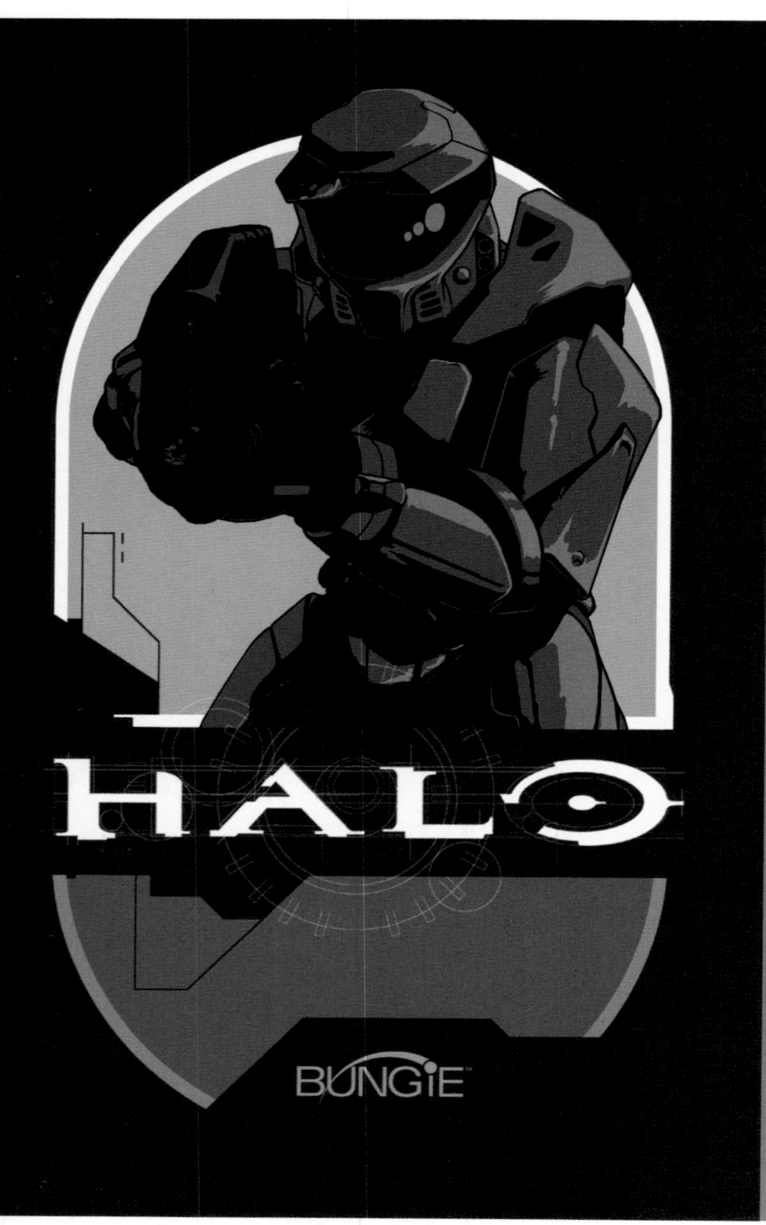

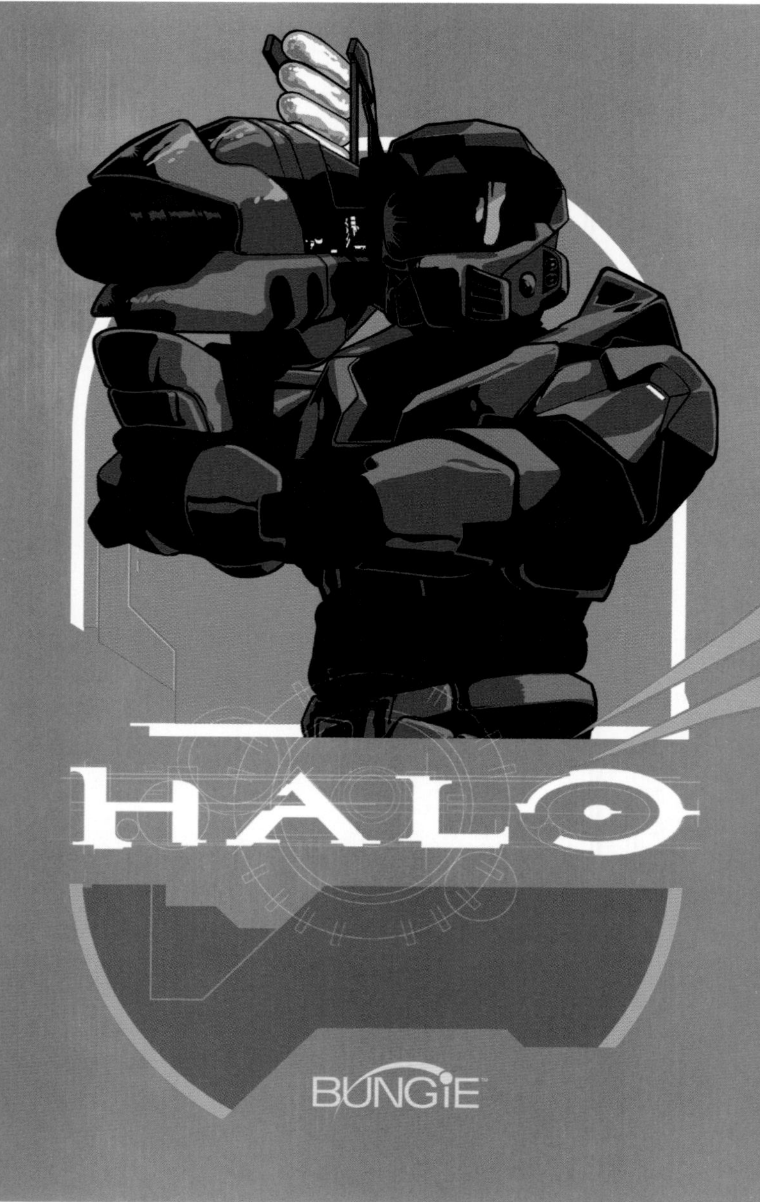

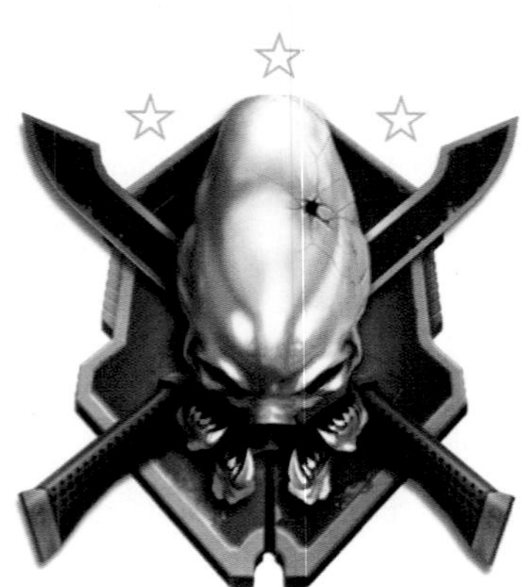

▲ T-shirt illustrations by Lorraine McLees.
◀ Legendary icon by Chris Barrett.

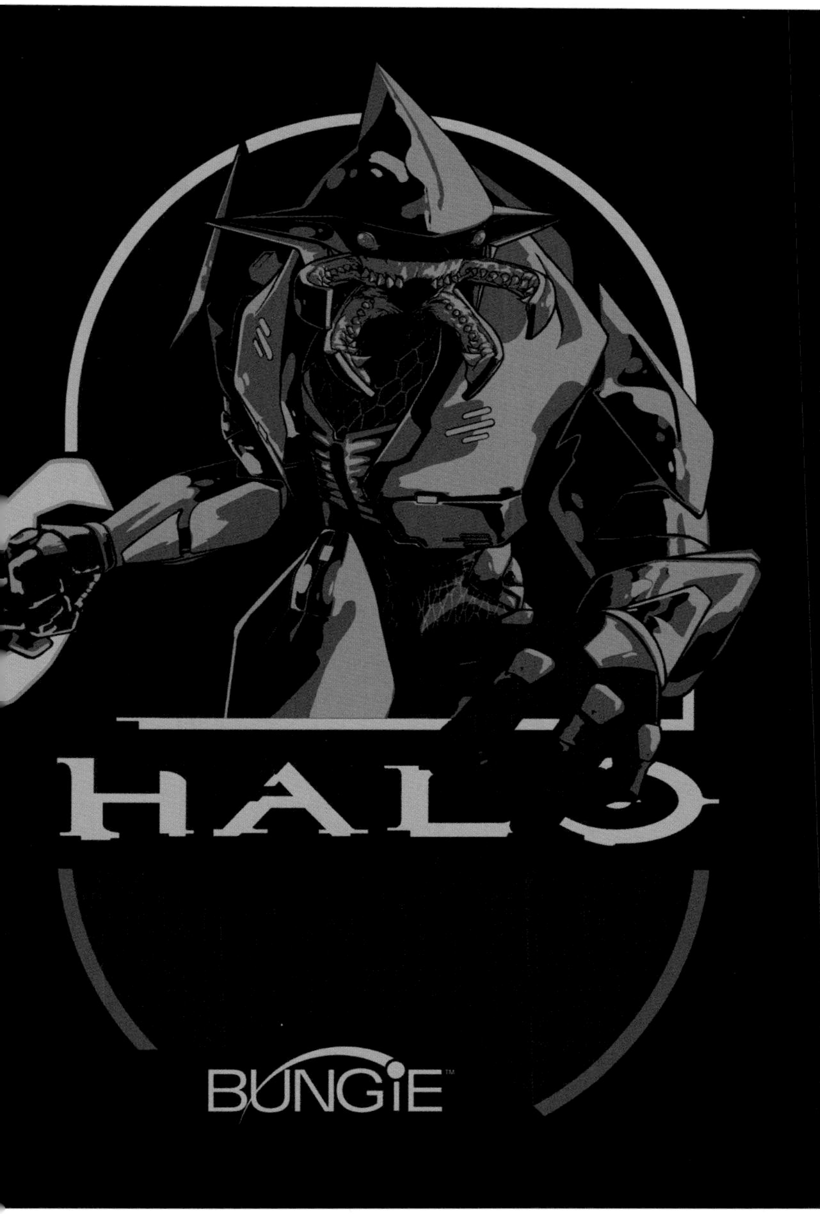

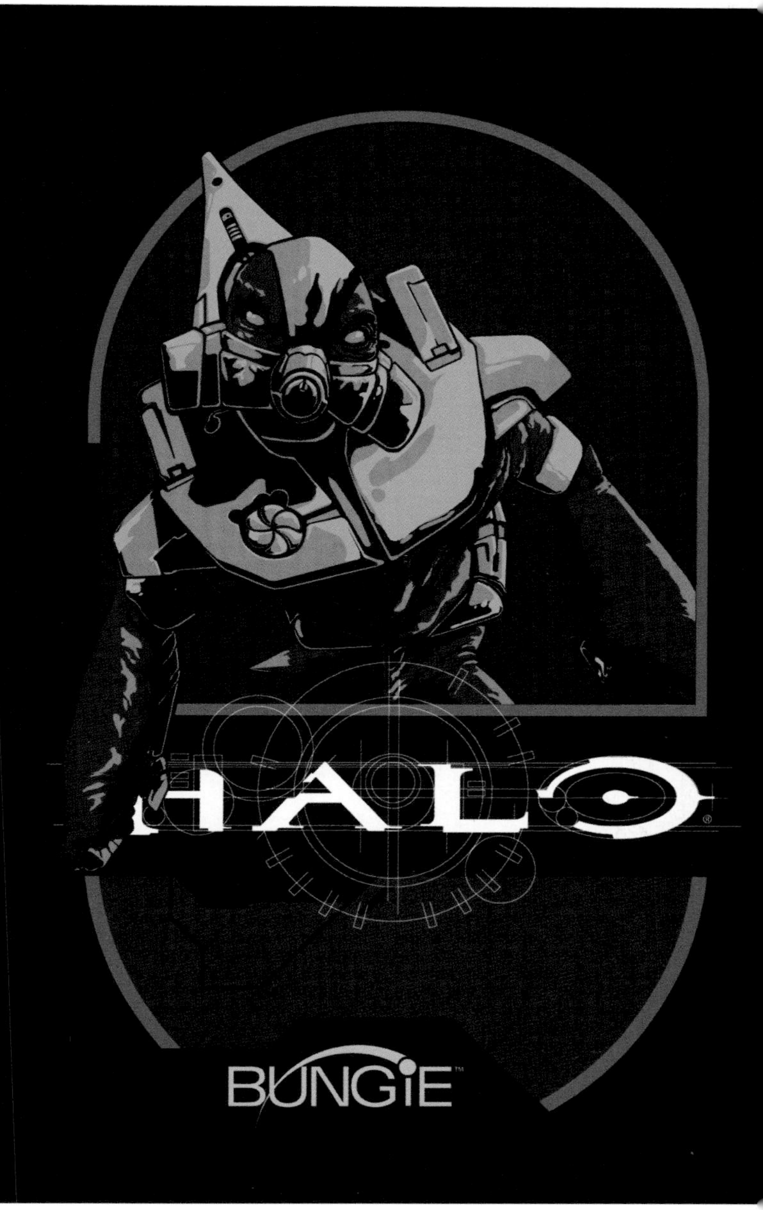

Flaming Ninja *Halo 2* team mascot by Shi Kai Wang.

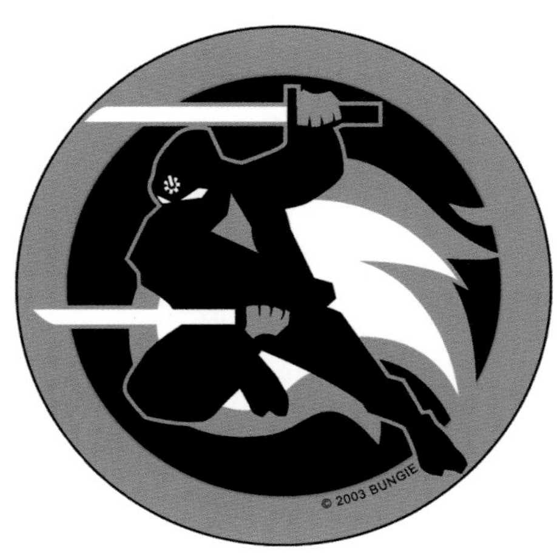

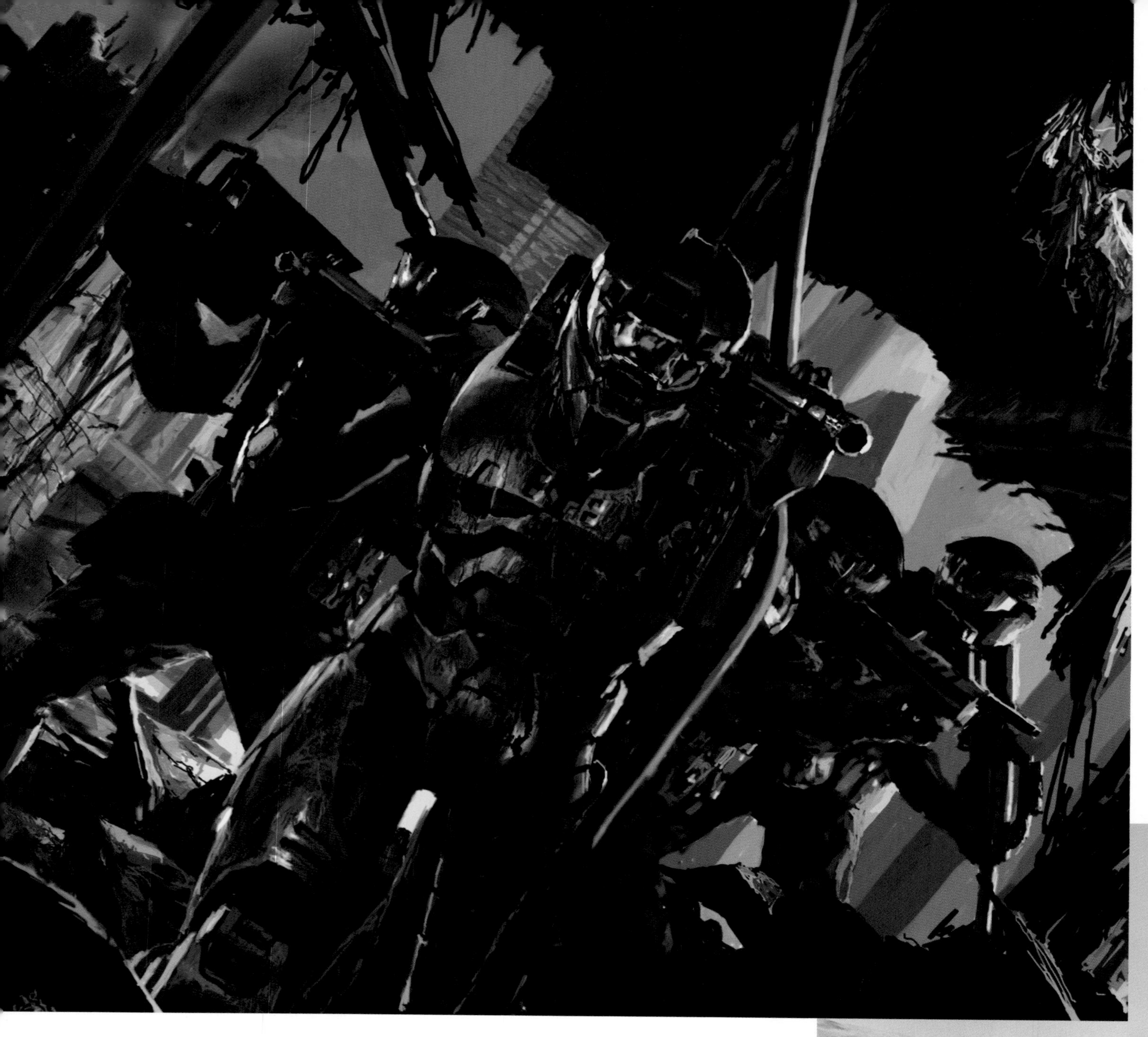

▲ Cover illustration for the *Official Xbox Magazine*, June 2003, by Eddie Smith.
▶ 3D illustration by Zoe Wolfe for bungie.net wallpaper gallery.

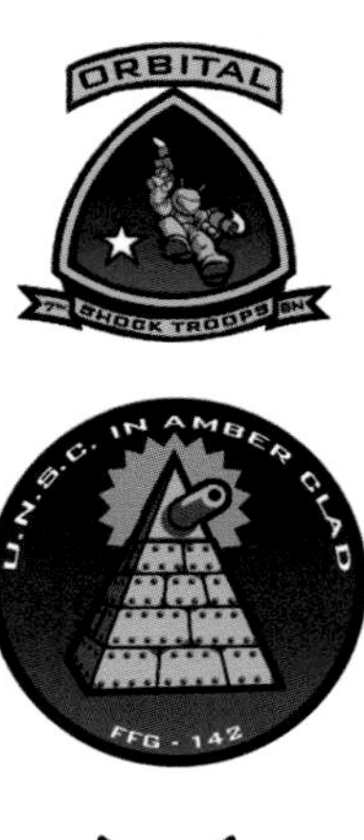

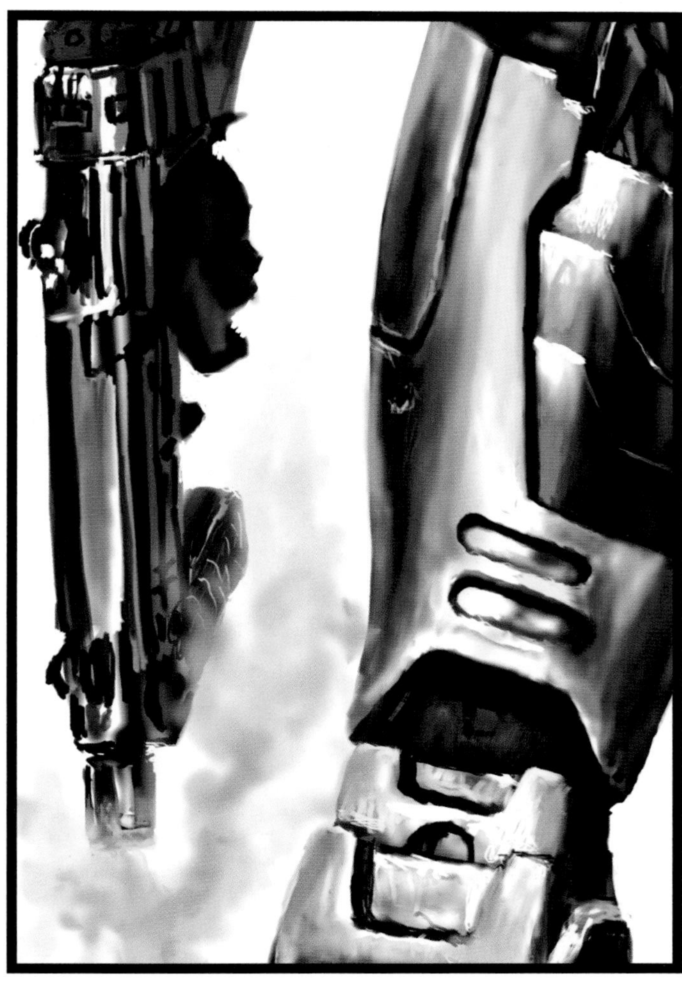

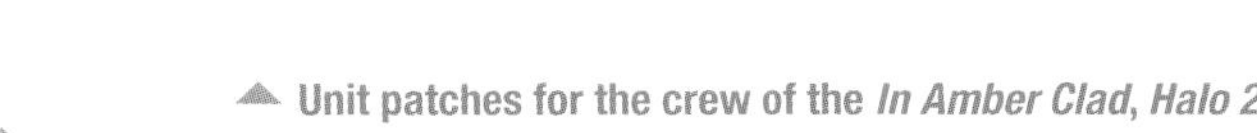

▲ Unit patches for the crew of the *In Amber Clad*, *Halo 2*.

▶ Tchotchke for media event at the 2003 Electronic Entertainment Expo.

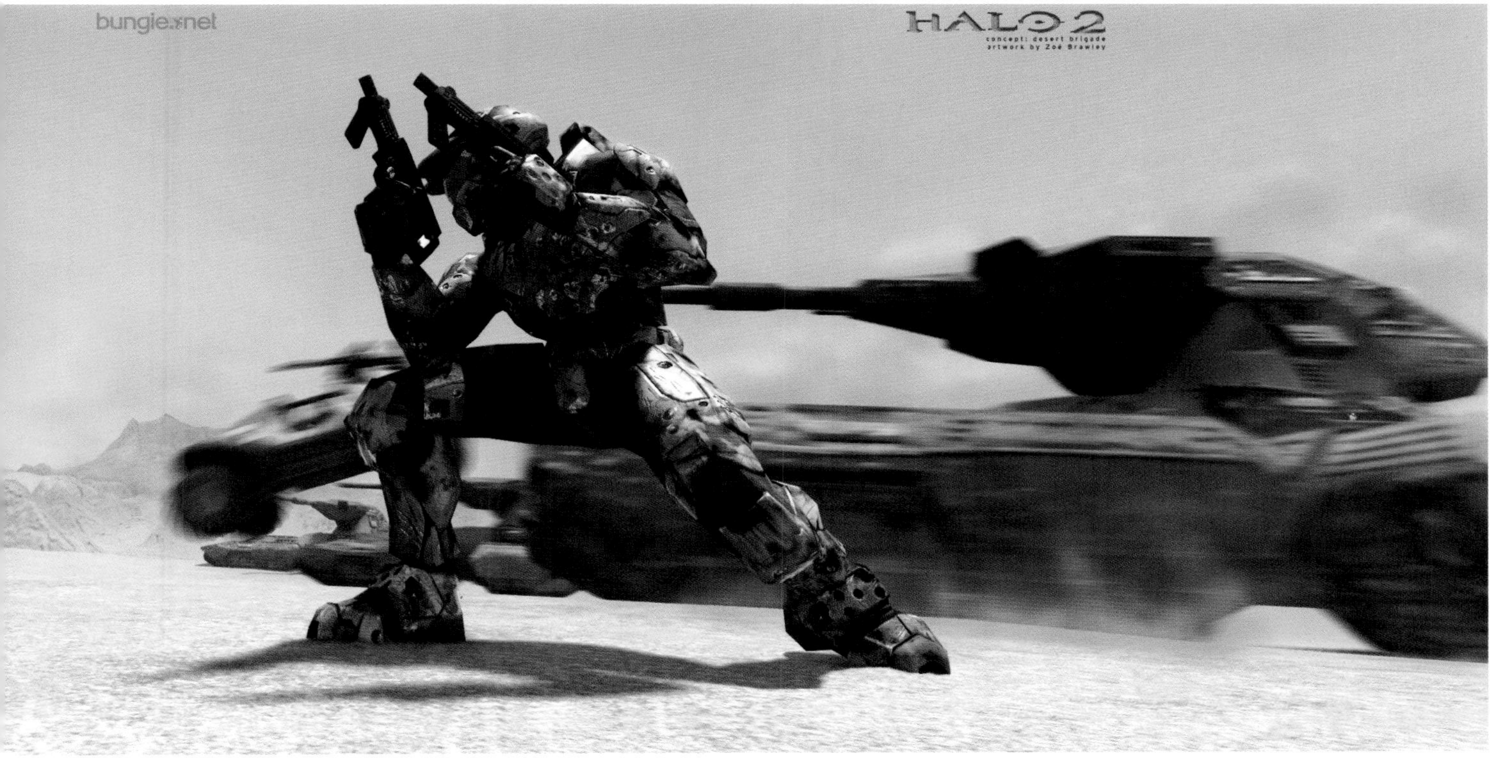

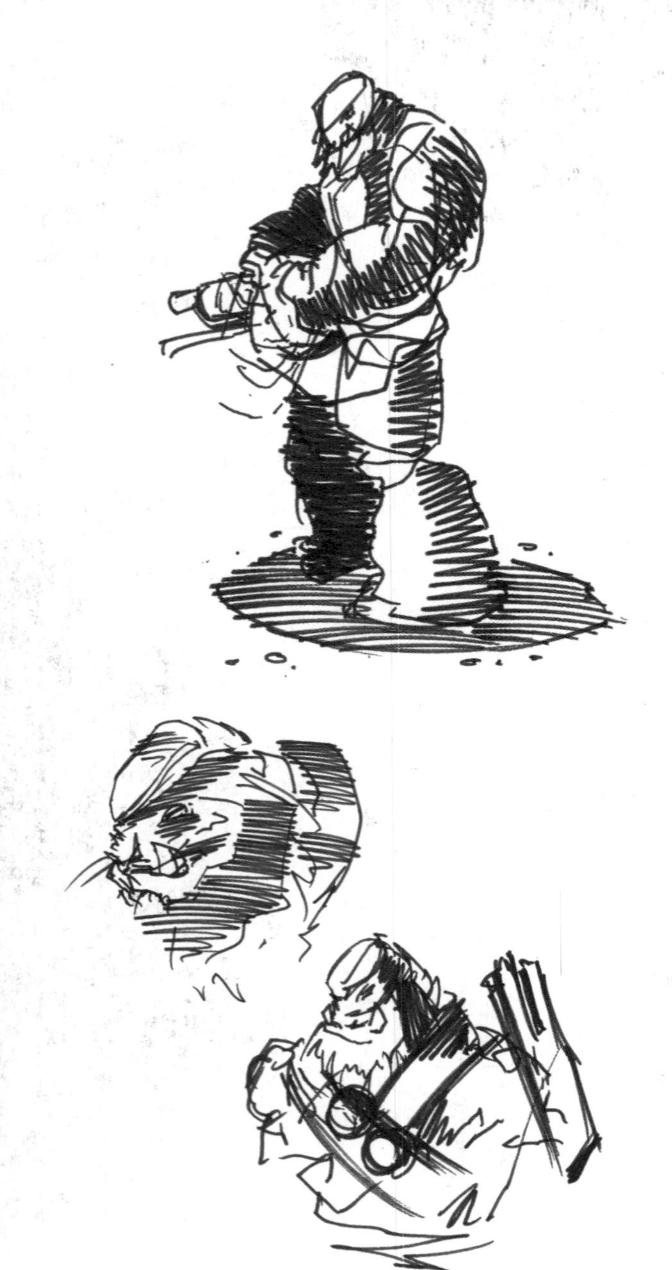

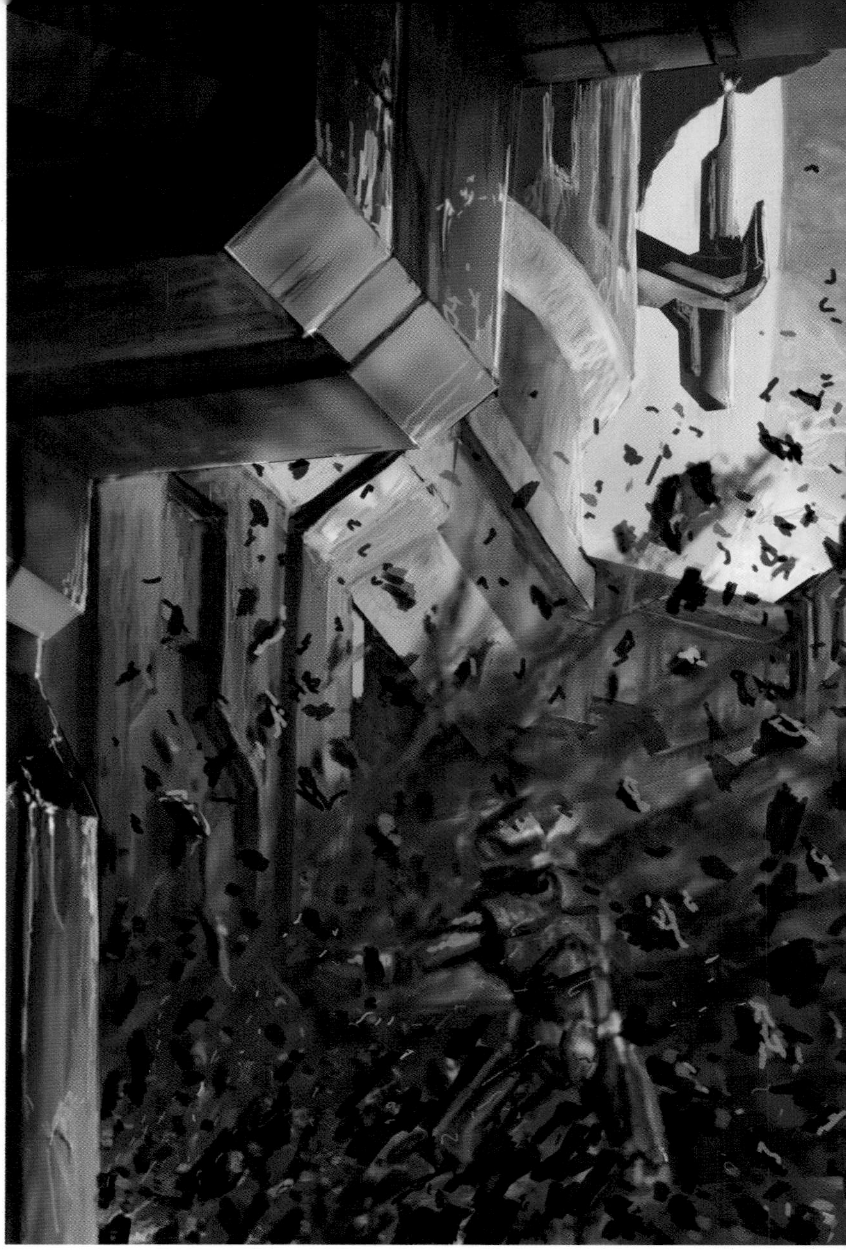

▲ Brute study by Nathan Walpole.
▼ Cinematic concept by CJ Cowan.

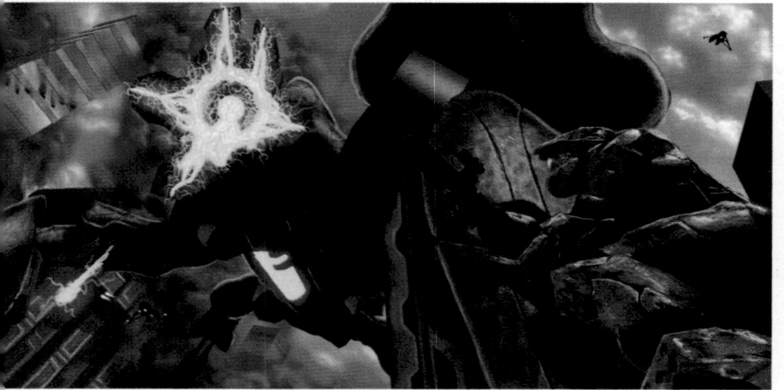

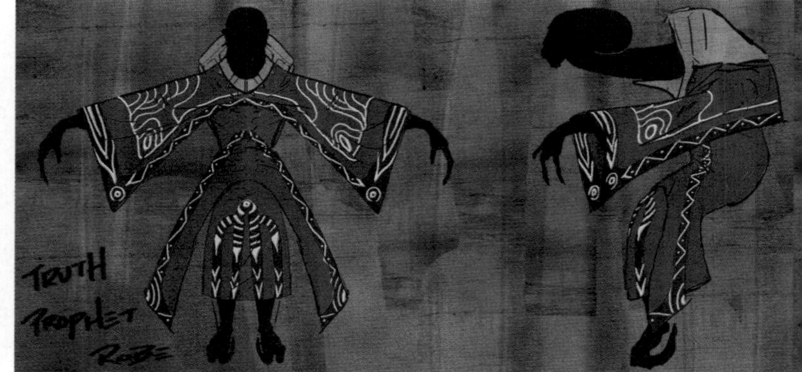

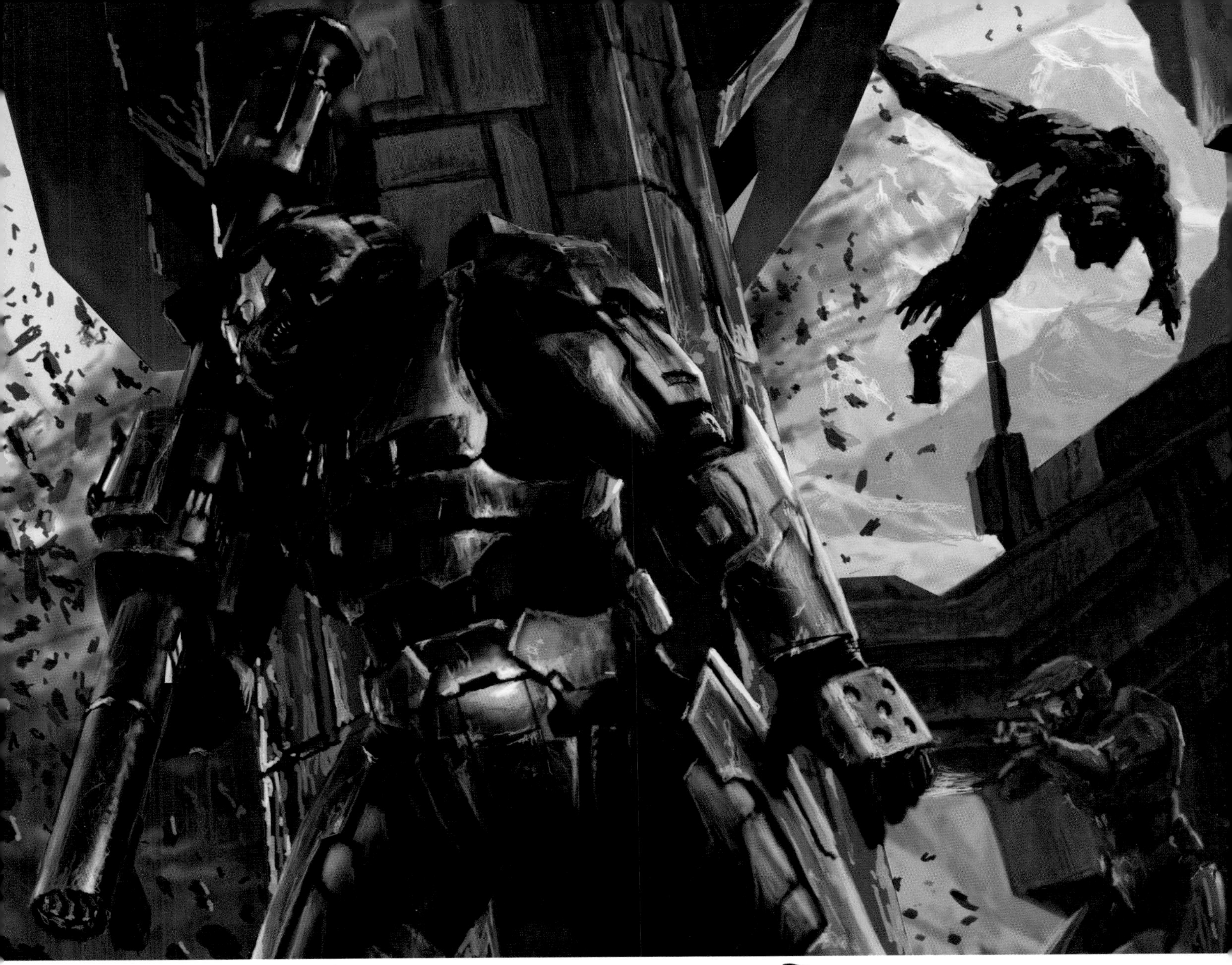

▲ Cover illustration for *Game Informer*, May 2003, by Eddie Smith.
▶ Brute animation study by Nathan Walpole.
▼ Prophet costume guide by Shi Kai Wang.

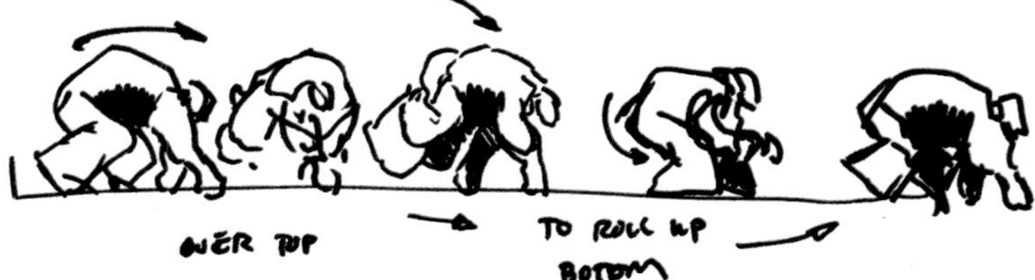

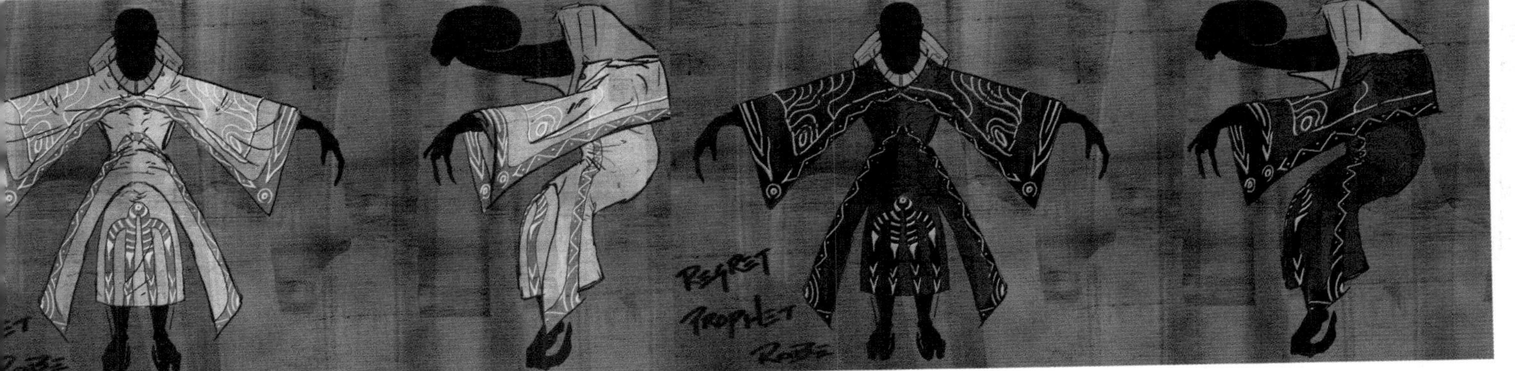